# THE SILENT CHILDREN

As she went to get a drink of water in the bathroom, she saw three small children standing half-naked in the darkness of the hallway. One was a girl of about eight or nine, and one a boy of five, and the littlest one, barely more than a baby, a little two-year-old. But they all wore cloth diapers.

And something even more shocking.

She noticed that at the edges of their mouths, thread had been sewn, and their eyes were closed, too, threads also, little black threads, and their ears and nostrils, all sewn shut. Ellen's heart beat fast, and she clutched the bathroom door for support. She was unable to scream, and she wondered for a second if she were dreaming.

Then the little girl reached up and drew the thread from her mouth, humming sounds coming from her.

And as she drew the thread, and as her lips parted slightly . . .

A small green fly crawled to the edge of her lips. Spread its shiny wings and flew, and then another emerged from her lips. And another. And another.

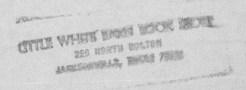

LITTLE WHITE DOVE BOOK STORE
250 NORTH BOLTON
JACKSONVILLE, TEXAS 75766

Other books by Douglas Clegg:
**GOAT DANCE**
**BREEDER**
**NEVERLAND**
**DARK OF THE EYE**
**THE CHILDREN'S HOUR**
**BAD KARMA (Writing as Andrew Harper)**

And coming soon from *Leisure Books:*
**YOU COME WHEN I CALL YOU**
**THE NIGHTMARE CHRONICLES**

# HALLOWEEN THE

# MAN

# DOUGLAS CLEGG

LEISURE BOOKS  NEW YORK CITY

A LEISURE BOOK®

October 1998

Published by

Dorchester Publishing Co., Inc.
276 Fifth Avenue
New York, NY 10001

If you purchased this book without a cover you should be aware that this book is stolen property. It was reported as "unsold and destroyed" to the publisher and neither the author nor the publisher has received any payment for this "stripped book."

Copyright © 1998 by Douglas Clegg

All rights reserved. No part of this book may be reproduced or transmitted in any form or by any electronic or mechanical means, including photocopying, recording or by any information storage and retrieval system, without the written permission of the Publisher, except where permitted by law.

ISBN 0-8439-4439-0

The name "Leisure Books" and the stylized "L" with design are trademarks of Dorchester Publishing Co., Inc.

Printed in the United States of America.

For Matt Schwartz, of http://www.horrornet.com.

This must be shared with Raul Silva, and for all of those people who love a tale of the fantastic and of terror on a chilly October night.

Thanks to my mother, Aileen Naomi Clegg, for introducing me to the spellbinding poetry of Edgar Allan Poe when I was barely out of diapers; and to my father, George Benjamin Clegg, III, for agreeing, when I was 22 and taking off to write and live in Paris, that a writer should have many experiences from which to draw. I thank them both for being nomads of sorts, and for instilling their shared sense of adventure in me.

Special thanks to Ed Gorman for introducing me to my editor, Don D'Auria, among other things Ed has helped me with over the years. Thanks to Don and my agent, Jake Elwell at Wieser & Wieser.

If you'd like to get in touch with me, E-mail me at DougClegg@aol.com or drop by my website at http://www.horrornet.com/clegg.htm.

# HALLOWEEN
## THE
## MAN

# *Prologue*

The shattering of glass and metal, as some unseen intruder broke the window, did not wake him.

*A voice in his head whispered, "Your soul."*

The boy shivered. The rain outside, and the wind that blew across the near-desolate room, across the old woman's face as she too lay back in some dream, he knew this but none of it could draw him up from sleep; the crunch and squeal of a door opening, of glass being stepped upon, all of this played at the edge of his consciousness, but he could not tug away from the dream that had grabbed him.

*The voice whispered, "Your heart."*

His eyelids fluttered open for a moment, and then the boy closed them again, as if the real world were the dream, and his inner world, the truth.

Even the mindpain was only a shredded curtain, blowing against a window of the dream.

The boy dreamed on. His inner eyes opened onto *the other world, the one of insane geometries, of orange light-*

*ning, of fire that rained from trees like leaves falling, of the birds rising from the water, their impossibly pure white wings spreading across the burning sky. As the sky filled with bloody swans, he saw the dark ram with its golden eyes shining as it galloped towards him across the surface of the unbroken water. Then the eels wriggling across the glassy surface, turning the brown water red with their wakes. The ram rode across their backs, its hooves beating like knives on stones. The Azriel Light came up from its breath, forming crystalline in the mist of air, and then burned across the world. What was unspeakable found voice and its bleating froze the air for a moment, hacked from the fabric of time as the secret of all stabbed at his ears.*

Someone tried to wake him from it. The mindpain came back like a bolt of lightning, burning along his neural pathways. The boy's eyes opened, his dream torn apart.

The man shook him awake and held a hand over his mouth. The room came back with its shadows of curtains and half-opened cupboards. The trill of a mockingbird outside the window. The shroud of dawn. The room that always seemed too small for all of them. The others slept on around him.

The man wore a dark leather jacket and jeans, his dark hair in need of a cut, and the smell from him was almost sweet—like sage on the desert after a rain.

"You Satan?" the boy asked in a hushed tone of reverence. Fear was not there. He didn't sense it. He didn't feel it from the man, and it wasn't within him. He knew, somehow, the man would be there. He knew just as he knew that his dream had foretold something.

"I could be," the man whispered, his breath all cigarettes. "If you keep quiet, you'll live. Understand?"

The boy nodded. The mindpain blossomed against his small skull. When it came on, as it usually did after one of the Great Meetings, it would blast within his head like the worst headache. Sometimes his nose would bleed from it. Sometimes he'd go into convulsions. He never knew how hard it would hit, he just knew it was PAIN. He knew it HURT. The mindpain didn't let go until it was good and ready to.

The boy felt something pressed against his side.

Cold metal.

"That's right," the man whispered. "It's a gun. I will kill you if you make a noise or try to fight me. Or if you try to do what I know you can do."

The boy began shivering, and wasn't sure if he could will himself to stop. He wanted to be back in his dream. It felt like ants were crawling all over his arms and legs. Ants stinging him all over, and then tickling along his neck. He wanted to swat and scratch, but he was afraid the man might use the gun. The boy had seen a jackrabbit get shot clean in half once. He didn't need to imagine it happening to himself.

But the markings on him, the drawings . . .

He knew they were moving, the pictures on his shoulders. He wished he could scrape them from his flesh. He wanted to tell the stranger with the gun about them, about how they meant bad things when they began moving, but the boy knew this would do no good.

The man grinned as he lifted the boy up, wrapping a shabby blanket around him. The boy's last view of what he had come to call home was the old woman lying there staring at him. Blood sluiced from between her lips, and tears bled down in rivulets from her eyes. The mattress beneath her was soaked red. Her fingers were still curled around a small amulet she kept with her, nothing more than a locket, a good luck charm.

The boy was too tired to fight, and weakened, too, by the previous day's performance. Mindpain always came after the show. Mindpain was like what the Great Father had called a hangover. It was the morning after. That was a problem for him, it sapped him of strength, and even

11

when he had tried to kick out at the man, he could barely move his legs.

The man would probably kill him. The boy knew this is what kidnappers usually did. He had watched late-night TV shows like *America's Most Wanted* and knew that kidnappers rarely kept a kid alive.

The boy tried not to think of the gun.

Tried to remember the Great Father holding his arms out, his hands open to him. ''I will be your comfort in the valley of the shadow,'' the Great Father had said.

This was the valley of the shadow of death. This kidnapper and his gun and his blanket and the red stain on the mattress with the old woman's mouth wide open.

Thinking about it, the boy winced. The hammering in his head grew stronger. Everything hurt.

The pounding of the rain on the roof seemed unbearable. It was a terrible rain, it had come at first as ice and then tiny pebbles hitting the corrugated tin roof, until finally, it was just water. *God is pissin' on us on accounta our sins, that's what the old woman who took care of him would say, her Texas twang increasing with her years.* She was dead now. She was in whatever Great Beyond existed, the boy knew. She was in the pictures that covered him now, as were all things that were no more. If the mindpain hadn't descended that night, weakening him further, he might've been able to struggle against this evil man who'd taken him. Even though the blanket covered the boy's ears, it was as if the hoofbeats of wild horses were beating down upon him from heaven.

The kidnapper threw him into the backseat of a car. Slammed the door. As they drove off, the boy glanced back at the place he'd called home and knew in his heart he would never see it again. Dawn was just bursting from the far horizon. Rain accompanied it, the first fresh drops hitting the car windows, dirt rinsing down. The pain in the boy's head grew, and he could feel the tingling begin along his back and shoulders. He knew that whatever was supposed to start, all the things that he'd been warned about by the Great Father, would come to pass now.

Through him, the radiance would come, like electricity through the idiot wires of the gods.

His skin felt molten.

# PART ONE

# THE STORM KING

*"Down came the golden ship, plowing into the fallow earth as if planting a new crop in a dry field . . ."*
*from* The Storm King: Intergalactic Knight, *Vol. 12*

# The Damnation Highway

*"It was drizzling and mysterious at the beginning of our journey."*
—Jack Kerouac, On the Road

# Chapter One

# The Kidnapper

1

*You can't ever take this back.*

The kidnapper heard the voice in his head.

*You can't ever undo this. You must now follow it through, what you've started.*

*You must now take it to its logical conclusion.*

*Try not to picture what you're going to have to do to the kid.*

The only emotion the man felt was an indefinable revulsion, not even fear, for an adrenaline rush overcame his cowardice. His sweat had dried up, his body no longer trembled with the knowledge of what he had to do. It was no longer a plan, or a plot, it was an action in fact. Yet he had to have control over himself, or he would lose it. He might just go over the edge, and then all that he'd worked so hard to keep in place for so many years—the lurker beneath his own skin—all would run wild.

If a place could have an aura, this one did, and it was

the aura that caused his revulsion. An aura of darkness, and it was almost like a physical heaviness to the place. A halo of nightmare, all around the periphery. He'd do right by the world if he poured kerosene at its edges and torched the whole place, and the dozen or so people sleeping there. The Rapturists, they called themselves, but for people of God they had quite an arsenal stored out in New Mexico. The Feds were already surrounding their Quonset huts just outside of Las Cruces, out in the dusty hills, ready for a Branch Davidian–style showdown, at least according to the media. But the Rapturists had pockets all over the United States and parts of Central America. They were a big family of loons whose religious zeal tended towards forming militias and announcing messiahs with every change of the weather.

This enclave, small as it was, and apparently as harmless, contained the only messiah that the man wanted:

The boy who they called Shiloh, or Prophet.

*Funny that no one's standing guard. Funny that they don't feel the need to protect their little messiah from men like me who might want to do something terrible to him.*

He had one final protection with him in case they did catch him, one little parachute of sorts.

*Don't think about it.*

*All you want is the boy.*

*Funny though that no one is waking up, and funny about that woman lying on the mattress. Too dark to really get a look, but why didn't she wake up? Why didn't she try to stop him?*

*Don't think about that either.*

*Don't think about what might have been done last night, perhaps as some kind of God ritual among them, some kind of Kool-Aid laced with People's Temple cyanide, or some other nasty little "let's go to Heaven together, shall we?" party.*

*These Rapturists are that crazy. Their whole sense of*

*religion is built around death anyway. No big surprise if by sunrise all of them will be found dead.*

All but the boy.

What had Fairclough called it?

*Oh yeah, the Azriel Light, which was suitably biblical since Azriel was the Angel of Death. The Azriel Light was simply a phenomenon of idiot humans going crazy and killing themselves when in the presence of the light of Holiness. Leave it to Fairclough and the Rapturists to describe their lack of survival skills with some bogus religious phrase. "The Azriel Light," the blonde on the Christian show had said, "is the warm glow of God's love, but it is not of the flesh, but of spirit. The flesh is a covering, like this blouse and skirt I'm wearing, and we must shed it to move into the eternal light."*

*Ah, gimme that old-time religion!*

This was a place of darkness. No dawn, and no damn Azriel Light was going to make it any brighter.

*I know another name for the Azriel Light,* he thought. *Moonfire.*

All he wanted was to get the boy in the car and get the hell out of this enclave of rundown homes out in the middle of a Texas nowhere. The stink was everywhere—Stony Crawford could smell it like the scent of old blood, the way you knew that something or someone was dead, had been dead a long time and had just lain there in the excrement of death as if waiting for resurrection. He couldn't wait to get out from among the shacks and mobile homes, and back into his car. And those cages, full of rattlesnakes, all still and eerie beneath the trailer that sat up on cinder blocks. Christ, that was creepy. People who would keep fifty rattlesnakes for their church social weren't people you wanted to mess with.

The kid stayed put, which was good for both of them. Stony had to make sure that no one followed.

*Damn Death Cult. Damn superstitious backwoods New Ager Gospel spouters believing in snake oil and storm clouds and little boys who make rain come down over parched land.*

He trembled as he slid into the front seat. Thought he saw a man standing off behind one of the shacks, just watching the spectacle.

*The Kidnapping of a Twelve-Year-Old Boy; The Miracle Worker Kid of the Southwest; The Boy Who Predicted the Assassination; The Boy Who Healed the Sick; The Boy Who Raised the Dead; The Boy Who Made the Blind See and the Lame Walk; The New Messiah of Texas and the World, Shiloh Incarnate.*

Stony had read all the cheap magazines and lurid newspaper reports, seen the television show that dragged the kid before the cameras while some platinum blonde with mascara for brains tried to suck money out of the viewers. ''The Rapture is coming, and Prophet is our savior!'' she cried. ''Send ten dollars, twenty, five hundred, whatever you can, be part of this great convergence of heaven and earth!''

They sold the kid's spit at fifty bucks a loogie.

*I guess I must be the Devil, for stealing the Messiah.*

*I must be worse than the Devil, because I'm gonna take this kid and . . .*

*Don't picture it. You weaken when you think about it. You start thinking stupid-ass warm fuzzy thoughts about the innocence of childhood and about love and about care and about how this is just after all a little boy, and for all you know you didn't even get the right little boy, you did what you did last time, you grabbed the wrong kid.*

The voice within him whispered, *You got the wrong kid last time, remember? You were a dumbass twenty-year-old then and you grabbed the tot and ran, and when you got out to the place where you were gonna blow him to kingdom come, turns out you had just grabbed some kid who was nothing but a kid. Ordinary. Sweet. Goofy. Scared. And you had to shut him up somehow, but you knew only killing him would do it.*

*So instead you just showed him something horrible. You showed him that place inside you that no one wants to see and stay sane. You let that kid see it, knowing it would fry his little four-year-old brain and then he'd spend half his childhood hoping that Hell wasn't going to open up right under his feet.*

*Some wonderful as shit world you gave that kid, the wrong kid.*

*And you're so damn sure this one here is the right one? Who's da monster, Stony?*

"I am," he whispered aloud.

## 2

They traveled by car, an old beat-up Mustang he'd bought for a hundred and fifty-seven bucks in a town farther south called Causeway Center. The old man selling the car had told him he was a fool to buy it even at that price, and it wouldn't take him all the way up the coast, but it might get him as far as North Carolina, and from there, "You're on your own. Only God or Fate is gonna take care of this beat-up old piece of scrap metal from there on." The old man reminded him—too much—of his own father, not in the eyes, but in the mouth, that jug-chinned hangdog kind of mouth. He hadn't really trusted the old man. He never really trusted anyone. But he double-checked his various maps, and he knew the Mustang was as good as any car he could find after he'd smashed up his other one. He didn't have a lot of cash left, and now he had this mission.

That's what it was. A pure mission.

Stony Crawford glanced at the glove compartment.

*Don't think about it.*

*Even thinking about it might make him know it's there.*

He ignored the image of it that his mind conjured. *Keep your mind on the road.*

In the rearview mirror, the boy slept. The backseat was outfitted with pillows and blankets. He didn't want the boy to be uncomfortable. He didn't want the kid to get too scared of him, not yet. The boy had dark hair, almost too long. His skin was a deep tan on his face, from the Texas sun. His pupils, when Stony had seen his eyes go wide, were large and dilated as if someone had been putting some sort of eyedrops in them to increase the boy's sensitivity to light. But otherwise, Stony had recognized the boy almost immediately. The shock of it almost threw him backwards. He'd been searching for this kid for just under twelve years, and finding him, he knew. He knew why the other kid had been the wrong one, because he'd been looking for all the wrong qualities. But seeing this boy was like thrusting his hand into a bucket of electric eels.

He had arrived at the small one-room schoolhouse on the edge of a shit-dust town, and seen the boy from the back of the room. That death stink was all around, and the idiots there had brought in three corpses, as if the boy would actually be able to raise them back to life. But oh, those fundamentalist believers wanted to know that either Christ or the Antichrist had returned, Hallelujah, it didn't matter which. They just wanted the fulfillment of a book written a long time ago, they didn't want the truth of what the boy was. They didn't want his totality.

Hallelujah, he makes the wine taste like water! Hallelujah, he maketh the lion to lie down with the lamb! Hallelujah, he knows the fires of hell, and the fate of the world is written upon him! Praise the Almighty, we found our l'il savior and now let's praise him before we put him up on some cross and kick the living soul right outta him!

But Stony had seen him clearly. Known him, known what he had to do with the boy.

*This particular child.*

His fingers tensed around the steering wheel. He tried an old relaxation exercise, but the fear of what he had to do came back to him.

He blinked, and in that split-second blindness,

*He saw the red birds burst out of the skin, spreading across the sky, swirling in the wind and then coming together again, a wall of fire, its heat so intense it melted glass.*

"*It was long ago, my friend,*" the comforting voice within him told him. The voice of an old friend, someone he had internalized over the years.

*Nora.*

"*A long time ago, and what's past is past. All you can do is look down the road and decide if it curves and if you'll take the curve.*"

It rained like the devil from Texas to Arkansas. The land turned from plains to hills, with great pine forests springing up. Even the rain seemed unnatural for northeast Texas, pouring down like the heavens had opened up. The trucks ahead of him splashed water up onto his windshield. The wash of color turning to gray-brown mud, splattering across his vision as the day grew darker with the overhanging clouds. The wipers swiped at it, but the road did not clear from the blur of water and gray.

The rain stopped just outside Little Rock. Traffic was light, and there were several motels along the roadside. Their bright red flashing vacancy signs beckoned to him, but he could not sleep. He could not sleep, and would not let himself rest. Because he knew if he did, then he might let the boy go. He might just stop, out of fear. Or out of a sense that maybe he was wrong, maybe all of it was a bad case of insanity, that his ever-present memory that swirled around inside him was, in fact, fantasy.

He might kill himself, in whatever way it was possible to do so.

*To sleep for a thousand years,* a voice in his head whispered. *To be part of the nothing, the emptiness, and the everything. The enormity of existence, spread across it like fire. To not have to be trapped inside this prison of flesh and bone.*

*Nora, in her inimitible way, scoffed at this voice of*

*dissent.* "*Oh Lord, there you go, ready to jump in a pond with a two-hundred-pound weight tied around your neck when all you have to do is take it off. You have made cosmic suffering an art, and you're just too talented in that direction. Stony boy, when are you gonna just take responsibility for yourself and turn these demons around?*"

By then, his hands were tense on the steering wheel. He hadn't slept in forty-eight hours, and he wasn't sure how much longer he could go. He tasted what he thought might be blood in his mouth. It wasn't just the fear or stress, it was the knowing. The knowing of it. Not of what had been, but of what must be done. He glanced in the rearview mirror constantly. He half expected to see a police car following him. Or maybe the people from that awful place back in a small Texas roadside town, a middle of nowhere, a blind spot on the map. The kind of place where things like this might take hold.

Those people.

The people who worshiped the boy.

"*These ain't real demons, they're made up by you. If you looked at them the way they really are, you'd see they're just wake-up calls from the universe.*" *Nora seemed to be there, within him.*

He knew that it was his imagination. Always his imagination. He'd let the voices come out, especially in this kind of situation.

*I am kidnapping a kid from Texas, and dragging his ass halfway across the country, I have a gun, I have a—*

*(Don't think it and it won't really be happening—don't look at the glove compartment.)*

"Why do you live in me?" he asked the Nora-voice once. Knew he was crazy for even asking one of the voices in his head about itself.

"*Because,*" *came her reply.* "*You won't let me go.*"

He tried not to listen to the chaos of voices inside him.

"I'm not crazy," he said, and then realized he'd said it aloud.

Glanced back at the boy in the rearview mirror.

*I am a kidnapper. Felony.*

*I may be a murderer. Felony.*

*Oh, but worse. There's a law beyond the law, and a justice beyond human justice.*

*Damnation is my only highway.*

3

At some point in driving, he began seeing things on the road, like movies sprayed across his windshield. Just images from the past, people's faces, the big summer house out on Juniper Point. He had to force his concentration to see the highway through them, to see what was up ahead.

*Moonfire burst across his vision—*

*The yellow-white moon, corona of red around it like sunbursts—*

A flashback as sure as if he'd dropped acid back when he was a teenager.

*Moonfire, searing, almost blinding him—*

*The vision of her.*

*Her face encased in a liquid white sac, the blue veins, like a spiderweb, through it. The pulsing of the life fluid.*

Then, it was gone as quickly as it had arrived. The road ahead was dark and straight.

The sky lightened as storm clouds became as insubstantial as a dream across the reality of midday.

The smell of steamy autumn in the air, the humid moss of a warm October, caught in his throat. After the storm, the moisture evaporated in the brilliant sun. He wiped his sunglasses off, looking up at the open sky. A vast big blue emptiness that stretched for miles. There was no end to it as he glanced across the horizon. No clouds ahead. Nothing in the beyond but clear skies, no apparent darkness. It was a relief, for the rain had been like the pounding in his head since he'd found what he'd been searching for.

When the rain stopped, the memories quieted.

The rain had been like nails hitting stones in his head.

Or the soft thud of nails in hands.

Sometimes, it was just rain.

"I'm hungry," the kid in the backseat said.

"Later on."

"There's a war goin' on," the kid said.

"Yeah, right."

"There is. Between Good and Evil, Heaven and Hell," the boy said as if this had been drilled into him since the age of three. "All of us is part of it, and my part is like a fire across the seas."

"And he bound the serpent for a thousand years and—"

"You know Scripture?" the boy asked, shocked.

"You ain't the messiah, kid, so just shut up about those chuckleheads we just left behind," Stony clucked. Then, "Sorry, kid. I guess you could say I'm just in a bad mood."

The silence in the car became overbearing. Stony switched on the radio. The choices were country or preachers. Country won, hands down. Stony tuned into the end of an old Charlie Pride tune, "Kiss an Angel Good Morning." The kid began singing along softly to it from the backseat.

4

"How about over there?" Stony pointed to the Waffle Hut off the highway.

"I guess," the boy said. "You still in a bad mood?"

"Kid, I'm always in a bad mood. Waffle Hut?"

"McDonald's would be okay."

"You want to wait for the next McDonald's? It might be a half hour."

"Okay, whatever you say, you're da boss," the boy said almost cheerfully.

"You don't mind that I'm taking you," Stony said after he'd parked in front of the Waffle Hut. "You don't mind that a stranger put you in his car and is driving someplace you have no idea of."

The boy shrugged. "You're the one with the gun, not me."

5

Inside, the Formica table coated with a thin layer of grease, the boy glanced at the spattered-plastic menu. "My eyes must be bigger'n my belly. I want everything I can get."

"Easy, kid," Stony said. "Keep it under five bucks, okay?"

When the waitress came over, she wiped down the table, took the orders, and the boy said, "Grits, two sausages, three eggs, two pancakes. Big glass of milk."

Stony checked his wallet. Depressingly few bills remained in it. A small photo from the past: the fifteen-year-old girl with the dark skin and dark hair. Pretty eyes. Sweet smile. Around her neck, a small gold cross. "Nothing for me, thanks. Wait, maybe some toast. Yeah, just some toast. Toast and coffee."

The boy glared at him. "I got to eat." He took a sip from the glass of water. "Your car is a shitkicker, mister."

6

He could fix the car every time it died—which it did, and often. Once, at a truck stop outside Memphis, he'd burned his right hand getting the distributor cap off. Acrid smoke filled the air, but he managed to toggle some switches and buy a new temperature gauge, and it ran all right for the night. The boy had to piss five times in the space of six hours, and still he refused to give up his two-liter plastic bottle of Coke, which he clung to as if for dear life.

On the road, no one really looked at the boy, who mainly kept to himself in the backseat, flipping through the stack of *Time* and *Life* magazines that had come with the car, pulling the blanket over his head when daylight came—and Stony assumed he slept. At the rest stops sometimes a nice big-haired Southern woman patted the boy on the head as he ran by her on his way to the snack machines. "Your son is a real popgun," one woman told him, smiling a smile full of Georgia peaches and Southern-fried warmth. *If only she knew*. Every few hours, the boy complained of hunger. He devoured two Big Macs at one sitting that night, and then downed a large fries, a Coke, and a chocolate milk shake. The kid was an addict for Coke, with a secondary addiction to Snickers bars. The candy wrappers littered the backseat, and when Stony stopped for cigarettes or gas or a decent cup of coffee, the kid always had to get him to buy some more Snickers. A healthy appetite for junk food for a twelve-year-old. At truck stops, the kid did his business, washed his hands, stayed near him. As if the boy were afraid of the rest of the world more than he was afraid of him. That was good. He knew the boy would stay with him. He knew the boy would stick to him like glue.

That frightened him when he thought about it too much.

He tried not to think of it at all. He was not a man used to showing his fear to anyone, let alone a kid.

They didn't say much, back and forth, front seat to back. It unnerved him to think of the kid in the back, wondering what it would all come to when they reached their destination.

They passed the Virginia state line at four A.M. Stony was tired, but he wanted to wait until the sun was well up before finding a place to sleep. The kid had no problem sleeping, and seemed to be content with watching the stars and other cars and the blur of trees and houses and the great white blank spaces of the highway north.

Finally, as the sun was coming up, and he was too tired to keep going, the boy asked, ''Where you taking me anyway?''

He almost cracked a smile, glancing in the rearview mirror. The boy's accent was Southern cracker. He would grow up redneck maybe, he would grow up and drive a truck and own a gun and maybe have a Labrador retriever in the back with some beer cans rolling around. He grinned—God, he was tired. Tired and restless at the same time.

''Hey,'' he said. They'd barely said two words to each other in nine hours. ''I'm thinking of pulling off the road and sleeping. You mind?''

The boy shrugged. ''Whatever. Long as I don't have to keep smellin' your nasty cigarettes.''

''Motel 8 or maybe an Econolodge,'' Stony said, keeping his eyes on the road and then glancing up at the boy in the rearview mirror.

For a half second, the boy's face changed, but it might've been the shadows of early dawn.

Might've been sleep deprivation, too, for all he knew.

Something shifted on the boy's face.

Could he have really smiled like that, that kid? Could he have smiled so it looked like all his teeth were sharp like little knives?

''Watch out, mister,'' the boy said.

He had swerved the car onto the shoulder. It skidded along the gravel. He took his foot off the accelerator, regaining control, and pressed down on the brake. ''Hang on,'' he said. But the car slowed easily, and came to rest at the roadside.

The boy whispered something, and it sounded to him like a prayer of some sort.

''What?'' he asked.

''The Madonna of the Highways,'' the boy repeated.

"Out there." The boy tapped on the windowglass.

Stony glanced out in the direction the boy had been looking. There was a closed-down roadside stand, gas pumps as ancient as the pyramids, with an enormous sign that read, SEE THE EIGHTH WONDER OF THE WORLD! THE MADONNA OF THE HIGHWAYS! WHO IS SHE? WHERE DID SHE COME FROM? WHAT IS HER MYSTERY?

"Can we go in?" the boy asked.

"It's closed," he said. "See? Sign says closed at five."

"Later on I mean," the boy said.

Stony said nothing. He glanced at the small shack, painted a brilliant sky blue with its tar paper roof coming off. The gas pumps, sad as they were, seemed more artistic than anything near them. Out in front, several statues of Greek youths, all cheesy imitations, flamingos, and plastic geese. On a wide, flat plywood board, a painting of the Virgin Mary holding the Baby Jesus. She wore a blue robe, and a diadem of stars across her forehead. The Baby Jesus held a red jewel in his tiny hand. The morning sunlight, coming up in the East, flashed across the chrome of old hubcaps that surrounded this painted plank, like round mirrors of distortion. Flashes of sunlight burned like fire on the round shiny metal.

A sign by the highway, FOOD-LODGING, 3 MI.

"You ever gonna tell me who you are?" the boy said, sounding only mildly interested.

He glanced at the boy in the rearview mirror. He was already bundling under the thin blanket, getting ready to fall asleep.

"Sure," he said. "Sure I will. Later on."

He wasn't sure if he would tell the boy anything.

He wasn't sure if he himself knew why he was doing this.

Why he was going home again with a boy he had taken from a shack in Texas.

The motel was a mom-and-pop outfit, twenty rooms. The middle-aged woman at the front desk glanced at the car parked in the shade off to the side of the parking lot. "How many are there?"

"Just one," he said. "I'm exhausted."

"Traveling all night?" she asked, slowly reaching for the key.

He nodded. "Going to Baltimore to see my sister."

"I've never been there, but I heard it's some place. I heard that the traffic's terrible," the woman said. She held the key up, its huge orange tag hanging down, jingling in her hand. "Room fifteen. First floor. If you open it without pushing, you won't get in. You have to push and turn the key. If you don't, you'll end up jamming the lock. Then I have to call a locksmith and it'll cost me twenty dollars for a room that only goes for twenty-two dollars."

"Yes," he nodded, holding his hand out. *Thanks for the Southern hospitality.*

"Fifteen," she repeated, "to the left and down. Put out your do not disturb sign for the maid."

Feeling slightly punchy, he said, "Couldn't you just tell the maid not to go there?"

"I'm the maid," she said. "But I'll forget, Mr. . . ." she glanced at the card he'd just filled out, "Rogers. I have a thousand and one things to keep track of this morning and I have yet to drink my coffee. You just put out the do not disturb sign."

"Sure," he said. Mr. Rogers. *It's a wonderful day in the neighborhood*, he thought. *That's me.*

"Fifteen," she repeated, as he took the key from her.

## 8

He kept the blanket wrapped around the boy, carrying him into Room 15. Once inside, with the boy snoring lightly, Stony locked the handcuffs around one of the table legs near the television set. Some inner compulsion led him to do this. He didn't think the boy would run, and the boy had acted so far as if they were old friends or family. But something within him told him that he needed to tie the boy down. It's not that he was afraid of the kid running away; it was what the kid might do to him, or at least attempt. The kid knew about the gun. He didn't know about the other things, like what was in the glove compartment.

He set up a series of pillows around the boy's head. Then he sat on the double bed. In seconds, he lay back, staring at the ceiling. He would have to fall asleep, but something within him didn't want to.

He watched three or four houseflies gather in the air just above him. He smelled the musty yet clean smell of the motel, hearing the buzzing of the large black flies. Somewhere nearby, he heard car doors slam open, the click of high heels out on the sidewalk as guests left their rooms. His eyes fluttered closed, but behind their darkness, he was still staring at the flies gathering in the still air above his head.

When he awoke, he was in a sweat.

The boy sat at the edge of the bed watching him. He held the handcuffs in his hands, free. "It's an old trick I learned from this book on magic tricks," the boy said. "You just raise your hands so the blood drains out of them. If you got small wrists and hands like I do, after about an hour, you get loose."

He felt the old fear, as if it had always been caged up inside him.

The boy reached into his lap, bringing up a wallet. "I

34

went through your things, too,'' he said matter-of-factly. ''You're a cop.''

''Yeah,'' he said. ''Sort of. I've been a cop, among other things.''

''Your name is Stony Crawford. You're twenty-eight, almost. You live in some town in Arizona.''

''Outside Winslow, yeah.'' A slight nervousness crept into his voice.

''Don't worry,'' the boy said, looking slightly beat, as if what he'd learned from the contents of the wallet was not what he wanted to find out. ''If I'd wanted to do anything I already woulda done it. I held your gun. I don't like guns all that much. So, am I under arrest or something?''

''No,'' he said.

''I don't get it. You bring me here, you're actually kinda nice and okay if a little squirrelly.''

''It's a long story,'' he said.

''You killed the old woman who took care of me, Stony?''

Stony Crawford shook his head. ''No. But I know who did.''

The boy glared at him. He started making goofy faces. Then he glanced at the clock on the bedside table. The boy shook his head. ''I guess we got time, you and me. You one of those men who does nasty things to kids?''

He shook his head. ''Jesus, no.''

''Then why? Why me?'' The boy, who must've been nearly twelve, looked wholly innocent for the moment.

Stony wondered, *How could he not know?*

It seemed so obvious, from the moment he'd heard the stories in the mountains, the miracles, the boy wonder, the little boy they called Prophet. Then, at a fair in the valley, nearly nine months before, they'd taken him down there to show him off, to show off that power that they knew radiated from him. He recognized the boy without ever having seen him before. Others would recognize him, too. The wrong kind of others, like the family who lived among the rocky crags at the Mentirosa Pass. The way the boy walked, the smile, the hair, the eyes. Almost everything about the kid. And then, those people who he was with, the wild people who had somehow kept him to themselves, like a totem, like a fetish. They knew too, which was why they kept themselves secret.

They even kept the boy's own identity secret from him.

"If I told you, it might frighten you," he said finally, sitting up. "Mind if I smoke?"

The boy shrugged. "Like I could stop you. That's a nasty habit. Mind if I take a leak?" Then he got off the bed and went into the bathroom. When the bathroom door was shut, Stony heard the tap turn on. He lit up his Camel, and breathed in the smoke. He was not a habitual smoker, but took it up in times of stress. Then he went and opened one of the small suitcases. Underwear, some colored T-shirts, and a newspaper. The newspaper was folded over on itself, a string tied around it. He pulled it loose, opening the paper.

*The New London Day.*

On the front page, a photograph of three men examining what looked like the foundation of a burnt-down house. A cloudy day. They wore rain slickers. Behind the men, a lighthouse. Nothing remarkable in that photograph. Beneath the picture, an article.

9

THE VANISHING ON HIGH STREET
*by George Crandall, Special to* The Day

*In the aftermath of Hurricane Matilda, the mysteries at Stonehaven are still unraveling. This is not an ordinary hit from a hurricane, and the fires along Land's End were not set by lightning. What remains the biggest mystery is the disappearance of an entire town, not unlike the disappearance of the Roanoke Colony in Virginia in the*

1600s. *Could everyone in this place actually have been swept out to sea?*

10

He turned the newspaper over. An ad for men's shirts adorned the back page. He didn't want to read the articles after all.

The hunting knife.

*Souvenir from a memorable night.*

A way to never forget what had happened. Or what he had done.

Slipped it back in the newspaper, which he wrapped over it. Tied the string around it. Dropped the newspaper back in the suitcase, shutting it.

"Some world," he said, as he squatted beside the suitcase. When he stood up, he heard the water in the bathroom.

After two cigarettes, he called to the boy, but there was no answer. This worried him. He went to the bathroom door, turning it, but it was locked.

"Open up," he said. He felt sweat break out on his neck, but he told himself to stay calm.

Was there a window in the bathroom? He couldn't remember seeing one, but maybe there was one behind the shower curtain. Shit, he hadn't counted on this. In the fourteen hours they'd been on the road, the kid hadn't seemed interested in running.

He took a paper clip off his wallet, twisted it, and thrust it into the lock. Turning it slightly, the door popped open.

The bathroom was empty, and as he pulled the shower curtain back, the boy huddled, weeping, in a corner of the tub, in his underwear, his jeans and T-shirt wadded up behind him like a pillow.

"What is it?" he asked.

The boy wouldn't open his eyes. "They used to do some bad things to me, those people down there."

"Like what?"

The boy lifted his arm up, showing him the scarred flesh.

"Is that a tattoo?" he asked.

The boy shook his head, working to keep his teeth from chattering. "It's them. What they do. If I touch it sometimes, they move. They know where we are. They're gonna find us."

"No," he said. "They can't."

"They can," the boy said. "They have the power."

The man shook his head, crouching down beside the tub. "No," he said, flinching slightly as he looked at the way they'd cut a design down the boy's side. "It's you. You have the power." He didn't want to explain this. Or dwell on it. Not till they reached their destination. "Let's get out of here and get something to eat. Okay?"

The boy's vestigial eyelids, like a gossamer skin, flicked down over his eyes for just a second.

The man blinked, too. Had he imagined it?

Or was it there?

He watched the boy's face, but the boy seemed to betray no knowledge of what the man had just witnessed.

# Chapter Two

## The Madonna of the Highways

1

"You get hungry," Stony said, watching the boy as he seemingly swallowed the sandwich whole. Stony stubbed the last of his cigarette out in his coffee cup. A thin ribbon of smoke curled up from it. The tar caught in his throat. His tongue tasted of ashes.

"And you get smoky." The boy tapped his fingers next to the ashtray. "That's three in a row in the last ten minutes. Maybe it's time to kick the habit, huh?"

"Just finish your sandwich, kid."

"I'm Steve. Them people, the Rapturists, they call me Prophet, sometimes they call me Shiloh, but they ain't my real names." The boy chomped another bite of bread and turkey.

*His name is Steve. Can't even call him that. Can't think of him as a little Stevie. Not with what I have to do.*

"I know," the man said. "I'm Stony. But my real name is Stephen, too."

"Yeah, funny, huh? They wanted to call me something else. But I knew my name. I wouldn't let them. They had all these weirdo names and stuff. Hey, I got a good joke. You know 'Confucious say' jokes? I love 'em. The old lady's brother used to tell me them. Here's one: 'Confucious say, he who fart in church must sit in own pew.' " He grinned. "Don'tcha think it's funny? You never been in church and wondered why they call 'em pews?"

Stony dropped a dollar bill on the tabletop, and slid out of the booth. The boy followed him. As he opened the door to leave the Biscuit Heaven coffee shop, he asked the kid, "Why'd you stay with them if you didn't like it?"

The air outside was fresh and cool, with a slight nip in the air. The parkway beyond was still green, with full trees thick with leaves. October hadn't hit the South yet. That's what Stony had always liked about the desert. On the desert, there was no October, there was only summer and hell.

"Where the hell else was I gonna go?" the boy asked. "You tell me. They took care of me, it was the place the Great Father told me to go to, and they treated me better than you do."

They got in the car, the boy sliding across the pillows and blankets in the backseat. The car stank of cigarettes and old junk food, and maybe a little bit of body odor as well. It had come with the requisite stink of old men and whiskey when he'd bought it. The layers of its interior smell were like excavations in an ancient cave. Stony rolled down all the windows. "Comfortable back there?" Stony asked.

"Mmm-hmm," came the reply. In the rearview mirror, all Stony saw were the kid's eyes shining like red marbles, reflecting the late-afternoon sun.

Stony scratched the back of his neck. "You're pretty

agreeable. I don't know who kidnapped who.''

"You ever hear that song, 'You Can Steal Me When You Wanna'?''

"Nope, can't say that I have." Stony had to keep telling himself that this was just a kid. This was a little kid. This was not some terrible creature. This was not some monster. This was a kid, and he was a kid-napper. Likelihood was, he would do something terrible to this boy before their trip together was over. Likelihood was, he'd take the hunting knife and plunge it into this kid's heart, or slice it across his throat. Likelihood was, the kid was just a kid who happened to be in the wrong place at the wrong time.

And what if it was all a big damn mistake?

*Self-doubt. The destroyer of all men,* he chuckled to himself.

"It's an old country song," the boy continued. "It goes like—You can steal me when ya wanna, but'cha cain't take me where I ain't already gonna." The kid's voice was a pretty good alto, and he even managed to put in the country twang and break his voice mournfully at the high note. " 'Cuz I been down this highway many times. And if runnin' off's a crime, then I better serve my time, cuz yoo-hoo can steal me when ya wanna.''

Stony clapped his hands twice. "You're the next Garth Brooks. So, you trying to tell me you wanted me to take you from that place?''

Then the boy glanced at the dashboard clock. "It's almost four. That roadside place closes at five. Can we go? I want to see the Madonna of the Highways.''

"Okay. Maybe for ten minutes. If it's cheap.''

"Sure," the boy said, grinning for once like a kid his age without malice or darkness or enigma.

## 2

The grin didn't fade until they'd paid the eighty-cent admission, and gone through the turnstile. "You believe in the Madonna?"

Stony laughed. "Well, I like some of her songs. *'Like a Virgin'*?"

"Ha, before my time, old man, before my time," the kid said, moving ahead. For just a moment, Stony figured the kid might escape through this maze of darkly lit rooms. He had to walk fast to keep up with the kid. The hallway was strung with the story of how the gas station curio shop had gotten hold of the Madonna, where she had been "Ven-er-ate-ed by man-y" the boy read aloud as he went. "Venerated sounds like venereal disease, which I only know about on accounta I heard that VD'll kill ya from the Great Father, who had it from time to time." They passed through several small rooms, each with various religious paraphernalia. "Lookit," the boy said, pointing to a glass-encased rusty nail. Then he read the placard below it. "This is from the Holy Land, Jerusalem. From the Place of the Skull, this is one of the nails from the kind of cross that Jesus was crucified on. Wow."

"No way," Stony said. "It's just a nail. Trust me, this place wouldn't have the real thing."

The boy shrugged. "I guess you ain't a believer," he said, and went off to the next room.

Stony glanced at the iconography along the walls, of saints and virgins and martyrs. In the next room, a poor imitation of a Bosch painting of hell, complete with little devils poking red forks at a naked Adam and Eve.

"Eve has a rack," the boy said. He pointed to something mounted on the wall. "What's that?"

A shamble of white feathers, a beak, all crusted over and dried up.

Stony walked over to stand behind him. "Looks like a dead dove."

"Gruesome," the boy said, a thrill in his voice.

A brass plate sat beneath the stuffed dove, its eyes perfect small marbles, its wings spread outward.

"The Holy Spirit came to them as a dove from heaven," Stony read aloud. He scratched the back of his head. "What kind of sick person put this display together?"

Then he noticed the bottle of water set on a high table. The water looked as if someone had put yellow and red dye in it. It was almost like a lava lamp. A banner beneath it read: "From the Miracle Waters of Lourdes, France, where the Sick crawl on their Knees for Miles to be Healed. One drink of this Water will Heal the Sinner."

Stony looked at the bottle for a moment, the red and yellow swirling mixture.

*The miracle of Lourdes.*

*The miraculous water of France, right up there with Perrier and Vichy.*

Then it struck him hard, like a punch in his gut.

*The miracle of Lourdes. The mother of God. The miracle . . .*

"Dead doves and holy water, weird, huh? I want to see the Madonna." The boy ran to the dark room at the end of the corridor.

Stony followed. He stepped into a room lit entirely in deep purple. The boy stood before a glass case.

*No,* Stony thought, *it's a coffin.*

A small shriveled mummy lay beneath the thick glass. THE MADONNA OF THE HIGHWAYS—TOUCH HER FOR GOOD LUCK! read the placard set atop the coffin display.

Her skin had tightened like papier-mâché around the small skull. The only modesty allowed her was a long blue cloth that was loosely draped across her bones, and then rested like a pillow behind her head.

In her arms, what might have been a mummified baby.

"This is ghoulish," Stony said. Then he laughed, clapping his hands together. "I can't believe how sick this is. This is some little old lady and some little old monkey they're trying to make look like the baby Jesus." He shook his head. "Some people will do anything for eighty cents a customer."

The boy tapped on the glass. "How can anybody touch her for good luck when she's in this glass coffin? Ain't this against the law?"

"You'd think."

"A dead woman all wrapped up like that," the boy said. "And a baby. Cool."

Stony Crawford glanced at the Madonna of the Highways, and tried to shake the image out of his mind—the image forming from the jigsaw pieces of the past.

*Nora's voice in his head whispered, "It's just something you see. It's not real. They're just pictures like movies or TV. Don't start fearing the dark, Stony, not now, now when you got so much light in you."*

*But behind his eyes, he saw the statue of another Madonna. He saw the crushed flower in her hand.*

### 3

THE MADONNA OF THE HIGHWAYS! SEE HER! TOUCH HER! FEEL THE MIRACLE OF HER EXISTENCE! WHO IS SHE? WHERE DID SHE COME FROM? HOW CAN SHE CURE THE SICK? HOW CAN SHE MAKE THE BLIND SEE? HOW CAN SHE MAKE LEPERS CLEAN? YOU MISSED THE TURNOFF—TAKE THE AMHERST EXIT AND GO BACK ON THE SERVICE ROAD 9 MILES. FREE LITER OF COKE WITH EVERY FILL-UP.

Stony glanced away from the last sign advertising the Madonna of the Highways. The road ahead was all that mattered. The road and the descending gloom.

"What's in the glove compartment?" the boy asked.

"Nothing."

"Why do you lock it then?"

"You try to get into it?" Stony asked.

The boy was silent for a moment.

The boy looked at Stony's reflection in the glass. "Who are you anyway? Besides your name and stuff."

It was time. The boy was not going to fight him. The boy was not going to try to run back to the others.

He told the boy, "Look at my face."

"Seen it," the boy said, but he turned around anyway. A slight recognition seemed to come across the boy's eyes, like the light of a distant fire. The boy walked over to him and touched his chin. The boy's fingers were cool.

"Are you my father?" the boy asked.

Stony Crawford's eyes were dry, and his throat seemed to go parched at that moment.

"Where are you taking me?" the boy asked.

"North," Stony Crawford said.

"What's there?"

Stony said nothing. He felt better for having let the boy find out these things for himself, he felt that somehow all this was a sign—as if the universe were not the malevolent force he'd believed it to be.

Stony finally told him when they got onto the New Jersey turnpike, and it was nearly dawn again.

"A town called Stonehaven, up on the coast almost to Rhode Island."

The boy cried out, briefly, as if something had shocked him.

"You okay?"

"It's the pictures on me. They're moving. It means something bad is gonna happen." But the boy said it as if this were nothing out of the ordinary.

"Why did they torture you?" Stony asked, keeping his eyes on the road.

"They said it was for my own good. That I needed to let something out. It itches when the pictures wriggle. Like snakes or something."

"It hurt bad?"

45

"No."

"You hate me?"

"No."

"I hate me," Stony said. "For what I did. For what I had to do."

"Whatever," the boy said. "Tell me about this place we're going to."

"Not yet," Stony said. "We'll be there soon enough."

"Tell me," the boy in the backseat said, and again Stony felt that something was changing—the boy's voice was deepening, and the turnpike ahead seemed less a road than a river full of trawlers where there should've been trucks.

"It's almost dawn," Stony said. "I'll tell you at dawn."

"Now," the boy said.

"All right, all right," Stony said. "I wasn't much older than you, back then, maybe sixteen—no, almost sixteen, but just fifteen. It was probably the happiest time of my life."

"Yes," the boy said from the backseat, his voice so startlingly adult that Stony felt a slight shiver as if someone had traced ice down his back. "I'll tell you about what you saw back then, Stony, I'll tell you everything that happened in that place. Because I know the secret, Stony, I know that secret. Sometimes it's good to take off the mask, Stony. Sometimes telling all is the right thing. Want me to whisper it to you?"

Stony kept his eyes front—an eighteen-wheeler was trying to cut him off from the fast lane, and the bright headlights in the rearview mirror were blinding in the dark purple predawn dusk. He felt the boy's breath on his neck.

"Here's the secret of your past, Stony," the boy said, only it was not the boy, not his voice, not the Southern cracker accent, not the uncertain pitch of a twelve-year-old, but the voice was much older, the voice of an October day, sweet with late sap, the yellow jackets buzzing around it, the smell of burning leaves in the air, of time itself, turned back years to that moment when he went from child to man. The voice seemed to be of a woman's timbre, and he remembered, with a shock, as if he'd forgotten the old woman, working at her loom, or sitting by the potbelly stove, sewing up trousers—it was her voice.

It was Nora. Only her voice was no longer in his head—

*At least I don't think it's in my head. I think I'm not going mad. I think I'm still sane, hanging on to that last shred of clarity before the wrecking ball inside me smashes it all to hell. Watching the kid form the words with his lips but with her voice—*

*Nora, is that really you? Inside him? Coming up from his throat like a bird escaping its cage?*

Then the boy whispered the secret of all that had ever happened to Stony Crawford.

And you want to know what he whispered?

*He whispered,*
*"Once upon a time, long ago,*
*there was a village by the*
*sea . . ."*

*"The mystery of our birth is the mystery of those who*
*brought us into the world. . . ."*
—Montague Thomas Jr., The Seven Seals of Mankind,
*1884*

# Chapter Three

# I Am Born

## 1

. . . And in the village, something remarkable happened, at least once that anyone knows of, but it may have happened a few times. Maybe never—you can never tell from legends whether there's much truth to them or whether they're just lies told by storytellers of a suspicious nature. There are many tales from the past, and many legends of Stonehaven. The one that began years ago and ended with the hand of God destroying the town—so say those who lived at its periphery and saw the squall, heard the wind, felt the power—began even before the beginning of Stony Crawford.

The village of Stonehaven was founded in 1649. Imagine the coastline then, with its ragged uninterrupted line of primeval woods, rocky slopes, the touch of the rich sea, and the scattering of newly settled villages above and beneath what was then known by an unpronounceable Pequot word which meant, "Walk Alone." This was the year that Charles I lost his head, and John Haynes was appointed governor of Connecticut. Silas Crowninshield was an Indian interpreter and displaced member of the gentry from Sussex, England, who was originally given the acreage that is now the village, as ten acres of planting fields off the bogs in what is now Wequetucket. Then, it was considered Old Pequot territory, a haven for Indians and rascals, but Crowninshield carved out a large seaside plantation by 1650. Others followed, exiles from the North, up around the bay in Massachusetts, a few families with gold, servants, and the ambition to create a purer puritan. There was fishing along the coast of what would later be called Connecticut, and the peculiarity of Stonehaven's geography—as if it were a thumb thrust slightly into a sound between a few barrier islands—made it an ideally inhabited place. The local Pequot Indians were, by and large, friendly, and in fact, none of the natives quarreled with the intruders taking the lands from Wequetucket Woods all the way to the water. The Pequots would not settle that land, although the new owners of it found it quite a successful place to live. In those days, the borough consisted of seven houses surrounding a Common. The various epidemics that broke out along the coastline on long hot summers would decimate the small population of the fledgling village, but children were born every season, and with them, hope. As the years went on, and revolutions were fought, the village grew to nearly two hundred homes.

In the 1800s, Spanish and Portuguese fishermen came in, and helped establish an even more thriving fishing trade than had been known before, but most of these families settled outside the borough in nearby Wequetucket, for real estate was hard to come by in the borough even then. An ordinance had been passed in the previous century, one that was never challenged, which limited the growth of the borough. Only the summer homes out at Juniper Point were added, and this because the Point was not in the borough proper.

The famous writer Arland Bishop, a best-selling novelist of the early part of the twentieth century, wrote a short article for *Liberty* Magazine on Stonehaven's charm. Bishop owned a house just off the cove, and wanted to attract his New York friends up to the borough with tales of its quaint and peaceful existence. But the residents of the village were none too pleased with his depiction, such as the line about "the local color here is both of New England and almost totally without color." Or his damning praise of the village's lazy approach to house maintenance, "The rooftops are in disrepair, the porches crumble, the clapboard warps, yet the houses are like its people. Sturdy, long-lasting, ill-tempered."

Stony Crawford's great-great-great-great-grandfather ran the Custom House near the heart of town, and many is the time his grandfather, when alive, would tell Stony of the old piggery, or the great fire out at Land's End, or the blizzard of '32 that just about wiped Stonehaven out, or the time the cove froze over with swans still stuck in it, and how his grandfather and four other young men had to go out with guns and put the birds out of their misery. "How we wept," his grandfather would tell him, "for their plumage was beautiful, and we hated destroying any kind of beauty. But they were suffering and there was nought else to do."

"Did they have to die?" Stony, age four, had asked, sitting on his grandfather's lap, looking up at the old man, hunched over, the twin smells of whiskey and cigars emanating from his yellowing skin and silver hair. Stony liked to reach up and touch the silver hair, watching the laughing eyes.

His grandfather touched the top of his head. "All of us die, Stony. I'll die someday too."

"I'll never die," Stony said, and was determined to mean it.

When his grandfather died, Stony Crawford's world changed, but there were things that had changed the world of Stonehaven before he had even been a glimmer in his father's eye.

2

Years before Stony came to be, in a distant country, a man of forty-two stood outside what appeared to be a cave, but on closer inspection was something of a cloister. Many nuns had lived much of their adult lives within these dark holes, and their paraphernalia had been abandoned when they had left nearly a hundred years earlier.

The man stood outside for a moment, before entering the cavern, with his workers and his feeble light and his absolute knowledge that a great and forgotten treasure lay within these rocks.

He had been sent to see what the workmen had found beneath the rough-hewn chapel at the heart of the cavern. The bones of some creature embedded in an amber-like substance, a hardened resin from forgotten millennia. The superstitious townspeople were calling it "dragon." Archaeologists from distant places assumed it would be the bones of some dinosaur. Word had just leaked out, and the man had arrived from London on the first flight he could book, and then had rented a car from Paris, driving all night until he arrived at what seemed to be a lost and empty village. It had taken him three hours, beginning at dawn, to assemble a work crew, for he knew that if he did not get what he had come for, and quickly, then others would soon descend.

Since he'd heard the reports from one of his search agencies, he had barely slept or eaten anything. His energy seemed stronger, even so. It had begun simply as a report of boys playing inside an old cloister. Finding the cave paintings. Finding the relics.

Hearing about the light of dawn coming from two hundred feet beneath the ground.

The Azriel Light, that's what it was called in one of

the old musty tomes he owned. Crowley? Fairclough was positive that Aleister Crowley had been the one to call it that, the Azriel Light, and the darkness that spread from it. Azriel, Angel of Death. Azriel, Servant of God. Azriel, symbol of the Radiance beyond understanding.

*Azriel, demon.*

*Azriel, Angel of Death and of the Magnificent.*

Finding a bit of what lay beneath the flooring that the French sisters had laid down years earlier, perhaps three centuries back. Beneath this, the rock wall had caved in at one time.

He knew he would find something in this dark stone world. He hoped it would shed light on the studies that had swept him up since he'd been a young man.

But when this man entered the flare-lit cavern, he did not expect to find what he had spent his life seeking. Only its shadow.

His name was Alan Fairclough, and he had once upon a time been a monk, and then an academic, and finally, now retired, a man of some wealth, acquired through inheritance, and much leisure.

He turned to one of the workmen. "I've had so little to celebrate these past few years," he murmured, half to himself. "And now this feels so close. So close."

"Oui, monsieur." The workman nodded, only half understanding the language.

In French, Alan Fairclough asked the worker if there was anyplace a man could go in one of the local villages to satisfy certain appetites. He attempted to make it sound as if he were interested in religious matters.

The workman nodded, giving him an address.

That night, Alan Fairclough tied the woman's wrists as tight as the torn strips of her blouse would go, and leaned over her, whispering, "You cannot even guess, *ma chère*, how long this night will be for you. But do not be afraid. I will not mate with you. I am saving you for something finer."

The nun, whose mouth had been sealed shut with putty and tape, closed her eyes and Fairclough was certain she had begun to pray.

This was in southern France, thousands of miles and several years from the small town on the Connecticut coast where a boy would be born one spring morning.

3

In the village on the Connecticut coast, in a secret place, there was a room that was always dark, lit sometimes with candles, but even they did not vanquish the inner night. Several rows of pews, side by side, an aisle running between them. Two small steps up to an altar made of primitively cut stone. The smell was thick, incense and musk. Some wild animal was caged nearby. Some beast from the nearby woods, snarling and snapping.

Upon the altar, a slaughtered lamb, its blood draining into a chalice kept beneath the stone slab.

The little girl, her eyes wide with terror, as her father guided her hand into the place where the animal's heart still beat. She brought her hand back swiftly, wiping it across her mouth, her small face, flickering in the candle-light, painted dark with blood.

Shadows flickered in the candlelight behind the altar.

The little girl looked above the altar and prayed that it would be over soon. When she opened her mouth to speak, her tongue seemed to give off words other than what she wanted to say, words that no three-year-old could possibly speak, and the languages she used were many.

On the altar, the obscenity began.

This was long ago, before there was light, before there was summer, before the day when Stony Crawford was born.

4

When you live in a village with just a few hundred residents, legends of births and deaths tend to take on mythic proportions. When Old Man Randall died, he didn't just fall down the front steps and go, he keeled over and cried out the name of the Savior three times, and as he lay bleeding, his nurse from over in Mystic saw a flight of starlings take off overhead and then vanish into fog. "Starlings carry the soul to heaven, but if a hawk was to get even one of 'em, then the soul remains earthbound," she'd tell folks outside the Stonehaven Baptist Church after Sunday service. She fudged on the story, because she had actually seen a hawk take out one of the starlings, and she suspected that Old Man Randall still tried to pull up her skirt when she made the rounds of her patients down at the nursing home in Ledyard.

When Tamara Curry's widowed sister Jerusha gave birth to twins, they weren't just stillborn, they were exhumed from Jerusha's forty-six-year-old body and breathed one gasp of Stonehaven air. Then in their angelic wisdom, they got the hell out of this awful world as soon as they could. Jerusha followed several minutes later. Even at a distance, myth bloomed like an April crocus.

It was said that when Chad "Mad-Dog" Madigan died in Vietnam back in the '60s, he raised his hands to heaven and called out to his girl Martha Wight at the distance of all those thousands of miles. She sat up in her chair on the front porch, clutched her heart, and heard his dying words, which were, "I'm gonna miss those tits of yours, baby."

Even the Doane sisters' Border collie's death was an event worth talking about. "He went out to the dock on the cove lookin' for Alice's old boat, and then he gave one last ki-yi and dropped down to the wood planks. He was gone. That fine dog was gone. It is a mystery to us why he went so soon. But he called to us one last time. As if to say, 'God take me!' ''

Angels visited the dying; Jesus came to those who wept; even Fiona McAllister swore up and down on a stack of Bibles that she'd seen a vision of Mary, the Mother of God, when she came down with pneumonia one winter.

Legends and belief intermingled, and from them grew a small village's identity within itself. The mythology of Stonehaven was as thick with significance as anything Homer had ever sung about.

Stony Crawford's birth was no exception.

With all the stories surrounding his birth, you would've thought Stony Crawford was the Second Coming. That's what mean old Tamara Curry said, her of the twenty cats and the prodigious breasts who covered them so well they looked like great pumpkins beneath her many scarves. She swatted Stony whenever she saw him, and she'd tell him, as she wiped down the counter at her ice cream store, that if he'd been born a second sooner he'd have hit the pavement and gotten brained and that would've been the end of his stealing candy from beneath her nose. "I wasn't there, mind you, but I heard plenty. I heard you were ugly and looked like a demon out of hell and all hairy. Disgusting that good women like your mother would want to bring you into this world, Stony Crawford."

His real name was Stephen, after his maternal grandfather, but even at birth, they called him Stony because it was in the borough that he first cried with life, laid out on the cobblestone walk. Being small-town New Englanders, and sea folk, and in a borough all but isolated from the rest of the Connecticut coast, they seldom mentioned how they felt about anything other than weather, work, and scandal. They had a history of silence, since 1698, when the borough was officially founded by a small group that included the Crowninshields, the Randalls, the Clements, and the Glastonburys, back when all of Stonehaven was literally a stone haven, from the rocky point to the granite of its quarries. The village was born in silence, and only later would it tell its secrets. As he grew up, no one ever mentioned that he was born on the same day that Daniel Madigan threw himself off the top of the Land's End lighthouse because of his unreturned love for Jenny Lee Baker, daughter of the owner of Baker's Dozen Bakery. Or that the Crown family had come early that year to their palatial summer home out on the Point the night before, and that their five-year-old daughter had bruises all over her body that no one thought to question. The summer people were different than the locals. They had different ways, different means. A bruised little girl from the big summer house on the Point was just a phantom as her family drove through town in the early evening. No one mentioned that Book Ends Books & Cards would be set on fire later on in the day, after the rain, when Alexandra Shoal dropped her cigarette in the wastebasket, and then her cocker spaniel knocked the basket over. Some later might've mentioned that this was Alexandra's way of collecting insurance, others might've said that it was her way of clearing her unsold stock of books in one fell swoop. And the cries of hundreds of birds, as if all of the swans on the cove had flown at once up into the air and had been silenced also at once—like a miraculous ascension. All was forgotten later. Even his own mother, Angie Crawford, didn't tell him the other thing that happened that day.

The only thing his grandfather would tell him about his birth was, "It was special. I saw a dozen shooting stars the night before, and I knew you were going to be someone I'd want to get to know."

They talked about the storm, and Johnny Miracle, and the beer, and the priest—whenever they talked about the day he was born.

Angie Crawford was on her way to the Package Store down on Water Street to get the weekend's beers when she felt the jolt within her. "I had been watching *The Holy Brigade* on Channel 9 just the night before, and they're all talkin' about how the Antichrist was comin' and me thinkin', with my big belly, oh Lord why bring another child into the world if it's going to hell so fast? And then, not ten hours later, I hear you knockin' to get out. I was wearing my whites," his mother told him, "because I was still on call even though I was eight months along." She dropped her purse right at the doorstep to the store, and clutched the edge of the doorframe. She tried to call out to someone for help, but the pain hit her fast. Her young son, Van, looked up at her and asked, "Mommy? What's wrong?" She managed to whack him on the behind with her free hand and told him to shut up because his little brother or sister was about to make an entry into the world. She looked out at the street, and saw people sitting in the tea shop across the way, all lost in their conversations. The rain was light even while the sky darkened with clouds. "I thought maybe there'd be time if I just held you in," Angie told him more than once, "because I know you were happy when you were inside me. You didn't kick the way your brother did. And oh, I was worried that we'd have those complications like I had with Van—he was blue when he came out, and all kinds of things had to be done. So I thought: I'd better get to the hospital and fast!"

His father was still out on the trawler working the lobster cages by the Isles of Avalon, and his grandfather knocked out from the previous night's medication, so his mother was pretty much on her own. After taking another sip from a Budweiser can, she left her little one, Van, with Martha Wight at the Package Store. The only man available to drive her to the hospital down in New London was Johnny Miracle. "He had been an idiot in search of a village, and he found it in Stonehaven, of course," she'd laughed when she recalled the day. Johnny was less a half-wit than a three-quarters-wit who could do two things

and two things alone: drive, and quote scripture. He also
had a proclivity for setting trash cans on fire around town,
so he was as much a nuisance as he was a fixture. Since
no one ever trusted him with their car, nobody was really
sure about the first thing, but the scripture rang in their
ears when Johnny went on his shouting sprees. And at
least once in everyone's lives, they'd had to put out one
of his little fires. Other than that, he occasionally swept
the streets, but was not much of a sweeper. Johnny Miracle was not true to his name, either. Usually whenever
he touched things, they had a habit of never working
again. "He is the AntiMiracle," Stony's mother would
laugh. Angie Crawford should've known better than to
entrust the birth of her second son to Johnny's aid.

As soon as Johnny got behind the wheel of her station
wagon, the car refused to start. Angie's water broke right
there in the backseat. "It hurt, but I just forced my knees
together. You wanted to come out, and I wanted to keep
you in, at least for another half hour." Between that and
the storm that began, seemingly out of nowhere (at least
that's how his mother always told him the story), raining
down in buckets, Johnny didn't know what to do. So he
got out of the car and began shouting for help. Not a hell
of a lot of help around Stonehaven Borough, midday in
spring when half the shops had not yet opened for the
summer trade, and most folk worked in neighboring
towns. The idle were there, as the idle always are, but
they did what the idle are best at and just watched as the
woman in the backseat of the green station wagon began
screaming.

Still, one person came to help. From across the town
square, Father Jim Laughlin had heard Johnny's bleating
call and Angie Crawford's cries. Some said it was the only
time they'd ever seen a Catholic priest sprint across the
Common with his white collar coming undone and only
one shoe on. "He was a handsome figure," Martha Wight
once told Stony, "he was only about twenty-three, a full

thick head of dark hair, a strong body from all that jogging he did, and you know he used to coach basketball at the Parish back in the summertime. I once watched him take his shirt off at the beach, and my oh my, Stony, if I weren't a good Baptist and he weren't a good Catholic priest, I might have had a notion or two.''

Father Jim was able to calm Angie Crawford in the last few moments as her newborn emerged, already bloodied and somewhat battered from the birth passage. Angie downed a couple of beers while the pain subsided, and later told her son that it had been one of the easiest of her births. "Of course, both you and me was stone drunk by the time it was over," she laughed. The young priest wept when he held the baby in his arms. Johnny Miracle, it is said, looked up to the heavens and the downpour of rain and cried out, "It's the bloodiest baby I ever saw in my life! It's the goddamnedest bloodiest baby I ever saw! I never seen so much goddamn blood!''

As Stony grew up in the village, he was often told details of this story by various townfolk who claimed to have been glancing out their windows, or sitting in the Blue Dog Tea Shop across the way. "Johnny Miracle is good luck 'cause God watches over drunks, babies, and idiots—and all three of them were there." Stony also grew up knowing that his mother was the one known as the drunk. He found out much later what no one, including his mother, would tell him—that the nurse's uniform his mother wore was soaked red before the morning was over. That she stayed in the hospital for four months after his birth.

That when he was just beginning to breathe the air of the brave new world he had entered, his mother's body was ragged and torn and his own father would not touch him for the first year of his life from blaming him for it. His father would never touch his mother again, either.

But the crying newborn could not know this, nor would anyone tell him.

Someone else was there, too, that day, at his birth.

A woman, who was not watching him, at least not watching him in the traditional sense. She sensed his birth more than anything. She sensed something about the baby that had just come into the world as she sat on the little bench under the granite eaves of the Stonehaven Free Library, the rain pouring hard. But her senses were sharp, and above the storm, she heard the baby's first cries as it entered the world. She turned to her older sister, and whispered, "It hurts to hear the way that baby cries, doesn't it? It just brings out the pain of living to hear it go on. It's like he knows he's come from a better place and now he's stuck here for the time being and can't do a damn thing about it."

Her sister, sitting next to her, took her hand. "Nora," her sister said. "Let's go on home now."

"No," the other woman said, reaching up to her face to pull the dark glasses from her eyes. "I want to hear him. I like the way he's crying. It's like a song, isn't it? He's telling us about the journey he's been on. He's saying that he knows where he's been and now he's moved on to us with the news."

Later, when they met, she would tell Stony about hearing him cry at his birth.

Later, she would make him feel as if just by being born he had done something remarkable for the world.

Only when he was fifteen, and fell in love for the first time, did he feel that the world had done something remarkable for him.

5

But until fifteen, Stony's life was like a shadow room. His first actual memory at home was when he was three. His brother Van grabbed his hand in the hall and drew him into the bathroom. "Shh." Van put his hand over Stony's mouth.

Then Stony felt the vibration in the door, as if some great force were shaking the house.

The stomp of a giant's footsteps.

Then, the shouting, his father's voice, in the hall. *"Damn it, Angie! I'm sick of all this, I'm sick of all this. I know the bastard's not mine!"*

"Stop that, he's here." His mother's voice was smoother. "Just stop it!"

*"I am so sick of working damn hard all the time and coming home to this mess and Van with his bike in the driveway and you gettin' fat and sloppy and that bastard eating the food I work hard for, wearing clothes I pay for, it ain't what I dreamed of for us, Angie, it ain't what I dreamed when we met and started out, you damn—"*

Then his mother's voice raised to a pitch. "Walter Crawford, you just shut your yap, you drunk old fool! I work hard too, and he is your son as much as he's mine, and just because he doesn't look like your trash family doesn't mean he isn't from you, you ignorant son of a bitch!"

Stony, at three, could not possibly know these words, but he knew that his parents were angry, and he knew that the bathroom door vibrated whenever his father shouted.

He looked up at Van.

Van whispered, "I wish you'd never been born."

6

His next earliest memory was crawling under his parents' bed during yet another fight of theirs, this time over paying the mortgage. As he shivered, trying to crawl as far under the bed as he could, listening to their screams—

He came across a small metal box. It opened easily, and in it he saw all kinds of money. He was nearly four, and knew well what money could buy (candy and toys). As he sat there looking at paper money, piles of it, rubber bands wrapped around it, he wondered why his parents were fighting about paying for the house when it looked like a lot of money was right there in the room.

He was thinking of bringing it out from under the bed. The box was his mother's—it had her name scrawled on the top. She had probably forgotten where she'd put it. He could stop their fighting right there.

But his father's voice, booming across the room, and then the sound of the slaps, and then his mother got so quiet it scared Stony.

He stayed beneath the bed until long after his father had stormed out of the house.

This was not all of his life. There were happy times, and times when his father was wonderful to all of them. His grandfather, on his good days, would walk with Stony out to the lighthouse and tell him old stories of the sea and of the village. All the stories were sweet, and tinged with a sadness that the world changed with time. "It's not the same place I grew up in," his grandfather would say. "It was once—not innocent, Stony, not that—but it was once undisturbed." Then he'd raise his fist at the summer homes. "Those summer people coming down here with their money and city ways. I don't care who owns this village. I don't care. It's ruining itself. But you—you, my boy—you will get out of here someday. Do the one thing that my daughter—your mother—was never smart enough to do. When you get older, get out, go see the world, don't let this village stunt your growth."

"Daddy says—" Stony began.

"Don't ever listen to him," his grandfather interrupted him. "Don't even pay attention. He's a bitter, unhappy man, and he loves you, but he is not capable of showing it. He and your mother crawled into a bottle a long time ago, and they don't seem to want to get out. Just let them be. You keep your joy within you, Stony, keep your candle burning even while, all around you, they snuff theirs out."

Then his grandfather's tone turned grave. "You're too

young to know about a lot of things, Stony. But when you get a little older, when you become a man, you'll find out things about your mother and father, and you won't like those things. You'll find out about what this village is all about. If I was in better health, I'd get out of here, and take you with me, something I should've done long ago before your mother got rooted here. We tie ourselves down, Stony, but we don't have to. Someday, you'll know why your father is so awful and why your mother is the way she is. But for now, trust that it will all come out all right, will you do that?''

Stony nodded, never understanding him. The old man's mind seemed to be erasing itself, and within months his grandfather didn't even recognize him anymore.

After his grandfather died, there were still good things. Christmas was always beautiful and magical. Summer was usually peaceful. Sometimes he thought it was perfectly normal that his dad sometimes hit his mother. Only sometimes; other times he thought he lived in a crazy house. But his mother didn't seem to mind all that much. Usually he didn't like it, but did nothing about it. He knew his parents loved each other, though, because of the way they looked at each other over the dinner table, or because of the flowers his father would bring home after a night of shouting. Once, he'd come home early from school in third grade, and his father was just getting in from the trawlers. Dressed in the heavy fisherman's mackintosh coat, his rusty beard spattered with bits of his lunch, his father gestured for Stony to come over to him. His father placed his arm over his son's shoulder, his breath thick with beer, and said, "You're a good kid, you know that, Stony? You're a damned sight better'n I was at your age." These were the only kind words his father had ever said to him, but they were enough to keep him warm during the more difficult times in the Crawford household. Other times, he'd sit up with his mother to watch her favorite TV show, *The Holy Brigade*. The man with the glasses reminded him of his grandfather, and he'd shout out about scripture and gospel and raise his hand up and call to Stony and his mother—it seemed like he reached right out of the television—to make them send in a donation. When the man on *The Holy Brigade* looked right at Stony and said, "We are raising a generation of vipers! It's true! Look all around! We have false messiahs, and you! What will *you* do about it?"—Stony was sure the man could see him as he picked his nose.

Once, when Stony was walking down High Street, near the bank, Johnny Miracle was sitting there on the revolutionary war cannons that had been rolled out on the cobblestones as a relic of old Stonehaven. He shouted the very same scripture at Stony, and it gave him the creeps. "No!" Johnny had shouted, "Don't run, boy! I wanna talk with you! God wants to talk with you too!"

Such incidents made up his childhood memories.

And there was his favorite comic book, called *The Storm King*. The Storm King had once been an ordinary farm boy in Kansas, but by accident had discovered his true abilities. He was a Rainmaker sent down by the inhabitants who lived beneath the frozen seas of Yog Arren, a moon of a distant planet. They were water element people, and the boy had been sent to earth since he was the last living son of the greatest of the Aquamers. All of his other sons had been slaughtered in the wars with the people of the Quillian Desert. But the boy who became Storm King found his powers, and took storms and lightning with him wherever there was injustice, wherever a wrong had been committed, "Wherever Evil Takes a Foothold, the Storm King and His Powers of the Cosmos Shall Find and Destroy It!" So said the advertisement at the back of each magazine. The Storm King had even gone to Hell and made the Devil beg for mercy as the rain came down and put out Hellfire . . . the Storm King had gone to the ancient garden of Eden, which was now a desert, and he'd brought rain to make it grow . . . the Storm King had gone to Mississippi and had called the great flooding river up, up, up into the sky so that it would cause no more damage . . . the Storm King had taken the tail of a cyclone and wrapped the water up into it like it was a handkerchief. No one on earth was more powerful than the Storm King, but he had one weakness, what he called his Achilles' heel.

He was alien, and a loner. There was no place in the world upon which he'd been set which would accept him, for although he was a savior, he also brought fear, and his very touch might mean death. . . .

And one thing alone could destroy him:

Moonfire, the Fire That Burns in Water, in Air, in Earth.

*It is an elemental fire, neither spirit nor flame, it sears and transforms those it touches.*

*Once the Storm King is touched with it, his powers lessen, and he becomes like all mortal men.*

He was an outcast from his own kind, and a creature who had to disguise his inner alien nature with a hooded cloak. The Evil Men and Women of Earth, when they discovered his Achilles' heel, would steal Moonfire from a Sacred Vault and use it against him. He would weaken, and they would then capture him. But he usually got away eventually and righted more wrongs. The Moonfire Effect, as it was called, was only temporary.

Someday, the little boy knew, the Storm King would come to Stonehaven, too, and right all the wrongs and vanquish those who caused Evil to exist. The Storm King could use the winds to suck out evil like bad blood from someone, or he could bring rain on a dying land, or he could chase evildoers with lightning bolts.

Stony Crawford had all twelve of the *Storm King* comic books, and knew each practically by heart. He took comfort in all this whenever the bad seasons came on and his father began drinking. Stony had favorite TV shows, and movies that made him roll in the aisles of the theater in

Mystic, laughing his head off. He had the world of his books, which he read over and over again, especially *The Count of Monte Cristo,* his favorite. He had his childhood friends, all of whom lived in other parts of the county but who attended the Copper Ferry school on the other side of Wequetucket. He had his Special Places, like the rotted-out old tree in the woods that doubled as a fortress, and the dock down by the Cove where he could sit back and watch the swans while he plotted his future escape from Stonehaven. He had his dreams of the future, and of rockets and jet-packs and intergalactic missions—all the things that boys growing up in the last gasp of the twentieth century cherished.

So even in the worst of his young life, there were both hope and comic books.

The boy grew, and when he fell in love, his life seemed to open up with a radiance he had never before known.

# Chapter Four

## Love Hurts

### 1

Remember how it tastes? The first time you really fall in
love, and you don't know then, no matter what happens,
that it's that first taste of love that is always best? You
don't know that truth until you're older and you accept
what life offers, then you forget. You forget that once,
when you were young, you burned with love.

*Burned.*

It's almost like that first cigarette you tried, a Camel
unfiltered, and it burned inside your throat just like love
burned inside your heart.

### 2

"You know what's cool about being fifteen?" his buddy
Jack Ridley from Copper Ferry High said, Jack's breath
an eternal cheeseburger-with-onions, his face peppered
with zits, his good looks still shining through undefeated

by adolescent ravages. Jack had grown up down the block from Stony, and only recently, when his folks divorced, had he moved out of the village halfway down the road to Mystic. Still, Jack was a villager, and sometimes Stony felt as if they were more brothers than Stony's brother Van would ever be to him. But they were hardly alike. Jack was cool, unlike Stony. Jack had always been cool, it was a halo around him, ever since third grade. He even smoked Kool cigarettes, and flashed the pack at Stony.

"What?" Stony said, but didn't give a damn because he was wondering when he was going to see that pretty girl again, the one who passed him the note in third period that read, *You're cute. You want to call me?* That pretty girl who just a few years ago had braces and no makeup and hair pulled back and worn in a braid so she looked dorky, only now she looked like the Babe of the Universe as far as he was concerned with her slightly crooked smile, those red lips, the Spanish eyes. How could a guy resist?

"Here's what's so great about being fifteen: Abso-fuckin'-lutely nothin'," Jack said, laughing. "Jesus, I just want to be away from all this . . . this bullshit!" He withdrew a cigarette from the pack, as if he didn't care if any of the teachers caught him on the last day of classes. He offered one to Stony, but Stony patted the pack of Camels in his breast pocket. They'd both begun smoking just because it was something they knew they weren't supposed to be doing. "Hey, what you doin' this summer? I have to go work for my mom in her office. New London, here I come. Pisses me off."

"Just gonna do the boring stuff."

"You gonna get some?"

"Please," Stony laughed, punching him in the shoulder. "I will die a virgin. My dick's gonna fall off before I'm sixteen from lack of use."

"Sure it will, the way you beat it five times a day, ya wanker." Jack grabbed the last of his books from his locker. He held each one up as if weighing their sins. Biology was the heaviest. Jack had drawn a picture of Mickey Mouse on the back of it. "Man, I just want to burn these. Burn fuckin' bio, fuckin' geometry, fuckin' Spanish. Wanna do a bonfire in my backyard? BYOLF. Bring your own lighter fluid."

"Look at her," Stony said, nodding as the Girl of His Every Thought passed by. "Huh?" he added, as if waking from a dream.

Jack nudged him. "I saw the way that Spanish babe winked at you. Lourdes Maria. She's sweet. Puerto Rican, Mexican, Portuguese, or Cuban, I don't care. She is the Latina goddess. She's fine. Fine as fine can be. But watch out—I hear she's got a ton of brothers all of whom want to make sure she doesn't date till she's forty. And you know those Catholic girls, it's the wedding ring or it's . . ." Jack kept talking but his voice became indistinct, and then Jack stepped off the edge of the world—at least as far as Stony was concerned, because there she was again. Looking at him. Moving in front of him so he could get another glimpse. As if from some great distance, he heard Jack's words, "She looks mighty fertile, Stony, she looks like she wants you too, kiddo, those breasts, those hips, those beautiful lips, her eyes—"

She was a goddess—

Like a dream passing by.

Lourdes. *La chica mas bonita en todo del mundo.*

Her soul was in her eyes, her depths were there, her mystery. Her body was small and perfect, her breasts cupped gently within her thin sweater, her hair sparkling with black diamonds, her grin infectious, her warmth like the sun.

She glanced back at him for a second, her dark hair falling across half her face. He just wanted to touch her hair and maybe talk to her. He wanted to be near her so badly he could taste his own frustration.

Time stopped. He felt it. His heartbeat was the only

sound, and all the other kids, they froze, even the air froze with motes of dust hanging. . . .

All that moved were her eyes, looking into him, opening him up, freeing him.

Then, time returned, noise returned, all the students scrambled to clear out their lockers, and Lourdes was half-way down the corridor.

Stony raced after her, practically knocking down Ariel Seidman and Ellen Tripp ("Sorry, Ariel, sorry, Ellen, I didn't—"), then he tripped over his Nikes and his big floppy blue shirt came half untucked as he caught up to Lourdes and asked her out, and then summer began, summer and the end of all things of childhood for him.

The beginning of manhood.

When love hits a guy whose hormones are already hay-wire, it hits hard and fast, and love can be the most enthralling of demons.

3

A flash from early June—

Sitting on the big rock by the pond in the woods, his hand up her blouse, his lips on hers, the pounding of sweet love in his head as he whispers too soon, "God, I love you, baby, I love you more than—"

"Hush." She stops up his mouth with her kisses. Then, laughing, she pulls away. Buttoning up her blouse, shrugging his hands away. "Give up those damn cigarettes, Stony, it's like licking an ashtray!"

He nods, and picks up the rest of the pack and its cellophane wrapper and flings them out across the pond.

"That's littering," she says sternly.

"I can't win," he grins, and for her (anything for her!) he jogs along the narrow path to the far side of the pond to pick up his trash. When he turns to look at her again she shouts, "You are nuts!"

A flash from late June—

Laughing, both of them, him wearing his big goofy swimming trunks, and her in her bikini that shows too much and all the other guys on the slim strip of beach out at Land's End are staring at her. Running through the water, the spray bursting around their calves. He splashes water at her, and she shrieks, and then chases him deeper into the icy water while some little girl floats by on a rubber raft shouting that there might be sharks in the sea.

A flash from late July—

Drinking ice cold beer stolen from his fridge, just enough to get a buzz, not enough to do damage, and they're out on the Cove in a little boat also stolen from a neighbor's dock. He says to her, "I never thought I'd feel like this about someone." She repeats it back to him. He kisses her big toe and tells her that she has got to have the most beautiful feet he has ever seen, with such perfect toes. She calls him a pervert, and he laughs, "Yeah, I'm so perverted I think I love you."

And then it all begins.

## 4

*Dear Stony,*
*I have heard that everyone has one GREAT LOVE in their lives. ONE GREAT SECRET LOVE. I didn't know till I met you that I would have one. I thought I'd always feel alone and maybe get married and have kids some-day but never really know REAL LOVE. I look at my mother and I think, THAT'S GOING TO BE ME IN TWENTY YEARS. Married with kids, cleaning, keeping my mouth shut, wishing something better for my kids. But when I saw you the first time, last spring, I knew just by looking in your eyes. I mean, I'd seen you before, you know that. But I had never really SEEN you. Did you know it too? It was like there was a chalk outline, or maybe a halo around you. When I looked in your eyes it was like looking into an ocean that was there*

*just for the two of us. I knew that you were the one. I knew that there would be no others. You are my ONE GREAT SECRET LOVE. I don't know if we will always be like this, but I know that I will never ever forget you. NEVER. I want it always to be like it is between us right now. ALWAYS. No matter what happens. And things do happen. I know that. I know that sometimes love is not enough of a miracle to cure everything. I just wanted you to know. What we did together is what I wanted. It was PERFECT AND RIGHT.*

*LOVE*
*LOURDES*

*p.s.*
*I don't love your smoking those nasty things. Kick that habit. I mean it.*

## 5

"Your hair," she says.
  "Your smile," he says.
  "Your muscles," she laughs.
  "Your legs," he grins. "Whoa baby, those legs!"
  "Your sweetness," she whispers.
  "You," he murmurs. "I love you best about you."
  *Fifteen! And it's your first time.* You know what that means, you know how forbidden and natural and mind-blowing it is, you remember the half can of beer that gave you courage, and the way your first love looked at you.
  Beneath a tree thick with summer green, so thick it's milk, not leaves, milk in the tree, mother's milk sap running down its humid bark. The heat of August on your back, the crawling humidity of night, the heat of August inside your own body as it moves like liquid. Fifteen! You lie beneath the spreading tree with your girl, not just your best girl, your *only* girl, and it's after midnight, and this is the experience that will blow your mind, the moment that takes both of you and binds you to each other and

throws away convention and bursts your boy and girl consciousness until your branches grow heavy with the green
of man and woman. You want it, not just the sensation,
but to get out of your skins, to change, to be more than
what you were a few moments before. You notice how
hairy you are, and how smooth and fresh her skin feels,
and you let that part of you, that delicious animal part,
take over and you let nature command. You close your
eyes because you want to be somewhere other than in the
sensation you feel, you want to be inside and outside at
the same time, you want to be cosmic and you want to
be small, and afterwards, as the two of you lie wrapped
in each other's arms, you shrink and the tree seems larger
above you, its hungry leaves flowing all around you.
Through its branches, you see the world now, filtered
through the veins and stems and twigs. Your hands feel
scored like the leaves, like the hands of an old man. It
has taken something from you, this summer night, this act
of passion.

Then you begin to look at her differently. She is already
not who you thought she was. Maybe it's love.

Maybe it's fear that there's a dream you've entered into
now, a dream from which you will one day awaken.

But now, you're fifteen.

After a while, you say, brushing off the dirt, buttoning
your shirt while she discreetly dresses, "It's almost morning. We'd better go home."

"Yeah," she says.

You say, "Tomorrow, we'll meet at Nora's. Okay?"

"Sure," she says, and you watch as she picks bits of
a leaf, crumbled up like ash, out of her trammeled hair.
You reach up and touch the edge of her face. You both
have gone over into the land of secrets.

Fifteen, Stony, fifteen, and already you wish you'd
waited because there's a closeness and a distance that
comes with the secrets. There's someone else living inside

you now, and what is left of you is only the cocoon that won't yet shed itself.

6

Dear Lourdes,
I love you like no guy has ever loved a girl before. You are the light of my world. You got my heart in your hands and I want you to have everything really good there is. I wish I had lots and lots of money to shower you with lots of gifts—like a Corvette or something! Or a trip somewhere just the two of us! It's going to be u + me till the end of time. I never felt this way before either. Want to go see a movie this weekend down in Mystic? And also I want you to meet my friend Nora. She's an old lady but she's really cool.
STONY, YOUR STORM KING!

*Within this note, a crushed purple iris blossom.*

7

You can't know Stony Crawford, at fifteen, without knowing the old blind woman who lived in the tarpaper shack in the woods. He met her when he was a little boy, not long after his grandfather had died. Certain times of the year his father and mother fought more than usual, and at those times Stony found it best just to make himself invisible by being wherever other people were not. She'd been outside doing her wash, deep in the old woods. He thought she might be an evil ogre, but she convinced him with the smell of a blackberry pie cooling on her windowsill that she was actually just a human being. When they got acquainted, she told him how she'd been there at his birth. He had not believed her, but found that he wanted to believe her despite the fact that people lied all the time. He knew they did, even in grade school. His father lied, too. He'd seen his father down at the Boatwright Pub drinking when he was supposed to be out on his trawler. He'd seen his mother lie, too, when she put him to bed at night and told him his father hadn't caused the bruise on her face.

But this woman in the woods, she told him what sounded like the truth.

She was named Nora Chance. People said she had been blinded when she was making soap with her mother, back in the '30s, back when soap was made of lye and suet and the lye had splashed up. She had rocked it, and it had sprayed across her forehead. Before she could even scream from the pain, it had gotten in her eyes. But she never told this story herself. When asked, she would avoid the question and instead go into one of her spins. It was what she called them—her spins, her stories. She'd sit down at her loom, blind and yattering away as she tossed the boat through the threads, making one of the blankets or rugs that could be sold down at Mystic. She did nothing the modern way. She would not have electricity, she would not have a telephone, she would not have anything but fresh running water and a modern toilet, which according to her, were the only true conveniences of the past one hundred years. She had a clothesline of candles, made the old way, with rolls of beeswax, hanging beneath the eaves of her low roof. ("Who the hell buys all these candles?" he'd asked once when he was fourteen and feeling bold, and she had scolded him for his language but had not answered his question. Then, once, she told him that she didn't care if the candles were bought or not, she made them out of devotion. "Candles bring light to darkness," she said.)

She was three-quarters Pequot Indian, a Mashantucket, and one quarter African American, a smart and nimble woman who had survived four husbands over sixty years. She had spent forty of those years weaving and taking in laundry, which she washed behind her home in a great black pot—thus she had been called the Bog Witch, for she had spent many an afternoon stirring the boiling-over pot with a great long stick, singing her old church songs. Spied by malicious children in the crackling woods, she was a wraith seen through the bog mist, calling to her demons beside the crumbling cemetery of the town's outcasts of yore. But Stony had known her since the days she'd saved his pet cat from drowning in the bog, and had brought the two of them in—boy and cat—to dry and warm themselves by her stove while she took out her knitting and wove the first story he'd ever heard another human being weave. It was like magic.

"There was a woman from upcountry," Nora Chance began, and upcountry was what the old-timers called anyone not from the sea. Stony was shocked, then, when he noticed that her backwoods dialect dropped away when she told her stories. "She and her man didn't get along. She had a little boy, about your age, maybe a little younger. Maybe half your age plus two. And her man, he was beating on the boy, too, so she had to run and get away from him. It was winter, and fierce. She took the train and wanted to go all the way to Boston, maybe, or Springfield. But going through the hills to the west, the storm became a blizzard, and the train had to stop a little farther on. It was in a small town, smaller'n Stonehaven. The train was surrounded by ice and snow. She thought to sleep overnight in the depot with her boy, but the train company had fixed it up so passengers could go sleep in town in farmers' homes. This was back in the days when that could be done, when you could sleep in a stranger's house during an emergency."

As she spoke, Stony lay down with his black cat, stroking her still-damp fur, watching the embers between the slats of the great potbelly stove. "The people she stayed with were good country people. He, a retired farmer, and she, a woman who had mourned all her life for the children she'd never had. They showed the lady, whose name I think was Ellen, and her son, to a small bedroom. Strange thing was"—and this was the point that Stony would learn was the departure from reality, the part that Nora Chance strung across her stories the way she strung a bright red thread through the grayness of some bit of sewing—''Strange thing was, Ellen noticed the green and black flies all along the lights on the walls and ceiling of the little farmhouse. In the room, seven or eight of them flew along the ceiling. She fell asleep holding her son in her arms—her little boy that still had bruises on his face and neck from what his awful daddy had done to him just the night before.''

''Is this gonna be a scary story?'' young Stony had asked.

''Don't interrupt me, child,'' Nora Chance chided him. ''I don't tell scary stories. All my stories are the truth, and they're about human love. Human love comes in all forms. Like this mother, Ellen, who loved her little boy so much she ran from his daddy just to keep him safe. Now, there's human love for you. So they slept all night, and she began to dream of flies. Flies all covering her and her little boy, flitting around his nose and mouth. Frightened, she woke up. It was early. It was almost dawn, but not yet. She glanced outside the window and saw the snow shining like broken glass on the farm. She got up, leaving her little boy wrapped up in the old quilt, and went to the hall.''

''Why'd she do that?'' Stony piped up.

''I told you, don't interrupt when I'm weaving a story,'' Nora Chance said. ''All will be revealed in the telling. As I was saying, she went into the hall because she was thirsty. And as she went to get a drink of water in the bathroom, she saw three small children standing half naked in the darkness of the hallway. One was a girl of about eight or nine, and one a boy of five, and the littlest one, barely more than a baby, a little two-year-old. But they all wore cloth diapers.

''And something even more shocking.

''She noticed that at the edges of their mouths, thread

had been sewn, and their eyes were closed, too, threads also, little black threads, and their ears and nostrils, all sewn shut. Ellen's heart beat fast, and she clutched the bathroom door for support. She was unable to scream, and she wondered for a second if she was dreaming.

"Then the little girl reached up and drew the thread out from her mouth, humming sounds coming from her.

"And as she drew the thread, and as her lips parted slightly . . .

"A small green fly crawled to the edge of her lips. Spread its shiny wings and flew, and then another emerged from out her lips. And another. And another."

Here, Nora Chance fell silent.

"Is that the whole story?" Stony asked, after a minute.

Nora chuckled to herself. "No, but it's enough for you now. Your cat's dry now, and it's getting dark soon. You two get off on home for your supper. I'll tell you the rest another day."

And so it had gone for six years, since Stony had been nine years old, wandering with his cat out in the woods. That cat, Liberty, had gotten hit by a car by the time Stony was fifteen, but even she had become part of Nora Chance's stories, woven into the tapestry of whatever tale had been begun the time before his last visit to her. He had begun getting her groceries for her when he was twelve and had the *New London Day* paper route for Stonehaven. He could ride his Schwinn around town, delivering papers, and make his first stop his last: the Watchman Goods and Package Store, where he'd pick up her orders of flour, sugar, ham, milk, and beans. Her diet rarely varied from this, other than the whiskey she drank—but she seemingly had a never-ending supply of this in her cellar.

All this he'd told Lourdes by their third date, and had taken her to meet Nora. "But how does the story end?" was the first thing Lourdes asked when she sat on the threadbare rug by the potbelly stove.

# Chapter Five
# Legends of Stonehaven

1

"Which one you talkin' about?" Nora asked, her nimble fingers still working around a needle and thread. "I got a million spins, some about Stonehaven, some about distant lands and fascinating folk."

"About the children with the mouths sewn shut," she said, for Stony had never finished the story for her.

"Oh, those children!" Nora said, and then quickly resumed a story which she'd actually left off telling years before. "Well, this woman named Ellen went back to her room to get her child. She was going to leave. She knew what kind of monstrous farmer and wife they were. The kind to torture little babies like that. Why, she was going to the police, she was going to find someone to take those poor children away from them. But the farmer told her the truth about it. See, he didn't torture those children. 'They been at their threads again,' the farmer said. 'Damn it, they ain't supposed to tear at the threads.' And Ellen,

82

she's fit to be tied. She's a ball of fury. The farmer tells her, 'They got the minds of flies now,' he says, 'They need to let them out, Lord, but that means I got to put them back.' And Ellen slaps him one and says, 'How dare you stand here self-righteous when you're such a monster.' And the farmer, he looks at her. He's crying. 'We love them babies,' he tells her. 'Only they ain't ours. Mama, she cried for years for not having children of our own. I thought she'd like to die. What was I to do? What is a man to do? So I thought, other people have children. They die. They get put in the ground. They just get left there.' So this farmer, see, he goes and digs up these three dead children. And he thinks: How does anyone know if someone's alive or no? What makes us alive? And he figures, if you move, you're alive. That's the bottom line. And for most folk, it's true. So he sews up these dead kids with maggots and such, and when the flies are born, they move. 'But,' he tells her, 'they got the minds of flies, and sometimes they got to let them out. But Mama, she loves them kids. It's love beyond choosing, lady, don't you know that?' "

"Oh, that's terrible," Lourdes said, shivering slightly.

"I ain't done yet, you hush," Nora Chance said, no longer tolerant of interrupters. "So this woman and her little boy go to get on the train. The boy's daddy is there, and he's mad and he drags them back home. Months later, she returns to the farmhouse. She's got her little boy in her arms. His daddy might have hurt him real bad. His mother, she loves her little boy too much to let Death take him. She tells the farmer, 'Love beyond choosing, remember?' and then the bundled-up little boy, he's so still he might be dead, a spool of thread falls out of his little curled-up hand, unraveling as it rolls." And here, Nora dropped the spool of black thread she held in her hands, and it rolled towards Stony.

"Oh my God," Lourdes gasped.

Stony clapped his hands. "See? She's the best story-teller in the world."

"That's a cool story," Lourdes agreed, leaning back on her elbows, looking up at Nora with awe. "Creepy, but cool."

"I got a thousand and one," Nora Chance grinned, her eyes never lowering. "Just like ol' Shehairyzade." Then she grinned, and nodded. "You children get on home now. It's almost twilight, I can smell it in the air. Twilight ain't good 'round the bogs."

And so it was that year, when Stony Crawford turned fifteen, that love came to him and swept him away, and Nora Chance, in telling the rest of her story from so long ago, blessed the union of the teenagers.

That was the summer before.

Autumn came in with the lobster trawlers, dumping its catch on the streets, the smell of brine and barnacle and seaweed across the cut-crystal day. Stonehaven was lovely in the summer, but like all New England coastal towns, did not bloom until the leaves had begun turning.

2

Are there places like this anymore? Where summer seems to last nearly as long as the school year, where the houses all have neat lawns, are made of brick or clapboard, all neat neat neat; where all the neighbors' children play together, play tackle football on summer afternoons down on the small beach by the cove, where there doesn't seem to ever be an end to the days until the fireflies themselves appear in the nighttime veil of purple as it descends after nine at night? Then the days shorten, until dark comes by five, and the chill of fall sets in, with the scent of rotting blackberries and crisp leaf mold.

Stonehaven, a small gem of a town, but a gem washed over by sea and years until it was smooth at its edges but sharp and prickly within, sat along a promontory of land

that poked into the Avalon Islands Sound. Hurricanes in
'38 and '60 swept the rooftops off the houses, and the
town clock off the old Meeting Hall, but by the time Stony
was fifteen, all had been replaced, all looked as it had
when much of it was first built in the 1700s. Officer Dennehy joked that the roads had not been improved since
then either. He'd sit out in his patrol car sipping coffee
from the Bess Eaton donut shop out in Pawcatuck and
watch the slow pace of the village, and then go back to
the station in Mystic and tell his envious colleagues,
"Well, again, the Village was quiet. I saw three pretty
girls, one black Mercedes, and I got a free lunch at the
Tea Shop just for checking the burglar alarm to make sure
it was working." His reports rarely deviated, except in the
odd suicide or petty theft and, at fifty, Ben Dennehy was
happy to lead such a peaceful existence as an officer of
the law. The best he could say about Stonehaven folk was
that they were good God-fearing people; this was also the
worst he could say about them. Down at the Water Street
Barbershop, where most of the older men gathered of an
afternoon, the stories of never-forgotten storms and wars
passed around like influenza, and the tales coughed up got
larger and grander, until they'd have had you believe that
all Stonehaven was crushed by Hurricane Donna way
back when, and that all the young men of Stonehaven
single-handedly won World War II.

The village had always continued, through history,
through gossip, through neglect. Stonehaven was all white
clapboard, dark shutters, weathered boards of the old
abandoned houses out by the railroad tracks. It was filled
with newly remodeled houses of the summer people, now
ghost houses too; its skyline consisted of the steeples of
three churches, the rotunda of the two-room library, the
flagpoles above the U.S. Post Office and the trees along
the Common—the square emerald lawn of grass that occupied the imperfect center of the borough. It was a community just half an hour out of New Haven, but none of

the children living in the town knew much about the great city an hour to the south, nor of Providence, an hour to the north, nor even New London, and much less of Mystic or Stonington, its nearest neighbors. Stonehaven was hardly even suburban, for the houses, houses with names, had all been built before the oldest man in town was born. The Josiah Bishop House, the Nathanial Greaves House, the Sarah McLendon house, the Randall house with its ancient slave quarters, the Portuguese Holy Ghost Society, the Custom House, even the tiny Citizen's Bank building (one teller, no ATM, and open one day a week, summers only) on Ocean and Water Streets had been built just after 1814, after the town was under attack by the British troops. Many houses were nameless, and some had not been built until 1900, but they all were weathered and lovely and the clapboard flaked with bad paint jobs by the end of summer. The scraggling woods on its eastern edge, full of bogs and ancient cemeteries, before the road led to the highway which led to the interstate—it was like the wilderness had not quite been burned back far enough by the early settlers of the region. It seemed so far away sometimes, as if Stonehaven itself had not progressed since the late 1600s, when it was founded. The town, as summer turned to fall, stank of the overflowing lobster boats that consumed the harbor as they spilled their clawing catches onto the long docks to the south side of town. The lobstersmell was so thick you could cut it, you could inhale it and choke on it, it would open up your pores and clog them with the red sea scum stink. Stonehaven, surrounded on three sides by water, a finger thrusting defiantly at the Isles of Avalon, all three, spotting the glass of sea where it beveled at the horizon. How many bare feet were pricked by thorns, how many hands and elbows stung by yellow jackets, how many faces eaten red by the powerful sun before Labor Day came and destroyed all devices of escape? And then, with fall, all the summer people left, and with them, the mansions out by the point became shells, dark at night, the luxury boats sat on stilts in the boatyard, the lunch and tea shops closed, and one boy would have felt buried alive, if it had not been for the intense love he had. The burning love that only the very young can understand.

It was all Stony Crawford wanted at fifteen, his pure white T-shirt blotted with yesterday's sweat, his swimming trunks waffling as he ran in his old torn-up sneakers, down the placid streets of Water to Seascape Terrace to Swan Drive, then across the bridge at the cove, to the other side, to the other neighborhood beyond the cove. Wequetucket it was called, an old word that meant nothing other than freedom from the village to Stony. Wequetucket was beyond all the white people he had once believed were the only people in existence in his real world. It was the other side, where the apartments rose up, where the people who worked the lobster trawlers lived, where his heart seemed to beat faster and faster as he ran. Spanish and Portuguese and Indian and Black— the colors and tongues and legends were endless, just outside the borough. It was a world where things happened. Where love happened. Where Lourdes lived with her mother—the rows of garden apartments, the highway, a causeway between bays, that connected Stonehaven to the outer world. To freedom. First down the streets of numbers, three, six, four, down alleys without names, across Barley Road and Myrtle Drive, to the Ninth Street Apartments. See him run like he's a match trying desperately to catch fire.

See him run.

3

"Bueno," her mother said at the door, but Lourdes Maria Castillo stood behind her, glancing over her shoulder. Her mother glanced back, glaring. "Lourdes, it's your amigo." Her mother shut the door and turned to her daughter. She waggled a finger at her, keeping her voice down. "You must make them call you first. A boy should never drop in like this. It shows disrespect."

"Oh, Mom," Lourdes said, exasperated, moving swiftly past her mother to open the door. The door creaked as she pulled it back and she felt a slight embarrassment at the smell of the hallway—the fish, always the fish from the boatmen.

Stony Crawford stood there, sweating, out of breath. His brown hair too long over his forehead, the shine of perspiration like glaze on his face. "I ran all the way," he gasped. His grin was wide and goofy. He waved hello to her mother, who had already padded into the kitchen. "Hello, Mrs. Castillo," he said, then he returned his look to Lourdes, who blushed at its intensity. "Want to go for a walk? We can go to the confectionary. I got some money."

"You should call first." Lourdes didn't smile. She looked slightly cross. She did her best not to look him directly in the eye—otherwise, she'd have begun laughing at the charade.

"Next time. I promise," he said.

"Okay." She nodded, continually glancing back towards the kitchen as her mother banged one pot against the other. "I have to do some chores later."

"I can help," Stony said, his voice deepening as he caught up with his breathing. "Tell your mom I'll wash her car."

"I heard that!" her mother called out from the kitchen. "Tell him I want it waxed, too!"

Lourdes grabbed his hand, giving it a conspiratorial squeeze. "Let's get out now while we can."

"I want you two back here by three. Understand?" Her mother's voice became shrill as it blended to Spanish, "Maria Lourdes, *entiendes*?"

"*Sí*, Mommy," Lourdes said. "*Promeso*."

Then she went out the apartment door, and when it was

shut behind them, he grabbed her and they kissed and she felt something wonderful blossom inside her.

4

It was always: to the lighthouse, to the lighthouse. Stony might drag her this way and that in the cool October night, she might linger down by the harbor where the trawlers creaked along, abandoned till the following morning, but it was always to the lighthouse, finally. The woods, too, or the cemetery, or out on the docks late at night when the sea was a flat gray glass and the few twinkling lights of the Isles of Avalon beckoned. But the lighthouse was better, for you could go inside and huddle in the low-ceilinged room, or climb up the tower and look out over the Sound. Or you could go out to the sloping hill that led to the rock wall before the sea, and lie camouflaged by shadows and land. The lighthouse no longer functioned, so it was the best possible place to make out and speak softly, for it was all dark there, at Land's End, across the cracked pavement of Lighthouse Alley, to the dead end marker. Leaping over this, to find one of the grassy bunkers that rose on the hillock over the wispy sea.

After Stony had told her of his love, and she had told him of her love, and they had done all the things young people are warned not to do,

*And in his mind, he felt Moonfire bursting yellow red almost a sunset—*

*Almost the pale light of a moon—*

she told him.

That night, he wept for joy.

Then, by dawn, he wept for fear, alone in his bed, knowing that the sun would be up in minutes and he had not slept a wink. He could hear one of the wild dogs of the docks barking as the trawlers pushed away, out to check their lines and cages.

Words could kill, sometimes, he thought then. Words could change everything.

Lourdes had whispered it sweetly, knowing that a boy might not like hearing the words. Knowing that this might destroy the wonderful thing they had together.

Knowing that this might destroy everything and take from both of them all they had ever dreamed possible.

He felt his heartbeat accelerate, and something that might have been adrenaline—or liquid fire—burst under the surface of his skin when he remembered the two most horrifying words any fifteen-year-old boy could ever hear.

# Chapter Six

# Consequences

1

"I'm pregnant."

"You can't be," Stony said, more startled than shocked, knowing that of course she could be pregnant. It was nature. It was their bodies reaching fertility, it was hormones and the terrible price that came with them.

She didn't say anything for the longest time, but he heard her breaths, slow and careful.

"I love you," he said.

In the morning, the full understanding of this hit him, of what it would mean to him and to his future.

2

Mid-afternoon, a couple of high school punks skip school, and one of them has a bright idea. "Let's pillage my folks' room. I know they always got a couple of twenties lying around," he says, and his name is Van Crawford and he's lanky and has ears that nearly stick out, but he has that aura of coolness with his knit cap on and pock-marked face and terminally hip sullen sneer. He knows these things about himself:

He hates life.

Hates his little brother Stony. Tolerates him but hates him.

Hates his mother.

Hates his father.

Hates the fact that he has to live at all among these fish-people in this fish-village.

HATE is tattooed on his ass, only he's never shown it to anyone in his family, but half the guys in gym have seen it in the showers after soccer practice. Not that Van is good at soccer, but hate can even fuel him through a rough game. He got drunk one night down in New London, and his buddies dared him to get a tattoo, but he decided that *hate* was the word he wanted emblazed on his left buttock for all eternity, although if he'd had his druthers he would've had a flaming skull tattooed there too, only he was too drunk and he couldn't afford it.

He sits on hate, he breathes hate, he lives hate.

If he could get drunk on hate, he would.

Van says, "Always beer in the fridge and maybe once we get some cash we can go on to Mystic and meet some girls or somethin'." He has this way of speaking that's half snarl and half cough, his voice is too deep, his eyes are set too close together. "I fucked Brenda last night."

"No way," his buddy says, his buddy named Del, who lives in a rundown old farmhouse with his lobsterman father, but way out on the highway, way out in the middle of nowhere. Del lives far enough out from the borough and the docks that he doesn't have the fishstink on him. "You didn't fuck Brenda." His voice, drunken, giggling.

"Yeah I did. I rammed it in and got her to moan real bad. She smells, though. She smells like barnacles down

there. Fuckin' townie. I didn't care. Just needed to get a
nut off,'' Van says.

"Holy shit. Think I can do her?''

"Fuck yeah. She ain't the kind of girl who's gonna
mind a few more,'' he laughs, and then they're rummag-
ing the fridge for beer, calling friends, lighting up the last
tiny bit of a joint and wondering when the hell their other
friends are gonna come over.

### 3

Van grinned stupidly, a can of beer in one hand, his other
clutched around his hunting knife. "Your knife is your
dick,'' he said, laughing. He lay back on his parents'
lumpy, messy bed, and looked up at the ceiling. "See?
And life is a great big pussy that you just jab at and slam
it home—'' He sliced the air above him. The knife flashed
silver in the overhead light. It reminded him of fish beneath water.

His friend Del Winter opened and slammed a dresser
drawer shut. "I can't find ten bucks in your mom's
dresser,'' he said, ignoring what Van said.

"You hear me?'' Van said. "I said your knife is your
dick!''

"Yeah yeah,'' Del said, pulling out a strand of pearls.
"Shit, your mom has nice pearls. We could maybe take
these to a pawn shop. You people in this village, you got
nice things.''

Van downed some beer. "Naw, they're fake. She don't
have nothin' of value, trust me.''

"Last week you found a twenty,'' Del said, dropping
the pearls back in the drawer.

"Yeah and last week she got pissed off 'cause she figured out I'd been taking it.'' He took another gulp from
the beer. He hated Bud, but it was the only thing his father
ever bought. So it was all he could steal from the fridge.

He sat up, looking at himself in the mirror above his mother's dressing table.

"Your knife is your dick and your dick is your knife," he said to his reflection. "Who the hell asked you?"

Giggling, sipping, swinging the knife around.

Del came over and picked up a new can of Bud from the floor. He popped it open. "You're gettin' shit-faced, my man."

"Yeah I guess I am fuckin' very gettin' shit-faced."

He set the beer down at his side, heaving a bit. It overturned, spilling the last of its golden contents on the white comforter. The room spun slightly. His reflection in the mirror wavered. "Your balls are God and your dick is your knife, that is wisdom," he said.

"Yeah yeah," Del said, chugging his beer down.

"I would like to kill that Spic bitch my brother's fuckin'," Van said almost solemnly.

"Yeah sure. Hell, I'd do more than just kill her," Del laughed, raising his beer in a toast. "I'd make her cream."

Van held his knife up. "Your knife is your dick," he said.

4

Van Crawford lived by a single code:
*Survival of the fittest.*
It was fuckin' Darwinian.

5

"Throw out your line," Van said, nudging Stony's arm. They were in the dinghy, which rocked gently back and forth on a fairly placid current in the cove. The sunlight was almost blue across the pockmarked sky, and swans rested like feathered bowls not far from their boat. "You'll get something."

"No thanks," Stony said. He leaned back against the

prow, and stared up at the sky. He watched the sun, wondering if he would go blind from staring.

"Something's up," Van said. He reeled in his line, and set his pole down in the bottom of the boat. "Tell me."

"No way," Stony said. Even when Van seemed warm and kind, Stony had not grown up for fifteen years in that house for nothing. He knew Van too well. Trusting his older brother seemed impossible at times.

"It's your girl," Van grinned. "You get some pussy?"

"Shut up," Stony said. "Shut the hell up."

"Use rubbers, that's my advice." Van slapped a mosquito on the back of his neck. "Damn skeeters ain't dead yet. It's fuckin' October and they ain't dead." Then, an afterthought, "Don't trust a girl to take the pill. They lie. They all lie about that. Dad told me even Mom lied to him. All women do."

Stony couldn't help himself. "Too late for that." Had he said it aloud, or muttered it? He glanced at his brother. To see what his face betrayed.

But Van was always on the lookout for the nasty side of things, and the deep dark secrets. "Shit," he said. "You're shittin' me."

"Shut up," Stony said. He reached down into the cooler and brought out a Coke. Popped the top, sipped it. Two swans circled around the dinghy. Stony tossed the birds bits of his sandwich, which they gobbled greedily.

Van shut his eyes, shaking his head. "All that you've known about sex, and you got her knocked up?"

"Shut up," Stony said. "We came out here to fish."

"I came out here to fish. You came out here to confess," Van laughed, and then, "Holy shit. Holy shit. Stony, your life is over."

And then Van said, "That bitch. She let herself get knocked up on purpose." Something tugged at his line. Bringing it up, it was a small bass. He unhooked it quickly, holding it in his hands. "That fucking bitch. Wequetucket Spanish Portuguese bitch trying to get a white

boy from the borough to take her and her bastard in. Just
like mom got knocked up and made Dad marry her. Just
like it's always been in this shithole. Jesus, these fucking
bitches. And you are such a dumb shit for knockin' her
up.''

*"Shut up!"* Stony shouted, his voice echoing across the
water. Geese flew up from the surface of the cove, rippling the sky as they went.

## 6

In the shower, Stony Crawford steps beneath the hot water, and turns it up hotter. He isn't sure if tears are falling
or if it's just the spray of clean hot water that almost feels
hot enough to clean off the dirty way he feels. *Don't
fuckin' cry,* he warns himself. *You cry and you might as
well be back in third grade.* He grabs the bar of Dial soap
and scrubs it hard beneath his armpits, and along his
shoulders. The water and soap run across the light hair on
his chest, and the smell is fresh and new.

All he wants is to be clean.

If he could, he would scrub the soap across his mind
to erase his memory. To erase the part of him that told
him he needed to somehow take care of this. To eradicate
the fear he had about the future.

The steam and heat are almost magical, taking him out
of himself for a few minutes.

*The Storm King is alone. If he touches someone they
might burn to a crisp or drown. . . .*

*And the Moonfire got him.*

Then the water begins to turn cold.

He stands beneath the cold water, shivering, wondering
what the hell he's going to do about the baby that he made
with Lourdes Maria Castillo.

96

### 7

In the pocket of Stony's jeans, a note:

*Things I love about you:*
  *I love your smile.*
  *I love when you get angry and stomp around like a big baby.*
  *I love all that hair on your chest and tummy. It's like you're a puppy.*
  *I love when you kiss me.*
  *I love when you tell me you love me and all the reasons you do.*
  *I love the way you mow a lawn! Hubba hubba!*
  *Your soul.*
  *Your purity.*
  *Your heart.*
  *I love how sweet and kind and considerate and wonderful you are Stony Crawford. Don't ever forget it. And we're never going to be like your folks or my folks. I think you're pretty special.*
  *Love ya,*
  *Lourdes*

### 8

He walks into the living room where his mother, in darkness, watches *The Holy Brigade*. The man with the glasses is shouting that false messiahs abound, that "we live in an age of miracles and nightmares, and God will send his fury down upon sinner and saint alike, and there will be war and rumors of war, and rumors of unnatural beasts from the seas, and of fire from heaven!"

His mother glances up at him for less than a second.

"You might want to pay heed to this," she says in a monotone. "Your father won't and your brother won't. But you ought to."

Then she takes another drink from her small flask.

9

*From the Diary of Alan Fairclough*

*. . . All my life I had been searching for this, but I did not think in my wildest dreams that I would find some evidence of it. We are raised with such beliefs in devils as children, but as we grow older, our imaginations die. Our beliefs transmutate like the consecrated wafer, but in reverse. From flesh to bread, we believe that symbols take over from imagination, rather than the opposite, that imagination creates symbols from the genuine creation. Ritual comes from our instinct, the way that salmon return to the rivers of their birth. Ritual is not empty. Ritual is full.*

*If this damn business with the banks had not taken over, I would have remained there at my retreat, but it's always the prosaic that draws one back from the abyss, time and again. I would not wish the hell of finances upon anyone. Let the poor remain happy rather than deal with the responsibility of money when one wishes to be a hermit in the wilderness, a scholar in the library, or a pilgrim at a place of worship . . . damn necessity . . . damn properties . . . damn worldly goods.*

*But without them, I could not have my home on the island, I would not have met these terrible yet wonderful people. I would never have seen the creature, or watched it open itself, change its geometry, go from beast to demon to beauty as if it could no longer keep to one shape. There is no god but the god of the flesh, and all sanctity runs from profane images. All flesh is profane. All flesh is sacred. All men are gods. Ritual is the key between the worlds of the Old and the New.*

## The Halloween Man

The town is a crucible, a place to observe the effects of our grand experiment, our foray into playing God, our need to move humankind forward, to stop the endless spiral of death that is mortal necessity. When I first saw it, in its cage, its arms strong, its eyes golden and fierce, I knew terror such as no man has ever felt. What must the ancients have known who laid eyes upon these beings! What must the holy sisters have felt when they heard its cries beneath their sanctuary?

And yet my terror turned to love and longing, for even in the darkest of daimons, the fire of heaven kindles and threatens to rage.

When I touched its face, it gave in, it put aside fury, softened.

Can I describe what I felt when I parted its warm flesh and watched the transformation beneath my hands?

When this business is done, I will return to America, to that crucible. The note I received from George Crown this morning was full of urgency. There is more, he told me, there is the beginning of the future now.

His note read simply, "It has taken hold."

# Chapter Seven

## The Life and Times of Alan Fairclough

### 1

Alan Fairclough raised his hand over the young man's face. The face was handsome. Alan would not hire anyone without a handsome face for this. He liked seeing the bruises beneath the eyes, the gashes that opened up above the lips. He liked turning the very beautiful into the very scarred.

When his arousal heightened, he went deep into himself, losing the sense of the physical world, and entered the domain of the gods.

### 2

*From the Diary of Alan Fairclough*

*The story of my life is not a tragedy, but an adventure from what we believe is true to the extremity beyond truth and minor distinctions of Good and Evil. There is no Good and Evil, there is only evil right now and good right now. How life, as it got its hooks into you, moved effortlessly from the sacred to the profane. All we can truly know of it is the Light, the ever-brilliant Light of Divine Essence. In the deepest cruelty, in the most saintly kindness, in the brutality of human conflict, the Light sparks again and again and again.*

*The purpose of my life, its mission, is to find the stone from which the spark can be struck and set afire.*

3

From his earliest years, Alan Fairclough had been destined for greatness. His father was Lord Early, whose ancestral fortune included three great castles in Scotland and Northumbria. His mother was Lady Elaine Romney, a diamond heiress whose grandfather had been South African Dutch and whose father had made a success of the Romney Ironworks as well as the mining operations in Africa. Alan attended Harrow, made the cricket team eventually, and then his world changed so swiftly that the shock of it had never quite worn off. His parents died in a sailing disaster off Majorca. Alan was pulled from school and sent to live with the only living relative who would take him. His aunt owned land in a particularly inhospitable part of northern Scotland. While Alan had been protected from the worst of life by his parents, his aunt was cheap and mean-spirited. To build character, she forced him to take freezing baths, and when he disobeyed her, she had him soundly whipped by a tall grim German named Ranulf. His work was to keep on top of fifteen tenant farmers and their rents. By the time he was seventeen, he had been won over by what he then believed was the nobility of poverty. He took to the streets, eventually joining a monastery and foregoing any material comfort.

But just before his twenty-first birthday, lying on his hard bench of a bed, he began to experience erotic dreams for the first time in his life.

In them, he held the poor young street girls in his arms, thrusting into them like a jackal. He tasted the first blood of virgins, and whipped them until their screams turned to moans of delicious surrender. In these stimulating torture dreams, he was Ranulf the German, not peach-faced Alan Fairclough the Good. Even in the dreams he was not a willing participant in the pleasure he felt. He felt as if he were being raped even as he slowly pressed a rusty spike into the nipple of an altar boy; he tried to resist, but was overcome by a greater force, which shoved him deep into the body of a beggar girl from Calcutta. . . .

When he woke from these dreams, he also resisted them. At first, he was disgusted with their vileness, then he was merely curious at his own nocturnal imagination, and finally, he grew to look forward to sleep and his night of dreaming.

As he was in the middle of an orgy of beating up a young hoodlum before raping the boy's mother, Alan realized with dread that the dream had the texture of reality. As if his memory had become a black hole, sucking in the material world around it until he could not tell what was substance and what was not. He felt his fist connect solidly with the boy's shoulder as a sexual electricity surged through his groin. . . .

"It's not a dream!" he cried out as the boy howled, blood bursting from beneath his left eye a split second after being hit. "It's not a dream!" He screamed at the boy as if it were his fault. Beyond the boy, the mother, her flowing dress torn down the middle, her hands tied to a metal pipe above her head.

Alan let the boy go. The boy ran to sit beside his mother, shivering. The boy was no more than sixteen. The boy held his mother, and both of them wept.

Alan, awake, stared at his bloodied hands. For the first time that he could remember, he began to weep as well. His tears washed the gray walls of the room, wiped clean the image of the woman and her son, until all he could see was night. All he could say was, "My God, my God, why hast thou forsaken me?"

Dawn arrived, eventually, without response. He untied the woman, and dropped five hundred pounds into her son's lap.

A small mirror, above a scummy sink, stood at one end of the room. Alan Fairclough went and looked at himself and saw a monster. Neither Alan nor his former tormentor, Ranulf, stared back.

The face was so inhuman he could not place it as anything other than a shadow.

Several weeks later, he embraced this image, and began his voyage to seek God in dark places. At twenty-one, he inherited his parents' vast fortune, and began discovering the extent of flesh, suffering, and pleasure.

But even these had their limits.

One morning he'd awakened, naked, with two young women and one young man sleeping beside him, curled beneath his arms on a stained and ragged mattress—their bodies so beautiful and fresh the previous evening—with the tastes of laudanum and marijuana soaking him. Then, in the noon sun slicing like a steel glint razor through the slats of the cheap wooden shutters—now, these bodies were great puddings of rot and disease, and smelled to him of excrement. He noticed sores along the man's buttocks from the whip, and one of the women had small knife slashes on her left side along her rib cage. The all-consuming flesh lay there, one great tangled body. He had hacked his way out of that den of melting skin. Rushed to his shower, wiping himself clean of the night's residue.

And the darkness enfolded him. Not the darkness of depression or regret or longing, but the darkness of a man who knows what is true about himself and his appetites.

With that knowledge, all youth abandoned him. All happiness faded, all satisfaction dissipated. He was thirty, then, and had already heard about the creature held captive in the caverns at Maupassane. There were stories of its cries echoing through the small village beyond the cliffs.

### 4

*From the Diary of Alan Fairclough*

*After all this time, to be so close to the legend, to its origin. I will find the creature if it's the last thing I do. I will experience the miracle of its existence. I will touch its essence and be transformed. The key has always been ritual, this is what men have forgotten, what has been lost. It is the ritual that turns the lock and opens the door.*
*My God is the Savage God!*
*I glory in His Presence!*
*I will find His Radiance!*
*Azriel, come! Come with your Light!*

### 5

Since these particular holy sisters had died or moved on two hundred years earlier, it had been difficult to track down the precise cavern, but Alan Fairclough had a great deal of wealth and he spent much of it excavating the area.

Then, at last, one of the local workmen found the first clue.

The remains in rock, crushed by some collapse in the caves several hundred years earlier.

"Beautiful," Alan had said, as the flares were lit around the remains, casting yellow and orange shadow. "Look at its shoulders. Look at its . . . magnificence."

It appeared to be a fossil to some extent, with the arms and spinal column of a human, but its skull, crushed and with the jaw separated, had the incisors of a lion, and what

appeared to be perforations along the forehead. The wings
that had been crushed behind it seemed like a pterodac-
tyl's, but this was Alan's fancy playing with him. He
could not tell for sure.

He knew that it was a daimon that the holy sisters had
kept within this darkness. Its secrets would never be
known.

In eleven months of painstaking excavation, he'd raised
the stones and carefully brought it forth from its resting
place.

When he beheld it in the light of day, his hair went
from jet black to pure white. His eyes, from sparkling
jewels to the dullness of cold stone. The light of the world,
he felt, had flickered and been worn down—both by the
majesty of this discovery and by the knowledge that it
was no longer part of life in the flesh.

It was on a trip back to his town house in Manhattan.
He'd heard a man say something quite remarkable. It had
been a regular afternoon at the private club, and the chap
mentioned something about a certain family. ''The
Crowns,'' the man repeated when Fairclough asked.
''They're in all kinds of industry. Arms, mostly. Very
charitable clan as well. Six million last year to the Save
the Children Fund.''

''I couldn't help but overhear—you said something
about . . .'' Alan Fairclough didn't even want to repeat it.
Perhaps he'd heard wrong.

''The beast? My brother saw it himself. Visited them
one summer,'' the man said. ''They have a pied-à-terre
up the coast a bit. My brother's place is on a little island,
right across the water from their place. He's selling his.
While he was doing some renovating, they had him and
his wife out to stay with them, briefly. He said for such
rich people they have fairly common tastes.''

''The beast,'' Fairclough reminded him.

''Yes, so my brother tells me that they own some creature that looks like the devil himself.''

Alan laughed. "Your brother—does he drink?"

The man went silent. After a sip of whiskey himself, he said, "Not these days. He died six weeks ago."

Alan Fairclough was about to inquire further as to this information, but suddenly it was as if the noise of the club—the laughter at terrible jokes poorly told, the chatter from the men at the bar, the tinkling sound of the piano keys being molested by a less-than-adequate musician— all had been overwhelmed by his thoughts.

*The beast.*

*The Devil.*

*Holiness.*

6

Fairclough had tracked down the Crowns' penthouse in the Lonsdale, off Central Park. He had no problem bluffing and bribing his way up to it, but was sorely disappointed when a lone butler met him at the elevator. The butler was extraordinarily handsome, with dark hair and round blue eyes, Black Irish if there ever was one, a trace of a scar running down beneath his left eye.

"I'm terribly sorry," the butler said. "The Crowns are in Bangkok this time of year."

"Liverpool," Alan grinned, recognizing the butler's accent. "I thought you'd be Irish, but that tone."

The butler half smiled. "Yes, completely. And you're . . ."

"A man of the world, home nowhere."

"I would've said Sloane Square with a bit of Scotland thrown in," the butler nearly laughed.

"Well, you are close to the mark, you are. Alan Fairclough." Alan extended his hand.

"Pete Atkins," the butler said. Then, as if remembering his own job, added, "They won't be back for another month. Not till this nasty winter is over."

"Business?"

"And pleasure, one would assume. Would you like to leave a message, Mr. Fairclough?"

After a moment's hesitation, Alan Fairclough said, "Yes. Yes I would."

He scribbled down a note, folding it once, and passed it to the butler. "How long have you been stateside?"

"Two years," Atkins said. "The Crowns are wonderful employers. Not like people say at all."

"They say?"

"The usual malarky. Nasty rich people and all that. They been like second parents to me almost." Atkins then held the note up. "You don't know them at all, do you?"

Alan tried not to reveal the lie. "We're old friends. Tell me, they still summer in New England?"

Atkins nodded. "Yes sir. Stonehaven. A lovely village I'm told, right on the water. From the pictures it looks like a castle to me. The property's been with them for hundreds of years. Come on, then," he said. Then he led Alan Fairclough into a modest parlor with three over-stuffed chairs, a long table, and a half dozen pictures on the wall. "It's called The Shields." Atkins tapped a photo. The picture was an old one. It showed a Bearcat in the driveway, and a white mansion behind it. A rich dowager and her driver stood in the foreground. "That's Miranda Crown. They called her the Queen. She died a ways back. I heard from cook she was fierce."

"The Crowns must have quite a history." Fairclough glanced at the other photos beside this one. One caught his eye. He stepped over to it for closer inspection. "This one," he said, almost forgetting himself.

"1914," Atkins said. "I know because Master Crown told me it was taken the morning his father was born."

In the picture, four men, one in military garb, stood outside the mouth of a small cave. "That's Master Crown's grandfather." Atkins tapped the glass.

"Where was this?"

"France. Outside Paris I think."

"The war," Fairclough said. "Doesn't look much like they're concerned with war, does it?"

Atkins was silent for a moment. "You say you're an old friend?" There was suspicion in his voice.

"Well, truth is, I lied," Fairclough admitted. "I know old friends of theirs from the club. I wanted to contact them."

"Good show," Atkins chuckled. "You had me fooled, just about. But I knew if you were an old friend, you'd know about them and war."

Fairclough didn't look away from the picture. "Yes?"

"Their girl, Diana, told me that they began all wars. I believe her."

Fairclough barely caught this comment. "I've been there," he said.

"France?"

"Yes," Alan whispered, almost to himself. "That cave."

7

Rupert Lewis was the name of the man at the club who had first mentioned what Crown possessed. Fairclough got hold of him through some easy connections—the Rafael Finches, with whom he dined occasionally, and with whom he often entered New York's seedier S&M clubs for a weekend of inspiration. On the phone, Fairclough asked, "Did your brother ever sell that summer place of his?"

"You have some memory," Lewis said on the phone, obviously barely recalling their conversation. "No, and now his widow can't seem to unload it either. It has some structural faults from a tropical storm three years back. It's quite grand, really, but his property is probably more valuable than the house itself. It takes up most of a small island. Less than a hundred acres. Interested?"

"Very," Fairclough said. "Make that extremely."

The next afternoon, Alan Fairclough drove up from the city, taking 95 the whole way, past the usual and better-known turnoffs where he had known others' summer places in Old Lyme or Saybrook, Stonington, Mystic—until he found Route 3. Then another ten miles down a two-lane road full of potholes and bumps, shrouded from sunlight by thick brambly trees shorn of leaves by winter. He thought he'd made a wrong turn—then the sun, a small cove, woods everywhere. He drove past boatyards into what he could only describe as the most quaint New England town, still fairly untouched by New York and Boston on either side of it, both gradually growing out like parasitic routes. But here, an abandoned Customs House that looked as if no one had yet thought to use it, a public library the size of a one-room apartment, three churches with perfect steeples, and the empty streets of a fishing village at midwinter. It almost made him nostalgic for something he'd never had nor wanted.

At Land's End Point, he saw the small islands off the coast, the three Avalons, and the smallest was no doubt where Rupert Lewis's brother's summer home ate up half its geography.

Then, losing himself again in the narrow streets, the clapboard and brick piles of houses along frosty lanes, he turned towards Juniper Point, and the row of enormous white houses that formed a horseshoe just the other side of the village. They were close enough to join with the Borough of Stonehaven as a unified architecture, but far enough away for luxurious privacy. These were Hamptons mansions in an antisocial geography.

A small brass plate attached to a low wrought-iron gate proclaimed, THE SHIELDS, ALL ARE WELCOME, NONE SHALL BE TURNED AWAY. Stables to the north of the house, a caretaker's cottage beside the six-car garage, a boatslip off the south end, and a lawn that was smaller than he had expected, with no garden to speak of. But the house, a Georgian fake, its columns too short, its windows too large, its flourishes barely regarded. . . . Yet it was magnificent. The Crown place was itself more than a feast for the eyes and soul.

It was a face of white carved from the very landscape that surrounded it, holding in contempt all that it held within its gaze: the Avalon Sound, the woods, and even Alan Fairclough in his small black Mercedes as he parked it in the circular drive.

### 8

His first impression of Diana Crown, who was then only barely five or six, was that she was rather homely and unkempt. He mistook her for the caretaker's daughter, until her hackles got up at this suggestion. Then she became a little tyrant.

"I am Diana Crown, daughter of Darius and Honor Crown, and right now, sir, you are trespassing." She still had that little girl lisp, but her vocabulary, and the authority with which she used it, seemed beyond her years. Her hair was blond, but matted impossibly with some kind of gummy substance, as if she'd been rolling in clay.

"Well, I am Alan Fairclough, and I'm buying the Lewis place out on the island. I wanted to meet your father if I may."

"Mr. Spencer Lewis?" she asked, eyeing him suspiciously.

"Yes, the very same."

"He was a very tedious man," the girl said. He chuckled at her words. "And just what is so funny?" she asked imperiously.

"Not a thing," Fairclough said. "You're charming."

She gave him a slight pout, and then turned to call out to her father. "Daddy, there's a Mr. Faircough here—"

"Clough, Fair-clough," Alan said, emphasizing the sound.

Diana grinned impishly. "Yes, I know. I was playing

with it. I prefer Faircough." As Alan Fairclough stood there, listening for the sounds of Darius Crown's footsteps, the little girl turned back to him, staring up at him soulfully with her nearly transparent blue eyes. "Last night I dreamed you'd come here, Mr. Faircough. I dreamed that I was standing up in my bedroom and I saw you driving up here in your black car. Only it was a nightmare. Someone else got out of the car."

"Oh?" he asked, wondering if she had ever felt much pain in her life yet, or if the pleasure of it was to come as she reached adolescence. "And who was it who was driving my car?"

"The Devil," she said. "But he looked like you. His eyes were like yours."

"I'll tell you," Fairclough chuckled. "He's a distant relative, from my mother's side. No wonder you saw a resemblance."

9

That had been years ago, and Alan still felt the chill of that first meeting with Crown and his family. The slow beginnings of trust that grew between them. Alan bought the Lewis place and fixed it up and found himself living more and more on the island, spending time visiting the Crowns in the summer and at their midwinter holiday.

He showed them the image that had been burned into the stone in the French cave, and they in turn showed him their secret, a treasure more valuable than all the riches in Christendom.

And he taught them the words of bondage, and what language their treasure understood.

Only Fairclough's appetite as well as his many financial dealings drew him back to cities, to London, Rome, New York, to the places of teeming masses where a half dozen or more bruised youths or violated maidens would not cause more than a raised eyebrow ... where he could practice his form of spiritual growth in relative anonymity. . . .

But the Shields, and the Crowns, always called for him in this little borough of darkness.

What he helped them do.

The atrocity, the glorious atrocity, the use and misuse of power beyond the sphere of human endeavor—he was part of something greater than anything any man had ever been part of.

If it took and held, as it seemed to be doing, the world would transform and slough off its old tired skin.

Alan Fairclough would shepherd the new age into being.

10

*From the Diary of Alan Fairclough*
*Seventeen Years Earlier*

*I felt only impatience as Crown led me into his study. I wanted to see. I wanted to experience. But he told me that he had matters to discuss with me first. The usual talk, the suspicious glances. My assumption is that Crown believes the bullshit he's spouting, his falling back on Judeo-Christian mythos, his reliance on words like* Satan *and* Fiend, *as if this could possibly describe what his treasure held. He is perhaps a madman, and his immense wealth has separated him from his fellow men. He believes his own hogwash. He has even created a chapel for it. He says that it remains trapped by the symbols of religion, but he must be mistaken.*

*If it is trapped, it is for some other purpose. For nothing in the world could hold this creature if it needed to escape this house.*

*Finally, after showing me the ancient drawings of Hell and Heaven and the conjuring of demons and all the ar-*

*cane foolishness that Crown in his megalomania believes, he took me into the chapel.*

*I can only describe the emotion that held me in its thrall as I entered that sanctuary. Fear? No.*

*Pure terror. I felt as if I were a child again, a little boy walking into some great and mysterious cathedral.*

*Crown has the accoutrements of his belief strung around what once must have been a quaint family chapel.*

*But I barely noticed the perverse nature of the place.*

*Instead, there it was. Caged and held like some side-show freak.*

*I spoke the ancient language known only to those most Holy Sisters, and who knows who before them.*

*The celestial language of demons and gods and all those who are the fire at the heart of the cave and are not the shadows dancing about it.*

*Its golden eyes opened and watched me as I stepped nearer. My bowels released involuntarily, and I felt a shudder of electric energy shoot up my spine. My nose began bleeding, but I didn't bother to wipe at it with a handkerchief.*

*I felt suspended.*

*For a moment, I felt disembodied and could not be sure that my feet touched the ground or that I was even breathing.*

*All sound ceased.*

*Should I write here of the great sorrow in those eyes? Of the weariness, and yes, even fear, but most of all, the sorrow?*

*And in that sorrow something more terrifying than this vision of a creature from either nightmare or fantasy.*

*It began speaking with my dead father's voice.*

*What was it, what did it show me, what did it say?*

*All this it destroyed within my memory, and all I'm left with is the image burned indelibly in my mind after this first encounter.*

## 11

The picture that he could not remove from his brain, through no matter how many sleepless nights, nor during those nameless hours before the first sunlight when all the world seemed in the same state of sublime panic that he felt within, that picture conjured itself in the blackness whenever he shut his eyes.

*A man screaming from a great oak tree, red sparrows pecking at his palms, feet, and eyes. Upon his head, a crown of fire.*

It was not until much later, replaying this image in his head like a dreaded movie, that Alan Fairclough recognized that the man on the tree was himself.

# Chapter Eight

## In the Summer House

"Can't you stop it?" the young woman gasped, as the servants held her down on the bed. She was trembling, her body spasming, sweat pouring off of her. Her back arched, and her blouse was shredded where she'd clawed at herself before they got to her. "Can't you stop it?" she began shouting, her voice soon going hoarse. "Somebody stop it!"

Her father stood over her, wiping a sheen of perspiration from his brow with a handkerchief. "Please, Diana, it will pass. You must let it pass."

"It's burning me," she cried, her arms breaking free of those who held her down. Tears streamed down her cheeks. Her skin flashed with an ashen glow. "Daddy, it's burning me! Get it out of me! Why can't you get it out of me?"

Her father stepped forward with his handkerchief and pressed it against her lips. Her eyes went wide with terror as she looked up at his calm face.

"You must fight it. Keep it in. You have to."

"It wants out!" she screamed.

Then he stuffed the handkerchief into her mouth, gagging her.

# Chapter Nine

## Nightmare

Stony awoke in a sheet-soaked fever, the sweat so filmy and thick it was like pond scum. Someone was whispering a phrase over and over, and he realized with a start that it came from his own lips. He felt a tickling around his nose, and when he felt it, he also felt the blood that dripped from his nostril to his lips. Grabbing a Kleenex from the box on the windowsill, he wiped at it. *Shit*. He sat up in bed, the end of the dream, just a hypnogogic trace, left hanging over him like a spiderweb:

*A memory of being four years old, and having cut himself accidentally with his brother's hunting knife while he was playing with it. But the blood didn't terrify him, what terrified him was that he thought he saw a small fire burst from his skin, from his blood, a momentary flash. Then it was gone.*

He sat up the rest of the night, unable to sleep. He looked out over the shingled rooftops of the neighboring houses, out beyond them to the sea, to its vast darkness. The light of the moon cut across it, like yellow lightning, and the word that he uttered seemed at first alien to him. It was the word he'd heard when he was half in the dream, the word that he'd said on waking. He said it three times like an incantation, as if it would bring comfort to his thoughts. "Moonfire," he whispered, "Moonfire, Moonfire." Something in the word itself terrified him, as if it were something more than a phrase from a favorite comic book. As if it insinuated something to him, something about the world around him that lay just beneath its surface. *Moonfire fuels the world. The thing that destroys the Storm King is the very thing that flows in the veins of all creation.*

At fifteen, he felt again like a very small boy, not like the man he knew he was becoming. What was a man anyway? A walking erection? A fur-covered caveman? His father? Sometimes Stony wondered what the hell it meant to grow up and be a man when he still felt like a little kid on the inside half the time.

He got out of bed, pulled on his briefs, and went to use the bathroom. In the bathroom mirror, he looked at the teenager in the mirror and wondered why the hell the little kid from long ago wasn't gone yet from his features. One final wipe at the last of the blood beneath his nose.

*Moonfire*, he thought. *Christ, all this stress is getting to you. Lourdes is pregnant, your school grades are dropping, your parents are assholes, and you're having nightmares like there's no tomorrow.*

The words of his English teacher came back to him: *"These are the best years of your life."*

*If these are the best years*, Stony thought, shaking his too long hair in the mirror, looking at the last bits of Kleenex still stuck underneath his nose, *what the hell is the rest of it gonna be like?*

It was as if a threat were contained within the word, but he could not decode what that threat might be.

In the back of his closet, he found the old half-empty pack of Camels that he hadn't touched for over twelve weeks. He had promised Lourdes he would never touch them again, but this was different. He wasn't going to get through this night without some nasty little crutch.

He lit one, and inhaled deep. It was good. It burned in his throat. The nicotine kicked in, and he coughed. Then he put the damned thing out. Even a cigarette wouldn't do it for him. His head pounded, and he felt ancient.

He watched the moon until the first light of day came up.

# PART TWO

# MOONFIRE

*"As the Outcast held up the metal sphere, a curious light came from within. 'Weep, O Storm King! I hold the mastery of the cosmos! Behold, THE RADIANCE!'..."*
*from* The Storm King: Champions of Darkness, *Vol. 6*

# Chapter Ten

## Initiation into the Mysteries

1

All human tragedies are tragedies of innocence waking. Stony spent most of September brooding, when he wasn't delivering papers and groceries and going to school. He felt as if he were living underwater at the public school over in Copper Ferry, a good five miles out of town. He'd sit in class, nod his head during Geometry, doodle during American History, watch his lab partner do all the chemistry assignments and then just copy from his notes, and pretty much sleepwalk from one end of the long corridor to the other. Half the time in gym class, while he was running cross-country, his mind was elsewhere, off in a private zone of worries and musings about raising a kid, or aborting a kid, or just ignoring the whole damn thing. When the bells rang between classes, he no longer saw the individual students, he saw the sea, the melting tide of faces, intoxicated with secrets or half asleep and moving zombie-like from English to Geometry to Spanish—

through the dingy, dirty halls, their giddy excitement at some scandal of adolescence, their surliness, their many faces making one face. Even his old best friend Jack Ridley was lost in the crowd, and he shunned talking too much to anyone. And there, among all of them, Lourdes Maria. Her face, the first time he'd seen her, the tan of her Spanish and Portuguese forebears, the hair dark as night, and her lips sweet. He was still wanting her. Her yellow sweater, and the small gold cross on the slender chain around her neck . . . But now, in the sea of others, between classes, he turned away from her, from the one he thought he had loved but now knew he had destroyed. Stony felt caught between a dream and a reality too complicated to handle.

Lourdes finally grabbed his arm one day, and he felt like he might wake up.

"We need to talk," she said. He could barely look at her. He resisted, and instead looked at her hand as she grasped him. Her fingers, with their red nails, the two rings on her finger—the other grandmother had given her, the one that she had bought for twenty dollars at a flea market in Mystic . . . the olive cast to her hand . . .

Stony looked at her for only a second, but as soon as he saw her eyes, those dark stones brilliant with an inner sun, and the curve of her lips, bright red lipstick glossing them, he could not look away again.

"We do?" he said, feigning good humor. He still loved her. He felt that in his heart. He knew he loved her. But he also knew that her having a baby meant that what he wanted his life to be, the dream of what he wanted his life to be, was not going to happen. What was going to happen: He would work at the cannery or on the lobster boats like his dad, and he'd stink of fish and come home to some cramped apartment or worse, a trailer out by Route 63—the trailer park nicknamed The Lightning Rod of God because of the way it always got destroyed during the frequent summer hurricanes—Lourdes would be prematurely old by twenty, there'd be another baby, he'd be in a prison of his own making.

Still, he loved her, and he wanted to try to find a better dream for the two of them. He followed her outside, and they sat along the concrete steps overlooking the blacktop where the ninth graders were doing calisthenics.

Lourdes pressed her hand in his. "You're afraid of all this, aren't you?"

He shrugged. "I know I love you. I know that."

She leaned against him, kissing him on the cheek. "Good. I love you, too."

Silence. She let go of his hand.

"You haven't come over much in the past few days," she said.

Another shrug. "I had a lot to get done."

He could practically feel her trembling, even though they were not touching.

"I found out something today," she said.

"What's that?" he asked.

"I was wrong."

"Huh?"

"I was just late. That's all."

"You mean . . ."

"Yeah. It's not what we thought." Then she amended this. "What *I* thought."

For the first time in a week, he looked in her eyes again. He felt like he'd been a jerk. He was happy, but something inside tugged him downward. He'd shown his true colors. Yellow. Cowardly. Chickenshit. She shaded her eyes with her hand—from the sun, not from his stare. He wished she'd smile. He wanted her to smile and throw her arms around him.

"I guess you're thrilled, huh?" she said.

"No," he shook his head, throwing his arm around her. "I guess I was just scared. I mean . . . I didn't know what I was going to do."

"Me neither," Lourdes said. "My father would've

killed me. Thank God, huh?'' He thought her eyes were getting watery, and knew it had been a terrible experience for both of them. *Dumbass! Stupid! Two idiotic kids getting in trouble. Thank God she wasn't pregnant!*

"Yeah," Stony said, and tossing his head back he stared up at the cloudless blue sky. "Thank you, God!" Then he kissed her. "Do you think I was acting like a jerk?"

Lourdes shrugged. "A little. I guess I would've too. But it's different when you think it's inside you. It must be hard to understand if it's not inside you."

At that moment, Stony felt alive again. Engaged in life, where he had disengaged two weeks earlier, when she'd first told him. "I really do love you. I was just trying to figure out how we were going to handle . . . all this shit . . .''

"Let's not talk about it again," she whispered. "I need to get back to English. See you on Friday?"

Stony nodded. As she got up, he grabbed her hand again. Squeezing it. Something seemed cold when he touched her.

He looked up at her face. "Are you telling the truth?"

She turned away and walked back into the building.

2

Van Crawford, hanging out on the steps of the Package Store on Water Street in Stonehaven, tossed back a Pabst Blue Ribbon, neatly wrapped in a small brown bag. His buddies Del and Rich the Roach took turns watching for Officer Dennehy, and then swiped the can of beer and passed it back and forth.

"I need some pussy, bad," Del said, wiping the sweat off his neck, watching one of the local girls go by in her daddy's Volkswagen. "It's been two weeks."

"Bullshit," Van laughed, making another grab for the can of beer. It was empty, so he tossed it in the trash and reached into the green backpack resting on the pavement. "Like you ever get any." Then, as he popped up the tab on the can, he saw her, walking out of the Stonehaven Country Store, a basket in her arms, her dress all of summer and sheer audacity—for he could see through it to her creamy thighs, and her breasts, too, like twin scoops of ice cream.

"Who the fuck is that?" he heard Rich ask, but Van was already transported—his heart beat fast, his tongue shriveled, and his dick seemed to ache with a longing he didn't know a body part could have.

She had nearly blond hair, to her shoulders, and eyes like blue stones, and a set of thick lips, juicy lips, and confidence—a sexual confidence, he could tell just by the way she walked, the way her head stayed high, the way her posture was relaxed but perfect. Her lips made him want to fuck her. There was no other reason for lips like that.

She had legs that were near perfection, and where her waist was narrow, her hips were wide. She looked like a sexual thoroughbred. To him, she looked like the whore bitch of the universe, the one who could take in all of him, drink him in, and he would never be tired of it.

"Jesus, look at her," Del gasped.

Van actually dropped to his knees, holding the beer can in both hands like a holy relic. "Oh sweet Mother of God," he said. "Bless the fruit of your womb. Jesus. Jesus." He grabbed his balls with one hand, looking up. "Man, I want some of that."

She was a stranger to town, probably a tourist. A day tourist. Someone from New York. A model, maybe. No, better than a model: a wet dream with legs. "Who the fuck is she?" Van asked.

"She's a Crown I think," Del said. "I never saw her much, but when I was a kid, remember? Didn't you ever see her and her weirdo family out on their boat?"

Van shrugged. "A rich bitch too. Cool."

His buddy Rich whispered, "Man, she's trouble. Leave her alone. She's a Crown. They're bad."

"Yeah, fuck you," Van muttered.

And then she stopped, watching the boys.

Van closed his eyes, almost embarrassed.

When he opened them, she smiled at him. It was a blessing, all right.

She smiled and nodded, as if she knew what he was thinking.

As if she knew what he was thinking, and it was all right with her.

He got up, dusting off his jeans, passed the beer to his buddies, and trotted off across the street.

3

Picture this:

*You're a horny seventeen-year-old boy and you are used to the dregs of teen girldom, of girls that lie deathlike on soiled mattresses while you slobber and push into them, of girls who smell like the docks, of girls whose makeup smears and beneath it you see the chapped lips, the small eyes, the skin not quite mottled, not quite smooth . . .*

*Girls like Brenda Whitley with her uneven boobs, and her barnacly taste, and her way of whining when you get to third base . . .*

*And then you see a girl who looks as if she just stepped out of a Hollywood movie, with a nearly perfect body, with sexual confidence, with an aura about her that's like fire from the moon. Hormone is her perfume and what lies at that goal there, that place you want to get into, is nothing less than the garden of paradise.*

*You think: Maybe she will get me out of this miserable existence.*

## 4

"What's your name?"

"Diana."

"Diana what?"

"Crown."

"Yeah, I guessed that."

"You know my people?"

Van almost laughed. The way she said, "You know my people?" It was as if she was talking about a tribe rather than a family. Rich people were so different. All the summer people were. They weren't from the same world as Van and his family and the other families who lived in town year-round. They occupied the same world, but they weren't from it. Summer people were always like that. They were from New York or Washington or even England sometimes. They didn't have boats; they had sloops. They didn't have maids; they had servants. They didn't have money; they had wealth. And they didn't have a home, but homes. Homes everywhere. One for work, one for summer, one for winter. The Crowns were like that— the Crowns were rich. A Crown had once stolen money from a railroad in the north in the late 1800s, and then another Crown had bootlegged liquor from Canada, and another Crown had even funded part of the Nazi Party in the '30s. There had once been a picture of Frederic Crown in *Life* magazine, standing with Adolf and Eva, and the caption read: "The Crown Prince spends Easter with the Fuehrer." This had been meant to discredit the Crowns, but in fact, it barely touched their lives. They profited from the war, they profited from the peace. The Crowns even set up a Jewish Refugee Fund in 1945, and then in 1960, Michael Crown reopened the textile factories on the Monangetowga River in Pennsylvania, and produced the popular Crown Cotton Shirt in no time. They were different from the rest—everyone in Stonehaven knew it.

They were a family with power beyond the ordinary doings of mankind. They owned property all over. Van heard that they owned half the shops on Water Street, maybe all of them.

And here, Diana Crown, in all her monied glory, her hair swept by pearl and her breasts raised in cups of gold. He could barely see anything that resembled a real girl to him, since the girls he was used to didn't have the shine to their faces, or the hips that begged to be squeezed in his filthy hands. She looked not only like class and style, she looked like she knew why God had given her this body, these tits, these lips, the fire he saw in her eyes.

Van had had poor girls and middle-class girls before, many of them—he was used to seducing all the local girls. He'd been unsuccessful more times than not, but there were always a few, the Brendas and Mary Lynns of the world he knew. He had never gotten into the panties of girls like Diana Crown. As far as he knew, there were no other girls in his limited knowledge of the world that were anything like this Diana. This earthy vision, with the purity of good genes and some inner intelligence, all bound up in a package of hormonal vampirism. That's what she was: a vampire. He sensed it. She wanted what boys like him could give a girl: not money, not prestige, but the flesh heat that Van dreamed of giving her.

And here she was, presenting herself to him. So easy. So available. So fuckable.

"I worked for your father one summer." His voice deepened, and he showed his appreciation for her beauty by looking down to her feet and then back up to her face. There were only two places he cared about, and they both looked delicious.

"You did," she said.

"I thought your family left after Labor Day."

"Some of us did. Some of us stayed. What's your name?"

"Van Crawford."

"Van Crawfish?"

"Funny. You're funny, Miz Crown."

"Don't call me that," she said, stopping. "Diana. Call me Diana."

"Sure, Diana. Sure. How's the house?"

"Fine."

"You going to stay through the winter?"

"No," she said. "Just till November First."

"Sure," he said. "Just till it gets cold. You summer people."

"Yes," she said, with a formality that irked him. He wanted to throw her down right then and there and tear her summer dress off, covering her face, and expose her thighs, just holding them apart with his hands. He would squeeze silver coins from her loins.

"You're thinking something, aren't you?" she asked. "I like a boy who thinks. How old are you, Van Crawfish?"

"Seventeen. Almost eighteen. Eighteen in two months. December Third."

"That's a magic age," Diana Crown said. "How old do you think I am?"

"Maybe twenty?"

"I could be," she said. "Here, let's go to my car. I'll need help with the groceries. Mind if I hire you for an hour or two?"

Van shrugged.

"I'll pay you twenty-five dollars," she said. Later, much later, after the trip to the grocery store, after a glass or two of wine, when she had brought him on to the screen porch of her family's summer house, and as he looked out over the water, she said "No, make it thirty dollars, if you'll take your shirt off for me."

He felt cold when she said it.

He felt October in his heart.

He began unbuttoning his shirt.

5

Later, when he began bucking into her, uncontrollably, as if she were milking him, as if he were a cow that she was drawing some strength from—but he didn't want to think this, not while his senses were frayed and spitting electric juice from his pores—later, when the sweat stung along his chest as they bonded together, he felt as if there were something that she was taking away from him. Some indefinable piece of him, the virginity of a part of Van Crawford that he had never been able to name. A hidden corner of his consciousness, a sprig of life, pressed into her ice-glazed fingers that aroused him still, even while he lay against her, spent.

"I want you," she whispered.

"You got me," he said, drawing back to look at her sweaty beauty, the curl of her hips, the gentle curves of her small belly, the breasts that all but cried out for his lips. "You got me."

# Chapter Eleven

## Village Life, Autumn

### 1

The threat of winter so soon, not in great frozen breaths of air, but in the fists of wind. It was October coming in, the chill increased, the townsfolk moved a little more slowly, but not so much as to be perceptible to an outsider. If it wasn't rain, it would be wind, and if not wind, then snow, and if not snow, then an overhanging miserableness—once winter announced its coming, there was no retreat. Other autumns might be mild clear through Thanksgiving, but this was not to be one of those seasons.

Guff Hanlon, with his furniture business, shut the shop down for the winter; his sons would take the rest of the inventory down to shops in Greenwich and Rye for the winter, selling them off at half price to the dealers. Guff then went to his winter job, as assistant librarian at the Stonehaven Free Library, which was all of two small rooms beneath a dome at the edge of the town Common. Guff was probably the tallest man in Stonehaven, at least for the months after Labor Day and before Memorial Day. He was six foot four, and strapping, even at forty-six, a barrel chest and a constitution like an ox, that's what Doc Railsback always said. "You'll live till you're a hundred and three, just like your grandfather," Doc would say, and Guff would wonder how that might be, since his grandfather had been down at Yale–New Haven hospital on machines for the last twenty years of his life. Guff's father had been lucky—cut down in his prime, hit by a bus in front of Grand Central Station in New York in 1961, a healthy man, gone at fifty. That was the way to go.

But Guff knew in his heart he'd end up like his grandfather, for his life was without event. He worked in his woodshed building furniture, he worked at the library because he loved books so much, he worked at home with his wife, keeping her calm through all the things she worried about, and he worked keeping his sons, both in their twenties, employed and active so they didn't run off and be lazy good-for-nothings the way Guff had for a good ten years before he straightened himself out.

"Well, good afternoon, Guff," Fiona McAllister nodded to him from behind the front desk at the library, as he slammed the screen door behind him, then shut the thick oak door against the slight wind.

Guff nodded. "Fi, good to see you."

"How's Marcy?"

"Just good. And Alec?"

"Just good, too," Fiona said.

"I guess I need to go down and clean up the stacks," Guff said matter-of-factly, his folksy New England way of speaking sneaking out as if this were a hook for a fish.

"Yes," Fiona nodded. Then, she removed her wedding ring, setting it inside a small card catalog file.

She always did this when she followed him down to that dark musty room below, where they made love as passionately as they could before he had to clean up, and she had to return to help someone check out a book.

2

James and Alice Evarest sat in front of the Evarest Bakery, on the small green bench. She had a small rhinestone-studded calculator on her lap, and was totalling the week's grosses, while James, his white hair covering half his face, smoked his pipe and noticed that the shingles on the barbershop across the street were falling loose, and he noticed that kids just didn't play football in the streets the way they had last year. Their afternoons were ones of boredom, and James often felt as white and unnatural as the flour that powdered his apron and shirt. The barber, David Smith, known as Cutter, busily sawed at the thick tresses of Mike "The Mule" Mueller, getting him down to a military buzz because Mike wanted to go to the Coast Guard Academy down in New London in another year, and he wanted to start looking the part.

The Railsback Butcher Shop, on the corner, was probably the liveliest place, because before five, the business was as fast and furious as at the Package Store down at the other end of the street. Housewives and the unemployed lined up on the sidewalk—it was Friday, and Butch Railsback, cousin to Doc Railsback, who was also second cousin once removed to Stony Crawford's mother, Angie, was all decked out in his bright white T-shirt and old ship's cook's white pants, but his huge apron that covered him thigh-to-neck was already bloodied in the battle of meat.

His great arms were muscled like a stevedore in overdrive, and he wielded the cleaver freely across the chopping board, turning a once crimson steak into the thinnest of slices for Mrs. Partridge's Steak Diane that she was making for Father Rimmer for Friday night dinner at her house with the Prayer Meeting Group. Butch was thirty-six and gorgeous to the town's women, as only a muscled and cocky hunk can be, and perhaps it was the spraying

blood of the meat, or the gentle way he took their orders—for his voice never rose higher than a masculine
whisper when he asked, "And what would ya like wit'
dat, Mrs. Partridge?" He had the good looks of his Polish
mother, who had been a blond and ravishing beauty,
trucked over from Albany by his father sometime in the
1950s, and Butch was a poster boy for meat and dairy
consumption—even his one lazy eye, the left eye, with its
milky blueness, could melt the heart of most of the
women and some of the men who stood in the line. *Chop!
Chop!* The cleaver to the block, the meat laid out, or
pounded down with his mallet, making the chicken soft,
the meat tender, and the pork edible. This was a town
thick with fish, so butchered mammal was prized like
gold. No wonder Butch was one of the wealthiest young
men in town.

When Angie Crawford made it to the front of the line,
she said, "Is there any good lamb this week?" She held
her purse in front of her, demurely, and tried not to glance
at the pretty-boy face. Butch here was eternally young,
for the image of who he was at this moment, this crossroads, was burned deeply and painfully into all who beheld him.

Butch leaned forward, tipping his white cap, scratching
just beneath the shock of strawberry blond hair that fell
across his forehead. "You want good lamb, huh? I maybe
might have a little, yeah, sure," he said, his accent thick
and sharp. He sounded like a thug from Boston. "How
much you want? I got a good side in da back."

"Oh," Angie said, "Nothing that big, maybe . . .
maybe a shoulder and a good leg."

"Sure," he said, but it was always "Sho-ah," and it
never seemed a word with him, but an expression of an
ox pawing the ground. "Hold dat t'ought." He held his
finger up, and went over and grabbed a clean blade from
his rack. Turning his back to his audience, Butch opened
up the walk-in refrigerator, and then walked down a hall-

way. He opened another door, but this was as far as Angie, or any of the others waiting in line, could see. Butch Railsback did not exist beyond the front counter.

When he returned to the front of his shop, he had a shoulder all wrapped up. "Don't got no leg right now. Might try back on Tuesday."

"A shoulder's fine," Angie said, opening her purse to root around for her cash. "Just fine."

"How're dem boys a yours?" Butch made small talk as he rung up the order on the register.

"Van is thinking of UConn next year," she said, fully believing the lie. "Stony's okay. He gets in some trouble sometimes."

"You can't be a boy wit' out gettin' in trouble, Miz Crawford, 'specially when dey're young like dat. Dey're like spring lambs, all hoppin' around." Butch nodded, passing the package across the curved counter to her. "You send him 'round 'ere if he needs some toughenin' up. Next!"

The Doane sisters, Alice and Mary, were out in their garden digging up bulbs and gathering up the broken clam shells that the seagulls had dropped onto the paved walkway. Their backyard ended abruptly at the seawall, and the inlet, still calm and glassy, was packed with cormorants and seagulls floating lazily on its surface. Alice Doane had a little used-bookshop at the front of their shared dwelling, but it was always closed after Labor Day—still, the occasional book fancier bothered them into opening it up for a few minutes.

Down the other end of the shops was the Ye Olde Shoppe, which was mainly for the summer tourists, but stayed open through December, because it sold Christmas decorations and spices and old-fashioned candles. Lorraine Paglia ran it with her son, Giuliano, but most days she ran it by herself while Giuliano sat in a corner of the shop, brooding. One display case, over next to the potpourri bags, all neatly tied up with ribbons, held thirty-six beautiful one-of-a-kind candles. *The Kind*, the small card beneath them announced, *That the Early Colonists of the Area Made and Which Cannot Be Found Anywhere North of Williamsburg, Virginia, or South of Stonehaven.*

This was an out-and-out lie on more than one count, but Lorraine was in it to sell to the last of the tourists, stragglers who got lost off old Route One and came across the village accidentally, charmed by its old houses and shops.

The candles were like long thin fingers, and the dappled wax overdripped layer upon layer across itself as it formed around the wick.

Nora Chance made these candles out at her little house in the woods, and she'd been taught by her mother, who'd been taught by her grandmother, and so forth, back into unrecorded history.

It was Lorraine who, that day, wanted some more of these, since her supply was running low, and she was worried that Nora might start to get better offers on the candles from one of the shops in nearby Mystic. And since Lorraine could sell them for ten dollars each when they cost her twenty-five cents a candle, this was not a profit she wished to lose.

As soon as she knew the school buses had gotten back into town, she picked up her phone and called up the Crawford house, hoping to find Stony at home.

3

Which he was, having just run inside, thrown his books down, and heard the phone ringing. Stony raced to get it, and said, "Yallo."

"Stony? It's me," and Lorraine's voice was so distinct, like a sharp clatter of silverware, that Stony didn't need to ask. "I need you to ride over to Nora's and see if she can get me twenty more candles by Monday. Also, tell her the Christmas shawls are not in yet, and they need to come in by November. Tell her I'll raise the rate. Okay?''

"Sure," Stony said.

"Good," Lorraine said, "and when you're back I'll give you a tip. All right?"

"Yeah," Stony said, dropping the phone back in its cradle. He always needed the money, from lawn mowing, raking leaves, running errands for the shopkeepers, sometimes even cleaning the sailboats for the rich summer folk when he could get the work.

He glanced at his watch. Nearly four-thirty. Nora would be having her afternoon tea.

4

These were the typical pursuits of a typical October day, but as with all life, and all towns, it was not all surfaces.

Calvin Stowe, who ran a tourist boat in the summer, spent most of his afternoon at the Fisherman's Catch, down on Juniper Point, drinking himself under the table before getting into his Toyota and checking out to see if any schoolchildren were available to come over to his house to watch his special movies. Sophia Randall, a descendant of Jeptha Randall, who was a member of one of four early Stonehaven families, waited desperately on the front porch of her Captain's Walk home, a home built first in the early 1700s, then rebuilt after the town was burned in the War of 1812, and further rebuilt in 1901 after the Great Hurricane came through—a house and a two-acre lot with history. Here she waited, wringing her small, perfectly formed hands, her face glowing with fever, her normal beauty reduced to a labored moment of intense anguish. Then a Harley-Davidson roared around the Common, and its rider parked it by the house. Rather than run out to greet him, Sophia retired within her home. The young man with the golden goatee jogged up the walk, leaped onto the porch, and only stopped once when he dropped what appeared to be a syringe and a small packet of white powder.

Down at the loading dock, where the lobsters were dumped unceremoniously from the overflowing cornucopias of the trawlers, four men, all under thirty, decided the fate of the summer girl who had stayed past the season—the girl at the Crown place, out by Land's End, the girl they'd watched from their trawlers, the girl who'd stood naked at her back window at five in the morning, watching the sea, as if she were just there for them to take.

Lyndi Potter, who lived on Cold Spring Road, almost out of the borough, in the small clapboard house at the north edge of the cove, had already begun kicking at her five-year-old son, Rupert, when he didn't clean up the dog piss in the front hallway. She raised her foot and aimed for his gut, and her son, who was wise in ways that most five-year-olds are not, remained silent and felt no pain.

Out on the lobster trawler marked *Angela's Bounty*, Gerald Crawford, Stony's dad, nursed the last of his whiskey, and wished to hell he had never gotten trapped in the life he had, with kids and a wife and all the weight of the world on his bulky shoulders. *All the weight of this damned gone-to-hell world.*

5

Stony Crawford rode his black Schwinn bike past all this, ignorant of what lay beneath the anthill of town, and then veered off Cold Spring Road, onto the dirt path that led into the scraggly woods.

The smell of a dead animal was nearby, a physical heat, as if the death of the creature created a larger life in odor. The woods stank also of the damp of the bog and marsh. He rode beside the ancient and crumbling stone wall that marked off the cemetery, and finally took the left fork of the path. As the withering grass grew higher here, and the leaves piled as if building new earth, he dropped his bike, walking the rest of the way.

Going to Nora's always made him feel like a kid again, no longer saddled with adolescence, but a more innocent and wonder-laden time. He felt the tug of adulthood at him most days, but he still enjoyed heading out into the musky woods to find her at her loom, or out washing her mountain of laundry.

The tarpaper was falling in several places from Nora's roof, and two dozen candles dangled from the roof's edge, setting. Her great black pot boiled over with soap and laundry, and there she stood, stirring the pot with a great thick staff. The smell of the soap could burn, but the breeze was going the other way, towards the bog.

"Nora!" he called, waving his hand.

Nora Chance turned slightly at the sound, nodding. When he reached her side, she said, "I knew you'd be coming along sometime soon. Your voice—I can't get over it. Last year you were still my little boy, and now you sound like a man of the world."

6

They sat in the front room, Stony on the floor with his legs crossed, his back to the warm potbelly stove, Nora in her rocking chair. In her lap, the freshly made candles. She rolled each candle into several squares of tissue paper while she spoke. "I got an October story for you, Stony. You know the story 'bout the resurrection?"

"You mean Jesus?" Stony asked, almost sullenly.

"No, not that one. I mean the resurrection right here in Stonehaven cemetery. Happened in 1746. My great-grandmother told me this story on her deathbed. She had heard it from her grandmother, who worked the Randall and Crowninshield places back then, and she was just a little girl when it happened." Nora nodded to herself as if she were just being told the story for the first time.

"Yes, that's right. Something happened back then. Nobody's liked to talk about it since, although you can bet some people in town like the Doanes and the Mainwarings and the Randalls and even the Slatterys know the story, 'cause no one forgets this story once it's in their blood. It's always in October, like now. You ever hear of the Reaper?"

"Sure. The Grim Reaper."

"No, boy, I mean the Reaper who used to live out at Juniper Point. He owned most of the land out there, and he was called the Reaper because he looked like Mr. Death most of the time. Pasty white face, gaunt like a skeleton dug out a hundred years after he was buried. He married a gal from up in Marblehead, brought her here back before the Revolution. She was a sickly thing, and they thought when she was gonna have her baby that she was gonna die. They spent three nights tending her while she gave birth, but that little baby near ripped that frail gal up and down like a bayonet, and they had to use knives—it was something awful. I heard that the folk in attendance fainted at the sight of what they did to that little gal just to get the baby out. Story was that a farmhand couldn't take her screams no more, and came up to the bedroom like he was possessed and raised his scythe over her belly, just ripping her open and pulling that baby out. The baby was all twisted up and upside down, his head turned, his legs misshapen. His gal survived that night, stayed in bed from then after. And the baby—it was a little imp of a thing, and from its first day would only drink one thing from its mamma's breast, and it weren't milk, oh no. The stories are terrible, Stony. Terrible. You want to hear more?"

Stony nodded. "Yeah."

"Good. Go make us both a cup of cat's claw tea, and I'll tell you the rest when it's steeping."

Stony rose, and went to put on the tea. "How can someone live who's been scythed open?"

142

"It happens, boy," Nora said, stretching her fingers in the air above her head. "I get so tired sometimes, working all day. Know how old I am?"

"Sixty?" he ventured.

Nora let out a big belly laugh. "No, not even close. Older than these woods sometimes. That's what I feel like. You getting the jar of tea?"

Stony glanced up at the crude wooden shelf, packed with jars full of jams and herbs and roots. He grabbed the cat's claw jar, and dumped some of it in the clay pot that Nora used for tea.

"How's that gal of yours, anyway?" Nora asked.

"She's okay."

"That's it? Okay?"

"Yep."

"You still cotton to her?"

"Sure."

"You know about nature and how to avoid it?" Nora asked.

"You mean like birth control?"

"I never said nothing of the kind," Nora said, shaking her head. "I mean nature. It always gets you into trouble."

"Sure," he said. When the tea was steeping, he brought her cup over to her. "Tell me about the baby."

"Oh, the Reaper's baby? It was something fierce," she said, her voice sinking into her familiar storytelling cadence. "That baby wasn't satisfied with his mother's milk, it had to suck her teat till blood run out of it. It was an abomination more than it was a baby. Old Reaperman, he accused her of sleeping with the Devil or some such nonsense, and took her to the tribunal over in Copper Ferry, which back then was called Copperfield, on account of the farmland near the water. There she was, this gal who was always fainting and sick and practically no blood in her, and there was that Reaper, holding up his baby Reaper with its snarls and sharp little paws and the way it was suckled with blood. They drug that gal off and hanged her up on Gallows Hill near Hartford, and the old Reaper went back to his house here in town and shot himself through the head with a little flintlock pistol. He didn't die, but lived for a few more years. The hands, they said that he had wanted to kill the baby too, but something human in him hadn't. The hands, they raised the baby out in these here backwoods, and nobody ever saw that baby again as far as townfolk knew. And then, one October—years later, when the Old Reaper was living up at the house on High Street, with his brother—a man came into Stonehaven. Well, it wasn't really a man. It was a thing—not much taller than a six-year-old boy, and all hunched over, and it stank like the bog, and it half crawled and half walked. It came up to that old mansion, and there was Old Reaper, Old Mr. Crowninshield, sitting in a chair, half his own body frozen, his mind barely there. And he knew. He knew it was his son, come back for him. Come back to punish him for what he did to the boy's mother. Come back for revenge. Reaper tried to cry out to his nurse, who was in the kitchen preparing a sandwich for him. This was in broad daylight, in the afternoon. People saw him, the young man. They say he had little horns on his head, but you can't believe everything you hear. No, he may have been deformed, but he was a man. And he went up to his father. His father was shivering like he was seeing a ghost. And that young man, all hunched over,'' Nora said, her eyes widening despite their milky whiteness, ''that son of his threw his arms over his father's shoulders and began weeping. And his father, that awful Reaperman, grabbed the scythe, the very one he always kept by his side, the very one a farmhand had used to open up this boy's mother—and that awful man brought it against his boy's neck and slit his throat while the young man wept for finding his father.'' Nora paused. She sighed, shaking her head. ''Tea's good, Stony.''

''Jesus, did that really happen?''

"As God is my witness," Nora said. "The boy gave one cry to heaven and then died in his father's arms. That evil, evil man. My own people saw this, for some of them worked in the house. They buried that poor boy just outside the cemetery, which is always a mistake."

"Why's that?"

"You don't know?" Nora clicked her tongue. "This is all Pequot land, boy. You white folks jump off your ships a few hundred years ago, and you think you understand the land? This ain't ordinary land. This is sacred."

"You mean like an Indian burial mound?"

Nora cackled. "No, nothing as stupid as that. Our burial mounds are sacred, and maybe a curse or two'll come out of them. Why do you think we let you people settle this land? Because of your guns? Because we were nice? No, boy, this land around Stonehaven wasn't just sacred to us, Stony, it was magic. It was absolute magic. You can plant anything, and it will grow. Ever notice that? You plant corn here and it shoots up high. Now, we gave you white folks the cemetery for your dead and the land to the water for your borough, but we told you not to plant in this one area. We all know about it, we know where to plant and where not to. But you, you and your families all forgot that. That Mr. Crowninshield, he should've known. Hell, the entire borough back then should've known, but even then it was thirty years after Stonehaven got settled. You don't bury your dead where things grow. We never have."

"You mean like the deformed guy was buried in this magic place and he rose up alive again?" Stony asked, half in wonder and half in wondering if she really expected him to fall for this bullshit.

"Nothing as asinine as that," Nora said. She rose up from the rocking chair, the tissue-packed candles in her hands. Her full height was nearly six feet, and she towered almost to the low roof. "Don't you know about what you white people brought to these shores?"

Stony shook his head, half smiling, hoping she'd laugh or grin or do something to show she wasn't getting angry. "No, ma'am. What'd we bring?"

"The Devil," she said. "And he took root here. He grew here just like the crops did. And it ain't ever been the same since."

# Chapter Twelve

## Nora's Story

### 1

This didn't end with the Imp's burial—for that's what they called the young man that the slaves and hands had raised up. Imp. There was a woman in town named Mrs. Randall—she was a coarse-minded woman who liked to create difficulties and intrigues. She made sure that Imp was buried in the bog, just thrown in, without ceremony. I heard she stood there, her cape across her shoulders, her old biddy white cap covering her hair. They said she didn't even let them weigh his body down with stones, but just let it sink and then rise, and float again. Eventually, it caught under the low-hanging branches of a birch, covered with leeches sucking the last of the blood out of poor little Imp.

And then it sank again into the muddy water and lay in the silt.

People in town didn't much want to talk about Imp, or of what had happened. You know how people are—once

# Douglas Clegg

a judgment is made, and a sentence carried out, we tend to find ways of agreeing with it, and we build up superstitious ideas around it. The summer went by, a swift and bountiful season. By the time the harvest moon came up, from sharp crescent to full, the maize and barley crops were doing good, and the sea's harvest was plentiful as well. Back in those days, Stonehaven still had the Harvest Festival on the Common, with music and even a little dancing—'course nothing like the party the hands and the slaves and the servants had. Our people were back in the woods here, dancing in the moonlight.

And something else came out that night to dance.

Something rose up from the bog, clothed in the slime and covered head to toe with leeches. In his hand, the rusty scythe that his father had used to kill him. His face was no longer his own—it was a mask, bloated and pulled by water and leeches and insect larvae—it was a face without eyes in its sockets, and when he opened his mouth, water and leaves poured forth. Yellow jackets burst from the festering sore beneath his chin. He was no longer just Imp, the son of that Old Reaper bastard.

He was the force of nature we knew about—we who knew about the magic land. But not just that force, but another, for he was born from the seed that the white man had brought to our land: the Devil was in him, the Devil as only my people could understand the Devil: an ancient god that you white people hold close to your bosom, not the opposite of your Heavenly Father, but a long-ago banished god, a god of the Harvest of Humans.

There is a name for this god, but it is long forgotten.

He is called by many names, Stony, but he is known by his actions.

On All Hallow's Eve, four hundred years ago, he first came from this bog.

He was the god resurrected by the magic of the land. God always has got to die and get reborn before he has his true powers. Everybody knows that.

He was the god of vengeance and the devourer of light.

And he is still here in the land, in the water, outside the churchyards and beyond the reason of man.

Waiting for his chance.

After midnight, he came, crawling across the land with the scythe in his mouth.

He is the father of scarecrows, come to reap the harvest of flesh!

## 2

Stony laughed when she screamed this last part.

"What, you don't believe me?" Her voice was slightly teasing. Her eyes were, as always, milky white. Sometimes he dreamed that they were the warm cinnamon she always said they'd once been. She grinned. "It's absolutely true. My great-great-great heard it from her great-great-great and so on and so forth."

"The father of scarecrows? That sounds goofy."

"It ain't goofy. You know what scarecrows are, don't you?"

"Sure. Dummies on sticks to scare off birds."

Nora threw her head back, laughing. "You *ever* see a crow scared off by a dummy on a stick?"

Stony thought a moment. "Not really."

"That's right. Scarecrows go way back. Old words, *sacrée croix*. Means sacred cross in French. They were statues of Jesus up in the middle of the fields. They protected the crops, at least in the Old World. But the scarecrow ain't no Jesus. The scarecrow is older. He's thousands of years old. He's the King that's been killed and his blood makes things grow. He's the Magic One. He's the Halloween Man. You got to understand that everything we know now is as under a layer of dust. But one day, each one of us sees clearly. I once saw—"

"You saw?" Stony said, and then regretted it.

"Yep, I used to see. I ain't been blind all my life. I

once saw a scarecrow out at the bog, let loose from its cross, looking for his mate.''

Playing along, Stony asked, "So who's his mate?"

"The Corn Maiden," Nora said, nodding her head as if this were perfectly logical. "You can't have a King of anything without a bride for him. That's why I have that." She took up one of the candles, pointing it towards the doorway. Stony glanced over at the little corn husk doll on the threshold. "It keeps him away from my place when he comes searching. He won't cross over a house where the corn doll is."

"You're making this up," Stony said.

"Maybe I am," Nora chuckled, but something in her tone did not feel humorous to him. "And maybe there's just a bite of truth in it. But when the scarecrow sees the corn doll, he respects her. He must die to be reborn, but she lives and is reborn through her children. She is the giver and taker of life. This is why male and female are separate: strength and recklessness together is a world beater. But they're like magnets—they both attract and repel each other. So he won't ever cross my threshold."

"Wait. You said that this Halloween Man was the harvester of flesh. So did he kill the Reaperman?"

"Oh," Nora's voice dropped to a reverential whisper. "Something much worse than that."

3

*The Rest of the Story*

So after midnight, he comes crawling across the land, the scythe in his mouth. Remember, this was both Imp and the Halloween Man in one body—the Halloween Man used his body to rise from the earth and the water. Imp shoulda never been buried in that old bog, outside the cemetery, with no blessing of any kind on his head. So in the night, that most dreadful night of the year, he comes, and into the twenty families; he crawls up the stairs on all fours, leaving a trail of damp and leaves and leeches. What he did in the night was laid out for all to be seen on the Common in the morning. As the sun rose, people came from their houses, victims of terrible nightmares. And since back then all the houses of the borough were around the Common, even those who did not leave their houses could see the terrible handiwork of the Halloween Man:

Strung like pigs, by their legs, twelve of the men and women from town, the most devout, those who in church cried out in tongues to God, those who kissed the foot of the cross daily, those who were most godly and worshipful, their throats slit, their blood dripping down, strung from the two great oak trees, the ground soaked with their blood. And between the trees a great cross had been erected, and on it, nailed with spikes, Old Reaperman Crowninshield—his eyes and mouth sewn horrible shut, and his nightshirt torn open.

On his chest, carved the words:

*I came to save you*

In his one hand, his left hand, tied as if a hook, was the scythe that had butchered the villagers. This hand was not nailed to the cross-beam.

Of course, the white people thought it was Reaperman who had done the killing. They always thought he was crazy, even though he was rich and mighty in the village.

But we knew. We who had been here since Man had first been on this land. We who had avoided planting on the Magic land, and instead planted near it, but away from it. We who buried our dead not in bogs but in sacred, protected earth—we knew it was the Old One, risen again for his night in the flesh of Imp.

It was a wicked time.

It was a great stain of death on Stonehaven, that night and morning.

And it took one of my own people to go find the body of Imp the next morning and do the work that would seal the Old One into that flesh until it returned to the damp earth and slept again.

It ain't in the history books, but that don't mean it didn't happen just like I said it did. Or maybe, Stony baby, it hasn't happened yet, but will one day. That's how legends are.

4

"Even if you made it up, it's a great story," Stony said, wiping his dusty hands off on his jeans. "A great story."

"I don't have to make these things up," Nora said, her voice tinged with a serious tone that made Stony look at her strangely. "They come to me. I heard them from my grandmother who heard them from her grandmother."

"But I don't believe in a Halloween Man or in the devil," Stony stated, slightly embarrassed.

"You believe in God?" she asked.

He shrugged. "I guess so."

"God ain't a guess. Either He is or He ain't."

"Well, I don't know yet," Stony said.

Nora grinned. "Good enough."

"Do you believe in the Devil?" he asked, trying to tease her. "The horny-tailed red Devil with the pitchfork in his hand?"

Nora stood slowly and went over to her front door, opening it. The last of the sunlight was merely a whisper through the tree branches along the bog beyond her property. "The Devil ain't just one thing, Stony. He's an army. 'I am Legion,' he says. He can be a woman, too. He can be a country. He can even be a summer's day. But the one thing you can be sure of about the Devil: He's the reflection of what we want."

"I'm not sure I get that," Stony said. He walked out to stand beside her on the porch. A flock of dark birds flew across the sky, blocking all light for a few seconds.

"You ever want something so bad you forgot everything else?"

Stony nodded. "Do you?"

"Ah," she sighed, and her sigh was like an ache on the breeze. "To have my sight back. To see you, the young man you are, the boy you were, the man you'll become. That I would want badly enough to embrace even the Devil." Then she shivered slightly. "Next time you want something that badly, look in the mirror and see who's gonna be waiting there for you. Could be the Devil, could mayhaps be the Halloween Man. Halloween's comin' up, maybe someone here's gonna take off his mask and show himself again, who knows?" Nora was grinning, her eyes seeming to sparkle even with their emptiness. She reached out her hand. Stony took it in his. Her hand was warm and strong. Her voice softened. "Tell me about your girl. Why didn't you bring her? You never bring her to see me no more."

"We've had some problems," Stony said.

"Stony," Nora said, pulling her hand from him. "You're hurting me a little with all that squeezing."

"Sorry. I didn't know I was doing it." He wanted not to talk about Lourdes. He wanted not to think about what he'd narrowly escaped. About what he had wanted more than anything else. "People think I'm nuts to like you so much, you know that?"

"Oh yeah," Nora said, her husky voice breaking like a wave on a rock as she laughed. "The old blind lady in the woods who won't get a phone or electricity, she's half-black, half-Indian, and all crazy. I *bet* they think you're nuts. I bet they're gonna start callin' you by your Indian name, Crazy-Like-the-Moon."

"Maybe I am," Stony said. "Yeah, I am crazy like the moon." He stood there with her for several minutes until she told him it was time for her to go say her prayers.

5

"Do you like to hunt?" Diana asked, riding beside Van on her steed, while he rode the mare. Van was having a hard enough time staying on the horse. He wasn't much of a rider, but he was not about to show her any weakness. Not her. She wore a tan riding outfit, her dark boots as shiny as a storm trooper's. Over her shoulder, a quiver full of arrows, and a small bow.

*Are we gonna play Cowboys and Injuns?* he wondered. *I'll be the big bad cowboy coming upon the helpless squaw. She will beg for mercy, and I will give it to her. Give it to her. Over and over. Give give give . . .*

"Yeah!" he shouted. "I love to hunt. Bagged lots of deer over at Blue Point last year."

"What else?" she shouted.

"What do you mean?"

"What other kinds of prey?" Diana slowed her horse to a trot, and then finally a walk. She kept perfect form upon the saddle.

*Rich bitch probably's been riding since she was three.* Van watched how her hips undulated as her thighs pressed into the saddle. *Mmmmm.*

"Well, shit, I've fished. I've shot some rabbits," Van said, but kept watching those thighs. Pressing down and in. Clinging to the horse's side.

"Little bunnies, how adorable," she said, her words dripping with sarcasm. "Brave of you. I come from a long line of hunters."

"Girls don't hunt," he said.

"Of course not," she laughed, riding ahead of him. "Come on, Crawfish!"

She was a bitch, but he had to follow. They had been fucking so much, he felt drained of any will to resist her. He wanted to be with her, inside her, around her. He hated most of the local girls, but Diana Crown was different. He wanted her to want him. Badly.

He pressed his heels into his horse's flanks, and the animal took off after its companion.

When they came to the edge of the cove, she held her hand out to indicate that he should stop. "Stay in the shadows," she whispered, as his horse approached hers.

The cove was full of swans. It looked to Van like a mirror with a bunch of zit pops on it, or the little flecks that hit the bathroom mirror when he flossed once a month. It looked like his mother's round mirror in fact, the one she kept in the bathroom, the one that made your face large and when Van looked in it, he could see all the pores and zits and invisible whiskers and ugliness on his face.

"They're like angels," Diana said. "Angels on the water."

She reached back and drew the bow from her back. It was crudely made, and fairly small. She took an arrow and set it, tightening the bow, her shoulders drawing back.

"Watch this," she said, letting an arrow fly.

Van thought she was magnificent.

Birds flew up, their white wings spreading as if one great white bird were bursting upwards to heaven.

As Van watched the arrow go, he saw the girl out on the dock.

*It was that bitch who was going to ruin Stony's life. That fuckin' cunt girl from out of the borough who had got herself knocked up. Probably not even by his brother, but by some immigrant boyfriend of hers.*

He wished he could shoot an arrow at her.

He closed his eyes. He wished Diana would miss the bird.

Hell, he *prayed* she would miss the goddamned bird and hit that bitch in the heart.

"Let's get out of here," Diana said when she was done. Her breathing accelerated, and she had the ruddy glow that Van had seen after he'd done her hard and good. "I got one. Let's ride back, I want you now." Quickly, she turned her horse around, and they raced back through the woods, Van clinging to his saddle horn, having lost the reins. He kept his head low, and felt that at any second, he would be thrown to the ground.

Somehow, he made it back to the Crown place.

Somehow, he ripped her riding pants open and pressed his face into that salt-sea moist garden that grew wild at the center of her womb.

# Chapter Thirteen

## The Swan

### 1

Lourdes stood at the edge of the dock, watching the cove as if half expecting some secret of life to be revealed to her. Stony crossed the bridge, and waved, trying to get her attention. They often met here, for his family didn't like her calling, and hers often left the phone off. He couldn't wait to hold her. It had been too long. He knew that despite the fact that they'd had a scare about the baby, they were lucky. Damn lucky. Look at her, he thought, shielding his eyes from the last of the sun. The sky sprayed pink and yellow light across the distant clouds. The trees along the opposite side of the cover seemed deep blue. Seven swans glided across the slightly choppy water, colored a blue-green like marble rippling. Lourdes wore her blue jeans and an orange sweatshirt, but might as well have been wearing the most beautiful gown—or nothing at all as far as Stony was concerned. He stepped off the bridge, onto the flattened yellow grass. Moving through the drying thickets that had, in the summer, been blackberry tangles, now just dry twigs. In his hand, a small flower he'd plucked from a garden on his way to see her. The closer he got to the small dock, the more he sensed something not quite right. Something about the way she stood, like a statue at the edge of the water, made him think he shouldn't give it to her. He pressed it into his pocket, crushing it.

When he called to her, she turned and he saw, even at some distance, the tears on her face. Later, he couldn't remember how he'd moved from one end of the dock to the other, but suddenly—it seemed—he was there, his arm around her shoulder, as if time had skipped.

"What is it? What's wrong?" he asked. He felt a shuddering from her. "What's wrong?"

She turned her face into his neck. Her hair smelled always of spice and lavender—he would know her from her smell. Sometimes she smelled of cigarettes, too. He didn't like this odor, except from her, on her lips. "What is it?"

She whispered something so faintly he barely heard. Had she said, "I'm dead?" What flashed through his mind was the baby they'd thought had been within her. "It's dead?" That was what she'd said. He kissed the top of her head.

She pointed to the water that lapped at the pylons. Something small and white floated there—like an old towel, thrown into the sea by some bather.

Then he saw it more clearly. It was a swan, not as large as the others that glided along the water near them. It was dead. An arrow through its back.

"It's dead," she repeated. Her tears became a current from her eyes to his throat as she pressed against him. "I was feeding it." She unclenched her fists and balled-up Wonder Bread dropped onto the docks. "Someone shot it." She pointed across the water to the thick woods. "Over there."

Her voice trembled, but what trembled within Stony was not the dead swan but his love for Lourdes. "It's all right," he said. "Probably some asshole over at the Parkinson place. Someone should shoot an arrow at one of those jerks." It was all he could think to say. When he looked at the swan, its blood black in the water, its feathers so brilliant white and somehow untouched by blood . . . all he could see was that something that had seemed so pure—something so innocent and wild—that had been cupped in his hands, in his and Lourdes's hands, now lay dead with an arrow through its heart.

The sun began to diminish against the sweeping clouds. Like dust whisked across a room, the light scattered. It was as if the world had turned over, a restless sleeper, and woken momentarily as Stony woke at that moment— a millisecond of time—a photograph of her face. Lourdes. He knew. She didn't have to say it. It was like a sudden flash of telepathy between them, or perhaps merely intuition.

*You knew all along. You knew even when she lied to you.*

Lourdes was still pregnant. He was sure.

"Why did you lie?" he asked, holding her closer. Now her tears blotted at his cotton shirt, mingling with his sweat. The river was between them—she cried, he sweated—and the reservoir held the truth. "Why?"

She didn't speak. She wasn't like him in that way. She couldn't go on and on with words and phrases and well-articulated thoughts. All she had was a telepathy in her silence. All that needed to be said was in the warmth and tears.

Finally, "Because I was thinking of getting rid of it." Silence.

The wind was icy and bitter, as it came down suddenly, and then the air calmed.

"But I can't do that. I just can't." Silence.

"Christ," he said. "What are we gonna do?"

"I don't know," she said. "I don't know." The crying stopped. He felt their two hearts pounding together—and then he remembered the third one—the baby. Would the heart be pounding there, somewhere between them? It had been four months. The baby was four months old now.

"Other people do this. All the time," he said. He reached up to stroke her thick dark hair.

"Yeah. I guess they do."

Then she said, "I don't want us to get married or anything."

"Why not?"

"That would be dumb. We'd be divorced in less than a year."

"Maybe," he shrugged. "Maybe not. People get married all the time. If it lasts, it lasts. You can't predict anything with much accuracy." He felt something overcome him, a feeling of how good life was, despite the terrible parts. Despite the fact that at fifteen he knew his life would change whether he wanted it to or not. A curious calm came over him. He wanted her, he wanted their child. He wanted what life was throwing at him. He loved her smell, her warmth, and as he held her close, he thought: *I could wake up with her next to me, her face, her smell, her warmth, every single day of my life. I could do this. I really could.*

"Shit, you can't even predict the weather," Stony laughed, feeling the rain come down fast and furious. "See? God is pissing on us!" The heavens opened up with rain suddenly, a crackle of thunder, a flash of light . . . pure rain began pouring down on them as they stood on the docks. He lifted his face up to the rain, laughing at its chill, opening his mouth to take in the drops.

"Why are you laughing?" she shouted, but began laughing, too.

Feeling completely insane, he began dancing around her, nothing brilliant, no steps, no special moves, just

160

dancing the way he felt children must dance when they're happy. He was laughing, and she began dancing too. The joy was absurd. He had gotten her pregnant, she was going to have a baby, they were far too young, it would never work. He'd probably work the lobster boats now, no college in his future, maybe no high school graduation. . . . They'd live in some tiny one-room apartment and she'd get fat from boredom and he'd get sullen from resentment, and they'd raise a goofy child. *We can get around that. I know we can*, something within him whispered. Nora had always said, *Everything can work out fine if you just plant your feet on the ground and look straight ahead. Nothing is a tragedy unless you buy it a suit of clothes and give it a free meal.* Something within him told him it would be okay, and better than okay, it would somehow make itself work. It would fall into line. There was a dead swan in the water, but other swans, together two by two, far off in the cove, ignored the dead and moved in tandem across the disturbed surface.

"Why are we so happy?" Lourdes shouted, clapping her hands together. Her dark hair was flying side to side, her hips moved in circles to an invisible Hula Hoop, her grin was enormous, infectious. *The world can go to hell!* Stony thought. *It can go to hell and we can be here dancing on this dock.*

"Because I love you!" Stony cried out, throwing his arms up in the air, the rain pelting them.

"You look stupid!" Lourdes yelled. Her voice echoed round. She was laughing too, drawing her hands up to her mouth as if to stop the laughter. "You look like a fool!"

"I love looking stupid! Let me be as dumb as they come! I dare the universe to strike me with lightning! Come on, lightning! Hit me now!" He almost jumped into the water, but when he got to the edge of the dock he thought better of it. He raised his hands up, looking at the sky as the pale blue clouds darkened above him. He wanted to reach up and feel lightning in his hands. He felt it all surge through him—the power of the world, the power of his youth, the power of love. It was insane what he was feeling, but he looked at the sky as if it held all the mysteries of the cosmos. "I know the secret of the universe now! I know it, yahoo! I know it! Life can do its worst and it won't touch us!" He began to jump up and down, rocking the dock. The dinghies tied to it bobbed up and down. Small fish came to the surface of the water, attacking the raindrops.

The raindrops felt fresh on his face. He closed his eyes, face up to the sky, and opened his mouth slightly to taste the freshness of the world. He imagined touching the clouds, his hands clutching at their vanishing . . . and beyond them, the moisture of heaven. *I am a Rainmaker!* he cried out within himself. *I am the Storm King! Come on, rain, hit me with all you got! Throw the bolts down on me and the buckets of tears and the drums of thunder! I am the Storm King, and I'm gonna bring the heavens down on us, down on me and Lourdes and we're gonna have heaven on earth right here and right now! I am in love and we are gonna have a child and it will be the most wondrous child this stinkin' piece of hellhole earth has ever known!*

2

Sweat all over Van's face, from riding the horse, from excitement, from a fever that grew within him at the thought of her touch.

"What is it you want from me?"

Diana wiped her hands across her skirt. She looked Van Crawford directly in the eye. "What everyone wants."

"People want different things," Van said.

Diana glanced out the window, into the darkness. "All I can get. It's all I ever wanted." Then she smiled. "Want to see something?"

"Depends," Van said. "What is it?"

"Our own private chapel."

"Shit, I don't want to see a church. 'Specially after what we just did."

"It isn't a chapel like you think."

"No crosses?"

"No Jesus, don't worry," she said. "Come on."

He followed her as she took him through the pool room, with its wide Olympic-sized swimming pool, the billowing cover stretched across it. Past her father's orchid greenhouse, and the small gymnasium full of weights and bicycles. One wall of the house was made almost entirely of glass. The glass was warped in some way so that when Van looked out across the dark water, it seemed to have flecks of yellow and green light dancing on its surface.

"Come on," Diana said. "My, you're slow."

"I'm coming," he said, slightly testily. He didn't like some girl telling him things, nagging him. His father got that too. He did not intend to end up in that kind of life. Diana was a rich girl with a hot body, but that was it. He was sure that as soon as he could, he would move on to some other local girl.

Finally, they came to a small door. It was curved in an arch, and looked positively medieval to Van. "What the hell kind of chapel is it?"

Diana turned, her mood solemn. "No teasing. What are you, Catholic? Baptist?"

"None of the above. A goddamned atheist," Van chuckled. He stepped forward, slipping his arm around her waist. He tugged her against him.

She pulled away. "You're something. Everyone is something. You a good Christian boy, Van?"

"I don't believe in nothing," he said. "How many times do I have to tell you? All right," he finally relented, "I believe in this." He pressed his hand down to the cleft between her legs, feeling that part of her that he most desired. She let out a small gasp. "And this," he said, reaching up to press his fingers around her left breast.

Then he covered her hand in his, and brought it down to the bulge in his jeans. "But mostly I believe in this."

He felt colder than he'd ever felt in his life, yet there was some spark he wanted to ignite. Something had been missing in his life up to this point. This shitheel town, this dead existence, the way he knew where he'd be if he just went along with things: He would be in a goddamned lobster boat looking at his old friends getting older, smelling the fucking lobster and crab on his skin till it got into his blood . . .

Warmth emanated from her hand beneath his, and he felt all of a fever there.

"I am your religion," Diana said, her voice turning throaty the way it had when they'd fucked before. "I am your church."

Her mouth pressed against his lips, swallowing his mouth up in shimmering moisture, her greedy tongue thrusting across his teeth as if trying to find the heat and excitement within his body. Just as quickly, she drew back from him. She reached her hand up and wiped her wet lips. "Inside," she whispered.

She turned her back on him again, but his body would not let her go. He wrapped himself around her back as they stood there, his lips finding her delicate smooth neck. She shrugged him off. "Inside," she repeated. She turned the key in the door, and opened it. The door swung outward. A musty scent assaulted him. A rush of warm air from inside the dark chapel. "Follow me," Diana said. She stepped into the darkness. It was too dark to see. Too dark, but still he followed her.

He stepped over the threshold.

Diana was already lighting a third candle by the time he walked down the center aisle between the pews. "Holy shit," Van said. "Oh my God. Oh my motherfucking cocksucking God."

Diana kept her eyes on the altar.

"It was a gift to my great-grandfather at the end of the

First World War. A token of appreciation.''

"Jesus," Van said, feeling the piss run down the inside of his pants leg. "Goddamn."

He closed his eyes. His mind was blank, he could not escape the darkness that surrounded him. He began shivering all over as if he'd been sprayed with ice water. But within that growing pain, something else pushed at the back of his head as if there were something in him, some darkness, waiting to find its moment of freedom.

"Once a person looks upon it, he will never be the same." Diana's voice faded even as she spoke, and then it grew and he wondered how the hell she managed to be talking inside his head.

Then he remembered how much he wanted this, wanted this kind of experience. To break free from this village and its small minds and the horrible existence that doomed him to a prison of family and dead ends. The darkness within him seeped across his mind.

Opening his eyes again, he felt the fear, like a thousand lasers, graze his skin.

# Chapter Fourteen
## Our Lady, Star of the Sea

1

It was as if something busted inside Stony Crawford. He squeezed Lourdes's hand, and pulled her along. They ran laughing across the bridge, towards the Borough. Rain pelted them like endless tears, and they were soaked to the skin by the time they made the Common. "The library!" she shouted, but when they got there, it was was closed. (BACK IN TEN, the sign read.) "No, there!" he cried, pointing to the church next to the post office. It was Our Lady, Star of the Sea.

"Oh my God!" she said as he grabbed her hand and pulled her. They almost slipped on the muddy grass. "I can't! It's sacred ground!" She laughed nearly as hard as he was, and her hand was warm within his grasp.

He drew her into the church, its inner whiteness like the bone of some desert animal. As soon as they got inside, they slowed, quieted by the statue of the Virgin Mary. It stood sentinel next to the font of holy water. They both stood there shivering before it, the chilly dampness soaking them through.

"Oh Mary," Lourdes whispered, nodding her head slightly, crossing herself. "You who are the blessed mother of God, bless this child." She pressed her hand to her stomach. Stony noticed for the first time that her stomach was getting a little bit of a paunch. The baby was forming. The baby was growing.

He went to her, pressing his hand over hers to feel it. "It's a lump," he said.

Lourdes put a hand over his. "Look at Maria," she said.

Stony glanced up at the statue. It was pure white, like ivory. The statue's face was almost expressionless. Round white eyes, Romanesque nose, rose-petal lips. It bothered him, all these statues that Catholics had. It seemed idolatrous. "I don't worship statues," he said.

"I don't either, you Protestant-atheist," Lourdes whispered. "It's not a statue I'm looking at. It's the idea of purity and holiness. It's a human face for that idea. Do you believe in that?"

Stony shrugged.

"I need to know if you do," Lourdes said, applying more pressure on his hand against her belly. "It's important to me."

Stony closed his eyes. The idea of God or Jesus or anything like that had always been abstract, like a cosmic tangle of nerve endings shooting out the birth of the universe and then pretty much staying in the background. He rarely attended church with his mother, and his father never went. But for Lourdes's sake, for her sense of religion, he concentrated. In his mind, he saw a woman who might have been the Virgin Mary, but then all the color drained from her face until she was white as bone. "Do you really think she was a virgin?"

"I think she was pure," Lourdes said. "To give birth to God, she had to be pure. Do you believe in purity?"

Finally, opening his eyes, he nodded. "Yeah, I do. You're pure." He leaned forward and kissed her lightly on the lips. Drawing back from her, pulling his hand away, he glanced at the statue. It almost felt pagan, not that he considered that so awful. He pulled the crushed flower from his pocket. It was purple and red. He pressed it into the statue's open hand. "Sanctify our love," he said.

"Silly, she doesn't need it." Lourdes grabbed the flower and set it up behind her ear.

2

Van felt the power of the universe thrust through his skin, burning his blood, sending him wild-eyed into the rainy night.

"The horses!" Diana shouted. "We hunt!" Her hair twisted in the wind, practically a mane itself. Her clothes clung to her slender form, outlining the breasts he had so recently sucked at, the belly he'd nuzzled, the legs, so smooth and refined, that he'd spread like she was the cheapest whore from New London . . .

"That's fuckin' crazy!" he laughed, but he raced her to the stables. "Fuckin' nuts, it's damn insane!" He shouted against the rain, feeling the spirit of her life overtake his, raise him up, make him feel as if there was a purpose to this damned existence.

He no longer felt like stupid Van Crawfish, the lout who could never understand why his mother disliked him so much, why his father disciplined him too harshly, why the whole damn town wasn't on its knees to him—

He felt bigger than life itself, and here he was, with a goddess from the summer houses, a fucking beauty, and they were mounting horses in a rich man's stable, they were riding out across the gravel road, through the mud of rain, beneath the sheltering trees, great canopies of orange and gold and yellow leaves above them, holding back all but a trickle of rain. The lightning brought instant daylight to the trail ahead.

Van felt like a goddamn god himself, he felt beautiful and strong and unstoppable. Within minutes, Diana had spotted their prey, a deer that bolted at the sound of the horses. But Diana had her bow out, and aimed an arrow—

She let it fly, and it was the most perfect arc—

Her fingers, the bow, the arrow as it moved, and the deer as it leapt up to dive into the brush, with the arrow that caught its left flank. And then another arrow, then another, and the horses seemed to know the trail of the woods, and followed the wounded doe.

Finally, feeling as if wings were on his ankles and a tidal wave of pure energy carried him, Van leapt down and grabbed the doe's throat, exposing it in the lightning flash. His hair was wild and floated in static wind, his eyes redder than he could've known, his grip on the deer's throat as the animal breathed its last—

"The knife!" Diana clapped, pure joy coming from within. She was so fucking beautiful, and it was all for her. He was going to finish off this deer for her. She had brought the animal down, and he would glory in the kill.

He reached around to his belt, bringing out his hunting knife. Unsheathing it, he raised the blade up. Lightning whitened the woods around them—

The trees, for a moment, seemed to be men and women, shrouded in cloaks, the branches and leaves their hair, their eyes on him as if in some solemn event—

The knife flashed as the early dark of evening returned. He brought the blade deep into the deer's heart, once, twice, raising it and hacking at the creature—

Blood flowed across his arm—

Diana, throwing her head back, laughing—

"More!" she cried. "More!"

Lightning flashed—

She held her hands near him to catch the spray of red. It felt like he had struck oil deep in the creature's wound.

169

The torrent did not cease for several moments as the woods went from white to black and white to black again.

His energy grew as he dropped the dead animal—his dick got hard, he wanted her all over again. It burned inside him, this unquenchable fire she had kindled. Both of them, covered with the animal's blood, like wine, her skin, her breasts . . . she crawled to him on her knees and their tongues entwined, their lips, their hands, he felt her buttocks moving rhythmically as they coupled against the carcass in the leaf-shattered woods as night and rain descended.

Just as he was about to climax within her, she drew away. "No, no," she whispered, "Later. One more creature to hunt tonight."

But his arousal began to hurt, he wanted to be inside her, not just his dick, but all of his body, his soul . . . he wanted to stay within her wet heat and not be outside anymore. Rage filled him, then exhaustion. He lay back on the blood-dampened animal. "I'm too tired to hunt. Too tired, baby."

He closed his eyes for what seemed like the first time in days, and the darkness behind his eyes exploded—shattering his mind—he saw *demons leaping from the fires of Hell, smelled the tortures of men, the cries of women as they were thrown into lava pits*—

When he opened his eyes to a flash of lightning, she was so close to him that her face was out of focus. "One more hunt tonight, and then you have me forever," she said, licking blood from his cheek. "And I have you."

3

Stony Crawford followed Lourdes as she passed the statue of Mary, and went into the main part of the church. The stained glass windows depicting the Stations of the Cross were dark with the pelting rain. It felt so clean, the way the rain hit the glass, the way the colors in the glass mutated from light to dark. It was as if they were being washed, yet kept dry by the church. A coldness settled into the church, dispelled only by a lingering scent of incense. Above the altar, a great wooden cross, with a nearly naked Jesus nailed upon it, agony across his gaunt features. It made Stony think of Nora's story about sacred crosses and scarecrows and the Halloween Man. Was the carving of the man any different from Nora's tales? Could one man, being tortured to death, actually be a god, and not just any god, but *the* God? It was as hard to swallow as the Halloween Man story. It was a nice legend, but how could it be? How could a man be God? Men could be monsters, men could be devils, but there was no way in heaven or hell they could be better than other men. Christianity was a nice fairy story. He would have to play along with it if he wanted Lourdes to love him, but he did not really believe in any of it. It seemed ridiculous. Virgins giving birth. Gods being crucified and then rising from the dead to point out their wounds. Drinking wine and eating bread and pretending it was blood and flesh. It made no sense at all.

Stony and Lourdes sat down on a pew, and she knelt to pray. Then she sat back.

"Someday maybe we can get married in a church," she said. "If we decide that's what we want."

"I want it," Stony said. He glanced at the saints and the windows, and no longer felt tied to the town or his family. The church was a world where they could not touch him. "Come on," he said. He stood up, offering his hand. She looked at him, questioning, but took it, and rose. They went to the railing before the altar. Kneeling down, he said, "I take you until the end of time to be my lawfully wedded wife."

She cracked a grin. Out of the corner of her mouth, she whispered, "You're crazy."

"To love, honor, and cherish till the end of my days,"

he continued. "To protect and care for in sickness and in health—"

"That's not the exact wording."

"Till death do us part. No, till God parts us, till you don't love me anymore, till the universes collide," he said, and looked up at the cross.

"You don't believe in God, heathen," Lourdes said, shoving him slightly.

"If you do, I do," he said.

"I do," she said.

"I do," he grinned, leaning over and kissing her, feeling his mouth open to her, and hers opening in return, not devouring as when they'd made love, but sweetly, as if inhaling each other's breath.

4

Lightning lit the church, the blues and reds and yellows of the stained glass flashing for an instant.

"I better go," she said after a while. The rain had let up, and they'd been kneeling at the altar for several minutes. He didn't want to let go of her hand.

"I'll walk you," he said.

"No, I think maybe I need to be alone. Just to think. We both have a lot to think about, Stony. If we get married—"

"If? Now it's official. Before God," he said. "You, me, and the baby. A family."

"Ah, I see." Lourdes shook her head. "You tricked me."

"There's no divorce in heaven," he said. He helped her get up.

Tears played at the edge of her eyes. "It's not a joke."

"No." He kissed her eyelids. "I meant every word."

"My father will kill me."

"Mine won't be too happy either."

"I mean it. He will."

. ''Then let's run away.''

"Don't be ridiculous."

"I mean it," he said. "I can borrow my mom's car. We can get away and I can get work somewhere. I've saved some money."

"From what?"

"All those rich people's lawns I've mowed," he grinned. The lie hurt. But he wanted to make her confident now. Right now.

"We'll talk about this later on."

"When later? You're beginning to show," he said. "They'll guess soon. You'll need to see a doctor and stuff too."

"Please," she said, wiping her tears back. "If we run away, we'll end up back here. And it'll be worse."

"Tell you what," Stony said, and he almost could not believe the words spilling from his mouth, but he felt an urgency. "Meet me at Nora's tomorrow morning before school. Maybe at seven. We can decide then, okay?"

She nodded. She looked at him curiously. "Okay. But I'm not promising anything, Stony."

"Okay," he said. "Let me walk you home, though. We can talk."

"No, I really want to be alone now, just to think about all this," Lourdes said, and touched the edge of his face sweetly before she left.

5

He remained behind, sitting at the railing, after she'd gone. What was he doing? What the hell was he doing? *Fifteen, married, kid, wife, responsibilities* . . .

He imagined his father's face, his mother's tears, his brother's disgust . . .

"Can I help you with anything?" a man asked.

Stony turned around. He hadn't heard the man come in. Not just a man. A priest.

"Hi," Stony said, fumbling in his mind. Was it illegal to go into a church without permission? "I was just . . . admiring your church."

"It's a nice one. We've lost a lot of the congregation over the years to the churches down the road, but this is one of the most beautiful ones, in my opinion." The priest was in his forties, and a light frost of gray had settled along his light brown hair. He walked up to the altar, extending his hand. "I'm Father Jim."

"Stony Crawford." Stony shook the man's hand. A very cold hand.

"I know," the priest said. "I was there when you were born."

Stony felt a slight chill. He had lived his whole life in the Borough and had never run into this priest before. He stood up. "Yeah? I've heard every story in the book about that day. How Mom was in the station wagon, and Johnny Miracle was yelling."

"Rain coming down." Father Jim nodded. "I heard Johnny from across the Common, and came over to help out. But you'd already come into the world."

Stony grinned. "Well . . ."

"You feeling all right, Stony?"

"Sure."

"You look a little pale is all."

"Maybe a little bit cold."

"Good," Father Jim said, touching him on the shoulder. "Well, if you ever need any counsel, be sure to come see me. All right? Catholic, Protestant, even if you don't feel very Christian, we're all one fellowship in the divine light. Do you understand?"

"Sure," Stony said. He could not wait to get out of that church. He had never liked churches all that much, and priests bothered him. Father Jim in particular, now that they'd met. Father Jim had something in his eyes that seemed less than priestly, and Stony was not sure what that was. He just didn't want to see it again.

"Stony," Father Jim said when Stony was halfway out of the church.

Stony turned. "Yeah, Father?"

"You look so much like your mother in some ways. It amazes me."

On his way back home, Stony thought that was the strangest comment of all, since he and his mother looked nothing alike as far as he could tell.

6

"What are we hunting?" Van whispered, his tongue lapping at the back of her neck.

Diana remained silent, crouching down beside her horse. The rain was letting up, and the moon, nearly full, shone across their domain of tangled vines and branches.

*I have my knife*, he thought, clutching it, unsheathing it the way she'd unsheathed his manhood just minutes earlier and wiped it across her womb—it wasn't a *pussy* or a *vagina* or a *cunt* with her—it was a womb, it was a sanctuary there between her legs. *And my knife is ready, we will hunt! I am a hunter of all I see!* he wanted to cry out, but remained silent.

A lone figure walked along a slight ridge near the opening of the woods.

"Our prey," Diana whispered, rising up on her haunches, bow and arrow in her hand.

Then she did something that confused him. Her voice was somehow inside his head. Like a mosquito wriggling into his ear, and moving to his brain, it tickled and buzzed at first, and then he heard her clearly—

*Who do you want to kill more than anyone in the world?*

*No one.*

*Oh yes you do, Van Crawfish, you want someone to vanish from the face of the earth.*

*No.*

*Yes. Don't hide from me Van, tell me who it is, tell me—*

*The bitch.*

*Who?*

*The bitch trying to stop Stony from having his freedom.*

*Her name?*

*Lourdes Maria. She's a Spanish bitch from Wequetucket, she wants to get her claws into him and bring him down.*

*You want to kill her, don't you?*

*Yes! Yes I want to kill that damn bitch before she does to him what my mother did to my father!*

*You want to take your knife and open her up.*

*Yes! I want to open up that bitch with my knife and make her blood spurt out like juice! I want to tear that baby out of her! I want to make her taste her own skin! I want her to suffer as much as a bitch like her can!*

## 7

Stony sat out on the back steps to his house before going in to supper. He was wishing he'd just grabbed Lourdes and brought her with him, that they had run off tonight, just to get it over with before either had a chance to change his or her mind.

He glanced up at the emerging stars.

Closed his eyes.

Life was beautiful. It was. He loved her, she loved him. In spirit, they were already married.

*It's starting now*, he thought. *My life. My real life. The future of all I will be begins tonight.*

*I've been bad before, I've done terrible things, but from here on, if you're up there listening, God, from here on, because you have given me such a beautiful wife and such a happy beginning to a family, I will never do bad things again. I won't lie, I won't sneak beers, I won't even look at another girl as long as I live. I won't be all the things that my dad and brother and mom are. I'll be the best damn Stony Crawford there ever was.*

*If . . .*

*And there's always an if, but you'd know that if you're really God and you're really listening.*

*If only you'll promise me that I'll never have to come back here again, not to these people, not to this place. Promise me we'll get far from here, just me and my baby and my baby's baby.*

Then, Stony felt it. As if God had answered. As if whatever ran the universe was in accord with his wish. He felt something inside him give, and an overriding calm came over him.

He felt a strength inside him, and all anxiety vanished for a few moments as a cool salty breeze blew in off the water.

"Thanks," he said, knowing that it was all his imagination. But he didn't care. He felt confirmed in his conviction and he knew that marrying Lourdes was going to be the right thing, and that he would be a good father and everything would turn out better than just okay.

*Sometimes, shit happens.*

*But from here on, miracles are gonna happen.*

# *Chapter Fifteen*

Lourdes stepped cautiously over a low tangle of dried vines, her feet smushing down in the mud. She felt stupid for not having thought to bring a flashlight. She usually did. *But then, you could walk through these woods blindfolded and you wouldn't trip over much.* She had been walking these trails her entire life. She had fallen in love with loneliness at an early age. Her family was smothering. Her four brothers hovering around, either teasing their only sister or trying to protect her. Her father, with his old ways, believing that she should never leave the house unchaperoned until the day she married. Maybe not even then. Her mother distrusted Stonehaven Borough as well as the apartments and gas station areas out where they lived. By the time Lourdes was seven, she had managed to sneak away on summer afternoons and just roam. She would spend hours gathering berries, or hiding from yellow jackets, or watching the shadows for fireflies. She created make-believe creatures among the trees, and every bog and pond contained a mermaid or two. She spoke with the invisible spirits of Indians, too, who she still believed, at fifteen, wandered between the thick bundles of birch and oak. Nothing scared her here. Nothing ever could.

These were her woods.

Within them, she felt protected, and knew every tree, every moss-covered rock, every pond and bog, every blackberry bush. She even knew the ancient stone wall that was full now of hibernating snakes, and she knew where the mosquitoes attacked the most aggressively in the summer and how to avoid them.

Now, following the thinnest of trails, the fallen wet leaves slippery like eelskin, the mud sucking at her sneakers, the only thought that frightened her was the idea that she and Stony would be running away from all this.

*Every childhood has to end.* It was something her grandmother used to tell her when Lourdes was eight or nine and asking about when she would grow up. *Every girl becomes a woman, and there is often sorrow on that day. Do not rush ahead to meet the woman you will become.*

*And now, this will be it,* she thought. *Tomorrow morning. He wants me to meet him at Nora's and run away with him. Like prisoners escaping. I just can't. But I love him. We're going to have a baby. We're going to bring life into the world.*

After their moment together in Our Lady, Star of the Sea, something felt even more sacred to her than it had previously. The baby growing inside her had a family around him, a father and a mother. The Virgin Mary had blessed the baby, and she and Stony were bound together at the altar, before the eyes of God.

It was stupid, she knew. As she crossed a thin trickle of stream, Lourdes felt what seemed to be a spark leap within her. *We are one. Stony and I are one. No one will separate us. Not my parents, not his, not anyone.*

She pressed her hands upon her slight paunch.

*(The baby!)*

*(Hola, hijito, your mama is in love with your daddy!)*

What would he be like? Or she? Would he have Stony's eyes, or hers? Her hair, she hoped. His smile. Then, a terrible thought occurred to her as she slowed to a stop.

*What if the baby looks like my father?*

*Or his mother?*

*(It's okay, hijito, you will be the most beautiful baby who was ever brought into the world. Don't worry!)*

Carefully avoiding the low-hanging branches which shivered as she touched them, Lourdes giggled aloud. She imagined a child with all the worst physical and mental attributes of both their families. Moles on the neck. Large ears. Crooked nose. Wolfman hairline (her Tío Ruly). Lazy eye. Nonexistent lips. Short and fat. Boxy . . .

She had to remember to make a joke about it with Stony in the morning.

*(Don't worry, hijito, you're gonna be as gorgeous as your mama!)*

All her life, she'd known she would one day marry and have children. Her mother had been only seventeen when she'd married, pregnant with Lourdes's older brother, Miguel. *Mom was two years older than me. Not that much different.*

*Please, blessed Virgin Mary, bless us three, protect us with your love and purity. Don't allow temptation or the shadows to fall upon us.*

Praying like this, in her woods, seemed as natural to her as breathing.

Lourdes's father had warned her not to ever think of marrying a *huero*. This was the word for the blue-eyed, blond-haired Anglos, but it encompassed all non-Latinos. Lourdes had an Aunt Elena who had married a *huero*, and they divorced within four years. "They never work out, ever," her father had warned. Her father considered Stony a *huero* too, and had told her so. This had led to the first actual fight she'd ever had with him. He called her every name imaginable and she had thrown those words right back at him. In the end, she'd cried and her father had gone off angry. Only her mother had comforted her, telling her that her father would eventually come around to liking the "Anglo boy."

*And now . . .*
*Marriage.*
*A baby.*
*God, what will Dad do now?*

The moonlight turned a small oval pond into liquid gold. Lourdes looked up for the source of its light.

The moon was huge and round, filling all the sky that could be seen beyond the greedy treetops. It was turning an orange hue, almost like a sunset. She closed her eyes. *Harvest moon. God, please make sure this is the right thing. Please help me and Stony.*

Without realizing it at first, Lourdes found she was saying the prayer aloud now in the cathedral of wood. "Please make sure our baby is healthy and help us learn to handle my family and all the problems we're gonna have. Mother of God, who looks out for babies and mothers, keep your hand upon me, let us have a good life together as you will."

Opening her eyes again to the expansive moon, she shivered. The temperature was dropping. She could feel a difference between a few seconds before and now. The smells of the bogs and wet leaves were almost humid despite the cold. She glanced down at her own dark reflection in the moonlit water. "Two in one," she whispered, touching her stomach. "Be safe, *hijo.*"

She turned about, thinking (Hijito, *you had better not make me sick tomorrow morning like you did yesterday*), when a flashlight beam blinded her.

She put a hand up to shield her face from the light. "Who is it? Stony?"

All she could see was a silhouette and the round white beam.

"Victor? Miguel?" But her brothers would not do this. Not at this hour. Maybe later at night, but not when it could not be much later than six o'clock. It wasn't even suppertime yet.

Then the flashlight moved up beneath the chin of the boy who held it.

A ghostly light distorted the features, but Lourdes recognized him. "Oh, Van, it's just you," she sighed. "You scared me for a sec."

Van grinned. His smile, wide and gap-toothed, reminded her of a jack-o'-lantern.

"So," he said, his voice low and almost a growl, "here's the bitch who's trying to fucking ruin my baby brother's life. I've been looking for you all day. I got a game we can play. You and me."

Then the flashlight shut off.

"Let's play 'Skin the Bitch,' " he said.

*Interlude:*
*Dawn, Several Years Later*

# Chapter Sixteen

## A Man, a Boy, and the Road Home

### 1

It seemed like yesterday. Tears streamed from his eyes, and he felt like an old man. He felt that awful thing inside, too, that thing that he'd managed to keep down within him, that terrible feeling that meant only bad things were going to happen.

He could not stop the tears, and when they had all poured from his soul, he wiped at his face.

The boy had told him all and more than he could himself remember. *Nora's voice from the boy's mouth* ... Every detail of his past life was laid bare for him. How could this child know? Had he been there? It was as if he had raked his small fingers through the hair of Stony's memory. Stony, now twenty-seven, driving a car up 95, nearly there, nearly to the town of his birth. Time had held and stopped as the tale had spun out, and he glanced in the rearview mirror at the boy. He was sound asleep. He had not been telling Stony the tale of Stony's past, of things Stony could not have seen, but somehow did see, and did know. He had known it all as if from a distance, watching—part of him that did not even know he was then watching the world unfold.

The sign up ahead indicated that the turnoff to what had once been Stonehaven was coming up. It didn't read STONEHAVEN BOROUGH, which once upon a time it had.

The sign merely read LAND'S END LIGHTHOUSE.

Stony took the exit. Dawn clung to the trees along the potholed road, the ghostly light of five A.M. filtered through trees and thin fog. When he hit one of the many bumps in the road, the boy called Prophet groaned in the backseat.

"You okay?" Stony asked.

"Yeah," the boy said groggily. "We there yet?"

"Almost. About seven miles."

"Good," the boy said. "I'm hungry."

"Still have some doughnuts back there. Water's in the thermos." Stony reached over and grasped the thermos, handing it back to the kid.

"I have to pee," Prophet said. He took the thermos and a moment later Stony heard him gulping down water.

"Okay, I'll pull over." Stony slowed the car to a stop.

"You trust me?"

"To pee? Sure."

"No, I mean to not run away."

"You haven't run yet."

The boy got out and stepped into the woods. Stony opened the glove compartment and checked to make sure the timing device was still there. He hadn't checked it since Texas, mainly out of an abnormal fear that he would take the small sphere and throw it out and forget his plans. Forget why he was bringing this boy back to this place. Why he intended to protect the world from what had begun when he was fifteen years old.

It was not much of a bomb, actually, something he'd

learned about by accident when the Feds from Phoenix had come into a small Arizona burg to handle some old fart building a bomb in his outhouse. Stony had been called in to help, on a local level. The old fart was named Jaspar Swink, and had spent half his middle age building small bombs and then sending them in gift-wrapped packages to little old ladies in Tucson and Phoenix from the Heavenly Fudge Factory. The little old ladies, delicately pulling off the ribbon, then unwrapping the gold paper, could not have been more surprised when the first thing they saw was a tiny clock and some C-6 all bound together. Swink had timed his devices perfectly. He was an amateur mathematician and logistician, and had determined at precisely what time the ladies would get their packages, and approximately what time they would open them. "They first have to look for a card," he had told Stony, sitting in the backseat of his patrol car. "They look for a card because they want to know who to thank. They hope it's their son or daughter or an old beau they'd forgotten about. Then they take one minute and look at the gold wrapping paper as if it tells something about the sender. Then they are two minutes unwrapping, to save the paper and ribbon. When they see the timer, either they will know what it is and throw it, or they will look at it curiously for the sixty-second margin of error I give myself. And then, my friend, *kaboom*. *Kaboom*. Little-old-lady confetti in every direction."

*Kaboom*.

Stony had salvaged one of the small bombs. He knew as soon as he saw it what he would do with it. He knew, in the months ahead, when he finally found the boy, what he would need to do.

It hadn't made him nervous having the device in the glove compartment. Swink had told him that he kept six of them regularly in the back of his Chevy truck. "You can have these C-6 devices for twenty years. You can toss 'em in the air, you can smash 'em with hammers. Nothing. Not until you attach a detonator. A spark is the only thing. You can even get it hotter than hell, but until it sparks, you got just a lump of shit in your hand."

Stony had asked him, "How big is the explosion?"

Swink winked at him. "How big do you want it to be?"

## 2

The boy opened the front door. "Can I get in up here with you?"

Stony shut the glove compartment. "Sure."

"Cool," the boy said. He slid into the seat, reaching back for the seat belt. "Your seat belt's broken."

"It's a lousy car. I bought it for practically nothing."

"Yeah, I noticed it's a piece of shit but I was too polite to say it."

"Actually you said it a few times."

"Oh, I guess I did." The boy grinned. "I feel I can tell you anything. Your car's a piece of shit and you are one twisted bastard." The boy chuckled. "It's just a joke. I don't mean it." The tattoos on the boy's arms looked like eels wriggling. It was just the morning's dim light playing tricks. Stony glanced back to the road ahead.

Stony felt a trickle of sweat at the back of his neck. He started the car up again, putting it in drive. They drove in silence for a few minutes. Then the boy said, "Why are we coming here anyway?"

Stony, trying not to think of the bomb in the glove compartment, said, "To end something that should've ended a long time ago."

"Oh," the kid said. "All that stuff you told me last night."

"I told you?" Stony felt his throat clutch.

"Yeah, I mean, this stuff about town and your girl and all that."

"Funny," Stony began, but stopped. *Funny, I thought you were the one telling me.*

"You know that man," the boy said.

"Which?"

"The one who took me to Texas in the first place. We had to call him the Great Father, but that was a crock. I mean, I remember him a little. When I was like three, and four maybe," the boy continued. They passed farmhouses, in disrepair, off the wild fields beyond the trees, like sentinels at the outer edge of town. The village. It was coming up. It was coming. He hadn't been there since he was fifteen. He hadn't been physically in this town in all those years. The memories should've been wiped clean, but they were fresh wounds. The sign to Wequetucket at the crossroads—where Lourdes had lived. The sign for the opposite direction to the community college. A small truck passed in front of him, narrowly missing him.

"Your lights are off," the boy said.

"Oh damn." Stony reached forward and popped the headlights on.

"He should've seen you, but it's a little dark still."

"A little. Sun'll be up in ten minutes completely."

"You think?" The boy glanced out the window to his right. They passed an old gray barn beside a pond, a light steam rising from it. "This is nothing like Texas."

"Why do you think he took you to Texas?"

"Well, we were in Mexico first. He had a place down there. It was nice. A big old house. I don't remember a lot of it, just that this one maid was really nice to me. We used to even play marbles sometimes. She liked kids. She had two kids, too, she told me, further south."

Out of nowhere, Stony flashed on a memory he had never had:

*A short Mexican woman, her face nearly serene, her hair tied back and up, her thick body covered in a blue dress.*

*Someone had taken a needle and thread and sewn her lips together.*

*When she opened her eyes, he saw that one of them had been replaced with a cat's-eye marble.*

The world flashed back to him, the road ahead. He slowed down as they drove beside the cove. "This is where I grew up," Stony said, ignoring the damning vision he'd had just a moment before. The cove was placid. The thickets had grown up and wild and died down with the death of summer. It was a dead place. No swans glided upon its surface. No seagulls circled overhead.

The boy gave a cursory glance to the cove, but his mind was on other things. "I remember when we went to El Paso because it was so hot that day. We had to wait forever at customs. It was so hot I could barely breathe."

"It gets hot down there, huh," Stony said. He searched the cove for swans, but there were none.

"Yeah, especially in the trunk."

Stony laughed. "You weren't in the trunk."

"Yeah. They put me in there. He told me that no one was supposed to know I was alive. I don't know why. But he tied me up and put me in the trunk. It was hot as hell. It felt like I was in there for nine hours."

"Jesus."

"Yeah. And even then they opened the trunk."

"Customs?"

"Yeah."

Another vision:

*A man in a tan uniform lifting the trunk lid, and his face beginning to turn waxy, and then his lips beginning to melt down like a burning candle.*

*Then, his eyes bubbling with heat.*

*Then, the screaming begins.*

"Why Texas?"

"Search me," the boy shrugged. "He had this thing about the Wild West or something. When I was six he told me that there were people out there who were believers. That's about all I remember. Sometime around then, he took off. Down to Mexico, I think. The people who got me, the Rapturists, I heard them talk about how the old guy was a pervert and he did drugs and shit. They said he was useless and old. Some of them told me that maybe the Azriel Light got him, but between you and me I always thought it was a bunch of bullshit. He's probably just livin' down in Chihuahua. It wasn't like I was real attached to him.''

"Alan Fairclough."

*The face of Alan Fairclough, its pockmarked skin, its shiny pallor, its eyes like mirrors.*

*Alan Fairclough was an it.*

"Maybe," the boy said. "Could be. I just always called him the Great Father. Ever since I can remember." Then, "Hey!"

Stony slammed his foot on the brake. "What?"

"You almost hit it." The boy pointed to the thin slice of road. A stag leapt from the woods, darting across the road. In the headlights and fog, it was a shadow of antlers and a blue-gray blur.

"Christ," Stony gasped.

"Whew. Hey, can you read?"

A sign on the old bridge that led to the borough: PRI-VATE PROPERTY. NO TRESPASSING. VIOLATORS WILL BE PROSECUTED. NO HUNTING. NO FISHING.

Someone had spray-painted at the bottom of this:
*No nothing*

"Pretty funny," the boy said. "Hey, I got a joke."

"Not up for jokes right now," Stony said. His unease grew as he drove across the bridge. The vibration felt bad here. It felt like no one had come here, no one would ever trespass here, if he could help it.

*You're a fool to do this.*

*Worse than a fool.*

*You are the most despicable being who has ever existed. You are the bogeyman and this boy is an innocent*

191

*despite himself. You are an abomination on the face of
the earth and you can't keep hiding behind who you make
other people think you are.*

*You are the Devil and Hell doesn't even want to let
you back in.*

*You will do something terrible to this boy.*

"Here's my joke. Okay? It goes, this guy is like a
punker freak and he's on this train. And his hair is all
orange and spikey and he has tattoos and he has noserings
and nails through his hands and feet and eyebrows and
stuff. This old man is staring at him. Real rude. And the
punk guy goes, why the hell are you staring at me, old
man? Didn't you ever do anything wild when you was a
kid? And the old man goes like, Yeah, I did, when I was
in the army I got stationed in Singapore and I got drunk
and screwed a parrot. I thought maybe you was my kid."
The boy howled with laughter.

Stony smiled. "That's a nasty joke."

The boy kept laughing. "Only if you think about it.
Think about it." His laughter was infectious. "I bet if
someone screwed a parrot for real they'd kill the parrot.
Or get their pecker bit off!" He roared louder, slapping
his stomach when he laughed. "Oh man that was a good
one!"

"I guess kids are different now. When I was a kid I
would never have talked like that to a grown-up."

"Kids *are* different now," he said. "Well, I'm different." Then the boy's laughter died. Quickly, he rolled
down the window. Inhaled deeply. "Oh man, I really
smell the ocean! It's so clean! Oh man!" he shouted,
holding his hand out the window as if trying to catch the
wind. "Smell it?"

Stony nodded. "Smells good."

"Smells like *everything*," the boy said. "I can smell
crabs and fish and all that clean cleanness." He laughed
at his words. "Cleanness of sea-ness."

"Look," Stony said in a hushed tone.

Stonehaven Borough came up with the sunlight over the sea.

What was left of it.

Again, he stopped the car.

"Looks like God smushed it," the boy said.

"You believe in God?"

The boy shrugged, looking at the ruins of the buildings. "No. I just said it because you were thinking it." Then the boy began shifting uncomfortably. "I don't want to go here. Please. Not this place."

3

"Don't do this to me," the boy said.

"Don't do what?"

"Don't take me in here."

"Why?"

"I can feel it."

"Feel what?"

"You son of a bitch. You brought me here because you want me to die here. You want me to know everything about what you did. All the evil things. All the nasty things. You brought me here to kill me."

"What is it you feel?"

"Torture."

"Is it the pictures on your skin?"

The boy nodded. His face was threatening to crumple, as if he had tears or nightmares or pains in his mind that rippled across his scalp and down his nose and eyes and lips.

"Take off your shirt. I want to see."

"Leave me alone."

"Just calm down. Take off your shirt. I want to see the pictures. I'm not going to hurt you."

The boy pulled the T-shirt off over his head. He looked sullen. No longer that happy kid of five minutes past. He looked up at Stony with sunken eyes. He seemed younger with the shirt off, more like a boy of nine or ten than his twelve years.

"On my back," the boy said. He turned around in the car seat.

His back was scrawny, his ribs stuck out, his shoulder blades jutted as if not quite in place.

Stony had not fully understood the extent of the tattoos. They were swirls of color all across his skin, interconnecting stained glass windows, faces, houses, the sea, and the heavens.

"Who the hell did this to you?"

"I don't know. Maybe he did. He always said I was born like this."

"Holy—" Stony gasped.

From the swirl of earth tones on the boy's shoulders, a face began to emerge as if from a pool of oil-slicked water.

It was a face Stony had not seen in twelve years.

"Lourdes," he whispered. His eyes felt heavy. A fog in his mind blurred his vision. He felt the tears as they coated his face, tears as he watched her slowly open her mouth in a silent cry.

Then the boy's back seemed to grow, his skin stretching, the picture of her face deepening, enlarging, until it was as if the skin was a canvas of the world, and Stony was watching her. No, it was as if he was in someone else's skin, raising a knife on a night of an orange-yellow moon, a knife that glinted and flashed and made a noise like a fist going into mud as the knife went into her breast.

4

*At first, it was the orange-yellow moon.*

*The Moonfire grew pale from this and stretched and burst.*

*Until the world of all he could see was lit by Moonfire.*

*The Moonfire.*

*And at its cold blue heart:*
*The past.*
*Alan Fairclough stood before him, his hand out.*
*"Come on, Stony. Let's go. It's all over here. It's time now. You'll understand. You need to know what this is really about."*
*Then the other pictures swirled around this one, Our Lady of the Sea, as he held Lourdes's hand, the stained glass windows dissolving in a rainbow of colors and then reforming as Nora Chance's old shack, the tarpaper roof peeling back in a strong wind. Stonehaven itself was there, with the lighthouse at Land's End, and the summer homes on Juniper Point, all mixing and then reforming into other shapes, other colors, other remembrances of a place of years ago—*

And then he saw his brother, Van, who was still seventeen, his body soaked in blood, his hands held up, a hunting knife gleaming in the moonlight.

# What the Boy's Skin Shows

# *Chapter Seventeen*

## *Skinning the Bitch*

### 1

Time was a river of blood and fire. Van Crawford waded through it, the jagged pebbles cutting his feet, his arms raised above his head. It was only clear, clean water, and he was up to his waist in it now.

He looked about. For a moment he thought he'd been in the woods near Stonehaven at night, but now he was in a place that was like a summer's day, with the heavy sun beating down on him. He leaned over and grabbed something that flashed and shimmered in the clear water. It eluded him.

Diana stood on the far bank, her blond hair hanging past her shoulders, her skin pale, her breasts full. She looked perfectly natural there, as if this was where she should be, naked at a river's edge waiting for him. "Catch it!" she said, when he glanced up at her. "We need it!"

He looked at her for a long moment, not wanting this dream to disappear.

(He knew it was a dream, it had the feeling of dream, and he knew that a river of blood and fire could not suddenly transform itself into a clear beautiful summer river full of silvery fish.)

Then he reached again into the rushing sparkling water, and grabbed it, wriggling, bringing it up to the sunlight.

*A knife.*

*It's not a knife, but a silver fish wriggling in his grasp.*

Its small mouth opened and closed upon air, its eyes staring at the spherical world as he squeezed it. It felt slick and slimy, and as it paddled its small fins at him, he felt a series of small stings run along his palms.

*(I don't believe it.)*

*Believe it,* she said, but she said it without being near him. *All it takes is your belief, your faith. Let yourself go, let it take over, let it move you.*

*(Move me? Where?)*

*To the other side.*

*(Heaven?)*

*Come over and find out.*

To Diana, crouched down on the far bank, looking down into the water. Flowers seemed to blossom from her silky hair. The sunlight created a halo behind her. "Come to this side, Van, come on!" she shouted gaily.

He glanced down into the rushing waters, and saw another face there, beneath the surface.

A face that might have been a young Latina girl of sixteen whose dark hair streamed behind her in the distorting current. The water turned red as it passed over her, and her left eye was red, as were her lips, red as a rose, red as blood. All was red.

"Lourdes?" he asked, holding the wriggling silver fish high. "Lourdes? That you? You okay?"

She opened her mouth in a scream, and several small flat worms spiraled out of her mouth, dispersing in the bloody water.

He glanced over at Diana, but something was wrong

with her. Her skin moved across her features like heat. Emeralds seemed to shine along her arms and shoulders in the intense sun, which felt warmer by the second. An unfelt wind whipped her hair back, until it looked as if Diana were going to be blown away, yet the air was calm where Van stood in the water.

Lourdes came up from the river, like a mermaid, like a dream, and wrapped her wet arms over his shoulders, closed her eyes, pressed her lips to his. His mouth opened at her tongue's insistence, and he tasted the warm water, and their tongues flicked over and under each other. Her flesh was sweet and firm, and her breasts pressed against him, making his manhood swell.

*Manhood.*

For that's what he was now, a man, it was his manhood growing, and Lourdes the Bitch was bringing it all out for him, the slut was making him do this to her—

## 2

He knows he's in some kind of fabric of unreality, of dream without the comfort of sleep, even as he raises the knife up. *Night, October, the woods, Diana, hunting, Lourdes, BITCH—*

It all comes to him.

The summer day rips apart like a paper screen, and the dark woods return, the freezing night, and the knife in his hand. Moonlight and blood splash against each other, across the fragrant skin of her, of Lourdes, of the girl who has flowers of crimson through her hair and down her neck.

## 3

*"And up," Van gasps, and down! The blade goes in— ooh, with a sucking sound—am I the only one who hears*

*it? The sucking sound of knife in breast and out it comes, up and down and all around—*

The night, the moon, he no longer feels like Van Crawfish, loser of the cosmos, the chill is under his skin, others look out from his eyes . . . he is more than just the son of a lobsterman and a nurse with fat ankles. The look on her face in the moonglow. The look. Eyes still so lovely and dark. *I can see why my baby brother fucks you, I can see why now, I couldn't before. You're something, you're a piece of work and a piece of ass and you have really pretty lips that curl around your white white white teeth when you scream, only I'm a-gonna cut that scream outta you through your lungs, Lourdes, Lourdes Maria Castillo bitch. You're really Russian, right? Lourdes Castillobitch. Ho ha ha ha. Mmm, listen to that knifey go cutting—lovely lovely music of squish and squash and gush and spurt—*

*She fights like a girl, hee hee ho—she raises her hands because she doesn't understand what he's doing or even why he's doing it, but the knife knows.*

*The knife always knows.*

*Rule of thumb: The knife has a mind of its own and is in fact pulling the levers in his hands. Officer, I didn't mean to plunge it into her fourteen times but she got in the way of my knife. She pushed against it over and over. I tried to pull back, but she kept coming at me with her skin.*

*Up and down and all around, the knife slices and dices and flays and makes the mushy stuff come out.*

*Can't scream no more, Lourdes Maria Castillobitch, can't scream, and I bet right now your eyes are going pink with blood and you're not even feelin' nothin' because you can only get cut so many times before it's just like a summer day in the park and nothin' can touch your pretty pretty skin—*

He looks back in the dark as he holds the wet body of the girl against himself and wonders why Diana isn't joining in.

What he sees behind him makes his hair turn white, and he knows it's turning white because he can feel it, he can feel the girl's blood all over him and how his skin is wrinkling and how his hair turns thin and white in just a moment, in the moonlight, in October.

### 4

*Holy Mother of Jesus! What the hell am I doing? Why am I doing this? Why is my hand doing this, bringing this knife under her skin, making her bleed, making her hurt?*

The other voice, that bored like a worm through the rotting fruit of his brain, told him,

*You're making love to her.*

*She feels so damn good! She feels so* hot, *writhing with your touch, with your thing going into her, in and out and in and out! Her whole body is* pussy*! It's all* pussy*!*

Again, the lightning flash of a summer's day with the crushing sunlight, all around the river, as Van's manhood rose up to meet her, to dip inside of her river, to fathom what mystery Lourdes held, inside her, deep within her, so deep it was almost like crawling up inside her womb. The river water splashed across his face, chilly, and it gave him goosebumps. He looked up at the sun as he drove into her, and thought he saw great birds flying there, so huge and massive they could not possibly be what he thought they were, their wingspans so enormous and broad—

Then the fabric tore, the hymen of the dream, and behind it, the woods, the blood, the knife, the girl.

### 5

Van felt his pecker grow huge, a mastadon pecker, so big and thick, but not even that—it was his skin moving outward, his flesh taking over hers as he pressed himself against her body.

Lourdes was beautiful in the red light, her eyes were glowing with lust, her hands swept over his back and buttocks as she drew him into her . . . into the red light . . . his flesh melding with hers, washed with the crimson moisture . . .

The knife was no longer a knife in his hand, it was a tool of the ultimate love, and he brought it to her and she accepted it like a flower in her hair. He gave her red poppies for her hair, and then the poppies sprouted along her neck, and shoulders. Her breasts became a garden, her belly a wild row of poppies blossoming.

"I love you," he whispered, tasting the opium that spilled from the prolapsing flowers, their petals curving and turning and spilling. He lapped at her for the sweetness of the drug, and still more flowers bloomed rapidly along her body.

Her breathing became faint, and she made a series of little moans as he held her, his face pressed to her neck.

*No wonder Stony loves you so much, you are so beautiful, you are so desirable*, he thought as he rubbed his face along her shoulders, tasting the copper opium.

# *Chapter Eighteen*

# *In the Night*

1

At night, along the sliver of coastline that is Stonehaven, the few lights of the village snuff out before ten, leaving the flash and spin of the lighthouse at Land's End to sweep the gently tossing waters of the Sound. The mist of October moves like fine motes of dust in an old room, across the moonlit waters, until finally even the amber moon's sheen dulls. Across the bay, on one of the three sister islands called Avalon, a richly modest two-story clapboard, an enclave made to look like a weathered Cape Cod summer home, glowed with its many lights flicking into high beam against the encroaching night. By midnight, the temperature on the island had dropped to forty-two degrees. The seagulls all perched along the rooftops of the three houses, and down on the paved driveway, the refuse of cracked clamshells and crabs dropped from great heights by the ambitious birds.

Alan Fairclough, his expression taut, stepped out

among the lights of his courtyard. Raising a small pistol, he fired at the birds. The gunshot echoed, and the gulls scattered into the darkness beyond the white lights. The three houses, interconnected with breezeways between them, had been his since his purchase of the island and all that was within it years ago from the widow of Spencer Lewis. Lewis had been a curious sort, a collector of rare religious artifacts, an obsession not unlike Fairclough's own. He kept the Coptic crosses and iconography in the smaller of the three houses, and lived completely alone in the largest. Fairclough's goal in life had always been majestic isolation, although he hadn't truly felt it before. He felt this even here, in these modest digs, compared to the places and manor houses of his youth. It was not mere aloneness, but a feeling that he participated in something greater, something more magnificent than any man had ever touched. . . .

It was a warmth, a heat he couldn't explain. The grace he felt illuminated his flesh, opened the pathways of his mind. . . .

He was more than just a man now.

He was a creature of history.

He was the engager of the future.

The midwife of a change in humanity, a ripple in evolution.

2

He had enjoyed his life on the island, punctuated occasionally by the arrival of a willing sacrifice to his pleasures, a youth bought and paid for to take punches to the stomach and face; a young woman or two who could be tied up and made to commit unspeakable acts. Alan Fairclough had grown bored with it all over the years, for the fire that was in his blood often thirsted for darker and more profound pains and eroticism. He'd gone from punching and molesting to more transcendent practices, the breaking of spirits and wills, the numbness that set in that was beyond pain. He winced sometimes, thinking of what he had done to them, how he'd disfigured them, how one of them had—

*Had—*

*Made him do something terrible to him. Something terrible that Alan Fairclough didn't even like to conjure up, the image that pulsed in his brain.*

The boy was a runaway who had lived on the streets of New York City for four years, living an existence in darkness and squalor. Pete Atkins, the Crowns' butler, had found him on one of his diligent searches for Fairclough's subjects. Atkins had called Fairclough that morning. "I caught one, sir. Young. Needy. Willing. Shall I send him up?"

It had been like ordering groceries.

But Fairclough's divine depravity had grown and festered like constantly retorn scabs over juicy wounds. "Yes," he'd said to the butler. "Tonight, if that's possible."

And then, several hours later, the Crowns' boatman had arrived on the island with a tall, lanky eighteen-year-old. His hair was long, his face was gaunt.

*"You look like me when I was your age,"* Fairclough had said. *"Just like me. You are all alone. You feel life has nothing to offer. You don't know where to turn."*

*The boy looked at him, hard jewels in his eyes. "Fuck off. Where's the money?"*

After payment had been made, Alan took him into the Dark Room.

*"Why the hell you call it a dark room?"*

*A flicker of a smile across Alan Fairclough's face. "It's where I develop."*

Sometimes, he could blank out his memory of what had happened in the Dark Room since he'd set it up, but other times the images came at him like flashes of a strobe light.

In the Dark Room, the other Alan Fairclough came out.

Not the man of God, or the man of the Devil.

What came out was the true Alan Fairclough, the one beneath the skin.

The one that got high from the feeling a razor gave him as he brushed a young man's back with it.

The one that waited until they begged to be killed, until they looked through the streaming blood on their faces and asked that he push the slender spike into their heart.

The one who never satisfied this request.

Until the runaway boy who had just become a man, and within six hours lay on the drainage floor of Alan Fairclough's Dark Room.

Fairclough pressed his face against his throat, feeling the last of the young man's life pour from him. "It's all right, it's all right," he cooed, "just sleep, just sleep."

When he rose from this, he went to the bathroom to shower off the blood. He was still in his fever, caught between an erotic dream of flesh torn by pincers, and fire escaping from the slashes of epidermal armor. There, in the mirror, he saw it.

He saw the thing of his dreams, the creature of red fire, its skull consumed in the burning.

*Me.*

*I am the Devil.*

*Not just a true believer in the Faith of the Almighty Creation.*

*I am the Arch-Fiend of that Creation.*

*I am the Abyss.*

*I am the Betrayer.*

The ritual of it all rejuvenated him. It was all in the ritual, that's what priests had always known, that was what all great religious men had known. Even the Holy Sisters of Maupassane, they had guarded it with ritual, they had held it with ritual until they no longer existed. But the ritual existed, still. The ritual would outlast all. The ritual was what brought the power to mankind. "Hallelujah!" he'd shouted, reaching up to wipe the blood across his face and smear it like jelly until his features were obliterated. "Praise God from whom all blessings flow! Praise Him, all creatures here below! Praise Him above, ye heavenly host! Praise Father, Son, and Holy Ghost!" His cries echoed and carried out into the night, and as the young man breathed his final breath, Alan Fairclough was certain that he had gone on to the true heaven. Then the old words came to him, the words of magic and truth, as they always did when the ritual of blood had begun, "pari nue sathath yog alaai tekeli tekeli lialuana—"

*When Diana came to him the following morning, she held him in her arms while he wept and she whispered, "It's going to be soon, my love. Don't be afraid. Don't be afraid. We'll open the door together."*

### 3

The lights in the courtyard between his compound's houses were as bright as day, which was how he liked it. The night bothered him now. The night no longer held warm dreams, but a vague terror for him that there was something Other out there . . . another Alan Fairclough perhaps, whom this one would not want to meet. The low roofs were bathed in flat white light that even the fine mist could not cloud.

Fairclough held up *The Anubis Mysteries*, a translation from the Coptic, reading the passages to himself again, eager for what was to come:

### 4

"The fire from heaven is upon the earth once in a generation. It has been known by many names, and before there were names, it was known by its radiance. When the first man walked upon this earth, it burst forth from the mind of Ra and traveled like a flaming arrow across the body of the earth. It parched the Nile, and blackened Isis's beauty. At the heart of its flame was the secret of the gods' powers, and man and woman both were struck as by lightning with its touch. It comes with the dying of the crops and the season of the barren land . . .''

He compared this with the Gnostic Gospel of Judas the Betrayer.

"As we sat together, my beloved master turned to me and kissed me lightly on the cheek. I said unto him, 'Why, Lord, do you touch me so?'

"And Jeshua ben-Joseph saith, 'Jude, you are closer than my brother to me. We were born of the same moment, and made of the same fire. Yahweh gives us this fire from the touch of his finger, and it cuts like a burning sword into your heart, and mine.'

"I said unto him, 'Lord, Lord, if we are brothers, why do you gaze with such terror upon me?'

" 'The divine fire is too much in you,' Jeshua said. 'In the miracles and healings, what was within me awoke something within you. You have been too close to me. You will betray me.'

" 'What is the nature of this divine fire?' I asked of him.

" 'It is that which darkens the sun. When Adam walked in the Garden, it came like a flaming sword from the archangel, to separate man from paradise. The Angel of Death possesses its radiance, and it is said that a man dying sees it but once and then sees no more. But it is within us now. Within you, within me. Its nature is to turn against itself.'

"I wondered at his words, and when the meal was done I said thrice, 'You are most wondrous in your supreme countenance, oh Lord.'

"Jeshua turned to me and nodded. 'It is in your nature now. Do what you must do.' ''

5

Then Alan closed the two books. All his life he had searched for this, all his life had been drawing him towards this place, this village, these people.

Finally, he opened the manuscript he'd purchased at great expense at private auction three years earlier.

*The Devil's Own, The Profane History of the Archfiend and All His Works*, by Cagliostro, recopied in 1923 by Aleister Crowley.

6

. . . It was in Paris that I first heard of the nuns of Maupassane. These Holy Sisters had lived in the catacombs of this city from the time of the Dauphin, but were expelled by the church for harboring various perversions among them. Several of the sisters were bound together and set afire in the Chambre Argent, but most managed to escape. Devout to the Holy Word of God and to Jesus, they were hid by good folk in the countryside of Bretagne, and then managed to resurrect their small order in a series of caves once inhabited by the earliest people of Gaul.

They had been there for at least one hundred years when I traveled by coach through the rugged and backward countryside with three very agreeable companions. One was the young Loup Garou, the wild boy of the Pyreness, so famous now that he had been educated at court. At seventeen, he was a strapping youth who, it was rumored, could speak with animals and birds. It was also rumored that he had been sired by the Devil himself, owing to his wolf-like demeanor and excessive hair. My other two companions for the journey were the ever-youthful dowager from that backward and savage country, Countess Erzebet Bathory, along with one of her lovely young maid-servants, Minoru. The Countess had some ugly rumors following her, one of which, to my great amusement, was the story that she was already three hundred years old, but through black magic had retained the youth of a girl barely out of her teens. We laughed about these tales, since Erzebet often commented that if she were truly three hundred years old, she would not still be depending upon her husband's money, for she would have soon run out of it, given his gambling and general licentiousness. She was quite amiable, and her maid-servant not only pleasant to look upon, but with a delightful wicked streak and an unusual tolerance for her mistress's constant caresses and pinches. The wild boy and she exchanged the longing glances of the very young, something which the Countess very wisely discouraged.

It took us six days to reach Maupassane, and not without some hostility were we four met by the locals at the tavern, owing to both the Countess's finery and infamous reputation, Minoru's childlike beauty, my own sorcerer's demeanor, and of course Loup Garou's notoriety. These country hicks believed that if someone were from Paris, he might very well be the Devil's own. We were deemed bad luck, and it seemed the only folk who would give us shelter were the Holy Sisters themselves.

It was among the sisters, in that cave, that I first came to learn how Good and Evil were twin aspects of the one Source of All. The sisters were of an order older than much of the Roman church, and had a creed which included the snake in the Garden of Eden, and believed that Christ on his cross was the fulfillment of temptation into redemption. The snake on the tree of Knowledge of Good and Evil was their emblem. "The snake is the fruit of the tree. Christ is the fruit of the tree," so went their creed. This heretical belief had divorced them from the true Church, but their connection to Rome was never quite severed. It seems the Holy Pontiff himself (or so went the local legend) had visited the waters nearby and spoken with the Mother Superior of the Sisters. He had not given

them his blessing, but had refused to allow the usual in-
vestigation of their heresy. The local priesthood did not
touch them either. They were a peculiar sect, and my traveling companions and I were looking forward to meeting
them. I, of course, was there for something I'd heard, the
rumor of a rumor, the spark of something I'd heard of in
the salons of Paris.

"It is said the Holy Sisters of Maupassane have a relic
with them that is more powerful than Rome itself," a
charlatan of disputed reputation whispered in my ear.
"They are witches more than nuns, and their convent
reaches down to the very seat of Satan himself."

These words echoed through my head as we were es-
corted into the famous caverns.

First, we stood in awe of the great and ancient paintings, depicting ape men hunting great horses and beasts
along a rugged plain. Then, the pictures on the rock wall
showed beasts with the arms and legs of man, but with
the antlers of Satan, and the tail and buttocks of deer, and
the chest of a bull. The Holy Sisters told us that these
frightened them at first, but that they were Brides of
Christ, and therefore Brides of Truth, they believed.

And finally, they showed us what they had captured
deep in the bowels of their cavern.

A glimpse of the eternal, there. I knew even when I set
eyes upon its fire that it was of the Devil, that its great
countenance, its jaws, its monstrous eyes, could be none
other than tools of Hellish design to lure even these Holy
Sisters into perdition.

One sister told me that there had once been two, a mate
for this one, but it had burned like a sword of fire across
the earth, returning to its home.

"If it had a mate," I ventured, "then perhaps it had
progeny?"

She took me to a farther well, and there, evidence of a
mating between a human and this terrible creature. I cannot begin to describe what I saw there. Were I to do so,

I believe I would go mad, for madness is its name, madness is its form.

We slept at the feet of the trapped creature for seven nights before departing. As we left, the Countess Bathory drew me aside and whispered something to me which I shall never forget.

She said, "These holy women will burn in hell until kingdom come for what they have done here. They are monsters of the worst sort." Then she offered up a curious smile. "Perhaps you and I shall see them again one day."

I must say that her words could not seem more true to this humble servant of the Arts of Spirit and Darkness. . . .

7

Alan shut the book when he heard the phone ringing. Slipping into his loafers, he got up from the porch table. He walked across the slight landing, up a half dozen steps to the central house. Opening the door, he flicked on the inner light.

Directly across from him, the huge stone with its fossil.

The bones crushed under some great weight, the wings splayed up and behind its hunched shoulders.

He went to the large oak table in front of the stonework. Picking up the phone, he pressed the speaker function, and set the receiver back in its cradle. "Yes?"

Out of breath, the woman on the phone gasped, "Oh, it's . . . yes . . . it's happening . . . it's taking . . . it's opening . . . I can feel it. . . ."

8

A gull cried out above the sister islands, and flew out across the water, joining a half a dozen other birds as they soared up and then down, skimming the choppy waters, and then up again, now at the mainland, over the towering lighthouse, over the shingled rooftops of Stonehaven.

Tamara Curry took her slingshot and aimed for one of the gulls. "You flying rats, get out of my trash!" she shouted when the small stone she'd shot missed the bird. She ran out to the waterfront behind her house, and began picking up the wadded-up papers the flying rats had scattered. "I wish my guardian angel would tear those damn gulls to bits," she muttered.

As the birds flew up, against the mist-covered moonlight, someone was crying out. It was a boy, perhaps a little boy lost in the woods, raising his voice to the skies.

No word could be distinguished in the sound, but folks heard it. Those who lived on the edge of the woods heard the cry.

Nora Chance, making her last cup of tea for the night, felt a pain in the back of her skull as if someone had just driven a needle of ice into her.

She reached for a bottle of aspirin up on the shelf over the stove, and tried to block out the memories that throbbed in her head.

9

Stony tried calling Lourdes twice, but each time one of her brothers picked up, and he hung up the phone. He stared at the infernal machine for another hour, willing her to call him. But it remained silent. Occasionally, he walked into the small living room, and glanced out at the street. Watching for her, or waiting for his mother to come home from her workday at the hospital, or his father from the bars. Made himself two baloney sandwiches and drank one of his dad's beers from the fridge. This gave him courage. Or maybe it was just a goofy feeling, he couldn't tell.

Have to follow through on this.

It won't just get better or disappear if I do nothing.

He went up to his small room, and looked through the closet. What do you take with you when you're gonna run off with your girl and never come back? His jackets all seemed inadequate. He glanced down at the jeans he was wearing. They were filthy and threadbare in parts. He drew out a pair of khakis and a flannel shirt. Okay, good start: clean clothes. On an upper shelf was a stack of Storm King comic books. He drew them down and plopped them on his bedspread. Tossed them around, opening one at random. The Storm King was fighting the Ancient Enemy, also known as the Outcast. Stony grinned. He hadn't looked at these since he was younger. He remembered his own imaginary battles in the backyard at eight years old with the Outcast. The Outcast had nine hundred eyes and seven arms, and each finger on his seven hands was a curved talon. One of the pictures showed the Storm King down on the ground, the Outcast slicing his talons through the air.

Stony tossed this comic aside, and opened another.

What he saw almost made him weep.

A note in a childish scrawl had been thrust between the pages:

*Mommy loves me I know*
*Mommy loves me I know.*
*I know Mommy loves me.*
*I am scared of her.*

A memory from years before flashed upon him.

Something he had forgotten, had burned out of his memory . . .

## 10

*He was seven and his mother and father were having another of their big fights. He and Van hid in the bathroom, and Van covered his mouth to keep him from crying out. Van had been doing this since as far back as Stony could remember—they'd duck into the bathroom because it was the only room in the house with a lock on the door. They'd lock themselves in, and Van would cover his mouth to shut him up. This time, Stony was tired of not being able to stop the fighting. So he bit down on Van's hand, and Van released him.*

*Stony unlocked the door and went running out of the bathroom to find his mother. As he ran into the center of their bedroom, it took him a minute to realize what his father was doing to his mother.*

*He was holding her down and punching her in the gut.*

*Stony stood there for a moment as if he could not understand what was happening, and then he began screeching. He ran into the middle of it and grabbed his father's arm.*

*"No! Daddy, don't!"*

*His father looked at him, then at his mother.*

*His father pulled away, shouted some obscenities, and stomped off. A minute later, the front door slammed.*

*Stony looked up at his mother. "You okay, Mommy?"*

*And something was different about her. She wasn't crying, she wasn't the Mommy he knew.*

*Something had come into her.*

*Stony knew it was the Outcast.*

*Something evil had seeped into her.*

*She said, "You fucking bastard, you ruined everything for us! Everything!"*

*Then, she lifted him up.*

Stony Crawford, fifteen, picked up the note from the comic book.

Closed his eyes.

*"You want to know what happens to little boys who ruin things for people?" His mother was shouting and crying, and Stony cried too, flailing his arms and legs around—*

*And she took him into the kitchen, and dropped him down, still clinging to his hand—a viselike grip. "You want to know what happens to bad boys who fuck every-*

thing up?'' Her voice was like bombs blowing up around him, and he couldn't see for the tears—

"Do you want to—" she began, and he saw the blue-hearted flame of the gas stove as she turned the front burner on—

And she took him up and brought the edge of his face down so close to the burner that the heat felt as if it were all around him

He could see the blue-white flame turning to yellow and then orange—

Moonfire, he thought. The Storm King could be destroyed by one thing, fire from the moon. It would take his powers away on earth. It was the one thing that could turn him to dust, to nothing . . .

He was numb and was perfectly quiet and still, expecting that the Outcast in the guise of his mother would now destroy him.

The heat on the side of his face grew intense.

But then she let out a small yelp.

She brought him back up, hugging him, her tears soaking his face and shoulders as she muzzled him, her breath all gin, her kisses smothering. "I could never hurt you, I never could hurt you, oh you poor baby, you poor baby, how could I hurt you? I'd go to hell if I hurt you, I could never—"

Stony set the old note back in the comic book. Closed it.

Time to go, he thought.

Time to leave all this behind.

I will never be like them.

## 11

In his parents' bedroom, he hunkered down. Beneath his mother's side of the bed, her candy wrappers and magazines. He pushed some of these aside, and felt around until he located the small box.

Drawing it out, he opened it.

The money was still there.

Because he had only seen it once or twice before, when he'd been too young to know how much was there, he was shocked to see that the bills were all hundreds. Why did she have all this here? Why hadn't she ever used any of it? Or did she replace it? Did she hide some of her income from his dad?

These were the questions he'd had ever since he'd first seen the little box beneath the bed. It wasn't even all that well hidden, yet covered with so much dust it looked as if no one had ever touched it.

"I'll pay you back someday," he said uneasily to the silent bedroom.

He counted out two thousand dollars.

It would be enough for a start.

He and Lourdes needed it.

His mother would understand.

She would.

## 12

Pulling on his heaviest sweatshirt, bringing the hood up, Stony left his home. He thought he might take his bike, but then figured he'd be better off on foot. He and Lourdes would catch the bus up the highway. *In the morning. It all starts tomorrow at dawn.* They needed to travel light.

The village was silent that night, or so it seemed to Stony. Perhaps he was feeling guilty for stealing the money, or perhaps his mind was too clouded with worries about the near future, but as he walked out along the damp lanes, the only sound he heard was a dog barking in the distance. The clapboard houses were dark, and only the smoke from the chimneys indicated that anyone was home. This was part of what he was looking forward to leaving behind, the life that seemed to close up on itself like a snail in its shell when night came . . . the way people in Stonehaven never seemed to exist once the sun went down. . . .

He looked at the neighbors' houses. The Glastonburys and their adult children took up three houses in a row. Stony had spent much of his childhood running between their houses during the summers, watching them sit on their porches with cocktails and lemonade, raising their glasses to him, nodding, but not ever really talking to him. And the Wakefields, with their German shepherd that got hit by a truck years ago, still mourning the dog after all those years as if they'd lost a son. The Railsbacks, who owned the butcher shop, used to give Stony old *National Geographics* to root through for pictures for elementary school projects. He had rock fights with their nephew when he'd come to visit for his summer vacations.

He had known all these people here, and now, he was not going to see them ever again. Not that he was close to them, but he could only imagine what the world beyond Stonehaven would be like. He knew from TV, but he was not stupid enough to think that television contained everything about the world. There was more to life than Stonehaven, and more than even Connecticut, more than New England. They could go down to New York by bus, maybe, and he'd get a job and they'd somehow get a place and raise their kid.

Somehow it would work.

It had to work.

*God, I hope I never have to come back here again with my tail between my legs.*

He took the route back to the Common, passing the library, feeling colder than the night air, feeling more alone than he had ever felt before in his life.

When he followed the roadside trail to the edge of the woods, he saw the feeble candlelight of Nora's shack glowing within the woods. Stepping over the ditch, and through the moon-scraped trees, he went to the one place he knew would take him in.

13

"Tired?" Nora asked, as she stood in the doorway.

"Yeah."

"I got a little supper still. Hungry?"

"No, thanks."

"Sleepy?"

Stony nodded.

"What time is Juliet coming?"

He almost grinned, but something felt heavy in his face. "Morning."

"Well, I got a sleeping bag with your name on it all ready. Come on in, Romeo."

14

Nora awoke in the middle of the night, clutching her heart. "Stony!" she cried out.

Stony sat up quickly, tossing the sleeping bag cover away. "Yeah? You okay?"

Nora gasped. "Stony, I can't tell you what it means, but I had a dream. Not a good one. It was a dream like one of my spins, and it was about Lourdes, baby. It was about your girl." Nora leaned over the edge of her flat bed, lighting a candle on the floor. Her eyes, white and empty, full of tears. "She's in a place of ice, Stony. She won't come tonight, or tomorrow. She's been taken."

"It was just a dream," Stony said. He rose from the floor, and went over to turn up the gas lamps. "It was just a dream."

"True," Nora whispered. "But dreams aren't for nothing."

They were both silent for several minutes.

"I can't really sleep much I guess," he said.

"After my dream, I don't think I can either. You want to just sit up?"

"Wish I had a watch. I wonder what time it is."

"I got an internal clock. I say it's four A.M."

"I'm hungry. You hungry?" Stony asked.

"Well, I see you recovered nicely from your starvation diet."

"Do you think they miss me yet?"

"Maybe."

"I know my mom'll miss me."

"Your dad, too."

"He doesn't miss people all that much."

"He'll miss you. I guarantee it."

"Van I won't miss."

"You stole some money, remember? They'll at least miss that."

"She'll understand."

"Will she?"

Stony snorted. "What's she ever gonna do with it, anyway?"

"Well, it was hers to decide that, wasn't it?"

"I think it would have just sat there till kingdom come. That's what I think. I think she would've squirreled it away until she was sixty or something, and then she wouldn't have known what to do with it."

"You think sixty's ancient, don't you?" Nora grinned.

Stony bowed his head. "All I mean is, it isn't young."

"Your mama was once your age. I wonder if she ever stole from anybody so she could be happy."

"It's not the same," Stony said. "I'll pay her back. Somehow." Stony went over to the small pantry, and glanced around at its contents. "You don't have any good snacks here."

Nora laughed. "You're feeling guilty."

"If I told you I was, would it matter?"

"You're just going to wait here till morning when Lourdes shows up, feeling guilty because you stole your mama's secret savings account from right under her nose."

"She's a drunk."

"And drunks should be robbed. You got a peculiar kind of morality. She's a drunk, you're a thief."

"I didn't ask for this," Stony spat. "Will you just quit with the nagging?" After he heard the echo of his voice, he said, "Sorry."

"For what?"

"For sounding like my dad."

"Maybe now you understand him a little better."

"I don't want to be from them."

"Can't help how we're brought up or who by."

"Like it never bothered you. You were raised by humble angel saints."

Nora laughed even louder. "Oh Lord, Stony, you are gonna have me bustin' a gut in a minute. Stop!" She laughed, waving her hands about. When she quieted, she said, "My father was a decent man. He never laid a hand on us and he worked hard. But he drank and caroused and more than once my sister and me had to go into one of the bars over in Somerville and pull him off some woman just to get him home in time for supper. And Mama was one of those long-suffering women. Lord save me from anyone who is long-suffering. She prayed all day long and worked her fingers to the bone. But a martyr is its own kind of hell, too. She turned suffering from a hobby into a lifelong mission. Martyrs usually take down a few people they care about because they want some company to suffer with. That was Mama. Family is putting up with each other's shit sometimes, I guess."

They were both silent.

Then Stony said, "How much shit are you supposed put up with?"

"I guess whatever you're willing to," Nora said. "Why'd you come to me tonight, Stony?"

"You know why."

"To run away with your girl and have a baby in some lonely place? To steal your mama's savings, just so you can get out of town for a couple of weeks?''

"I guess."

Nora sighed. She wiped her long fingers across her face. Then she patted a space next to her on the bed. "Come on, sit up here, Stony."

"I'm fine where I am."

"Of course you are. I forget sometimes that you're nearly a man. Remember when you were a little boy and you'd come out here to hear all my spins? We'd sit on the rug in front of the stove, or up here in my quilts, or out on the porch. . . . Those sweaty summer nights. I'd tell you all my stories. Seventy years' worth.''

Stony nodded. He walked over and sat down beside her on the bed.

"Well, I miss those times. Can't turn back any clocks, but I miss that little boy. But you can turn the clocks forward if you want. I want you to think of yourself in fifteen years. You're thirty. You have a good job maybe. You and Lourdes are happy. Your boy is your age now. And he's going to ask, 'Dad, how did you and my mama meet up?' And what are you gonna tell him? How you fell in love with his mama? About the purity of that kind of love? About how you never loved any woman except his mama? About how men do the right thing, no matter what?''

Stony looked down at his hands, curled upward in his lap. He remained silent.

"I'm not gonna tell you the right thing. All I'm going to tell you is you're welcome to stay here till morning. When Lourdes comes, you two need to talk. Then you need to think about that boy or girl of yours in fifteen years and what you're gonna say to that child."

Stony got up and went to fix a peanut butter sandwich at the table. He glanced out into the dark night. If there'd been a phone, he'd have called Lourdes and told her that he was going to come get her. He would've told her that it was all right to steal his mother's money because it was worth a little time in hell for their happiness. It was worth some guilt. It was worth a little lying and stealing and pretending that they were doing the right thing. The universe wanted them to. The universe was made for those who took when the time was right, who jumped and grabbed what it was they needed for happiness. Happiness was all.

He saw his reflection in the window. It barely looked like Stony Crawford anymore.

### 15

The calls of night birds in the woods punctuated the more distant horn and warning bells of the train as it passed up from Mystic on its way north to Providence. The temperature dropped to thirty-eight, a jagged wind grabbed the last leaves on the trees along High Street, rushing down the narrow lanes that grew perpendicular to it. The oaks and maples held onto their colors for a future fight with the early winter wind off the sea. Clouds moved across the face of the moon like a bridal veil, to cover her beauty, to protect her chastity, to increase her mystery.

Johnny Miracle! The voice boomed from the gathering clouds. Johnny Miracle! Again, like a clap of thunder through the trees that scraped the hazy moonlight.

Johnny Miracle stood shivering on Water Street, just outside the Blue Dog Tea Shop. The voice was both inside and outside of him. It boomed louder than any surf he'd ever heard.

"What?" he asked, looking up to the sky. "What?" The sky was swallowing every utterance from his mouth until he was sure it just sounded like the bleating of lambs. He glanced at the passersby with their baby in a stroller, and at the old lady watching him from behind the Harper Real Estate Office sign. Oh, but they were ghosts! It was late—no one was watching him, no one was on the street, but in flashes of lightning he saw them—people standing

there, mouths open. . . . He blinked, and they were gone,
these Watchers, these Spies for Them.

Them were the evil ones, Them were the people who
made him *do it*, who made him *do it*. Johnny often struck
matches against them, struck matches to the burned bits
of leaves, set fire to small trash cans, burned his fingers
at times, too. Fire chased off Them, fire made Them
scared. He always kept his pockets and busted-up old
shoes full of packs of matches just so he could strike
Them in the face with the fire if it got to that point. Them
were so scared of fire it amazed him sometimes. God told
him fire purified things sometimes. God told him fire de-
feated the darkness and if anyone was darkness it was
Them.

Alone again, in the night, he raised his hands up to the
sky as the first drops of rain began to fall. He tried to
strike some matches against the dark, but the rain
wouldn't let him. "Lord God!" he bleated, "What have
you done here?"

And the voice that came back to him was a whisper,
tickling his ear.

The voice was always inside his head.

Every night for the past fifteen years.

16

In his head the images roiled and spun like multicolored
taffy, turning in upon itself:

*The man with the red eyes like rats, holding his hands
as he stood in front of the church, as the people in the
church raised their hands up—*

*As he, a boy, looked up at the man with the red eyes,
who was dressed like a priest but not really a priest, the
boy knew, not a priest like the way he remembered
priests—*

*And how they'd pressed the blade to the lamb's
throat—*

## The Halloween Man

*He was seventeen, working in the butcher shop, a strapping young man, ready to take on the world. The Crowns had paid for his upbringing and now he lived in their caretaker's cottage. The world was a terrific place, and Stonehaven, the home of his ancestors, was the only place for him. And then they brought him, that night, that night of Halloween, that night—*

The flashes grew more intense—

*That night—*

*"It's something you must do," Mr. Crown had told him as he unbuttoned Johnny's shirt, a starched white shirt that Johnny had bought for twenty dollars from the mail-order catalog. Diana was there, such a pretty little girl, smiling up at him. Mr. Crown gave him the piece of paper and told him to lick it. "Like it's a stamp," Mr. Crown said, and Johnny licked the paper, which had a sugary taste to it. Then he started to feel funny, the faces in front of him became flowers and then it was like everything turned into a big cartoon. "Lick it more," Mr. Crown said, and then someone pressed Johnny's face into the paper, and his tongue swirled around on it.*

*Someone said, "We should've just put it on a sugar cube."*

*"Or injected it," a woman chuckled.*

*"Oh," Johnny screamed inside his skin, "I wish I had my matches! I'd burn 'em all to hell if I had my matches on me, I would!"*

*"Shut up, he's like my son," Mr. Crown said, and this made Johnny feel proud. "He'll take it all."*

*But Mr. Crown now looked like Mr. Magoo, and Diana looked like Little Orphan Annie, with blank eyes, and some of the people in the chapel looked like they were out of* The Flintstones *and* The Jetsons.

*Johnny hadn't even struggled as he was told to pull his jeans down, too. The blue jeans melted off of him, they went down like seawater around his feet—*

*Naked, he stood at the altar, and four of them held the
struggling woman down—*

*Struggling?*

*Was she?*

*Was she struggling?*

*She shimmered, too, a ripple on a golden pond—*

*Like silver fish darting beneath the surface of a glass
lake—*

*The screams began and he looked at her mouth.*

*But they didn't come from her.*

*(She's not a her. She's an IT.)*

*It was the cartoon characters that held her—their skin
blackening and crackling—*

*But Johnny was gone somewhere too, he was in the
swirling pattern of the stained glass window, the window
with the picture of the angel holding the flaming sword
to shut off the Garden of Eden.*

*And then he felt the rumbling within his flesh, as if his
molecules were bubbling and transforming and getting all
twisted up and bouncing around until, for a moment, as
he felt the intense heat all around him, he thought—and
this was one of his last coherent thoughts—that his skin
was ripped off and he stood there at the altar, a figure of
blood and bone and meat, looking out at all of them, all
the cartoon characters as they sang praises and he felt
his brain scramble—*

*And then, nothing.*

17

"Johnny," God said, or was it Mr. Crown and Mr. Magoo
together telling him things? It may have been the man
with the red eyes, but it seemed like God. God had so
many faces, and Johnny could always see through the normal face to the inner one where God lived. Sometimes he
was so jumbled on the inside he didn't know who was

who, but God always came through. "Johnny, remember what time of year it is?"

He nodded.

"It's time," God said. "What happened was wrong. What we all got caught up in. It was a terrible thing to do. But it has to play out. We can never go back, can we?" God handed him a plate of food, which included a Burger King Whopper and coleslaw. "I got you some things. I forgot about the pear. Maybe tomorrow."

"Am I a sinner?" Johnny asked, his voice like a bleat.

"No, you're not. You're a good man. You've always been a good man," God said. "We just reached too far, that's all. It's something we should've stopped years ago. Maybe the moment it started. I was too caught up in it. I'm the evil one. But to experience it—"

"No you're not," Johnny giggled, picking over the coleslaw. "You're God, you can't be evil."

God gave him a look that he couldn't figure out. "I just wanted you to know that I am sorry for what we all did." Then God pulled his hat on and got back in his car.

God drove a Thunderbird, and kept the windows down, even as cold as it was.

Johnny watched the T-Bird dissolve along the road, and then the air shimmered with its vanishing.

# Chapter Nineteen

## Flesh and Lust in the October Palace

1

Diana Crown stood in the half light of the hallway, naked, and put her hand on the back of Van's scalp. She grasped his hair in her hand.

"Drink the blood, which is holy," she whispered.

Forced him down on his knees before her. Brought his head to her thighs.

Smeared the blood on his face.

"Did you love it?" she asked.

"Yes. God yes, I loved it." Van Crawford, his eyes wild and quivering in their sockets, his hair matted, his face crimson. "Baptize me, baby, baptize me in the holy blood!"

Diana smiled. Almost innocently, she said, "I think you may have killed her, Van. That's very very bad."

Tears sprang from his eyes. "No, I loved her, I promise. I loved her and I gave her red poppies to wear all over her face and body."

"She's dead, Van. Her heart stopped beating," Diana said, her voice firm and cold. "But I understand, baby, I do, come here." She let go of his scalp, and held her hands out to him. "Come on to me, Van." And as he rose up, her arms enveloped him, pulling him to her. "How I love you, my strong killer. Driving your knife into her, the heat I felt, the thrust in every wound, the taste of her life—"

"Oh, yeah," Van said, his tears drizzling down across his bloodstained face, pushing the rusty liquid into his mouth, down his throat. "Oh God, but I didn't mean to hurt her—"

"Hurting is good sometimes," Diana whispered, pressing her lips against his ear and biting down ever so slightly. "Pain is a ritual we all must endure."

2

Van didn't know what had come over him, but he was chasing her up the stairs, up to the master bedroom where he'd first entered her, first made her feel like a real woman, she'd told him, taking her on the bed she'd said had been her mother's. That had excited him further, and now, bounding up the stairs, two at a time, after her blood-stained flesh, watching the curves of her small, high breasts bounce as she went, her ass like smooth melons, he was going to have her again.

He was going to conquer what seemed just beyond his grasp.

She was giggling like a schoolgirl, her hair red, her skin red, too, slick and shiny as he pressed himself to her. She had surrendered, his Diana, his Diana of the Hunt who had stood by and watched him press his knife into the garden of Lourdes, had—

*Remember what you saw?*

*Remember when you turned in the dark?*

*Turned and saw something there—*

231

*Something other than the girl you know as Diana Crown?*

The voice was like a worm in his mind, but he ignored it as he took her up in his arms, and the room was spinning. Her legs surrounded his waist, and his pants began dropping to the floor almost of their own accord. He felt more powerful than any boy of seventeen had ever felt before. He felt lightning inside him, muscles of steel as he held her, as he pinned her—

*Beneath her face, in the dark, in the moonlight, you saw her.*

*You saw the cracks along her eyes, along her lips...*

*What was it you saw, Van Crawfish?*

*As you push yourself into her, into her depths, into that woman who changed in the October moonlight as if she were not a woman at all, but something made of red bright lava—*

*It was the blood!*

*No, it wasn't blood, it was something else, something that looked out at you from the skin you now hold—*

*Lava.*

*It was like a fuckin' volcano burstin' out at you—*

And there it was again, as he held Diana in his arms, awkwardly shoving himself into her flesh. There it was in her eyes, as if the thin layer of her iris were pushing outward and something that looked like the pink of inner flesh showed through. Pink and then orange, then red, then ... And as she pushed him backwards, onto the bed, he saw lying next to him the body of Lourdes Castillo, and he screamed, ''What the fuck have you done to her?''

# Chapter Twenty

## The Tales of the Stones

### 1

When the sun came up, Stony began to regret his decision to run off, but he still didn't think he could go back home. He stood on the little wood porch that overlooked the bog, a mug of cat's claw tea in his hand.

"Second thoughts?" Nora said. Nora had gone back to sleep for a bit, and had only just awakened. She emerged from behind a screen, where she took her sponge bath in a large aluminum basin filled with cold water and hog-fat soap. She looked refreshed in a pale pink sweater and dungarees, and poured herself some tea before joining Stony outside.

"Maybe," Stony said, when they'd started walking out across the flagstone path in front of her shack. "I just wish Lourdes would show up."

"Maybe she's having second thoughts too. Or maybe she's just sleeping. She didn't steal money. She has less to feel guilty about." Nora grinned, reaching out to find

Stony's shoulder. When she did, she drew him close to her. She smelled like lavender and vanilla. "She'll come. Don't worry."

"Yeah, I guess," he said. He was uncomfortable with her touch. He pulled away.

"Watch out that you don't step in that mud," she said.

He glanced over at her. "Sometimes I wonder if you're really blind."

"Sometimes I do too," she said, her grin growing broader. "Let me tell you, you live seventy years at the edge of these woods, you learn where the mud seeps and where the prickerbushes are real fast. Listen, Stony, seeing as how it's Sunday and the last day of October, why don't you lead me over to the stone garden? I need to pay my respects."

"You got a stone garden? I never saw it," he said, eyeing her suspiciously. "What you got up your sleeve?"

"Oh, nothing," she said, almost gravely. "Just something I think you should see before you run off with your girl. Follow me."

2

She led him around grasping vines and fallen and rotting trees, between laurel, and around undergrowth. "Mind your feet," Nora said as she took him down a narrow strip of muddy land between a pond and sticker bushes.

Then he saw it.

A rusty gate, barely noticeable for the tangle of dried vines that clutched at it, stood in the middle of a clearing. Ferns grew up around it, and within: a circle of stones.

3

Some of the stones were large, some small, but all were neatly arranged. When they went through the gate, Nora stepped carefully over stones the precise location of which

234

she must have memorized. She knelt down in the middle of the circle, and patted a small place beside her for Stony to do likewise.

"What is this?" he asked, squatting down upon the damp moss-covered ground.

"My family," she said. She felt along various rocks, and then lifted a small stone. "This was my sister, Angelina. She chose the stone herself when she died. It's not like we could afford expensive grave markers, Stony. And Mama never wanted any of us to be buried in the village. She said all my grand-daddies and grand-mamas were put in the sacred place, not in those devil places."

The stones around him all had initials carved into them.

Then, as Stony glanced about the soft earth, he noticed the slight mounds. The stones formed a small circle, but radiating out from them were the mounds. "It's a graveyard."

"Yes sir, Mr. Crawford," Nora said. "My grand-mama told me that all of us Chances and Owldeers—that was my grand-mama's side—were buried here clear back to before the village even existed. Back when I could see, I used to tend these graves and mow down all the new growth from the woods, but as you can probably tell, the woods have reclaimed much of it."

Stony nodded, noticing how even further away, where the prickerbushes grew, the ground was raised or dropped like a brief trench. "Amazing."

"I come out here when I'm troubled, to pay my respects, to put things in perspective, sometimes," Nora said. Then she picked up a small stone, and held it out for him. "Take it."

Stony hesitated.

"Feel it first. Feel this stone. They say stones can speak if we listen."

No initials were carved along its edge. It was nearly smooth.

"Let me spin a story for you, Stony. One last story.

One I've been saving for a long long time, but now that you aim to be a man, I think you can hear this one. I think you're ready. Many years ago," and Nora began her final tale. "You listening, Stony?"

"Yeah," he said.

4

"Stony, now, you got to listen to this one. And not just listen but really hear it, you understand? This is the last spin you're ever gonna hear from my lips, because this is the last one I know. I told you all the others. But I been holding back on this one.

"A woman who drank too much gave birth to a baby. The baby didn't have much of a chance. The baby was too small, came too soon, the baby was twisted around and backward inside this woman. It wasn't the baby's fault. It wasn't even the woman's fault, even though her drinking didn't help. Didn't help that she got kicked in the stomach that morning either. But it was just life doing its worst to the most innocent of us, I guess. This baby, he tried to get born, but he couldn't. He mighta had two minutes of breathing clean air and seeing daylight, but then the Lord took him back. Maybe it was the Lord's plan. Maybe it wasn't. But this baby did not breathe too long or suffer more nor less than any of us will suffer in this life."

5

"Was it yours?"

"No. Nor was it one of my friends' or relatives' child, but I come from a long line of guardians of the innocent lost." She pointed to another grave. Stony glanced at it. The initals carved in it were *IMP*.

Nora leaned back on her haunches. "Remember that story about the misshapen Crowninshield boy?"

"The Halloween Man," Stony nodded. "Sure. He slaughtered a bunch of people and crucified his father."

"That's the story that's told. But there's a deeper truth to it. The deeper truth is, Imp knew that something was in the blood of this town. Something that turned bad the way milk turns sour, the way flies hover around a corpse. He was almost killed by the people of this town, and something maybe from the Devil got into him and he went on a rampage. But we knew, we who were of the slave families and natives, we knew . . . it was the earth here and it was the darkness within some of the people who had founded Stonehaven in the first place. Both within and without. That family called Crowninshield and the Randalls, they weren't just nice Puritans coming here. You know their history? They got expelled from the Massachusetts Colony."

"Witches or something?"

Nora smiled gently. "We woulda been lucky if they'd a been witches. No, these folks were too good as Puritans. They were too close to the source of divine evil."

"I never heard of divine evil." Stony would've laughed at the term, only Nora looked too serious.

"It's worse than any other kind. You know how a fire can warm your bones in a hearth? But that same fire, if it jumps, can burn your house down? That's what divine evil is. It's the power from the source of all, taken out of itself. That's what those people did. That's what Imp came from. That's what he tried to destroy. But it got him, too, finally. But not before he fathered a child. Deformed and twisted just like him, that child fathered a child and so on. Imp had a bloodline."

Stony looked at her curiously. "Maybe we should get back." He glanced beyond her, towards the trees beyond which was her shack. "Why did you bring me here?"

Nora put her hands on Stony's shoulders. "Your mama and daddy are not who you think they are."

Stony, holding the small stone from the grave, felt

237

something squeeze inside his head—a pressure he hadn't felt before. Swiftly, it became a throbbing headache. Then he felt warm, too warm, warm like he had a fever.

Nora leaned closer, her breath against his face, her glassy white eyes almost seeming to watch him. "The stone in your hand, that is who you were meant to be."

"What? I don't get it."

"A baby was born fifteen years ago and breathed for only a few minutes. Then he died. His mother was in a station wagon down on Water Street. The rain began to fall. I could not see, but I saw within my mind. I am the last of my family here, I am the last who knows the true history of this place. I was afraid I might die before telling you. But you and this girl are going to start a family, and you need to know."

Stony looked at the rock. It was as if something in his brain were squeezing, like a sponge, and it hurt so badly he couldn't make sense out of what she was saying to him. He looked from her to the stone, and back again. He was not even sure if he could breathe. "What—I don't— what is . . . If this is my mother's baby, who am I?"

Nora wrapped her arms around him. He tugged away.

"You're angry," she said.

"I don't believe you."

She drew him back to her, her arms around him, pulling him so close, her heat, her love, it was smothering, it was something he'd never felt. . . . His mother had never even held him like that . . . not like that . . . not where he felt both safe and afraid. . . .

He felt her breath near his ear as she whispered the damning words.

"You're from the bloodline of the Halloween Man."

6

Stony pushed her away, and Nora fell back slightly. He stood up, brushing dirt from his knees. "Shut up, just shut up. You and your stupid stories. Your stupid stories all these years I been listening to and buying into and making believe, because I thought you made up—''

''You're a man now,'' Nora said. Her voice was deep and firm. Nothing about her face betrayed any emotion. ''You should know. They should've told you, but I know they never would have. Not until it was too late. And now—''

''Stupid bitch,'' Stony snapped. Then he said, ''I'm sorry.'' Then he was almost afraid to ask the next question. He stood over her, not knowing where to turn. Who else could he trust but Nora? Who else would ever tell him . . .

And then all the fights came back, the nasty knock-down-drag-outs of his childhood, of his father screaming, ''That bastard! Ever since he was born, things just got ruined for us!''

And his mother, holding him over the flame of the gas stove, his face so close to it. *The Moonfire burning, weakening him.*

It was almost a surge of relief that went through him now.

''So who is my father? My real father?''

''Your birth father is Johnny Miracle,'' Nora said. ''And he, in turn, is the descendant of Imp.''

Stony caught his breath. He felt blood pounding through his body like hammers. His heartbeat zoomed. He felt feverish, his hands trembling. ''I came from *him*?''

''Don't judge that man,'' Nora spat, and for the first time Stony felt venom in her tone. ''Do not dare to judge that man! He is from a sacred bloodline. You too are from that bloodline and you should look at what it means. You people in town with your cold ways and your white attitudes, judging those you'd best not pass judgment upon! Your birth father is a man of divinity, and if you knew yourself better you would understand. . . .'' Then she knelt down again. Her tone softened. ''It's too much for you to

239

understand. Sometimes I don't even believe or understand it.''

"Who's my mother then?"

Nora was silent. "Something I know nothing about."

"Is it someone in town?"

Nora closed her eyes. She brought her hands up to cover her mouth, as if wanting to keep something in, to keep it from escaping over the dam of her lips. A hissing sound came from the depths of her throat. Tears pressed from her eyes like wine from grapes. She brought her hands down to her lap, holding them together in a fist of prayer. "I wanted to never have to tell you any of this. I wanted you to grow up and I wanted to hope that all these years it could be forgotten. Buried like the baby from your mama's body, buried beneath that stone. But I can feel them, I can feel them."

"Feel who?"

"Them. Those people."

"Who?"

"The ones who own Stonehaven," she said. "The ones who did this."

"Someone owns Stonehaven?"

"They've always owned it. They own every piece of property in the village. They've owned it since the village began."

Stony brought his hand up to Nora's face. He cupped it beneath her chin. "I always wished that you were my mother. I mean, I sort of wished that my mother was like you."

"And I wish I'd had a son like you, Stony, as badly as I've wished for my sight to return, I've wished for that," she whispered. "But I'm not your mother."

"I know. But in a lot of ways you are."

When she calmed, she said, "I told you all those spins about the children with flies in them, and about the ice-house of damnation and about the Halloween Man, because you needed to know. Your mind needed to work those stories out.''

"What were you trying to tell me?"

"It's not everyone in town that knows. Some are strangers, and have only come here in the past thirty years. Some commute in the summers from New York. Some just don't know. But others do."

"What's so secret?" He felt the chill of morning seep into him, and the sun's light felt cold on his back as it cut a swath through the trees.

"You've always heard about how you were born, Stony. And it's almost the truth, what you heard. You've always heard stories about how things happened before you were born and it's almost the truth . . . but I have lied to you. So have others. Oh, I have lied like the worst sinner on the face of the earth."

Something went placid like the calm surface of a pond, only inside him. "I don't care. I forgive you. I really do. What is it? Tell me. Tell me the truth."

She opened her white round eyes to him, and began.

# Chapter Twenty-one

## Nora's Past

### 1

This was back when I could see just like you can. I had pretty brown eyes flecked with cinnamon. They were my best feature, my mama told me. They say the eyes are the windows of the soul. My windows were always sparkling, I can tell you.

You know we got two lives, sometimes more. I don't mean like reincarnation, I mean like we have our life of innocence and then it rams right into the real life, the life where innocence is just a mirror—looks nice, reflects a lot, but it ain't the real thing.

I was not a God-fearing girl when I was growing up. I ran wild, and had men right and left. I was always down in Wequetucket at one of the roadhouses. I never finished grammar school, and never worked. My mama was always chasing me with a broom, and telling me I was going to hell. When I was seventeen, Mama threw me out of the house. I lived in the streets most nights, searching trash cans for food, or going to the back doors of restaurants for scraps, like a dog. This was over fifty years ago, and I can tell you that in a little village like Stonehaven, black girls with no jobs were not well-treated. I drank too much, too, which always got me in trouble, and then one day this nice man told me that he needed someone to help with his sick wife. I refused at first, but he told me I'd have a warm bed to sleep in, a roof over my head, and three meals a day. Plus all the liquor I could hold when I wasn't working. Something about his offer got to me, and he seemed not only kind but also enormously wealthy, at least to me. "I ain't no nurse," I told him. He told me that was all right, his wife didn't need a nurse, mainly a companion to sit with her, perhaps play cards. This sounded like the easiest job in the world to me then.

I went to this man's house. Did I just say *house*? Stony, it was a castle. It was the biggest place I had ever seen the inside of. Marble and big fireplaces and views of the water and martinis as big as lobster traps. No fish-stinking men pawed me, no cheap whiskey, no sleeping under a gutter while the rain got under my bones. My room was small to this man who took me in, but looked like a room at the Ritz to me. I had my own big bed, and a private bathroom with a full tub. I thought I'd made it. My mama, she thought I was his whore, but she didn't understand. The man never touched me. I spent mornings and afternoons sitting beside his wife. She seemed to be in a coma to me, but sometimes she'd flutter her eyes open and look at me almost serenely. I'd sit there and sometimes talk about nothing but the weather and what was in the magazines. Or I'd turn up the radio and we'd listen to the good shows, and I'd laugh when Jack Benny came on, and she'd flutter her eyes open. Easiest living I ever had. I was drunk half the time and I didn't have nobody looking over me really. Sure, sometimes I had to spoon-feed the old lady tapioca or wipe spit from her lips. But someone else did the bedpans, and another nurse was there for her at night. I never asked what was wrong with her, since I figured you don't kill the golden goose, right? It was their business anyway. I was just happy to have a spring of comfort and good living.

Then, one morning, I had me some beer. It was a hot summer day. Beginning of June. A cold beer with a little lemonade in it. I came up to her room and drew back the heavy curtains. "Rise and shine, my mama always said," I told her.

When I turned around, the bed was empty.

It had been neatly made.

I stood there looking at the bedspread as if I didn't understand what this meant.

I went downstairs, looking for one of the other servants, but couldn't find anyone. I had never looked around the house all that much. Never had much interest in it. But I had gotten a little attached to the old lady, lying there practically dead but still *there*, still a resident, if you know what I mean. She was really the only person I ever spent time with in that house. The servants didn't talk much to me—they were too good for me, I guess. So I figured, oh Lord, she died, or they took her down to the hospital or something. I wandered from room to room, trying to find the man. But everyone was gone. I went into the kitchen, made me a cup of tea, and sat for a bit. It was just too silent. Too damn silent.

I was feeling a little bad, too. I mean, I had this gravy train in this house, I could have whatever I wanted there. And now, if the old lady was dead, I'd be out on the street again. I didn't want that. I went over to the liquor cabinet and pulled out a bottle of gin. Uncapped it, took a good swig. Then another. I started crying and crying.

Poor little me! I thought. Poor little Nora Chance! Poor little girl whose mama didn't love her, whose men had abandoned her, and now this old white lady went and died and took away Nora's only shot at living the high life! Poor poor girl!

I was wandering that house, in a daze aided by booze, and then I see this door that looks like the door to heaven or something. The place was spinning around from all my drinking. I see this door with an arch, and it's all dark wood. Around its edges are these cute little carved angels, and in the middle of the door is this inlaid picture of the Virgin Mary, Mother of God. I look at her a long time. She's a white woman, too. I think, damn white women and their fluttering eyelids and their sleeping in bed all day listening to the radio and then dying in the middle of the night.

I say to Mary, "Look, you may be the mother of baby Jesus, but you ain't got the right to take away the old lady from me. She was my bread and butter." I raised the last of the gin up and just splashed it across the picture of Mary.

Then I'm feeling repentant, drunk and sorrowful. I just blasphemed the Virgin, I know my life is a damp hell, and I need to get down on my knees and beg Jesus' forgiveness right then and there. Words from my childhood come up, words of preachers, words of my mama, the words I saw written above the little chapel door:

*Bless the fruit of her womb.*

And I'm thinkin', now what the hell does that have to do with nothin'? The fruit of her womb? What fruit? She's made out of stone, this particular Virgin. I open that little door, and walk into this room. Only it ain't just a room, it's a little chapel with pews and banners and little stained glass windows, and I walk down and then drop to my knees. I look up at the cross, only there ain't no cross, or it ain't where it's supposed to be.

The chapel gets cold, real cold. I'm weeping and asking Jesus' forgiveness, and then I hear something moving behind me.

The door closes, and the room gets real dark. Some kind of smoke comes at me—it's incense, it stinks, and I start coughing. When it clears, a yellow mist seems to come off the altar, and I go up. I know I'm drunk, so I know this is half me and half a miracle, because I know now Jesus is there with me. I know how wrong I've been. I see the error of my ways. I'm begging Jesus! Beggin' him! ''Help me, Lord! Help this poor sinner Nora Alice Chance!''

My voice echoes in the room. I'm raising my hands. The bottle goes crashing to the floor.

And I see something behind the altar as I crawl up to it. The altar ain't ordinary either. It's stone slab on stone slab. And as I crawl up to it, penitent sinner that I am, I see metal behind it, some kind of metal box. A big one, one almost as big and long as the altar itself.

I pull myself up and I see the mist coming off the top of this box. It's made of copper or something. Looks real old, all hammered out, and it has this . . . this figure sort of dented out around the top . . . this thing sort of sleeping in the picture, as if dead, and I think it looks like one of those Egyptian mummy cases, you know, and I'm wonderin' what in hell these Crown people are up to.

This gets my curiosity going, and I look at it for a minute, thinking it's strange.

And then I hear someone weeping from within the box. Or maybe it's just a child outside the chapel. Or maybe it's some animal in it.

And then, I see its hand reach out from the small square window on the copper box. Bars like a prison there. The hand.

2

*Nora took a long breath, pausing in her story. Then she continued.*

## 3

I don't remember what I thought then, whether I wondered if this was a child playing a game or if this was someone trapped there—

But it didn't matter. The chapel door opened and light flooded the place.

I turned around, and there, standing in the doorway, was the man.

"What the hell are you doing in here? I told you never to go wandering," he said.

I didn't know what to say.

"Look, half-breed girl," he said, as he swiftly walked towards the altar. "You come into my house and I clothe and feed you and ask so little of you, and now you betray me."

He walked right up to me, grabbing me by the back of the neck with one hand, and slapping me hard across the face with the other.

Then he looked from me to the box.

"You see it?" he asked. "It's what you came in here for, isn't it? You want to see what has been forbidden from mankind for centuries to get near, don't you? You want to gaze upon it, you drunken whore."

I pulled away from him, but he grabbed me around the waist. I was too drunk, I felt like I had no strength at all. I started screaming and kicking out, but he lifted me up and then threw me down in front of the box.

"You want to see it! You want to!" he's shouting. "Then look! Gaze upon its radiance!"

He opened the door to the cage, and for ten seconds I saw what seemed to be the burst of a thousand suns. Dazzling yellow and green light, and within it something else.

A being.

A creature.

Something that you only read about, but never see.

And then, the colors melted, the light dimmed, and a pain shot through my eyes as if someone had taken their thumbs and pressed them deep.

I was thrown back, and the wind got knocked out of me.

When I came to, the light still seemed dim, and I had a pain in my eyes. I was lying in bed in my room, and two of the servants were holding my arms and feet down.

The man leaned over me, his eyes wide and blank as if he were not looking at a human being but at a thing.

In his hand, a small blade that was bright orange with heat.

"She's coming to," he said. "Quickly."

Someone pushed their hands down on my forehead and the flat side of the red-hot blade came down on my left eye. As I screamed, I realized that rags had been stuffed in my mouth. I felt as if I were choking. Then he raised the blade and brought it to my right eye.

### 4

"I wandered for days in these woods, until my mama found me. I had been sleeping in the mud, eating grass and weeds, talking to myself. If someone had shot me then, it would have been a kindness. But my mama was a good woman. She took me in, and she and my sister never spoke of what happened, and neither did I. I learned to make candles and bring in peoples' wash, the old way, the way a blind woman could. And my mama built this shack for me so that I would never again have to go into that village. She told me the old stories, and she gave me the corn doll for protection," Nora said. "She warned me about the village, but I still went back sometimes, Stony. I still wanted to know what that was, that light—as if by some miracle the old man could bring my eyes back to me."

Stony remained silent. "Who was it?"

"It was Mr. Walter Crown. He got killed doing some business deal in the Far East, years ago. But his son, who is now Mr. Crown, was eighteen by then, and took over the duties of the family. But before they were Crowns, they were Crowninshields. And it's they who own this two hundred acres of land called Stonehaven. The lady I had sat with, her name was Miranda, and she was Walter's older sister, not his wife. I don't know what became of her that day, whether she died or whether—as I suspect— she was destroyed by the demon in that cage."

"It couldn't have been a demon. Nora, come on," he said, almost playfully. "Come on. Demons? Monsters? That's for movies and junk."

Her face seemed to shine, as if there were ashes and fire beneath her skin. "I saw its hand, Stony. It was almost a human hand, but it had this . . . this . . . smoke coming off it. And when I beheld it . . ."

Then he said, "Why are you making all this up?"

Nora pushed herself up from the ground, using one of the large stones to help balance herself. "Truth and lies get mixed up with people, Stony. You know that. But I've been preparing you your whole life for who you are and what you're part of. You are a Crown. You are the son of Johnny Miracle and a Crown. And the Crowns are of the Devil. It's a blessing that they gave you up to your mama and daddy rather than letting you be raised by those Devil worshipers."

Stony squinted at her as if trying to understand. "This is ridiculous. This is totally ridiculous. If this happened . . . if this really happened . . ." He shook his head violently. "Not that I believe it, it's totally nuts, but if this did happen, why would they give me up?"

Nora reached over and held his hands still in hers. Her face, lined and dark, was nearly calm. He knew she was not a liar. She had never been one to lie outright. She was a storyteller, but had always separated her spins from the truth of things. He wanted her to be lying to him. He wanted it badly.

"When you were born, Mrs. Crown could not give you life. She could not take care of you. They needed a mother, and they needed a mother who would keep this secret. And I suspect that the woman you call your mother never told you that she worked as a nurse in the Crown house the year you were born."

"Why are you telling me this?" Stony asked, feeling numb.

"Because you are going to be a father soon, and a man. There are things you must know," Nora said, her voice gentle. She reached up to the sky, her hand balled into a fist. "I vowed to God I would tell you everything when you came of age. I vowed I would not let them do to you what they intend." Her voice grew in strength, and a cold wind blew down through the trees, bringing with it damp brown leaves. She turned her face upwards, sweat shining on her dark skin. "I am not gonna let this lie live any longer. It has eaten at my soul as surely as if a wolf had crawled into my bed. I will not let them have the little boy who I came to love as my own son!"

# Chapter Twenty-two

## The Village, at the End of October

### 1

So many things happened that morning in Stonehaven Borough, so many threads that invisibly emanated from Stony Crawford, that to know everything, one would have had to spread like fire from house to house, to see the Indian corn on Alice Evarest's front door, which she had just finished nailing up, and the fat little jack-o'-lantern she'd put out, hoping that the teens in town didn't throw it into the street for just one Halloween night—

*Yes, Halloween,* Johnny Miracle laughed within himself, hanging onto a tree branch. *All Hallow's Eve! It's glorious, it's glorious and it's coming in the wind, all has been foretold, all that has been until now will be—*

From his mouth, words that were mangled, spreading like the red leaves of the nearby birch across the drying grass of the Common. He struck match after match as if trying to set the air around him on fire.

2

Down at the Package Store–cum–General Store, Martha
Wight had the cheap plastic masks and flimsy costumes
of fairies and goblins and superheroes from half a dozen
comic books all hanging from a wire above the dry goods.
Few children came in to buy them anymore, and even
fewer would be trick-or-treating. Times had changed, and
even though some of the adults would have Halloween
parties in the houses on High Street, the children more
often than not were warned of candy corn gone bad, or
Snickers bars stuck with heroin needles, of apples poi-
soned and studded with razor blades by wicked witches
right out of Disney's *Snow White*. But the old ways of
Halloween still showed through the cracks in Stonehaven.
The multicolored corn strung across doorways like mis-
tletoe, the pumpkins and stacked sheaves of straw leaning
against the sides of the clapboard houses, the pumpkinhead scarecrow that the Doane sisters set out on their
porch swing, all of it bespoke a remembrance of the harvest. The sons and daughters of Stonehaven had harvested
the sea for centuries, from the now near-extinct whales
off the islands, to the lobsters, crabs, clams, mussels, her-
ring, and cod that they were still supplying to restaurants
along the coastline.

Harvest and bounty were two words that were strong
in the soul of New England, and Stonehaven for all its
isolation was no exception. The sea and the earth had
provided all that the town had really needed for centuries.
All outside influence was superfluous at best; at worst, a
curse. The forests of the area had provided the material
for boats and housing, the granite quarries to the south
had laid the foundations and sidewalks, the bounty of sea
and woods and field had fed the original founders of the
village, and although now tourists in the summer tossed

coins in the local coffers, you'd never see this acknowledged.

Tamara Curry was the only resident who did not love the signs of Halloween as it approached. She felt it was far too pagan, too far removed from Jesus and the Bible. She told this often to Fiona McAllister at the library when she went to get her romance novels from the paperback section. "It all comes from witchcraft," Tamara said, pointing across the desk to the poster of a big orange moon with a witch flying across it. The text of the poster read, *Halloween Is for Scary Reading,* which Fiona tried to point out to her, but Tamara would have none of it. "It's worshiping the Devil, bottom line," Tamara said. "And I only wish we were living a couple hundred years back. They knew what to do with Devil worshipers back then."

"You know," Fiona said, a sly smile across her lips. "It used to be assumed that a woman with a lot of cats was a servant of Satan."

"My cats are all Christian cats, you know that better than most, Fi," Tamara huffed. "All of them been baptized good with the sign of the cross and no one can say otherwise, and blessed. You know how they're blessed." She grabbed her books and stomped out of the library.

Walking down the granite steps, and then across the Common, she saw what seemed to her to be one of the signs of the Devil in Stonehaven itself.

Johnny Miracle, sitting up in the great old oak tree.

"That tree has been there for hundreds of years, Johnny, you just quit polluting it." She raised her fist at him. She was in a bad mood now, what with Fiona's smart mouth making a blasphemous joke about her cats. "You—you—spawn of the Devil!" She spat.

Johnny Miracle smiled, as he usually did when someone yelled at him, and waved from his perch among the thick autumn-gold tresses of the oak.

Douglas Clegg

3

Stony heard Nora calling to him, but it was too late—

He had to run, he had to run and get the hell away from her. Something was wrong with her, maybe living in the woods had gotten to her finally, maybe it had been there all along—her insanity—but the stories she was now telling could not be true, they had to be the imaginings of a crazy old woman he had got too close to—

He ran across the mud and damp leaves, nearly slipping at points, wondering why the hell Lourdes hadn't shown up—if she had, if she *had*, he would never have heard Nora's ravings—

Nora, whom he had *trusted*! Nora, who told him these crazy stupid things that could never be real! Nora, who believed in demons and devils and old Indian curses and old slave ghost stories, and was not logical—and had no electricity, for Christ's sake, she didn't even own a phone or a TV, how could she possibly know *anything* about *anyone*!

When he got to his house, he flung his bike across the yard, and ran up the steps. Throwing open the door, he shouted, "Mom! Where the hell are you?"

He took the stairs two at a time, and when he came to the landing, his mother stood there in the doorway. She wore her bathrobe, and her hair was greasy and hung in strands around her face.

"Stony? Something up?" she asked, almost suspiciously.

He pulled the roll of bills from his pocket. Taking off the rubber band, he threw the hundreds down at her feet. "Where the hell did you get this money?"

She was silent. She looked from him to the floor. Her lips trembled. "What you been getting into?"

"I want to know where the hell you got all this money. Two thousand dollars. In a box under your bed. I saw it when I was four, and it's been sitting there ever since. You can't pay your bills on time, but you have two thousand dollars in cash sitting in a box under your bed.''

"Your father put you up to this?" she asked, her voice a whisper.

"No one put me up to this and I don't give a damn what you think, you just tell me about this money. And tell me about when you worked at the Crown place. When you worked as a nurse there.''

"Who told you that?" she asked. "What *liar* told you that filth?''

"Just you tell me. Never mind anything else.''

"Don't you come into my house acting like some nasty little man,'' she spat. "You don't know nothing about what my life is. And you going through my things and taking money. Money I been saving for you and Van all these years.''

"For me and Van? Is this how much it cost to keep you quiet? Is this how much it cost for you to raise me up? I know who my father is, Mom. I know I'm not your son! I know that's why Dad always fought with you, because he knew. And you knew too. You knew and they paid you off and now you're gonna tell me just what it is that's so damn secret that no one in this town is giving me a straight answer!''

"You just shut up, you bastard," his mother said, her voice stranger than he'd ever heard. She pointed to the money. "That is blood money, and you are lucky that your head wasn't smashed against a rock the minute you were born. I'll tell you who you are, you bastard. I'll tell you how you changed this family when you were born. How my husband would never touch me again. How I've had to pretend I cared about you when you didn't even smell like a baby, you smelled like nothing when you were a baby, you wouldn't even cry. You just stared at me like you knew everything, and I had to put your mouth to my breasts and it would turn my stomach when you suckled. It would make me want to vomit.'' Her mouth was a snarl. ''My son had to *die* and you have to *live*, and I had to take care of you because of this money that I can't even touch because I know what I did. I know what I was *part of*!''

Stony dropped to his knees. He covered his ears.

''You want to know it? Did that bitch in the woods tell you? Did she? I knew she would one day. I knew she couldn't be trusted. Did she tell you that you would be dead today if not for me? Did she tell you that I lost my little boy the minute he was born and then I had to decide in one minute if I was going to take you? And all I wanted was my little boy and something in me thought that you could be *him*. You could be *him*. And I spent the past fifteen years of my life pretending to love you, to love you, and hoping that it would somehow just work, but even your brother Van knew early. He told me when he was six that you had something wrong with you. He told me that you looked like other babies but you had something that made him think you were evil. And I knew you were, but I just pretended for so goddamned long! And I tried to kill myself but I couldn't! Even though I hated you, I knew you were a baby, and I knew that God would send me to Hell for eternity for killing myself and abandoning my children! Jesus tells us to bear our burdens gladly, but I couldn't! Not with you!''

Stony dropped his hands to his side. It felt as if steam were building inside him, and he felt a ripple—a movement within him that he could not identify, as if his blood were heating up, as if the sounds of distant waves crashed along his bones and muscles. He opened his mouth and the words that came out did not feel like his. ''Tell me who my mother is! I want to know!''

''Listen, you little ungrateful bastard, the only reason I took you is because a priest put you in my arms and gave me that money, because I needed to know that I could get away from here if I ever had to. I took that money as payment for you and your sorry sniveling little ass and now you throw it up in my face. Now get the hell out of my house. Get the hell out of my house!'' Tears streamed down Angie Crawford's face, and she looked uglier than he had ever seen her, uglier than he thought any human being could look. Her eyes were wild, her hair tossing up and down as she shook her head, as she slammed her fists against her stomach, screaming.

### 4

In the Castillo household, Lourdes's mother turned to the police officer from Mystic who had shown up early and said, ''She hasn't come home all night. I told you people something happened. I told you last night. She's a good girl. She doesn't stay out all night. Something's wrong. I bet it's that boy. That boy from the village. That village has always been bad. He's been up to no good with her.''

This was the most composed she had been in nearly nine hours, since she'd sent her sons out into the woods and to town to try to find their little sister.

### 5

Others in town detected a slight change, as if the coming winter had just drawn a breath closer, for frost was in the air, frost and something about the light of this day that seemed on the verge of going out completely.

Stonehaven Borough was arranged in a series of neat and tiny paths, all crisscrossing as if part of a labyrinthine design. At its heart, the Common with its old library, and at its autumn-yellow edges, the Post Office and churches. The old Customs House on High Street, the apartments above the few stores in what might generously be called downtown Stonehaven, the old venerable captains' and their widows' houses along Water Street . . . all intersecting, all winding around each other until, smaller and smaller, the village ended at Land's End. There, the glassy water surrounded the stubby finger of rocky land. The gulls and cormorants rose and fell with the water, and Guff Hanlon was taking his morning constitutional before going back into the village to work his winter hours in the public library. A few boats were out upon the shining waters, and the Isles of Avalon were just gentle slopes of haze out in the Sound. Guff saw, as he rounded the tip of Land's End, what looked to him to be a strange light coming from over at Juniper Point, back by the summer mansions. The light was yellow-green, and flashed for only a few seconds. But it was enough to startle him. He checked the position of the sun in the east, and thought it might just be light glinting off one of the windows of the Crown place. Something about the light seemed interesting to him, so he went and sat at the edge of the water, crossing his legs on one of the large rocks that shored up the point. He watched the summer homes from this great distance for a few minutes, and then decided he had just imagined it. For nothing could produce a light quite like the one he'd seen.

He was about to get up and continue his walk, when he saw the light again.

And something else, too.

Later, as he pushed the cart of books down the oriental rug in the center of the Stonehaven Free Library, he gave a nod to Fiona McAllister. She wore her low-cut peach blouse, and the tan skirt he liked so much on her. She followed him past a few early-morning patrons, into the narrow hall of the book stacks. In the dark, dusty room, he turned to her. She tried to kiss him, but he kept his distance. "Something's wrong," he said.

"What is it?"

"It's not you. It's me. I saw something this morning. Something that bothered me. No, wait, it didn't bother me. It . . . terrified me."

She put her arms around his shoulders. "Tell Mama," she whispered.

Guff shrugged her off. "Not now, Fi. Not now. I thought the Crown place was on fire this morning. I thought it was burning . . ." Then tears poured from his eyes, and he no longer looked like a man in his mid forties, but like a boy of nine. "I wanted it to burn. I wanted it to . . ."

"You imagined it," Fiona said, trying to comfort him. "Don't say these things, Guff."

"No," he said. "I saw it in the clear light of day. It's getting stronger . . ."

"Oh, baby," she said sweetly, and this time, he fell into her arms, and she kissed him all over, she kissed his neck, his closed eyelids, his nose, his lips, his chin. His tears mingled with hers. "It was a long time ago," she whispered. "A long time ago. We were all so young then. All so young and innocent. It's all right. It's a good thing."

"I was there," he moaned, a little too loud, not caring if others heard him. "I was there. You . . . all of us . . ."

6

"Where the hell you been?" Del asked. He had just managed to escape the school bus, and was down at the docks by eight-thirty A.M., drinking beer and skipping stones across the water. He had his wool cap pulled down almost over his eyes, and his sweatshirt was covered with seagull shit.

Van stood over him, not exactly looking at him, not exactly looking through him either.

Something was funny about the way Van looked, but Del couldn't quite figure out if he was just dirty or what, on account of the way the sun was gleaming so damn hard and striking the water too, so it made flecks of light dance around Van's face.

And then, as Del shaded his eyes, he knew.
*It's blood.*
*It's goddamned blood.*
*And Van—his face, his hair, all crinkled and wrinkled
and white as a worm—*

Van was soaking, his clothes, his skin, and he left a
trail of blood as he stepped closer to Del and took a beer
from the six-pack. Van hunkered down beside him.

"I'm fucked," Van said.

## 7

The village had its own morning bustle, as Officer Dennehy walked shop to shop with a picture of Lourdes Castillo in one hand, and a Styrofoam cup full of coffee in
the other. He stopped first at the Package Store, and
walked among the rows of wine bottles to the cash register. Martha Wight, her white hair flecked with pepper,
sat flipping through a copy of the *National Enquirer*, cigarette in one hand nearly singeing the pages. She glanced
up, a ribbon of smoke curling around her craggy features.
"Ben?" she said.

"Good morning, Marti," he said. He set his coffee
down. Tossed the photo on her counter. "She's been
missing since last night. Parents are worried."

Martha Wight gave him a curious look. "Never seen
her before. She from the village?"

He shook his head. "Wequetucket. But she was over
here yesterday. You got any rock candy?"

"Never seen her before," Martha repeated, giving a
light shrug of her bony shoulders. "Rock candy's over in
the jar." She pointed to a series of small jars on the far
counter. "You eat enough of that stuff, your teeth're
gonna fall out."

"Too late. Half of 'em are already gone," Dennehy
said. He walked over, lifting up the lid. The rock candy
was blue, and on strings. He lifted one strand up, popping

260

a bit of it into his mouth. He glanced around at the costumers and the liquor and magazines as if he'd never seen the Package Store before. "You probably know every kid in town, huh? Probably always trying to get some beer or candy or something?"

Martha Wight shook her head. "I don't sell no beers to minors, you know that, Ben. These kids. They're all the same. This one probably run off with some boy, or just took off on her own. They run wild." Taking a long drag off her cigarette, she raised her eyebrows. Exhaling a powerful lungful of smoke, she added, "If I see her, I'll send her home."

The cop hit three more shops, but reached a dead end on all of them, until he came to the Railsback Butcher Shop.

Butch Railsback, hacking at a side of beef, his apron smudged with blood and entrails, glanced at the picture. "Yeah, dat's Angie Crawford's boy's girl. Lourdes. Like that miracle place. Lourdes. She's a cutie. Hope she's okay. She and Stony, dey're prob'ly off somewheres to-get'er."

Then Officer Dennehy asked, "You know, that's what the girl's mother said. But when I stopped by the Crawfords' a half hour ago, Angie told me she had no idea who this girl was."

Butch shook his head. "It's her. I seen 'em together, kissin' behind my shop. Maybe Angie never seen her before. Could be. Could be Stony boy don't take his girl home to meet Mama."

When Dennehy was out on the street again, he noticed that more than a few shop owners seemed to be watching him.

As if waiting to see where he'd go next. He waved to each of them and thought, *Dear Christ, what a beat I got. Save me from old New England and the way they watch and wait and then never really step in with information until it's too late.*

8

The kitchen at the Crowns' house was long and wide, meant for entertaining company with dinner parties. In the early part of the twentieth century, it had been used precisely for that. Dozens of the almost-rich, the almost-famous would arrive in droves in the summer. Coming from Manhattan or down from Boston were the flappers and their feckless beaus with slicked-back hair, the charmed circle that the Crown family drew to them— never men as powerful as Crown, never women as wealthy as Mrs. Crown—but those who needed something from them, or got something just by being among the Crowns. Nouveau-riche movie stars, oil tycoons, upscale gangsters and their mink-glazed molls, all gathered for frolics and dalliances, and the kitchen was often the center of the hive as illicit liquor was more often than not hidden in one of its secret compartments beneath the long sink with its six faucets. You could almost hear the echo of laughter and gaiety as couples ran around the cooks, dipping their fingers to taste the sauce, or uncorked another magnum of Dom.

But the wild times and parties had ended, and within a few years, the summer home became a reclusive place. By the time Diana was born, so little entertaining was done there that they no longer employed a cook in the summer.

Alan Fairclough stood in the kitchen, and poured himself a glass of aged Scotch. Sipped it, looking about the place. Glanced at his watch. Eight-thirty A.M. He had slept well, and was not surprised by her call two hours earlier. "It's happening. I can't believe it, but it's happening," she'd said, her voice thrilling, her excitement palpable.

"All Soul's Day's coming," he had told her. "The rituals are the fine-tuning."

"Yes," she whispered. Then, after a pause, "There's a lot of blood."

"That's all right. Don't let it worry you. This is part of the plan, Diana. There's nothing to fear. You know that better than anyone."

"I'm not afraid of it. I'm afraid of—"

"Of losing yourself to its totality. Don't be," Fairclough said softly. "Look, I'll have some breakfast and then I'll bring the boat over."

Then Diana said, "I did the ritual. Just like you taught me. I wasn't tainted with the sacrifice."

Alan smiled, glancing out the window of his home, across the Sound, to the thrusting finger of Stonehaven, and the great white house at its edge. "Purity. Did he love her when he did it?"

"I think so. Yes. It . . . it almost brought . . . it out . . . in me," she whispered.

"That's all right, Diana," Fairclough said soothingly. "It's natural for that to happen. It's nothing to fear."

Now, two hours later, in the grand kitchen, Alan Fairclough felt as though everything he had ever searched for was at hand. Everything he'd ever believed in was coming true.

In a few moments, Diana Crown appeared in the doorway to the kitchen. "It's happening," she said, sweat along her forehead. "Just like you said it would."

Alan raised his glass. "Sometimes one has to prod these things along. For the sake of religion."

Her face could not be more perfect, he thought. What she was, what was within her—

*The magnificence of it.*

All his life he'd been searching, and to find it here, among this family, tucked away . . .

"I have something for you," she said.

"Him?"

Diana nodded.

Alan tasted the bitter fire of whiskey at the back of his

throat. "Do you think he has much fight in him? Last night must have been . . . well, exhausting to say the least. You had to push him over the edge, no?"

She shrugged. "Does it matter?"

Alan Fairclough grinned like a little boy on Christmas morning. "Oh, infinitely so. I want to give him a sporting chance."

# Chapter Twenty-three

## Van

1

"What's all that?" Del asked, but looking at the blood on Van's shirt, he didn't need to be told. The smell was enough. It was like sticking his face into an open wound.

"I fuckin' killed her," Van said, and then began giggling. "Shit, does that sound goofy. I killed her."

Del cocked his head to the side. Took another swig of beer.

"It was not like killing her, though, Del. Man, you got to believe me," Van said, his words coming out rapid-fire. "It was more like making cosmic love to her, it was like fucking something that opened like a flower. It was sweet. I know it was wrong to do, I know it was bad, man, but it was not like killing her, it was like she whispered to me to make holes all over her and then she opened them all for me—for me, man, for fuckin' me—and then she said, well, come on in, Van, baby, I want you inside all my flowers—she was like this *garden* . . ."

265

Both of them were silent for a moment. Del heard the cries of the gulls overhead, as they dropped crabs and clam shells along the pavement behind them.

Van popped the tab on a beer can, his eyes squinting as he glanced around at the sun-spotted water. "I'm fucked, man."

"Is this a joke?" Del asked, and then it struck him—of course it was a joke, man. Van was always playing pranks and shit. One time he pissed on six different doorsteps in one night, and another time he took a dump on Tamara Curry's back porch just so that when she went to feed her cats in the morning, she'd step right in it. Van was a fucking genius at practical jokes and stuff. "I know, you went down to Railsback's and got Butch to let you wipe like a dead pig or something all over you and that's the blood and shit." Del raised his beer can, "Good Halloween costume. Me, I'm goin' as Dracula, but you—Man, you are one sick mother, but my hat's off to you, dude—"

Van's expression flickered like there was a translucent mask of happiness over a face beneath it. A face that was like imploded flesh, like someone had stuck a hand grenade down Van's kisser and pulled the pin, only it blew up behind the skin.

"I mean, it's pretty freaky for you to do this for a damn costume, but man, it's gonna scare the bejesus out of the bitches from Wequetucket if we haul ass down there tonight—" But even as Del said these words, something about them felt hollow, as if in saying them he was hoping to cover up whatever black hole Van was sitting in.

"I killed that bitch who my baby brother knocked up," Van said, his lips quivering, as if all the awfulness of the previous night had just hit him. He squinched up his face, looking like a wizened old man for a second. He drank the rest of the beer.

The sunlight felt good. Del looked out across the water to the south. He could see Stonington and Mystic down that way, and some trawlers pushing out to the east. The curve of land, and the yellow-gold of trees as their brilliant colors swept the sky with a chilly breeze, all seemed part of the world of normal life that gave Del some comfort. He didn't look back at Van. "You're shittin' me, man."

"No, man, I'm not. I really killed her. Look, she was walking home through the woods. Like she always does when she and Stony get together. Remember when you and me spied on them?"

"Yeah," Del said, wanting to chuckle at this memory, but something icy caught in his throat. "Yeah, I remember. Last summer."

"Yeah, he was getting some off her, and whore that she was, she put out good. Well, it was like that, only it was me and Diana—"

"Something's wrong with that bitch," Del interjected.

"And then something got inside me, man. It was like I had swallowed some yellow jacket or something and it was all jiggly inside me and I heard these voices—"

"You're looney tunes, man."

"Shut up," Van snapped. "And then, it was like she gave me permission, and I had this knife, this knife—"

Del glanced over at Van. Van drew a large hunting knife from his belt.

Several strands of dark hair were stuck to the blade.

"And it was like she gave me permission, like that bitch Lourdes gave me permission to jab her, only it didn't seem like a knife, it seemed like my wang each time I entered her and it didn't seem like I was stabbing her, it was like—like—I was doing her—" Van caught his breath. Del wasn't sure if he was weeping or laughing, but suddenly Van raised his hands over his head, the knife held high. "I'm gonna kill myself right now, right now, man, I need to take myself out!"

"Shit!" Del said, pivoting to the side to make sure that he didn't get stabbed.

Van dropped the knife. It clattered to the dock. Then be bent down, wobbling as he went to retrieve it.

"You really kill her?" Del asked, and wondered if he could get up and run fast enough to get away from his friend, who looked like he was Charles Manson on a bender. "You really *really* kill her?"

"I stabbed her so many times, dude, that she squished when I hugged her," Van whispered. Then, exhausted, he grabbed another beer, sinking back onto the dock. "What the fuck am I gonna do?"

Del, considering his options, shrugged. "Whatju do with the body?"

Van, a gulp of beer in his mouth, sprayed it. "Shit!"

2

Alan Fairclough took his time walking up the stairs. His morning glass of whiskey still in his hand, he glanced out the windows towards the stables. It was good to be alive at the end of the two thousand years since God had descended, it was good to be alive when the Age of the Spirit was upon the world.

It was good to be the priest of the new age.

When he came to the bedroom on the second floor, he felt the old excitement. The tumescence in his groin. The feeling of youth within his muscles. That surge of energy that always accompanied his blood sport. The Crowns had, over the years, supplied him with a steady stream of youths and maidens, and it brought out the minotaur in him. He loved sparring with an athletic young man, a young man who felt that he could easily take out the old bastard who tried to punch him.

But Fairclough enjoyed the sport too much. He'd let the boy have a hit or two at his expense, and then he'd begin the battering. The bewildered youth wouldn't even understand what was going on, what this would lead to. Wouldn't even guess at the power that grew in Fairclough, the pleasure that burst from his brass-knuckled hands as he pummeled a face into pulp. Or the girls, how he could torture them just by holding them down and doing nothing but slicing a gentle razor against their fine brows.

Killing was not his game.

The youths were paid and sent on their way, hustlers and whores all to some degree, paid handsomely for the privilege of Fairclough's brutal touch.

But this one, this boy, this Van Crawford, who had done the sacred duty, who had shed the innocent blood of the lamb—

Who had unwittingly begun the work of the Gods—

He would be delicious.

His pain would be like communion wine.

*To know the light of God, one had to know darkness first.*

Alan Fairclough opened the bedroom door, and saw the blood-soaked sheets, the indentation where Van had rested his head in the night, and the bloody footprints to the window.

Out the window, he saw the red stains along the flagstone walk.

"Damn it," Fairclough said, setting his glass down on the windowsill.

"He'll be back," Diana said minutes later, when Fairclough came storming downstairs, shouting curses. "He needs me too much. He needs what we have. I know him inside and out now. He'll want me again."

3

Within a matter of minutes, her words proved true.

Glancing up, Diana saw what seemed at first the face of a deranged clown, his hair matted, his face pale with redness around his eyes and nose. Van. He'd been crying. He was incinerating himself from the inside out with his

269

need for her. His hunger. What he got from her was like
an addiction, and he needed his fix.

She leaned over the sink, reaching up to push the window out slightly.

"Please," he said. "We need to talk. Let me in."

4

Van's hunger for her was immense. Away from Diana, he
felt weak and spent, but close to her . . . breathing the
same air . . .

His brain felt as if it were at war with itself. The blood
dripped from his scalp, blinding him as he went down the
hall. Always, the house was in shadow, as if the Crowns
did not want too much light in their sanctuary.

Van wiped at the blood on his forehead. He tasted the
fire of his own fever.

*The fuckin' bitch! Look what she made me do! She sent
me to Hell! She's such a fuckin' cunt! Oh my God what
she made me do!*

He looked down at his hands. The blood burst and sup-
purated like lava wounds, flowing across the palms, trick-
ling down his fingers. Stigmata fountains—and in each of
his hands, a mirror. In the mirror, a reflection, not of a
face, but of a mask. A mask ripping apart like paper, it
showed the yellow fat of life beneath it. Something gibbered and spat like a creature made entirely of nerve endings.

*That's me!*
*That's fuckin' me!*

He screamed, slamming his hads against the walls.
"No! You can't do this to me, you fuckin' bitch!"

Diana came out into the hall. Reaching over, she flicked
on the hall lights so the morning shadows were wiped
clean.

He had expected to see her in the light of day, a monster.

270

But she was not one. She was still beautiful, too beautiful, too damn alluring, her hair falling loose along her shoulders, her eyes full of sunlight. She wore a beautiful sheer white dress, showing off her pale thighs. *Didn't she know what she was doing to him?* She probably had not even slept, yet she looked stunning.

"You didn't even say goodbye, Van Crawfish," she said.

Couldn't she see the hell he was in? Couldn't she feel the pain that shot out around him like an aura?

"I almost called the police on you," she added.

"Ha!" He laughed, clapping his bloodstained hands together. "That's a good one!"

"Look at you," she said, her voice low, "coming in here, out of control, tracking blood, reeking of dead meat."

She stepped forward and he saw what he had seen in her in the dark the previous night, the thing that had zapped his brain somewhere, the thing that didn't seem right, for when he looked at her, it wasn't like looking at a woman at all, not a woman named Diana Crown, but it was like looking at a dark creature with golden eyes that shot fire—

He remembered then all that he had seen, all that had been wiped clean from his brain in the past month, since he'd met her, all that had somehow hidden in his mind, as if it was too terrifying to contemplate—

"You're a fuckin' devil worshipper!" he screamed. "You made me do that last night! And that thing you got in the chapel! That thing from Hell! Oh my god, I'm gonna go to Hell! You're makin' me go to Hell!"

Then Van thought he heard footsteps coming up swiftly behind him, but when he turned to look, someone slugged him hard in the jaw and he thought:

*Damn, it's true! You really do see stars—*

A tall, skinny old man stood over him, holding the oar

from a boat. "You piddling little fuck. Time for me to have a little fun."

Van tried to push himself up, but could not.

"There's nothing I like better," the man said in a clipped British accent, "than a local boy with a high tolerance for pain. Ah, what I will do with you, Mr. Crawford, will open up vistas you now only imagine. When the pain becomes too intense, like fire, it numbs. Then you don't feel anything. I would never want to get to that point. I want to almost get there, Mr. Crawford. Almost. Just to the brink. Just enough so your nerve endings continue to scream for as long as possible. But don't worry. I never kill a boy unless he begs me to do it."

The man dropped the oar. It clattered on marble. The man crouched down over him, holding his face up. "You know what I get from this? No, of course you don't. Let me tell you my little secret. I get closer to God, Mr. Crawford. I get a little closer to the secret of creation. It's one of the rituals that's necessary for me to feel anything at all. I get what you might call a 'charge' from it. Permit me to introduce myself. I'm Alan Fairclough, and this, my friend, is your finest hour."

The man raised his fist and brought it down, but that was only the beginning.

5

Eventually, it was over.

Eventually, the man named Fairclough, whom Van had begun to call God, stopped slapping him, hitting him, whacking him, kicking him.

Eventually, Van lay in a heap, and was not sure just how long he lay there, or even if he was still alive.

The last words he heard from Fairclough were a wormy whisper in his ear:

"Now, Van, you have proven satisfactory. Thank you. Should you live, I'd advise you to get out of this house soon, before my appetite returns. If you're too weary to leave, I'm sorry, but as you know, sometimes the blood and the fight are enough of a charge, even without the kick inside, that little feeling you must've gotten when you stabbed her—what was it? One hundred and six times, yes, that was the number, one hundred and six times, but you know, that was part of the ritual too, Van, that was part of opening up something that God has sent to us, and I thank you.''

Perhaps an hour, perhaps two, passed before the will to live flickered within Van Crawford's soul. All that was left within him longed to just make it right, to just somehow make it right again.

# Chapter Twenty-four

## God, Stony, and Johnny Miracle

1

"You said I looked like my mother," Stony Crawford said, his face flush, his eyes almost wild, his hair falling across his face as if windblown.

The priest glanced up from his desk. "Stony," Father Jim Laughlin said. He closed the magazine he'd been reading. Picked up the rosary, fingering the first bead.

"You said I looked like my mother," Stony repeated. "What did you mean?"

"I—" Father Jim began. Then, "Have a seat."

"Just tell me."

Father Jim nodded. Closed his eyes. "All I meant—"

"Not Angie Crawford. I already know. I know Johnny Miracle is my father. Who is my mother?"

"When I was younger—" the priest began.

Stony interrupted. "Listen, I don't want to hear your private history, Father. I want to know who my mother is."

274

"I can't tell you that."

"Well then who can?" Stony asked.

## 2

Johnny Miracle climbed down from the tree when he saw God coming with the teenager. God always wore a smile for him, and God always took care of him and brought him food.

Johnny ran across the Common, and greeted God with a great big bear hug that made God groan slightly. Then God said, "Johnny, I want you to meet someone. Someone you probably have watched grow up here—" and Johnny looked at the boy, the tall gangly kid he'd seen ride his bike down the streets so many times. Johnny nodded to the boy, whose face seemed to be set in stone.

Then God said, "Johnny, this is your son."

Johnny Miracle felt as if his breathing had stopped, as if his whole body had split apart, as if God were touching the lining around his heart as it beat. Tears came to his eyes without his knowing fully why; he bit his lower lip to keep from shouting.

"My son," he said. "My son."

## 3

Stony felt nothing but pain in his head, and a feeling as if he were somehow a ghost and not real anymore.

"All I want to know—" he began, but before he could say another word, Johnny Miracle grabbed him up in his arms, hugging him tight. Stony pulled away, but Johnny's grip was stronger than he'd expected. It was like being hugged by a grizzly.

"My son!" Johnny shouted, weeping, his smile as big as a jack-o'-lantern's. "My son!"

After Stony managed to extricate himself from Johnny's grasp, he asked, "Who's my mother?"

Johnny Miracle didn't seem to hear. He raised his hands up to the sky and shouted, "Thank you!" Then, looking at Father Jim, "Oh, God, thank you thank you thank you!"

Stony waited for the shouting to die down.

"Who is my mother?"

"Oh." Johnny tilted his head to the side as if rattling the marbles around in his skull. When he spoke, his voice was its usual slurred nonsensical sound. What Stony's mother—*not my mother, not anymore*, he reminded himself—had called "Village Idiotese."

"Oh, your mother, your sweet mother, she was sent by God Himself, she was an angel, she was all beautiful and pretty and when they mated us—and they were all there, my son—oh, when they mated us, it was like heaven and hell meeting in the middle."

Stony glanced at Father Jim. "Who are they? Who's he talking about?"

Father Jim hung his head down. "I can't speak of it, Stony. All I can tell you for now is, you were brought into this world, and you needed a family. You needed the Crawfords. You didn't need the Crowns—"

"Fuck you," Stony said, suppressing an urge to punch out the priest, feeling his fifteen years bubbling with steam that needed to get out and quit with all this bullshit adults were passing around.

"Don't you talk to God that way!" Johnny Miracle shouted, his idiot grin turning maniacal. He raised his arms and swatted at Stony, clipping him on the chin. "Don't you ever talk to the Lord Your God that way!" He swung his fist through the air wildly, but Stony ducked. "No son of mine is ever gonna—"

Stony was already running, running but not knowing where he would go, running past pumpkins piled on doorsteps, past the Blue Dog Tea Shop, past the Package Store, past the policeman who shouted for him, past the streets, back to the lighthouse at Land's End, back to where he could forget that this morning had ever occurred.

*Wake up! Wake up!* he shouted inside himself. *It's a dream! It's a nightmare! You're gonna be late for some math test! You had too much of that cat's claw tea at Nora's and now you're hallucinating in her shack! None of this can be real, none of this can change so quickly! Nobody has been lying to you all your life!*

When he reached the tall yellow grass behind the lighthouse, he looked across the Sound and screamed at the top of his lungs just to get it out of himself, just to let it go.

He looked back to Juniper Point, to the Crown house—The Crowns.

He sat down on the ground, and lay back, staring up at the hazy sunshine.

*Oh Lourdes, wherever you are, I hope you're far from this, I hope you're at school, sitting in Chemistry class wondering why I'm not there. Wondering why, because you decided not to run away with me, that it was all foolishness. And you're sitting there wondering why you can't tell me about how you couldn't slip out of the house this morning, or how you had to tell your mother you were pregnant and she and your dad threw a major fit and now they won't let you talk to me anymore. . . .*

*Lourdes Maria, I know you'll understand all this, all this bullshit. I know you will.*

And then something snapped inside him, so loudly it was as if a twig had been stepped on near his ear.

Something snapped, and he felt the world going black.

"See? I knew it was a dream. I knew it," he muttered, and then pinpoints of dark and light fluttered in front of his eyes. A pain inside his head seemed to burst—

He thought he heard the hoofbeats of distant horses galloping along a shallow surf.

Then he blacked out.

*Inside a dream, he saw the cove, and Lourdes stood out on the water, wearing the dress she wore to church. She held her arms out to him, but when he stepped onto the still water, it turned red, and the swans all rose, their wingspans enormous, as they took to the skies.*

*He glanced up, watching the beautiful white birds, and saw fire erupt from their wings until the entire world burned from their beating.*

Then Stony Crawford opened his eyes. His head was throbbing. He wiped at his dripping nose. His hand came back bloody. "Shit," he muttered, sitting up. He'd only been out a few seconds. He felt exhausted.

Officer Dennehy said, "Hey, kid. Stony, right?"

The policeman stood on the edge of the path by the lighthouse.

"You okay, kid?" the cop asked.

Stony sat up, heaving a sigh that felt larger than his six-foot frame. "Yeah, I guess."

Dennehy stepped off the path, walking over to him. "Let me help you up, okay?" He squatted down, and put his hand under Stony's elbow.

# *Chapter Twenty-five*

## *The Cop*

1

"I've been looking for you all morning," Dennehy said. "You want some rock candy?"

Stony shook his head. He leaned back in the seat, glancing out the window to the Sound. Seagulls dove down and up from the choppy waves. "I've been around."

"You okay? Looked like you passed out. I don't smell any alcohol . . ."

Stony felt very arch. "Let's just say I'm having a shitty morning."

"Hmm." Dennehy cocked his head to the side, considering this. He popped a piece of the transparent hard candy into his mouth, crunching down on it. His back molar hurt, and he knew this probably meant another root canal for him.

"Why've you been looking for me?"

Dennehy brought out the picture of Lourdes. "This your girl?"

Stony nodded. Then, ''Something's wrong?''

Dennehy shrugged. ''She's missing. Know where she might be?''

''You tried her home?'' Concern in his voice. The teenager was worried. Dennehy could see right away that Stony had little to hide; but he did look like someone who hadn't gotten any sleep for a few nights.

Dennehy gave him a flat stare. Then, ''Kid, you look like you've been through hell. What's up?''

''You don't want to know.''

''Sure I do.''

''No, you really don't.''

''All right. So tell me about you and Lourdes Castillo.''

''She's my girlfriend,'' Stony said. ''We were going to run away together this morning. We were gonna get married.''

''Whoa. So what happened?''

''She never showed up.''

''Tell me about you.''

''Why?''

''Because,'' Dennehy said. ''Geez, kid, this village is full of you die-hard New England types. Get back into the world. I'm here to help. I'm here to find your girlfriend. I ain't the enemy.''

Then, both because Stony didn't know what else to do and because something in him felt like he would burst, he opened his mouth and let the story out, beginning with the revelation from Nora, all the way to the encounter with Johnny Miracle and Father Jim.

Afterwards, Dennehy said, ''Holy shit. That is a mother of a morning, kid.''

''Yeah.'' Stony nodded. ''It's Halloween and I keep hoping it's all a big joke on me.'' His voice cracked, fragile. Dennehy had a sudden impulse to drive the kid the hell out of the borough, down to Mystic, pass him to his sister Irene to give him a big bowl of clam chowder and a sandwich, and tell him to wait down there till Dennehy could locate his girl. If half of what the teenager said was true, this was not exactly the best time for his girlfriend to go missing.

Dennehy started up his patrol car. Voices from dispatch mumbled from his radio, but he turned it down. "Stony, tell you what. Let's go out to her family's place and maybe we can figure out where she might've gone. Okay?"

Stony shook his head. "No way. If she's not there, I don't want to have to take bullshit from them too. I need to find her."

Dennehy drove back up to High Street, taking the curve a little too fast, almost hitting a lazyass cat that stomped proudly into the street and then ran like hell when the police car was on it. Then, on impulse, he pulled over again. "Listen, you want to go take a nap or something? My sister's got a spare room down in Mystic and you really look like you need a few hours of shut-eye."

Stony shrugged, his eyes blinking closed. "No, I'm fine, seriously."

"Yeah right," Dennehy sighed, as he drove on out of the village, out to Route 1, down to old Mystic and the gray clapboard on Greenmantle Drive where Irene would already be making lunch.

The teenager in the seat beside him was already asleep before they'd even reached Wequetucket.

2

Stony awoke in darkness.

Sweat trickled down the back of his neck.

He heard voices out in the hallway. A needle-thin shaft of light from beneath the door. For a moment he thought he was a little kid again, and his parents were fighting, but these voices were more soothing.

"It's only been four hours, let him sleep some more," the woman said.

"Yeah, but he's got to go back, he can't stay here." It was Dennehy's voice. "Besides, maybe his girl is looking for him."

"Why are you so concerned?"

"I just am. He's been through hell."

"That cockamamie story you mean," the woman huffed. "He's a teenager. Teenagers make up stories sometimes. You were like that."

"No, Irene, I know he was telling the truth. Nobody lies about that kind of stuff. And you know about those stories—"

"Oh, good grief, and you believe them. A bunch of fundamentalists in Wequetucket spread a rumor nearly twenty years ago about devil worship in that village and—"

"It's my beat. It's a weird town. I've seen a few things—"

"And you're a cop. You gonna tell me that you believe that a bunch of Satanists are living over there? The evil rich people who use the villagers for their sadistic black masses?"

Silence. Stony stretched, sitting up on the featherbed. He swiped at the sleep in his eyes, and tasted the sourness of the last of some dream in his mouth.

"You know I don't believe that," Dennehy said. He cleared his throat. "My point is, maybe this kid should never go back there. The situation with his family, with his—"

"That's not your business," the woman said. "Remember the last time you tried that? What was her name? Natalie?"

"Stop it. I did what I could for her."

"Yeah, and now she's a ward of the state and probably will never be the same again."

"Well, they beat her. They probably would've killed her."

"Maybe. Maybe." The woman's voice softened. "You

282

can't save everyone, Ben. You just can't. Whatever that boy is going through, you have to let him.''

"It's just that . . .''

"Ben?''

"It's just that . . . I was there, Irene. I was there the day he was born.''

"That boy?''

Silence.

"I was doing my rounds, just wandering, and I heard the mother screaming, and I went over. . . . It was raining hard. It started raining so hard I couldn't see straight, and when I got there, the priest was there, and others were there, too, the Crowns, and well, lots of people, maybe ten or twelve, and it was like they formed a protective circle around the mother and I swear, Irene, I really am positive I saw two babies. One all bloody and the other all clean and not precisely a newborn and . . .''

"Ben?''

"Both of them were crying. Both of them were alive. But the priest, he—''

"No!'' the woman shouted, and then Stony heard a muffled cry.

"I could not believe my eyes. I would not believe them. But now, with this kid, fifteen years old, Stony Crawford, and the story he told me . . . It all fits.''

"They killed the baby? You're sure?''

"That's the sad part. I'm not sure. The rain, it was so hard, and I couldn't really see, and then later I asked somebody—maybe Marti Wight, or that woman with the cats, Curry—and they told me there was only one baby. That I'd imagined—''

"And you'd been drinking,'' the woman said, her voice softening again.

"Yeah, that was before. My six-pack suicide badass cop breakfast. Back in the bad old days.''

"Oh, Ben,'' the woman said. "Oh my God. I'm sure

this isn't like that. Nothing is that bad. People aren't that terrible.''

Silence.

Dennehy said, ''Aren't they?''

Stony got up out of bed, and went to the window. He pulled the blinds up, and saw a little garden in the light of early evening. Beyond it, a pack of trick-or-treaters, all about three feet high, were walking along the sidewalk of the opposite street, one of their fathers guiding them with a pumpkinhead flashlight.

Carefully and quietly, he lifted the window, feeling the chill of night brush past him.

3

To get from Mystic to Stonehaven was a five-mile hike, but Stony grabbed the six-fifteen bus up Route 1, jumping off just beyond Stonington, and then walked the final two miles along the dark slender offshoot highway that went into the borough. He thought of going on up to Wequetucket to see if Lourdes had returned home, but decided that if she had, it might be good if she stayed there awhile.

His blood was boiling, and he felt an anger surge through him that he hadn't known before.

There were lies and lies upon lies, and he felt a fury at his family, and at the village that had raised him up only to slap him hard when he'd nearly reached manhood.

As always, Halloween night in the village rarely meant children trick-or-treating, it almost never meant anything other than darkened houses with their harvest displays out on front steps. The few kids that did trick-or-treat were usually taken up and down one block, but the neighbors tended to not open their doors, preferring instead to leave out bowls of candy for the little kids to grab up in their bags. Stony felt a breeze come up as he walked alongside the cove, over the bridge, into the village. The temperature had dropped several degrees in just a few minutes. He drew the hood of his sweatshirt up. He noticed that he stank, which came as no surprise since he hadn't showered in twenty-four hours, and his exhaustion and anger seemed to come out of his pores. When he finally reached his house, it was nearly seven at night. It was silent, empty. His mother would still be on-shift at the hospital down the road, and his father would probably be drinking with his lobstering buddies down at the docks. *Well, not really my mom and dad*, he thought. The idea of it was vaguely comforting. *Fuck 'em all.*

He took the longest, hottest shower of his life, and felt like he was scrubbing the past off his hide, Ivory-soaping all the memories, rinsing the badness that had infected his life.

He watched the filthy water run down the bathtub drain.

After he dressed, he went downstairs, and tried calling Lourdes. Her mother answered. "Bueno?" she said.

*"Hola, Señora Castillo, es Lourdes en casa?"*

*"Stony?"* Mrs. Castillo asked, and the voice was one of suspicion. "That you?"

"Yeah," he said. "Is—"

She cut him off. "What have you done with my daughter? Where is she? Why was she not home last night? What did you—"

And then the line went dead.

Stony stared at the receiver, trying to make sense of what she'd said.

*Last night?*

*Lourdes hadn't even come home last night?*

Stony felt the presence of someone behind him, perhaps a slight sound had clued him, perhaps it was the fetid breath. . . .

He turned.

Van stood there with the phone cord, unplugged from the jack, in his hand.

"No calling out. Not right now. Not right now, Stony

baby brother. I done something real *real* nasty.'' Van dropped the cord.

In his other hand, his large hunting knife, unsheathed.

4

"You trying to call her? Ha! You ain't never callin' her again!'' Van, his face barely recognizable beneath a mask of blood and torn flesh, stood before him in the living room. "I killed Lourdes. I killed her.''

"Bullshit.'' Stony felt his heart leap, felt something scratch at the back of his throat. His limbs felt heavy. This was pure hell, the day and now the night, this was pure hell, and he had somehow been plunked right down in the middle of it. His world had turned into a nightmare of questions and confusions, and now, this . . .

"She's at the Crown place. They put her in this bed. They're sick fucks. Diana Crown is . . . is . . . she's something fucked up, Stony. She got this thing in her eyes. She got this power!''

Then Van drew something from his pocket.

Passed it to Stony.

It was the small purple flower that he'd given Lourdes, that she'd put in her hair. *Last night. Standing in Our Lady, Star of the Sea. Put it into the Virgin's hand, but Lourdes had laughed and said how Mary didn't need it, and had put it in her hair. How beautiful the flower had looked in her dark hair.*

Only it was no longer purple.

It was red and small and pulpy and smelled of blood. Three long strands of black hair were entwined around it as if they'd been pulled out violently at the roots.

"What the—'' Stony looked from the flower in his hands to his brother.

Van grinned, half his teeth rotted and yellow, his white hair almost on end. In his hand, his hunting knife. "You know you're the one doing this to me. You are. I can feel you inside me making me do this!''

Stony stepped back, sure that Van was going to plunge it into him.

''I never fuckin' liked you, baby brother,'' Van giggled, and then he thrust the knife into his gut, twisting and turning it as he brought it up to his throat.

Van Crawford spilled across Stony's shirt.

# *Chapter Twenty-six*

1

"Jesus!" Stony cried out, falling back, wiping the blood off him, tearing his blue shirt off, pulling his soaked jeans off. The blood seemed to go right into him, into his skin, into his throat. He felt the electricity of his brother's life go through him.

A bloody grin spread across Van's face, and he drew the hunting knife out just as if he still was there, still inside that bloodied and chopped body, and he held the knife out to Stony—

*Take it*, a whisper within him said.

*Take it. Use it on them. I couldn't. I'm not that strong. You're the strong one.*

"No! Van!" Stony shouted, his skin soaked with his brother's blood, watching the last of his brother shivering, falling like a marionette whose strings have just been cut, falling down in a heap of dark red-brown mess. Steam rose up from the body.

Some wire overheated in Stony's brain, and he felt as if he were teetering on the edge of a chasm—

*It's just a nightmare, none of this can be happening, none of it. All of it has to be a joke, a trick, a dream.*

Feeling a power surge through him, he held his arms out and screamed at the top of his lungs. His voice echoed. The screams came back at him, multiple screams, all with his voice.

Stony felt a strange rumbling inside him, as if a volcano within his own body threatened to erupt. I'm going crazy. I'm watching this going crazy. It can't be happening. This shit doesn't really happen. He held his hands to the side of his head. *Don't lose it now. Don't lose it. Find Lourdes. Somehow you'll find her. She can't be dead. She has our baby.*

Then a deep calm swept over him. The room shifted, as if cleaning something horrible from it. The body still lay there, the cheap blue carpeting soaking up the pour of blood.

But Lourdes was his only thought.

Stony went and grabbed clean clothes from the hangers in his closet. He put them on. *Don't think about this yet*, some part of him instructed. *Don't think about what you just watched your brother do. Lourdes is the only thing you need to think about. If she's in some trouble, if she's at that house, then you need to find her.*

2

He took his mother's station wagon, the station wagon that had contained the mythic story of his birth, but not his—oh no—the birth was of some other Stephen Crawford, this one, this Stony was born in the Crown house. Every damn thing in his life happened at the Crown house, only he hadn't known it, and now it was all so fucked up he didn't know which way to turn. He had only driven a car once before, with his old friend Jack the previous spring, driving out on the dirt roads down in Wequetucket once, in Jack's father's car, just dirt roads, and he'd learned how to use the brakes and all the other fun stuff, but now he didn't care if some cop pulled him over. Who the hell cared? Ha ha ha, Officer Dennehy, my brother just drove his hunting knife from his nave to his chops and you're worried about me driving without a license?

Something had become so calm, so peaceful, as if his sense of—*God? Was it God? Or was it just his sense that nothing could be this bad, nothing could be worse than his brother driving his hunting knife into his own stomach and (don't think it, don't conjure the image up, something inside is gonna erupt if you think too much about it)*—

The hunting knife was on the car seat next to Stony. He couldn't even remember taking it from his dying brother, he could barely remember thinking that he could use the knife. He barely could remember holding the knife in his hand. . . .

*His sense of something he felt he must have always known, always felt inside, his differentness, his stranger in a strange land sense, his feeling that he was like the Storm King, from another place, from another family—*

*Johnny Miracle and—who?*

*Who was his mother if not the woman named Angie Crawford? Who was she? Why couldn't Nora tell him?*

He almost crashed into the black iron gate at the Crown driveway. Opening the car door, he got out and looked at the mansion. How could Lourdes be here? Dead or alive? Why would she be in this place where she knew no one and no one knew her?

At the second-story window, Diana Crown pushed the curtain aside. She pulled the large window open, and the chilly October wind blew her hair back.

"Get out of my way," he said to her as she greeted him at the front door. "Get the fuck out of my way." He held the hunting knife up.

"Stony, you don't need to be upset," Diana Crown said. "It can all be explained. It's all set up to be—"

"Just get the fuck out of my way," he said. "I don't even know you. Who are you people? Where's the room? Where is she?"

"Upstairs," she said. "On the left. The first bedroom."

In a daze he walked up the stairs. It seemed to take forever to get to the landing. Once there, he turned left, counting the paces. This was too unreal. It was not really happening, but he would play along. It was just a big Halloween joke, it was just—

Then he saw her—

In the bed—

The mattress soaked.

*What the—*

*What the fuck—*

*What the fuck did they do to her?*

Then, he thought the wildest, craziest thought—

*Van lied. He killed himself in front of me, but he fuckin' lied! That bastard!*

Lourdes lay on the blood-soaked bed.

*Lourdes, alive . . .*

*But her body—*

"My God!" he shouted, "What the fuck have you done to her?"

*—like a whitish pink larva of pulsing liquid around her face and neck.*

*Through a layer of mucus-scum, her face. Her body, covered with translucent skin, with a clear liquid—*

*Veins running outside her body—*

*—To areolas and what seemed to him like the abdomen
of some kind of insect larva—*

*Like a coating around her—*

*Like a protective shell—*

*But her eyes, fluttering open—*

*Beneath the layer of pulsing clear liquid, and blue-red
veins branching out to the edges of the new skin that
covered her from head to toe—*

*Blood pumping—*

*She can't even see me.*

*She doesn't even know where she is.*

*She's in some kind of womb.*

*She's—*

A nearly clear pinkish liquid drained from the six dark
areolas on the left side of her body. The liquid environment that covered her seemed to flow upward to her face.

Her mouth opened slightly, and for just a second he
hoped—no he prayed—he would hear her voice just once
more—

But then, her lips shut slowly, almost a smile on her
face, almost a look of perfect calm across her features,
and her eyes closed again.

# PART THREE

# OUTCAST

*"The Storm King, weakened by the Outcast's Moonfire sphere, cannot bring himself to save his earth-parents' farm. The earth is doomed. . . ."*
*from* The Storm King: The Burning Citadel, *Vol. 2*

*Interlude: The Dead Village*

# *Chapter Twenty-seven*

# *Twelve Years Later*

1

"Holy—" Stony shook his head. It all came back: the year, his age, the moments . . .

*Her face beneath the watery pulp that covered her like a mucus membrane clouding over a wound.*

But he was older now, late twenties, the past was a whisper, a photograph.

The pictures on the boy's back stopped, a last image of Lourdes's face still there, her face beneath the yellow-white pulsing sac. She looked strangely peaceful. She was at peace. Some kind of peace in the picture. It had to be peace, he told himself after all these years.

The boy called Prophet pulled his shirt back down. "Seen enough?"

"This is evil," Stony gasped. "All of this. Coming back here, what you are."

"What I am is what you made me," the boy said.

"Smoke?" Stony asked ironically, drawing a pack out

of his breast pocket. The car smell came back, the filthy old Mustang, then the road they were on, at the rundown bridge overlooking the cove.

"Kids can't smoke."

"Most kids can't do a lot of things that you can do." Stony lit up the cigarette. The smoke filled his lungs, but tasted awful. "Christ, Steve. I can call you Steve, right? I don't go in for this Shiloh or Prophet BS."

"Yeah. Sure. I like Steve."

"Christ, Steve, that's some etching you got on your skin."

"As long as I can remember, I had it. The Great Father said that it was the map of the world."

"He would say something like that." Stony felt the sweat soak through his shirt. "I wish Mr. Fairclough were still around, Steve. I'd like to expand his horizons, so to speak."

"What are we gonna do here?" Steve asked, almost innocently. He glanced around the battered chain-link fence that had been clumsily erected with its no trespassing sign, and then some wiseass, probably a kid, had cut through the chain-link and made it look like a big exploded spiderweb. On the road, the fence had been totally torn apart. Hungry vines pulled back what was left of it.

"We're gonna go look at the houses."

They drove down what had once been Water Street, its dark pavement potholed, roots jutting from overweening oaks. The Common was nothing but dirt, and the trees that had been torn out at the roots lay rotting, sprouting lichen and fern as if the woods just to the northwest of the village would take it over after all these hundreds of years. What had been the Stonehaven Free Library was a pile of rubble. "That's where the P.O. was." Stony pointed across the Common. "Three churches stood over there." But the churches were still there, only their steeples and crosses had come down, their doors torn off their hinges, their stained glass windows blasted out years earlier.

"I want to see the ocean." Steve clapped his hands together. "I never saw the ocean."

"Okay," Stony said. He drove the Mustang out to Land's End. The car was at its last gasp. Stony could feel it in the bump and lurch as it moved over the jagged road. He thought he smelled oil burning, but none of the warning lights worked on the car, so he could not tell what precisely was going wrong. Everything was shot on this old classic, but it had done the job that Stony needed doing. It had gotten them here.

Along the road, nothing but the foundations of houses, rubble, as if the bomb had been dropped. Nature had begun to reclaim this territory. A slender new growth of trees grew above tangles of berry vines and dried grass. Hedges had gone wild, and snaked and burst around the old granite stones. Then they came to the seawall, and the Sound.

"Wow!" Steve shouted, rolling his window all the way down. "Look at that! I never seen the Atlantic Ocean!"

"You still haven't, this is just Avalon Sound," Stony said. "See those islands?"

"Barely."

"That's where you were born," Stony said, closing his eyes, trying not to bring it back.

He didn't want to remember it.

"Let's get out of here. We have somewhere else to go," Stony said after a minute. The air was fresh and clean, and as it pushed out the cigarette smoke in his lungs, it brought back too many sensory memories. The taste of fresh fish, of saltwater when he and Lourdes swam on the small beach, the same air he'd breathed when they made love and created this boy.

Douglas Clegg

2

The car died a quarter of a mile down Juniper Point, so they got out to walk. Stony wrapped the small bomb in newspaper. Then he brought his bags out and put them on the hood of the car. Opening them, he brought out the hunting knife.

"This was my brother's," he said. "Before him, it was my father's. It's soaked in the blood of innocence. I figure that's as good a mythological weapon as any. You ever hear any Greek myths?"

The boy—*No, think of him as Steve. You can. He is Steve. He is your son*—shrugged.

"Well," Stony said, as he drew the gun out and stuffed it into his belt, "there was this guy who had to go kill this really awful woman. She had snakes in her hair, and half of her was lizard, and her eyes turned men to stone. She was a monster called a gorgon."

"I knew women like that in the Rapturists," the kid joked.

"Yeah, well, this one was dangerous, and this guy had to go cut off her head without looking her in the eye."

"Kind of cowardly, you ask me," Steve said.

"True," Stony laughed. "See that house down there?" He pointed with the knife.

Steve nodded.

"It's the house where they kept your mother."

Steve took this in, and then looked up at his father. "Why are you doing this? You brought me all this way, and I can't figure out why."

Stony opened his mouth to say something, but thought better of it.

3

"I've made people die before," the boy said as they began walking towards the ruins of the Crown place. The morning sunlight slanted across the horizon and seemed to flatten the woods to their left. It was almost like the picture on the kid's back. It was almost unreal. "I've made them hurt."

The magnificent day was a good one for confessions.

"I know," Stony said nonchalantly. "It's the Moonfire."

"The what?"

"Moonfire. It's like exhaust. Those people back in Texas, where I took you. They were already dead when I came, weren't they?"

Steve nodded, a tear coming to his eye. "They called it Azriel Light. The light from the Angel of Death."

"Shit happens," Stony shrugged. "They brought it on themselves. You can't turn the key in the door of the tiger's cage and not expect that maybe now and then the tiger's gonna jump you."

When they reached the house, Steve said, "You're gonna kill me, aren't you? You brought me here . . . to kill me."

"You don't even know what you are," Stony said. "After all you know, you don't know that much."

"I know they worshiped me."

"Weaklings. Idiots. Fools," Stony nodded. "And those who weren't, like Alan Fairclough, used you. He was weak in his own way."

"I am a prophet," the boy said.

"Of what?" Stony spat, almost laughing.

"Of . . . of . . ."

"They sold you a bill of goods, kid. Truth is, you're my son, but you should never have been born."

"They told me my father was evil."

"Did they? What's evil? Hurting? Killing?"

"If killing is righteous—" the boy began, but Stony reached out his free hand and grabbed him by the shoulder.

"What do you mean by righteous killing?"

"If killing is ordained by the living god and if it flies like a lightning bolt to sinners!" the boy shouted, as if by rote.

"Then kill me." Stony shook his head. He chuckled mostly to himself, remembering the drama of childhood and how it made every kid feel like the center of his or her own universe. "Kid, you have a lot to learn about how people sometimes use you, don't you? People who claim they believe in Jesus and God and then they do really terrible things because bottom line, Steve, everybody wants to be King of the Mountain. And to be King of the Mountain, you have to kick everybody else in the ass."

Steve looked hurt. His face crumpled as if he were going to cry. They had spoiled him, those cultists. They had massaged his little growing ego until it was stunted and misshapen. *Fuck you, Alan Fairclough, for doing this.*

"They didn't use me. They loved me."

"And you loved them." Stony nodded. "I saw that old woman in the shack I got you from. What did you call her, Gramma? She take care of you when you were sad? But still, when I went in to get you, you'd already killed her. Okay, maybe it was the 'Azriel Light.' Those biblical names sure cover up a lot of sin, don't they? She hemorrhaged right there. I didn't even have to fight her. She was gone."

"Sometimes . . ." the boy said. "Sometimes it gets out."

"Yeah, it leaks, I know. I learned just like you did. Sometimes, when you do something you think is good, it leaks. You think you're healing somebody, or making the rain come down on parched land, or you—"

"You save a puppy's life. That's what I did, I saw a man beating the life out of a puppy, and I—"

"Sure, I know," Stony cut him off. "Been there. You think: If I just get him to stop, if I just make the puppy all back in one piece again, no bleeding, then maybe it won't leak this time. If I just make it so that little girl's legs aren't all twisted, it won't leak. If I just help that old man with his pain, maybe . . ." Stony let his voice trail off. "I've lived as far away from other people as I could most of my life. Just so I wouldn't let it leak."

"You said . . . you said you were from some town."

"Yeah, but when you're like us, kid, you're not from anywhere. My P.O. Box is in Winslow, Arizona. But I live up in the desert, farther out than that. Away. But even then, it's not far enough."

"How do you stop it from leaking?"

Stony squatted down in front of the boy. He held his shoulders. Tears came to his eyes without him even knowing why. He blinked them back. "Son, you can't."

4

The sign in front was no longer there, and the house itself resembled the Parthenon after the centuries and the tourists, for its columns stood, its roof had been rebuilt, the walls were still up, but it looked as if its meat had been sucked right out.

They walked in silence through the gaping hole of the front door.

A purple darkness permeated the house. Some windows were boarded up, others were still rimmed with the jagged teeth of broken glass. Rat and bird droppings were everywhere, as was trash—moldy bits of food, torn and wadded papers, something that might've been human excrement wiped across the walls as someone tried to write an indecipherable graffiti phrase. Tattered curtains fluttered like moth wings in the morning breeze. The stench was strong and rose and fell with the air.

Finally, Steve looked up at his father and grabbed his arm for comfort. "It's breathing."

Stony glanced down at him.

"The house. It's breathing."

Stony felt his skin change, and goosebumps rose along his arms just with the kid's voice. He glanced up at the ceiling, which undulated slightly. "It's her," he said. "It's like residue is still here."

"Who is she?" Steve asked.

"She is what we've come to destroy," Stony said. He hefted the thing in his left hand, the thing wadded up in newspapers. "In this unclean house. Your Great Father and the others were here. I even had a hand in it. Look—" He pointed to a corner of what had once been the living room. It dripped with some viscous liquid, like a light slow drizzle of rain.

He felt the hallway tremble slightly.

"I'll bet some Crown heir is still around, keeping track of this place, watching for omens." Stony heaved a long, drawn-out sigh. *Christ*, this was the moment he'd always dreaded, coming back to this place. "There's a chapel here. That's where we need to go."

5

*Now*! he thought, do it *now*!

When he walked in behind his son, into the darkness of the Crown chapel, Stony set the newspapers down on one of the pews. Then he reached into the pocket of his leather jacket and withdrew the handcuffs. When they clinked together, Steve turned. His face, even in the shadows of the chapel, was visible. His expression was not one of shock or fear, but of resignation. He held his hands out.

Stony got down on one knee, and looked up at his son's

face. His beautiful doomed son. The boy who should never have been brought into this world, and was not meant to be here, just as Stony should never have been born.

He handcuffed the boy's left wrist to his own right wrist.

"Bound together forever," he whispered, and touched the side of his son's face. "You and me, kid."

"I guess we're gonna kaboom?" Steve asked. "That's why you brought me."

"We have to," Stony said, reaching up to comb his son's wild hair from around his eyes.

"Is it 'cause it's evil? The Azriel Light?"

Stony thought a moment. "No. It's because it was never meant to be here. It should never have been here on earth."

"Yeah," the kid said, sighing.

"You know how different you are?"

Steve nodded slowly.

"Do you love me?"

Steve nodded again. "I always wanted a dad."

"I love you too, Steve. You are my only child. Your mother was beautiful then. She was the most wonderful and beautiful human being on the planet. You look a little like her."

"But I should never have been born," the boy said, his eyes glistening with tears. Stony could not resist. He tugged his son close to him, and hugged him hard. Perhaps the tears had all been cried out, for his eyes no longer filled with them, but he felt as if his soul were weeping, he felt as if his entire flesh and spirit cried out to the universe, *Why have you led me here? Why have you done this? What did this boy ever do to deserve this?*

He squeezed his son until he was afraid he would hurt him. When he drew back, his son's inner translucent eyelids closed over his eyes briefly, then opened. The tears were gone in him, too.

"I always thought I was some kind of alien, like from another planet," Steve half grinned, but then his face fell again, a flat line. He was resigned to this fate.

"No, you're not from another planet," Stony comforted him as best he could. "You're from me and your mother. But you were part of something terrible, like an experiment these people did. You know the Rapturists? How they used you for their beliefs? Used the Azriel Light too until it got some of them? Well, these people, that Fairclough and the Crowns, they had tried to do to others what they did to me, and to your mother and you. But it never worked. It never 'took.' It almost did sometimes, I guess. They tried it before, but . . ."

And the images came to him, images he couldn't possibly know, but they came nonetheless as if the history of what was within him showed him the attempts—the girls with their bodies burning, the boy of sixteen who caught on fire at his crotch and it spread up his belly, up to his face until he was a pillar of fire— "It didn't work, not until the rituals were used, and then all they needed was one or two, just enough to bring it into the world. Just enough to make it flesh where it was not wholly flesh before."

"What was it?" his son asked, but Stony didn't answer. He felt what the boy had said; the Crown place was breathing, and as he looked at the jagged empty eyes where the stained glass windows had been, he saw how the membrane had grown across it, a stained glass of its own, a pulsing life taking over the house, unable to die, unable to do anything but survive.

As Stony unpacked the small bomb that the mail-bomber Swink had taught him to use, the boy watched carefully. It was a cheap device, and he might've used it earlier, but he knew that he owed it to Lourdes and to their son to do this here. This earth, this place, was tainted with the past crimes against nature. This was the unholy sanctuary. To bring it back to where it had begun, just as

Fairclough's ritual had tried to do. To bring it to a cursed spot, an unclean place, a land even the natives had shunned because it was the devil's playground, it was the place of *Walks Alone*. As he brought the bomb out, careful of the wires, careful of the small timing device that would set off the spark, his son whispered, "Dad, I love you, don't do it, I don't want to hurt—"

He set the timer down. Ten minutes. That was enough time to say goodbye to the world, to his son, to what had taken over this house.

9:33

He glanced at the digital watchface, at the melting liquid that pooled around the altar of the chapel.

9:25

He heard the breathing, as of some monster, an architecture of a being, all around them, containing them.

9:00

Nine minutes, and it would be over.

Nine minutes, and then peace.

It was an eternity until the timer got to five minutes, and Stony felt as if he could no longer hold in what he'd held for so many years, over so much pain and distance.

"There must be some redemption!" he shouted at the darkness. "It can't be for all this pain! It can't be for all this nothing! There must be a purpose!" He slammed his fist down, bringing his son's hand down too, and the boy cried out as if hurt. "There must be some redemption! I don't believe that I could come this far and not find it! I did not imagine it! I know what happened here! I know what I set free!"

Then, all around them, encompassing the chapel and its shadows, a woman's voice. "I knew you would come back."

Stony turned, and saw her face for the first time in twelve years, the face that lay beneath the face, like the developing butterfly inside the pupal sac, beneath silken layers of cocoon.

A vision of a ghost of a shred of memory, and then gone.

*Lourdes.*

In less than seconds, Stony Crawford relived that night, so many years buried, so quickly resurrected in her glance.

*Comes the Halloween Man,*
*Reaping*

# Chapter Twenty-eight

## All Hallow's Eve

### 1

*Halloween night, and he is fifteen, and he watches as the nearly clear liquid pulsates along the blue and red veins within the outer covering, the thin sac, that surrounds Lourdes's body. He is weeping, unable to touch her, afraid of hurting her with that thing—that liquid environment floating around her, pulsing and flashing with red and pink and blue. When his weeping is over, the other one, the one called Diana Crown, touches him lightly on his shoulder.*

"She's more beautiful now than any human being has been since the dawn of mankind. Your son won't let her die," Diana said. Her breath was warm on his neck; he moved forward slightly to get away from it.

"What have you done?" Stony gasped, and felt as if he were choking on his own words. He could not take his eyes off Lourdes. It reminded him for a moment of Snow White, the fairy tale he'd read as a kid, sleeping in her glass coffin. That's what it was like, it was like she was sleeping under glass, or under some stream—

Diana chuckled lightly, but her voice was strangely soothing. "Nothing. It's your child inside her that does this. If you were to try to open the covering, it would kill her and the baby instantly. This keeps her safe. That's what you want, isn't it? What you—and I—have within us, you were able to pass on, to ensure our survival in this species—"

"This species? You . . . and . . . me?"

He turned to face her. He was beyond shock, beyond tears. He felt a coldness grow within, as if he were turning to stone.

Diana Crown was beautiful. Sure, he'd seen her around town in the summers, not often, but now and then while he rode his bike past her house, or saw her in town picking things up at the Package Store. Sure, she'd always been beautiful, but in a cold and not appealing way to him, but now he saw something else. Like smoldering ashes beneath the surface of her pale skin. She wore a thin white dress, opened down the front so he could see the curved edges of her breasts, her smooth whiteness—

Her eyes, pale blue and full of some inner radiance.

"Who the hell are you, anyway?" he asked, or thought he asked, but could not hear his own voice.

Her smile curved, and she seemed warm and more familiar than he wanted her to be. *It's a dream. I'm in some dream.*

"I'm your sister," she said, reaching her hand out to touch his. When she touched him, he felt a jolt of electricity. He struggled to pull away from her, but it was as if the electric current held them fast together.

Then it stopped.

And he knew.

2

She spoke inside him now, and as she spoke, the images of what she spoke of played across his mind—

*"We are half brother and sister, Stony. I was born five years earlier than you, and my mother was my flesh-and-blood mother. My father—well, this will be difficult to understand—but there's something not right in me that is right in you. I did not turn out as well as they wanted, the Crowns, but they loved me and raised me, since I was of their flesh. But I was there when you were conceived, and when you were born, Stony. It was the most beautiful act ever committed with a human being, it was a moment of triumph for those who live only in the flesh, these animals all around us. Your father—"*

*"Johnny Miracle?"*

*"Yes, he was handsome and smart and—"*

*"Johnny was smart?"*

*"The act of a human coming into contact with divine fire can destroy that human, but it did not destroy Johnny. He has a bloodline of fierceness, he was forged from the bloodline of a god older than any these humans know of to worship, the same bloodline the Crowns came from. They were originally Crowninshields, Stony, a noble family, and before that, their name was Sacrecroix, and before that it was—"*

*"You're joking. You're crazy—"* Stony gasped and in his mind he saw a thick nail being driven in by a flat rock to a man's wrist on what might've been a cross in a large and seemingly endless garden. *"Jesus Christ—"*

*"No, not Jesus Christ, Stony. Far older than that, in the fields of western France, a god that walked the granaries and gardens and all that was planted, a god who was king for a season and then was inhaled by certain men, a god that was ritually killed every season, whose blood drained into the earth—"*

313

"Stop!" Stony pressed his hands over his ears, opening his eyes to try to stop the sounds and images that came after him.

"It is only legend that says that Johnny is from the same bloodline, it is only legend that says that Johnny is the first son of the first son of the first son—going back to all the Sacrecroix—"

Scarecrow. Nora's words came back to him, the words spat across his mind. Sacrecroix, Scarecrow, Crowninshield, Crown, the lineage of the Halloween Man.

"And you, too, are the first son, Stony, and so is your child in Lourdes's belly. You are descended from the Kings of the Gods. Do you know why they call him Johnny Miracle? Do you? Do you know that he died when he was seventeen, hit by a car out on the highway? And they took him for dead, these people. They took him for dead and they buried him and he rose from the dead, he scraped his way up from the earth like a madman, and he came back to town covered with the dirt of his own grave, smiling as if none of it mattered, all his wounds seemingly healed. That was his miracle. But only his first, Stony. His second was his fertility with your mother."

"Who is my mother?"

She grinned. "Your mother and my father are the same being. There is no differentiation of sex in the realm of pure radiance. But you are finer than I am, Stony. I was not born of her womb but of the seed of her loins. You were born from within her, you were nourished from her blood, you were made flesh from that which is without flesh. I have waited so long for us to meet, to talk, Stony. I have waited so many years to truly love my brother."

3

The voice died within his head.

Diana stood there, seeming more ordinary now. The

dim light from the bedside barely illuminated the bedroom.

"It's in you, Stony," Diana said. "The reason why she won't die. It's in you. You planted the seed of greatness, of divine fire inside her. . . . She is no ordinary human now, she has been touched by the gods."

"What the fuck—" Stony said, fighting the urge within him to collapse, to wring the last ounce of strength he had left within him. "What are you talking about?"

"You are the Halloween Man, Stony. You have the bloodline within you, and your mother was—"

Stony pressed his hands to his ears to drown her out, his body shaking involuntarily, the sound of wild horses stampeding inside his head, the feeling that a crack in the world had taken hold and was growing, and all of hell was seeping from it. "*What the fuck is going on?*"

She reached up, touching the center of her forehead. "It's time, Stony. Time to take off the mask, to show who we are, to run free. The feeling you'll get will be like breathing for the first time in your life. Both of us. The rituals—"

"Rituals?"

"Rituals are the keys that unlock the many doors," she whispered, her fingernails pressing into her skin. A thin line of blood ran down from where her fingernail cut into her skin. "Fairclough knew them. He knew how to open . . ." Then she smiled, her teeth shining white. "You know, Stony, I was there when your brother stabbed her. Your girlfriend was beautiful too, with blood. He slammed it into her over a hundred times. Her blood burst out from all over her body, soaking us through, baptizing us in her—"

Stony felt something surge within him, and he brought Van's knife up. "Just shut up!"

"That's the knife," Diana said. "That's the one. Did your brother tell you how he felt when he killed her?

315

How he got aroused from it? How he felt wave after wave of—"

Stony stepped close to her, holding the knife threateningly. "Just shut up! I don't want to hear—"

Her voice within him, and the images, telling and showing him everything—

*Van slicing the knife into Lourdes's breast—*

*The look of terror, the pain, the fear as Lourdes tried to scream but the knife went into her throat—*

"No!" Stony screamed, squeezing his eyes shut, and when he opened them he had already brought the knife down into Diana's flesh.

He stared at it a moment. At his fist around the knife. *Oh my God, what the fuck is going on? What have I done? What is this?*

He looked into her eyes.

A calm flooded him, as he saw warmth and yes, even love within the blue pools of her eyes.

"You have done what you needed to do," she whispered.

Coming to his senses, he drew the knife out of her and opened his mouth to speak, but only a thin stream of air escaped his lips.

He heard a tearing as of paper, and then the sounds like liquid and mud splashing—

Diana Crown tore at the place around her heart, where the knife had come out—

A split of flesh ran from it in spiderweb patters across her flesh, up to her face, around her eyes—

She was—

*Oh God, no.*

—pulling off her skin, while splits in her face ran down the length of her chin, and then her neck, and where the openings grew—

*MOONFIRE!*

*MOONFIRE!*

*Something within him smashed like a doll, and he felt himself curling up in a fetal ball—*
DON'T WANT TO LOOK AT HER.
DON'T WANT TO SEE HER.
NOT WHAT SHE'S BECOMING.
NOT THAT.
*The nausea rose in his stomach, up to his throat, but he held it in, forced it back down—*
DON'T LOOK AT HER, IF YOU DON'T LOOK YOU WON'T SEE—
''Flesh is just a covering, it's our upholstery,'' the thing that had been Diana gibbered, as the last of the Moonfire shed the bleeding elastic skin—
*THE OUTCAST STARED AT HIM WITH EYES OF MOONFIRE.*
*What the hell are you?*
*What the hell is that?*
Her body turned to what seemed like spinning and burning molecules, thousands of tiny fireflies spiraling amongst themselves in the shape of the body of the young woman who had been . . .
Had been . . .
*Opened. Set free.*
Inside his mind, she answered him, *We are what men have only dreamed. We are touched by the divine fire, Stony, you and me. Thousands of years ago men and gods mated, but the age of magic and gods has long died, until now—until now, Stony! You are the strongest, but you don't know it, you have within that weak flesh of humanity the divine fire of other worlds! We are the first to take, and your child, growing inside her, is the future. Do not fear for her, for she feels nothing. It is like a deep sleep, and when she awakens, she will remember none of this, but she will give you a child, and that child will be of our kind—*
*They tried for decades for births, but none took. Young girls burned up from the fire, and could not conceive . . .*

317

*but then we took, you and I. . . . They thought I wouldn't make it, but I did . . . and now you, too . . . and they . . .*

Stony shouted, "Who are they?"

The creature that stood before him, fire like an aura around its form, opened its mouth and said, "The devout. The faithful. Those who believe and have been touched by it."

"By what?"

The creature's light wavered, turning blood-red, its eyes feral and sharp. "Your mother. Your real mother."

"Who is my mother?" he shouted, and as he did a strong wind broke against the window, bringing with it a small bird that broke its neck, breaking through the glass. The wind blew the window open, the curtain fluttering, and it seemed as if air was sucked out of the room as the wind thrust across and out again.

"Who is my mother!"

Then the thing that was Diana was caught on a gust of wind, and shimmered before him—

What was beneath her skin, fragile as glass stained red and yellow—like sparks, separated—

*Let your mind go, Stony. Be free. Let the Halloween Man out of his prison, the Sacrecroix, you who are most sacred, most loved of the Eternal, you are part miracle and part human and part God, rain down on them all, your torture is in the secret. Let it out, let it go—*

*You are Holy.*

Like red red poppies bursting into bloom, petals blowing—

*Humans sacrifice themselves for us, Stony. We are Gods. We are the future of life. We are Creation itself!*

—out across the night sky, like blood spattering along a sheet of wind, and then the thousands of bits of red light that had been Diana returned and glowed across the surface of the ceiling, which began dripping with droplets of crimson.

He felt fear in the back of his throat, a tickling up and down his spine as the blood spattered the top of his head.

*It's in the blood, our power, our light, it's mixed with what humans have now. We are eternal and we are mortal at the same time.*

And then Stony was no longer afraid, no longer terrified, no longer within the grasp of a nightmare.

The flesh that had contained what was inside Diana Crown fell like dust to the floor. Her skull cracked as it hit the floor, and the jaw dropped. Steam rose up from the last of her viscera.

He turned to what Lourdes had become, to the bedside, and knelt down beside her. The sweat had dried on the back of his neck. He clasped his hands in prayer and said the two or three prayers he could think of.

Above him, red sparrows flew from the ceiling, reforming across the bed from him, forming again as Diana Crown, in a vision of molten silver, an aura of yellow fire around her body. "The rituals are complete, brother. And now it's the night of the harvest. We own all of Stonehaven, and all who dwell there are meant for our pleasure."

"What the fuck are you?" he gasped.

"I am a god." She licked her shiny lips. "And I hunger for my flock."

Her metallic skin glowed red, and burst again like sparks from a fire, like fireflies, no, like burning wasps all heading to the open window. Her voice was like wasps, too, a humming of words. "Join me, brother, join me, and I will show you the the pleasures of freedom that even the gods don't know!"

Stony rose up and ran towards the swarm, but the spiraling lights flew out into the night, across the strip of water, to the village. "No! Diana!"

He heard a single scream, as of a child who has thrust his hand into a nest of yellow jackets.

319

4

He prayed to Lourdes, *I am not going to let them hurt you. I know you can hear me, Lourdes. I love you. God, I love you more than anything. You, me, and our baby will get out of this somehow. Somehow* ...

Then he began to hear more screams, echoing across the water, coming from the village.

He reached out and touched the shimmering edge of the sac across Lourdes's face. A thin ripple, like gelatin, ran across its surface. Her eyes opened, blank, staring out into the watery nothing surrounding her.

*It's protecting her.*

"Lourdes, I'm so sorry. I need to go. I need to go find help. Somehow ..." Stony wasn't even sure where to go for help, who to turn to. He thought about the cop from Mystic, but it was too far. Part of him wanted to run off into the woods and just hide. He thought of Nora, wondering if she could help—but how? How can you fight a nightmare? How can you stop what Diana had become?

And then his own voice within him told him:

*You are the Halloween Man.*

*Remember the story.*

*Remember what he did.*

*The story wasn't everything, was it? The story wasn't about Imp killing children, or about crucifying an evil man. The story was not about revenge, even though that's how Nora told it.*

*No, the story was told to prepare you for something.*

*The Halloween Man ... Sacrecroix ... the bloodline ... Sacred. Holy.*

*The story went that they killed Imp, and buried him. But he rose from the dead, with a greater power within him. And he went on a bloody rampage.*

*Or did he?*

*Perhaps what the Crowninshields were, and what the*

Randalls, and all the other old families in the village
were—

—*was evil.*

And the Halloween Man stopped their evil once. They
had found ways to revive it, they had found some great
secret for their evil, their beliefs, some way to bring a
supernature into Diana, into him, too.

Nora's words in his head:

"*The Halloween Man . . . He's thousands of years old.
He's the King that's been killed and his blood makes
things grow. He's the Magic One. He's the Halloween
Man. You got to understand that everything we know now
is as under a layer of dust. But one day, each one of us
sees clearly. . . .*

"As the sun rose, people came from their houses . . .
even those who did not leave their houses could see the
terrible handiwork of the Halloween Man:

"*Strung like pigs, by their legs, twelve men and women
from the village, their throats slit, their blood dripping
down, strung from two great oak trees, the ground soaked
with their blood. And between the trees, a great cross had
been erected, and on it, nailed with spikes, Old Man
Crowninshield—his eyes and mouth sewn horribly shut,
and his nightshirt torn open.*

"*On his chest, the words:*

"*I CAME TO SAVE YOU*

" *. . . And it took one of my own people to do the work
that would seal the Old One into that flesh until it returned to the damp earth and slept again. . . .*"

"I've got to find Nora," he said aloud.

*All this time she's been trying to tell me who I am, to
warn me.*

5

Gerald and Angie Crawford were at it again, fighting like
cats, unaware that if they had but moved from the kitchen

into the living room, or even the narrow hallway, up the stairs, they would've seen the blood on the carpet and on the floor, and upstairs they would've found their dead and mangled son, Van. But instead, Angie was shouting at Gerald, who stank of fish, whiskey, and another woman's perfume; while Gerald was shouting at Angie because supper was late and the house stank and where the hell were the goddamned kids anyway. When the kitchen window burst wide, glass flying, what Angie thought at first was a meteor brushed past her face, burning her skin slightly.

Angie looked at Gerald, and he at her. Their eyes were wide, but Gerald's took on a suspicious aspect as if he were about to blame her for this meteoric intrusion as well as everything else.

The fiery ball burst upward in a column, and when Angie stared at it long enough—surely minutes went by, she told herself, surely it's hypnotizing me in some way—she felt as if the room were spinning. She heard Gerald shouting from across the room, but the beautiful fire branched out like a tree and suddenly she was not in her house at all, but shot back nearly twenty years to when she worked her night shift at the Crowns', checking to make sure old Mrs. Crown had her oxygen on right, taking her blood for tests, massaging her legs when they swelled up too much. Angie turned, and there was little Diana Crown, not more than three years old, a smear of blood on her face.

"What happened to you, dear?" Angie asked.

Diana, looking like the most perfectly made little girl doll in the world, looked up at her with those innocent eyes and said, "I just drank blood from Father Jim. He let me."

Angie stared at her, wondering if she should smile or laugh at the little girl's joke.

And then, behind Diana, Mr. Crown stood, dressed in a dark suit. "Hello, Angela," he said, nodding. Then he grabbed Diana's arm. "Come on, little moppet, we have to go to the ceremony."

"Someone getting married?" Angie asked.

Angie heard a strangled sound from poor old Mrs. Crown from the bed, and she turned to look and see what was wrong.

Mrs. Crown, who could no longer speak, opened her mouth slightly, and it reminded Angie of a fish pulled out of the water. Her eyes went wide with some kind of terror.

Angie was sure that Mrs. Crown was mouthing the words *Kill me.*

Then this vision memory from the past burst into fire, as Angie heard Gerald screaming, and she was back in her kitchen, and red and yellow hornets circled around her husband, moving so fast it almost made him look like he was bound up by lasers spinning around him.

Then he burst into flames, running to her, falling against her, tearing her flesh apart with his burning fingers and teeth.

She fought him off as best she could, but the fire ran all around her, slicing into her, and when her eyes melted from the heat, she tasted the red-hot coal of death.

What had been Diana, now Azriel Light, burned across the house, and from that house, burned across the grass to others, dancing wildly as rain began falling from the sky.

As the light singed the doors and melted windows, screams along the village rose in the night, and strangely enough, as the sounds carried across the water to Mystic and Stonington and other boroughs and towns along the coast, the screams took on the quality of hymns, as if an entire town were somewhere in the distance singing the praises of the Lord.

6

Stony went and looked down upon Lourdes, whose eyes fluttered open and closed as if some invisible current pushed her eyelids back and forth.

"I love you, Lourdes. Somehow I'll make sure you're safe. I promise."

Then he ran as fast as he could, out of the bedroom, down the stairs. He thought he heard some kind of singing—but how could there be singing?—from another end of the mansion, but he didn't stick around to find out. He ran out onto the porch, down the steps, and into his mother's car. Starting it up, he drove down the gravel road.

To his left, he saw what looked like houses burning out along Land's End, but he didn't care, he didn't give a damn about what happened to anyone—

All he cared about was Lourdes. Lourdes and why.

Someone had to tell him the why.

7

Nora's shack was dark and silent. He pushed through the front door, out of breath, and quickly grabbed one of her long matches, lighting the candle near the front door. When the feeble light came up, he carried it around to her bed and work area, but she was not there.

But there, on the small table next to her bed, a note she'd begun, and then left off in mid sentence. In a scribbled handwriting, the best that Nora had ever been able to do, owing to her blindness:

Stony,

Forgive me. I wanted to

He set the candle down on the note.

He was beyond any feeling, as his mind seemed to push down on itself.

After a minute, he left the shack, walking on foot through the dark woods, back to the station wagon.

The screams from the village grew louder, and he knew that the thing that had been freed from Diana's skin was taking its harvest from the village, and he cared less than he ever thought he would care about anything in all his life.

He longed for sleep, and even death.

Even death would be a relief now.

*But Lourdes.*

*Your baby, too.*

*I just want to die.*

He heard the wind push Nora's door closed, and then open again. He turned at the sound, and the candle went out in the breeze. Silhouetted against the moonlight, in the doorway, a stranger.

"Stony," the man said from the doorway, his accent clearly British. "Let's go. It's time for you to know who you are." Then, "She needs you. Lourdes needs you. She won't survive without you being there."

As if this were the most normal thing in the world to say, the man added, "Look, it's starting to rain. A storm is coming from out at sea. Let's go, Stony. It's time for you to meet your mother."

8

Clouds gathered around the enormous harvest moon, and the scraggly trees grasped at its light. They walked along the old path, alongside the bogs, through the woods. The rain trickled down, the wind died for a brief while.

Stony felt a great heaviness grow within himself. His urge to run had long passed; his urge to die was still there within him. Lourdes—his only thought. He would go back, and he would get her out of that place, that mad-house, this nightmare. He could not leave her there. . . .

The stranger walking beside him might've been fifty,

325

thin, his hair silver and cut short, dressed in a white shirt that had mottled dark stains across it—the moonlight seemed to make him glow as if he were absorbing the night. "I know this all must be a shock. We should've prepared you better—"

"Who are you?" Stony asked with no interest in his voice. He glanced down the dark trail, watching the way the moonlight jagged along the tree trunks and branches.

"Alan Fairclough. I am the—"

"I don't give a fuck." Stony kept walking slightly ahead of him.

"One day you will. Part of the ritual was not preparing you. If we had, you might not have mixed with us. You might not have created a child. Do you know what that means?"

"You one of the devil's own, too?"

Alan Fairclough didn't answer until they'd reached the edge of the woods, with the Crown mansion ahead of them. Several cars were parked in the driveway now, and the house was completely lit, its outside lights glaring. The wind picked up, and the rain began to come down faster.

"Are you Satanists?" Stony asked, knowing that there probably were such things, but even when he asked it, he doubted any worshiper of Satan could be this terrible. He doubted anyone could be as evil as the people who had been inside this house.

"We're not of any devil," Fairclough said. "You and your sister are part of something that will change the destiny of humanity. It will probably save us, too. Our future, anyway. There was the Age of the Father, and then the Age of the Son. Now, Stony, it is the time of the Holy Spirit. It is the fire from heaven that comes among us."

"Why did you do this to Lourdes?"

"I didn't. It was your child growing in her that did it. If it makes any difference, the child has also protected her from death. You believe, don't you?"

Something went calm inside Stony. "Yes."

"She's beyond any hurting. She's in a beautiful dream, and when she wakes, she'll be holding your child in her arms."

"This is all crazy—" Stony said.

"You know deep inside it isn't. Part of you knows that what your sister told you is true. You've never felt like part of the world, not like other boys did. You've always felt separate."

Stony kept his mind's eye on Lourdes's face. "My brother said he killed her."

"He thought he did!" Fairclough shouted, raising his fists to the wind and rain like a madman. His voice became like a storm, as he cried out against the night, as the clouds covered the brilliant moon until a harsh gray shadow covered the earth. "It's the beauty of it! It was a ritual, Stony! Rituals of sacrifice are nothing new, and after every sacrifice, a rebirth! Lourdes was reborn as the mother of your child the moment that your brother thought he had taken her life away. It was proof of your son's divinity. If he'd been purely flesh, they both would've died, but they didn't, he wasn't, and his life created protection for his mother."

Stony took a long slow breath. "She doesn't hurt?"

"Not one bit."

More screams carried on the growing wind.

"What's that? More tricks?" Stony asked.

The man shook his head. "No. It's Diana. She's on a rampage through the village. No one can stop her, not once she found release from flesh. She is like a ravening wolf among a flock of young lambs. She's not like you, Stony. They didn't know the rituals when she was born. They didn't know how to make the sacrifices. She is the shadow of what you are. The Azriel Light within her is darkened—"

"Cut the bullshit."

Fairclough turned to Stony, and his grin seemed enormous in the shadowy light from the house. Then he slammed his fist into the side of Stony's face. Stony felt as if he were flying across the gravel, and when he fell, stinging pains blistered along his back and arms. Fairclough went over and lifted him up, kissing him on the forehead. Stony struggled to pull away, but Fairclough had a strong grip. Stony hawked a loogie as hard as he could, hitting the man right between the eyes. Fairclough looked deep into Stony's eyes and whispered, "I am the one who set the ritual at your conception. I am the one who coaxed your mother into a form for taking the seed of Johnny Miracle and carrying you for nearly eight months. If you wish to despise someone, despise the woman who raised you, whose silence was bought cheap. Do not fuck with me, little god, for I know the ancient words, I have the knowledge, I have gone through the portals of Hell and the smashed gates of Heaven just to bring you into this world. I have smashed the brains from boys twice your size. You have a power within you, but you are still made of flesh and blood, and I know a hundred ways to make boys like you suffer for their insolence." Alan Fairclough set Stony down again, pushing him forward. Stony glanced back. Fairclough's face was pale and shiny, like a worm's, in the house lights. The man gestured forward. "Go, boy. You want to protect your girl, your baby, you want to know the mystery of all of what you are? It's in there. I can show you. Mankind is dying out, you can see it, you can feel it everywhere. We've lost touch with the divine spark, the fire of creation, ancient savagery. We have lost it, we are destroying all that is fertile. Men used to walk with gods, Stony. Men used to sacrifice to the Almighty. Abraham took his son Isaac to be sacrificed to God. He did, in fact, did you know that? But the words were changed to make it all nice and sweet so that God was no longer a force of the cosmos, but merely a nice father sitting in the clouds. When the Age of the Son began, we put ourselves higher

than the Divine, we set ourselves up as gods. That is unnatural. That is blasphemy. No, man is doomed as a species, but you, and your progeny . . . What I did—what I
did with the Crowns, with what they sheltered—what I
did was I brought the rituals, I brought the means of com-
munication with the Divine. We midwifed the gods when
we brought you into this world, and through you and your
children, slowly, over time, mankind will be saved. Diana,
she was brought forth in ignorance. These Crown people,'' he said with contempt, ''they have no respect for
the rituals, they think they're all just so much ancient
history, but there's a reason that religion, in all its forms,
exists, Stony, it exists to create a bridge to the gods, to
God, to the divine fire—the ritual is the way of controlling
the power rather than just setting it loose upon the
world—''

The screams from the village continued unabated.

''Listen,'' Alan Fairclough said, cocking his head to
the side. ''That is what she is. She is like electricity without a wire to conduct its flow. Her fire leaps from tree to
tree, house to house, a wild talent of the gods, but without
control, without conscience. But you, you were born with
the rituals, with the respect for the power, with the old
words and keys.''

''I don't know anything,'' Stony said, now crying, not
wanting to, feeling such great pain within him, such agony, as if his bones longed to push outward from his flesh,
as if his blood wished to burst from its veins and arter-
ies—

''Ah, but you do not know what you know,'' Alan Fairclough said. He threw his head back, opened his mouth,
and began ki-yiing like a wild dog, and through the howling sound, crazy words. ''Ya thaeia nue pari sothga,'' he
sang into the rain. Stony's ears began ringing as the words
were intoned.

''Within you, they mean things. They are the language
of your spirit.''

"No!" Stony shouted, thinking he might run, thinking—he had the knife, he still had the knife, thrust into his belt, he could draw it out—

Fairclough pushed him towards the driveway, almost making his knees buckle. In the driveway, so many cars, as if they'd begun a party inside the mansion. Stony recognized some of them—the Glastonburys' Volvo, Mrs. Doane's Buick Skylark, Tamara Curry's Subaru—what were they all doing here? Why? Fairclough's voice softened to an insinuating whisper as they stepped up on the porch. His words came out rapid-fire, spittle flying from his mouth as he declaimed, "All Hallows', Stony. This isn't just happening by chance. This is the harvest from the ancient days. It is the rite of passage for you. This is the night when gods may walk with humans. It's the space between the two worlds. The birth of Christ was not in December, Stony. And it wasn't in midsummer, as many scholars seem to think. No, it was at the end of the harvest, and across thousands of miles, harvest kings like your Crown ancestors were being cut down with scythes in fields and resurrected within days at the same time the Nazarene cried from the cave in which his mother gave birth. Gods are never born in grand palaces, they are born in stone, they are cracked like egg yolks from the shell of rock, from the earth, from the place which is both beneath our feet and controls our lives. And she is at the heart of it. She is growing stronger after centuries of weakness in her captivity."

"Diana?" Stony asked, entering the foyer, glancing briefly up the stairs, wanting to see Lourdes so badly, to hold her, to never let go of her.

"Not your sister," Fairclough said, coming up behind him. "Your mother."

# *Chapter Twenty-nine*

# *Mother*

### 1

"In there." Alan Fairclough nodded to the open door of
the chapel. Over the arched doorway, Stony read the
words, *Bless the Fruit of her Womb.* The door was open,
and the sound of voices singing died almost immediately.
The chapel was lit with dozens of candles. The smell of
a dead animal permeated the place, mingling with the
thick smoke from a powerful incense. The walls within
the chapel were carved from rock, and the effect was of
a cave that had been transformed into a small church.
Great stained glass window light mixed brilliantly with
the candlelight within and the flashes of distant lightning
without, the saints and the Virgin and the crucifixion and
many martyrdoms, all arranged in beautiful colors. It was
not that much different from the main section of Our
Lady, Star of the Sea, only on a smaller scale.

Stony saw a lamb, its throat cut, on the great stone slab
of the altar.

The candles were tall and thin, and Stony had never seen so many in one place. When he looked at all of them, thrust along the stone wall, among the stained glass windows, on small holders at each of the pews, something about the candles themselves seemed to tell him something.

*(But they're tall and white and old-fashioned, and you only know one person who makes them like that.)*

The chapel was full of people, some of whom he recognized as he passed, others he did not know. Martha Wight was there, and Tamara Curry, her breasts bulging under a low-cut dress, a fat gold cross hanging atop her mounds; Father Jim nodded to him, a half smile on his face, his hand held out as if for a handshake, which Stony declined; Butch Railsback the butcher and Fiona McAllister from the library sat side by side; others, too, and then strangers, all dressed as if for church in their Sunday best, suits, ties, some of the women wore hats, and a few of the older women wore white gloves as well.

Stony laughed when he saw his friend Jack Ridley, his best friend growing up, the friend who had shared all his secrets, or so Stony had thought. Jack winked. "I knew you'd understand," Jack said, somewhat nervously. "It was all ordained from—"

"Fuck you, traitor," Stony said, shaking his head. He reached into his belt, drawing the knife out.

Stony held the hunting knife up, vaguely threatening in case anyone tried anything, but they just sat quietly watching him. Not as much fear in their eyes as he'd been hoping. Not as much fear as he himself was beginning to feel all over again.

Alan Fairclough stayed behind him until he reached the foot of the altar. Then he went around Stony, beckoning with his hand.

Stony shivered now, knowing that no matter what happened to him, the knife would not defend him if these insane people leapt up and attacked him.

As he approached the altar, the dead animal across it, he remembered Nora's story about coming here. About being shown this.

About seeing the thing in the long metal box.

And there it was.

## 2

A dark metal box, jewels embedded along its lid. The outline of what looked like a Renaissance angel crudely battered along it, a round halo surrounding its flowing hair. It was the size of a small coffin, with slatlike windows in its sides and a reddish glow as if of burning metal from within.

Alan Fairclough went and stood behind the altar.

"You have something trapped inside there?" Stony whispered, unsure what he was feeling.

"Not trapped. It contains the divine fire."

"What is it?"

Then Alan Fairclough brought Stony's hand to the top of the box. It was warm. "It is her. Your mother."

"How?" Stony trembled.

"Let her out. You can. You alone, her son, can let her out."

"But . . . I don't understand . . . I don't . . ."

"She is the Great Mother who searches the world for her children," Fairclough said, and his words took on a quality of chanting. "She is the Eternal Mother, she lost her daughter to the Underworld, Her son, Her son is come amongst us."

"Her son has come amongst us," the people in the congregation whispered.

"Come amongst us to bring new light to a dying earth," Fairclough intoned.

"To bring new light to a dying earth," the people whispered.

Then Alan Fairclough opened the cage, and Stony saw

the dazzling light that was like a blue and yellow fire in the shape of a body, and wings—

*An angel?*

*She's an angel?*

her eyes were large and warm

and full of some pity

as if a terrible sorrow had overtaken her

as if she looked upon him with a knowledge of loss to come

She reached her burning arms out to him, and they dissipated into thousands of points of light spinning in the air, surrounding him, covering him like fireflies. They were hot and his body erupted with sweat, but she didn't hurt—

*MOONFIRE!*

He felt her embracing him, all over, within the light, within the warmth that was her fire—

and words from another language whispered in his ears,

words he understood as if it were the language of his dreams—

Others saw Jesus, or a great white-bearded figure, or a cosmic kaleidoscope, and the congregation rose up as one and began singing hymns, speaking in tongues, shouting hallelujahs to the creature that surrounded Stony.

3

"My son," she said. "I love you so much. I love you so much, and I weep for you."

*But who are you?*

*What are you?*

The light that encompassed him shimmered, and thickened so that he could see nothing but light, and within the light—

*What are you? Are you an angel? A god?*

And then the laughter began, not the laughter of the

sweet mother's voice he'd heard but something terrifying, like the growl of a wolf in the dark or—

*Other*, the voice came back, a deep growl. *Just say that I'm Other than you. That I'm something that has been held in stone, something that once walked freely, and these . . . these humans . . . centuries ago*—

And the light became pictures, moving, and Stony saw:

*Perhaps fifty young children screaming, tied together with thick ropes, while several men pushed an an enormous rock over the mouth of a cave. With the ensuing darkness, a buzzing sound, and then a light, and then thousands of black flies flew from among the rocks, into the children's faces, into their mouths, their eyes, eating at their skin while they screamed*—

"I have been called the Lord of Flies," the voice said.

*The men outside the cavern, dressed in little other than animal skins, covering their ears while the children screamed*—

*And then the Holy Sisters inside the cavern, blessing and consecrating the cavern and the creature that moved beneath them in a dark pit*—

"I have been called the Eternal Enemy," the voice whispered in Stony's ear.

*You're the devil?* Stony tried to speak but his mouth wouldn't open.

"No, I am none of these names, I am the Mother of all Life and I am its taker, I am the Father of Dreams and Nightmares, and I am the source of all that breathes—" and the voice was like lions roaring in his ears. "I was in the Garden when man and woman were created, not in flesh, but as bacteria and fungi, a flesh born of decay which must return to it. I was superior to all that lives in the flesh then. I still am. And you are my son."

*Are you God?*

Again, the laughter, only now it seemed like the laughter of a thousand children.

*I am that I am,* the voice said. *And you are my son.*

Then she stood before him, and the awe he felt made his entire being shudder.

At first it seemed to be the statue of the Virgin from Our Lady, Star of the Sea, but its flesh burned with life, and her eyes were warm with red blood.

"Good and evil are within my glance," she whispered, red tears flowing from her eyes. "Do not judge either, for life is made up of All. Men and children shall live and die, but my power—our power—comes from the source of all creation."

And within this vision, he saw others:

*A demon from hell with a great wingspan like a dragon's—*

*A creature with a human face but with stag's antlers on his thick-haired scalp and deer's legs—*

*A beautiful woman with hair piled high, naked, three rows of breasts along her torso—*

*Another woman in her place with many arms and legs moving swiftly, a necklace of skulls around her neck, a curved blade in her hand—*

*A lovely man wearing flowing white robes and great swanlike wings settling behind his golden hair—*

*I am the image of all that men have worshiped, but I am unknown to man—*

Then, the Virgin Mary stood before him, in blue robes, her eyes doelike, her lips full and gently curved upwards—then this even split into infinitesimal bits of light.

"Do not be afraid of what you have within you, my son. They fear it, because they fear death, but you need never fear death."

"What about the others?"

"Others?" the being asked, the light wavering.

"Those we love?"

Again the laughter. "I gave birth to you, my son, so that you would raise a generation against those who have kept your mother prisoner for so long."

"How do they keep you?"

"With the metal, the rock from the caverns, with the rituals passed from ancient sorcerors, with what little magic men have."

"But if you're all-powerful—" Stony said.

The light flashed red and then a deep blue.

Then Stony whispered, almost to himself. "You're not a god. You're just some creature. You're something . . . something that doesn't belong here. Something that should never have existed."

Again, the Virgin Mary stood before him, her tears of blood coursing down her beautiful face. She reached out to him, her palm upturned. "I am and have always been. As you too shall be."

And then Stony felt a swift pull on his flesh, as if a giant vacuum was sucking at his pores, and the light whooshed by him in the wind, shooting upwards and then down again.

And there at the chapel, in the candlelight, Alan Fairclough stood beside him.

And the creature of burning light, the shape of the beautiful woman, leaned over the dead sheep and began licking the blood from its neck.

4

Alan Fairclough reached out to him. "Stony, we did this for all of mankind."

"It's a monster," Stony spat. "It's a goddamned monster. And you—you and the Crowns have been *feeding* it."

"No," Fairclough said. "It's a goddess. It's the Mother Goddess. It's an Angel from Heaven."

The creature licked its flaming lips as it wolfed down parts of the sheep's throat.

"Don't you see what it's doing?" Stony said.

337

Fairclough nodded, smiling. "I see the Divine Fire accepting our sacrifice."

"It's some kind of monster, and you're breeding it, for God's sake, you made me part of it! All of you!" Stony turned towards the congregation, and without wanting to, felt that surge of energy, of some inner fire that he could no longer hold back. He shouted at the top of his lungs, "You used me to make a son, you used Johnny Miracle to make this cave-dwelling monster breed! You're bringing it into the flesh when it's just been a vision, a fire. It's an element, not God—you damn evil—"

And then he saw her, at the back of the chapel.

Nora, standing behind the last pew.

"Oh shit," he gasped. "Not you, Nora. You aren't one of these—"

He walked slowly, carefully down the middle aisle between the pews, as the faithful turned to watch.

5

"You're not one of them," he said coldly, as he approached her. "Tell me you're not one of them."

Nora was silent.

He held her face in his hand, raising her chin slightly so that he was looking down into the milky white of her eyes.

"They brought the devil with them. I told you," she whispered softly. "But I've always hoped it was an angel from God."

"It's not the devil. It's no angel either."

Nora attempted a grin, but it grew faint. "I could never fight them, Stony. I tried. But I couldn't. From the moment you were born—"

"No more lies, Nora. No more spins. No more tales."

"Please forgive me, baby. Please forgive me. I should have told you before, but you weren't ready. You weren't strong . . . even now I'm not sure. You're so young."

He cupped his hand against her cheek, her tears dampening his fingers. "I can give you something now. You know that."

"Don't," she said.

"I can do it. I can feel it now. I guess I could've done it before, but it—"

"Hadn't been awakened," she finished the sentence for him. "I know. Some things are not meant to be awakened within us. Don't—"

Then he pressed his thumbs lightly against her eyes, barely touching her eyeballs.

"No," she murmured, "If that part of you wakes up—"

But it was too late.

It felt like he held a rose, a small rose, a rosebud so tiny and pink in his hand that when it broke open, he felt the warmth of creation—

Her eyes, cinnamon, looked up at him.

"The blind shall see," he said, remembering a line from Sunday School.

6

"Stony," she whispered, seeing him for the first time, seeing the face she had loved like her own child all the while he'd been growing up. She reached over and touched the edges of his face.

7

He felt a prickle of heat run along his skin; then a series of sparks where her fingers touched him.

Her eyes grew wide with terror, as if the first thing she could see after all these years was a horror greater than anyone would want to see.

A rushing sound filled his ears, as of the beating of thousands of wings—

"You've let it out," she gasped, drawing back from him as if from a fire. "It's the light of creation. You can't let it—"

Her body slammed back against the wall, her arms splayed as if some great invisible pressure forced her into that position. "You let it out! Stony!" she cried, but the wind that had pressed her like an insect to the wall stopped up her breath. "That's why it gave birth to you! That's why! It had to travel through you!"

"No!" he shouted, but the very force that grew from him held him back. "Nora! No!"

"It was waiting for you to do this! It needs your miracles! You let it out! Stony! No! You have to put it back—" She screamed, and then the tears from her newly born eyes turned to fire, running like lava down her face, devouring her features in its wake.

Nora's face steamed with the growing heat, and he knew just looking at her that she was trying to be brave, maybe for him, maybe for those who watched. Trying to fight back the pain.

*Oh please let me take it back*, he prayed. *Please.*

And then, she was a fountain of blood.

8

Where she had stood moments ago, a mass of pulp and blood and bone. He couldn't look at it anymore, nor could he weep, nor could he think clearly. Was he shivering still? He couldn't tell. The world shivered. Covered in her blood, he turned towards the congregation.

"A miracle!" Tamara Curry shouted, pointing back towards the altar. "The Angel of God has given us a sign!"

At the altar, the creature of light had shifted, and had become a handsome angel, wearing a great white robe, with a wingspan that covered most of the altar. The golden light burst from it like the dawn.

Stony held his hands up as he stepped forward up the aisle. His eyes were dark, the blood matted in his hair.

Alan Fairclough cried out, "The miracles of the Living God! Praise his Name!"

"His name is Glorious!" the congregation shouted.

"You're worshiping a monster!" Stony shouted.

The angel of light shifted again, and the Mother Goddess stood at the steps of the stone altar, a crescent moon upon her golden hair, a blue robe covering her pale skin. Her hand was raised in a gesture of supplication.

But Stony saw the blood on her lips.

And the lamb on the altar—something was wrong—he couldn't see it well, his eyes went in and out of focus.

It was no lamb at all.

*It was his brother Van's body, laid down, eviscerated, opened, fed upon.*

The monster had already eaten the eyes from their sockets, and his nose had been gnawed upon. His throat was a bright red gash.

*But they can't see it*, he thought. *They can't see what it's done. All they see is a goddess or an angel. All they see is the energy they give it.*

*They probably didn't even see Nora's body when it burst. They don't know what it has done.*

9

He feels a wind go through him, a wind of light, a wind of darkness, and he's running, running towards the very thing that will kill him, the very thing that brought him into this world, but he doesn't care, for he thinks of Lourdes and his unborn child and all the fools who have been destroyed and distracted, putting their faith into such as this—

341

## 10

"You bitch!" he shouted as he approached the creature. "You fucking breeding bitch with your magic and your light."

As he reached her, he slammed his hand into her—

And his hand swarmed with the thousands of fireflies.

"They keep you in a box because they own you," he whispered. "They raped you to have children. You aren't powerful. You're just energy. You're just—"

The howling of wolves filled his ears, then the sound of locusts as millions teemed overhead, and the burning light rose up from where the creature had stood and hovered.

A whisper in his ear:

*But she was right, Stony. I needed you to let me out, to set me free—*

*Your sister couldn't do it, she was made wrong, she was not formed as well as you, she was not of the flesh in as many ways as you are—*

*But you, my child,*

*You are the embodiment of my radiance, and now you're making a child to be the New Adam for the world of Earth, so that we may walk again as gods in the light of day, in the dark of night—*

*Let me show you the wonders of the gods—*

And then the light split apart and swooped down upon the people in the pews and the cries were so loud that Stony's ears began bleeding before he had even turned around to behold the terrors.

Warm rain fell from the ceiling of the chapel, and as it fell, Stony looked up and saw the light holding them, holding the villagers. Tamara was screaming, trying to grasp the stone walls, and Martha smashed her fists against her breasts in agony, and Father Jim, his hands clasped in prayer as he floated just beneath the ceiling—

the invisible pincers tore at them—all who had come to worship their demon god, flying above, their skin being ripped open with lasers, their blood pouring down upon the chapel floor.

*It rains blood, son, and power is in the blood—*

*They trap their power within flesh, but will shall release them from that cage*—his mother watched from beneath her encompassing light, whispering fondly to him as if he would enjoy the carnage.

Another whisper, not from his mother, but as if Nora were there, inside him, a whisper of strength—

*"The power is in the blood, Stony, the strength is in the blood, remember. . . ."*

And then her voice died within him, and he no longer cared if he lived or died. In a flash of lightning, the chapel returned to candlelit silence. The villagers were gone. Alan Fairclough, reciting some words silently to himself, stood alone at the altar.

The creature, all burning with radiance, crouched upon the altar like a harpy, her leathery wingspan wide. She began cleaning her face like a cat.

All along the ceiling, their bodies were strung across what looked like razor wire, their torsos ripped open, their eyes torn out.

"Why do you bring me to witness this?" he asked.

But the creature at the altar dissolved again into shimmering light.

# *Chapter Thirty*

# *The Stone Cage*

1

After several minutes, Stony turned and left the chapel. He walked back through the long corridor, to the open front door. He looked out across the driveway to the woods, and above, the night sky. The rain poured, and seemed the only thing that would wash away the blood and the terror. He stepped out into the storm.

Closed his eyes.

Wished it all away.

Opened his eyes, and it was still there.

He dropped to his knees. Clasped his hands together in prayer.

*Please God, help me stop this. Help it end. It's not the way it's supposed to be here.*

2

The Moonfire is his one weakness.

But when he is burned with it he uses its energy and destroys the Outcast—

The words came to him, remembering the Storm King of his favorite comic book. Moonfire.

*The divine fire. Within me.*

It was in his mind—a new myth for the Storm King—a way of fighting that had not been imagined before by him. A way of drawing strength from the very thing that burned away who Stony Crawford was—

I AM THE HALLOWEEN MAN!

And in that second, he knew why Nora had told him the story of the slaughter on Halloween night so many years ago—

She was telling him that he could fight this.

She had warned him that he was enough, that the Halloween Man was not the evil one, but the force of the god in the flesh, the real power.

He had already let it out. But he was the power. He was the one with the power. That thing at the altar was weak. It was trapped, it was held. Only he could let its power go free. . . .

*Inside me. Moonfire.*

Stony closed his eyes, and brought the hunting knife up to his chest.

*It won't hurt if you're fast.*

*If you believe, you can do this. You can do anything.*

He remembered the strange smile on Diana's lips when the knife went into her. She wanted to be released. She wanted out.

Do not fear death, the creature that was his mother had warned.

The blade went in deep, and the pain was ice-cold, and

spread like broken glass through his veins, through his flesh.

### 3

He opens his eyes and watches the fire—

The Moonfire bursts and crackles along the edge of his skin—his skin blackens—burning—the Pain, oh please God don't make it hurt so much—He doesn't resist—he lets the power come out completely, destroying the flesh that was Stony Crawford—like molten lava—

Destroy my weakness!

Destroy this cage of flesh!

### 4

His consciousness lay within the stream of fire as it pissed down his pant legs, down to the ground. The burning sap formed a pool beneath the blackened body of a boy of fifteen.

Then it re-formed again, bursting up from the ground in a tower of flame.

For a moment, he looked back at the body of who he had been.

Seared flesh, a mouth that lolled open, empty sockets where the eyes had melted . . .

*Now, bring me back, bring me a new skin.*

*A new skin to cover the Moonfire.*

*Stronger flesh than human flesh, armor against my mother.*

He felt the change within his form, as if his consciousness alone could determine what shape his physical body would be. It hurt, it felt like small slivers of glass being shoved into nerve endings, and if he'd had a mouth, he would have been screaming—

But as terrible as the pain was, it brought a numbing with it that was like ice.

And then he'd formed the flesh around himself again.
He was Stony.
He felt his own true power, the power of one who had
died and been reborn, as much a god as any man had ever
been.

5

*I'm sorry, Lourdes. I'm sorry, my baby boy. I'm sorry,
Nora. I wish I had never been born.*
As much as something within him told him to escape,
he turned around and walked back to the chapel.

6

Inside, all was silent. The candles were extinguished.
Alan Fairclough stood alone by the savaged corpse that
lay upon the altar. Hanging from the low rafters, the torn-
open bodies of people from the village that Stony had
known since as far back as he could remember.
"You must accept that these people were meant to
die," he said.
"Just shut up, you freak," Stony said, walking up to
the altar. "It's like exhaust, isn't it? I gave Nora her eyes,
but something worse comes out afterwards. I make something good happen, but something terrible comes from it."
Alan Fairclough said nothing.
The fire creature glimmered from within the metal coffin behind the altar.
"You have to ask yourself," Stony said, "why would
it let itself be kept in a coffin made of what—lead?—
from the very cave it had been trapped within for hundreds of years? Why would it wreak this small amount of
havoc, harvest these sacrifices, play into your fucked-up
sense of religion if it had all this power?"
"We cannot question the gods," Fairclough said.
"I can. I'm the son of this thing. I can question any

fucking thing I want,'' Stony laughed. ''How could a creature with unlimited power be tamed by human beings, and kept in dark stone and in—this chapel, what is it made of? I'd guess the same rock as the rock from those caves, am I right?''

Fairclough nodded.

''You think this is really an angel from heaven, don't you?'' Stony asked.

Alan Fairclough nodded. ''As much of an angel as there can be. As much of a god as has ever existed.''

''You'd think an angel would want to return to God.'' Stony shook his head, smiling. ''But not this one. This one likes to be kept in the dark, kept away from heaven, away from most anything but the few sad people who worship it.''

''There were others, I have the fossilized remains of its—'' Fairclough began, but when Stony shot him a mean look, he kept quiet.

''I don't want to hear any more of your crap. You don't mind that all these people died, and died horribly, do you?''

Fairclough shrugged. ''Human beings die.''

''I could kill you.''

''I know.''

''You don't care?''

''I don't love life over all things, no.''

Stony went around and looked at the metal coffin. ''Sort of like a vampire, huh? Comes out to drink blood and goes back in to snooze.'' The fire flickered from within the small windows. ''I think I know something about this thing now. I think I know a little bit about my mother. I think I know what she's afraid of. I was afraid of it, too, but I don't have to be. I'm solid. I'm flesh. I even killed myself out there, but I re-formed. I can't be killed. But unlike her, I can't float away, either, I'm going to forever be flesh and this creature all in one. But not her. She's just that fire. She's form without flesh. She's got to be afraid—''

"She's afraid of nothing," Fairclough said with malicious pride.

Stony shook his head. "Oh, no. I think Mama's afraid of the one thing that won't keep her inside a stone cave or chapel. One thing."

"She's all-powerful. She's the divine fire," Fairclough muttered, but Stony sensed his nervousness.

Stony grinned in his direction. "Is she?"

"What—what are you thinking?"

"I'm thinking that she needs to be set free," Stony said, and he lifted the lid up. She was there, like a young girl—like Lourdes, a beautiful fifteen-year-old girl, lying naked in a bath of fire.

*My love*, she whispered.

"Look at you," Stony said. "You eat, you run wild in here, and now you're exhausted. You need to rest after all this, don't you?" His voice was almost sweet. He lifted her up in his arms, carrying her. The fire tingled across his shoulders and arms, but the pain was nothing now, all pain was gone.

"What are you doing?" Fairclough asked.

"I'm setting her free."

"No, you can't, you've seen what she can do—" Alan began.

Stony turned. His eyes bore through Fairclough. "You want to see what I can do? You want to see what I'm capable of? You know, I don't even know what I'm capable of yet, but I'm willing to find out. Are you?"

Alan Fairclough held his hands up in a peacemaking gesture. "Please, you can't let it out now, Stony. You can't. It can do terrible things. It has been trapped for centuries. . . ."

"Get the fuck out of my way!" Stony shouted. "I'm letting it out. I'm letting my mother go back to where she came from!"

Fairclough reached over and grabbed Stony's shoulder—
smoke rose from where he touched the boy.

A vision flashed out like lightning

Fairclough saw it—

*He was crucified against a tree, his hair on fire—*

"I'm a god now, remember?" Stony said. "I'm your
worst nightmare. I shed my skin, I let it go, and now I'm
back from the dead. To be king, you have to die and be
reborn, right? Well, say hey to King Stony."

He carried the creature out into the night.

7

*Don't,* it whispered inside him. *Please, I don't want to—*

"You don't want to return to your own source, Mother?
After thousands of years imprisoned by these sheep?"

"Please," she gasped, and he felt her weakness, the
body that had been fed and then its energy spent as it had
bled its own followers.

"I wonder why, Mother? Why would you want to be
here among men, trapped in rock?"

He took her to the doorway, and laid her down on the
grass just beyond the front steps and the columns. The
rain poured across them, the lightning flashed over the
trees.

She looked up at him, and he could tell she was trying
to burn more brightly, to shift into some creature, some
power—

"All Hallows' Eve," he whispered to her as he stroked
his fingers through the sparks of her hair. "The old rituals,
the harvest, when the gods would be killed, sent back to
the other worlds. Sent back to where they belong. Demons, too, souls traveling between the worlds, it's the
right time for that, isn't it? That's why Halloween is important to you. That's why you need the sacrifices. Why
you've been trying to mate with humans all these centuries. Because you want to be here, you know what will

happen to you in the other place. Call it heaven or hell or the idiot frequency of the divine superhighway, I don't give a damn. You have power here, but there, you're probably nothing. You gave me my humanity, so I wouldn't have to go there, so that I could have power here. It's Halloween you fear. But Mother, it's time for you to take off your mask, too. It's time for you to move on."

"Please," she whispered, and he almost responded to her pain—

Its pain, for the humanoid form no longer remained as the rain poured down, the cleansing rain, and then her light burst across the grass like a brush fire, up the trees, across the woods.

Stony held his hands up to the sky.

*I am the Storm King. Bring on the storm of storms tonight. Take the fire back to heaven!*

He shut his eyes, grinding his teeth together, willing himself, willing what was of his mother within him to transform.

He burst into thousands of bits of red and yellow and spread out across the land, following her trail as she tried to find a rock, a cave, a basement, something to hide within—

And each time she did, her fire spreading after her, he brought her out again, into the storm that grew as he felt the power grow in him.

Until finally, at the Common, with the rain pouring hard, her light turned silver, he felt her inside him.

*Why do you do this to your mother?* she asked. *I carried you and felt the pain of human birth just so that you would live.*

*Because,* he told her, *you do not belong here. Not with us.*

*But you are of me.*

*I'm more of them,* he said. *Return to where you belong.* Her body turned to an enormous lightning bolt that grew from the burning grass and shot slowly towards the blackened sky, drawing streams of white electricity from all corners of the village and surrounding woods. For a moment, it was as if the most brilliant daylight erupted from the corners of the earth, and the village of Stonehaven seemed at the center of the light.

Stony covered his eyes.

8

People in the village, the nonbelievers, those who had never been inside the Crowns' summer house, nor had they mingled much with those who had, waking in their beds, looking at the blazing light—they saw the most beautiful thing they'd ever experienced.

And then the pressure of air was too much—oxygen was sucked inward through some unseen vortex . . .

Stony saw them, the men and women and yes, even children, turning in their beds, looking at the bright daylight outside their windows—

Bodies prolapsed, or sucked forward into emptiness, houses were crushed in the path of the divine Moonfire.

*Moonfire.*

He felt a suction from above, as if he were at the center of a cyclone, and he knew that it would take him, that he too would ride the elements to heaven, or to the sky, to the space between worlds where he belonged.

Then the pressure slammed him back against the ground, into the mud, and he watched in horror as trees uprooted from the earth around him, and the earth shook, rooftops of houses smashed down, windows shattered.

And then there was an unearthly silence.

He looked back towards the Crown place, and the mansion remained, seemingly untouched.

*It's protecting her.*

*It's protecting Lourdes and the child.*

When he stood, finally, he saw that Stonehaven was on fire. A green-yellow lightning bolt, so large it looked like a highway among the roiling clouds, shot across the sky off into an infinite darkness.

The storm raged on, and Stony Crawford lay back down in the mud until dawn.

9

"Stony?" the man said.

He opened his eyes. The sun's light had just come up. It was Alan Fairclough standing above him.

"It's all right. It's over."

Stony tried to open his mouth to lash out at the man, but was too weak to even utter a single word.

"Yes, I'm alive. I told you, I am the keeper of the rituals. I will teach you some of it, Stony. I will teach you many things. It took a lot out of you, what you did. It did your mother, too. It's a terrible gift, Stony. You can't throw it away. And you're not like she is, you won't get caught up in the ether. Your element is the element of earth and water as well as fire. You are, for better or worse, one of us in as many ways as you are one of them."

Stony tried to muster every ounce of strength, but he felt like he was dying. A tremendous battering in his head, a ringing and the sound of hammering, all came up when he tried to move.

"Don't try to speak, just rest. What you did must have taken a lot of your power. It may be years before you gain it back. But do not worry, you have something to live for, after all," Fairclough said. "Lourdes is still alive, and your child within her is strong. You are the future, Stony. You and your son. We who are merely human are now part of a charming history." Alan Fairclough lifted Stony up from the mud, and carried him as he would carry a newborn across the muddy Common, past the smashed houses and fallen trees, out to the dock behind the Crowns' summer place, to a small motorboat in which lay the sac-encased Lourdes, her belly grown large with their son.

# *Epilogue*

## *Journey's End*

### 1

At a distance of twelve years, Stony Crawford reached to the ticking bomb and pressed the button near the timer. One minute to blast off, to kaboom, and he could not do it. He knew he should, but he could not.

*For Lourdes.*

*For our child.*

Stony turned to his son, Stephen, and said, "He lied. How could I have put my trust in that human monster? You were born two months later, in winter, but I awoke one morning and found . . . what was left of . . . your mother." He closed his eyes, remembering the body, less a girl's body than a cracked-open encasing for an incubator. Clear liquid had sluiced from within the burst stomach, and her face was all but obliterated by the glaze-like network of fatty tissue and veins. "Fairclough had taken you, newborn, in the night, and had left me on the island with just a small boat and provisions to last a week or so.

I was still too weak, and I could not let what was inside me out again. . . . I didn't know what kind of bloodshed . . . I was like a walking bomb . . . By the time I returned to the mainland, I had no idea where to go, how to find you. And I had to survive. Ben Dennehy and his sister helped, they took care of me until I knew I had to run from them too. Knew that the Moonfire in me could not be near full-blooded humans. I did things to survive that no man should ever have to do.''

"And then you found me."

Stony nodded. "After all these years. Hunting, searching, trying to sniff out Fairclough's trail wherever it might lead."

"To kill me?"

"I thought so. Then. Not now."

"I am a monster," the boy said.

"Both of us," Stony added.

"You stopped the bomb."

"I don't want you to die. Not for something you were no part of. You're only a quarter of what my mother was. You're half Lourdes, and a quarter Johnny Miracle, too."

"But this house, it's . . . it feels like it's breathing," his son said.

Stony glanced around. "It is. It's what's left of that Halloween night. The residue of her being."

"We should end it all," his son said. "After all that happened here, this place shouldn't be standing, should it?"

"Right," Stony grinned, feeling the melancholy of his memory seep through him. He touched the edge of the bomb, and the timer started up again. Ten minutes. Enough time to get a good ways away. "Let's go."

"Where?" Steve asked.

"Where no one will come after us. Where no one will worship us," his father said.

2

The small boat that Stony had left the island on was still docked behind the Crowns' house. They ran together down the landing, out onto the small dock. Stony quickly unraveled the holding rope, and started the motor.

3

"What are we going to do there?"

Stony shrugged, unable to predict the next few days, let alone the next few years. "I guess we'll wait for what will come. I can come to shore for food and what we need to live on."

"But it's bound to come out in me someday. The Devil."

"Maybe. And it's not the Devil. It's not Evil by itself. It's Evil because it's untamed. It's evil the way the wind is evil or the lightning. It's a force. But you have will."

"If it does come out, what if—I mean, what if other people come and it gets loose?"

Stony glanced at his son, and saw Lourdes there in his eyes and his hair. Lourdes Maria Castillo, with the crooked grin. *I love you because of your hair.*

*Your eyes.*

*Your muscles,* she whispered.

*Your voice.*

*Your heart.*

*You spirit.*

*Your love.*

"I don't mean to hurt people, but it seems to always happen around me," the boy said.

"I'll teach you how to let it out and still control it. We'll find out what our purpose is for the future," he said. His son grinned, a boy, only a boy, with his father, headed for the farthest of the three Isles of Avalon.

"Here," Stony said. He reached into his pocket and withdrew a piece of paper. It was loose-leaf paper, with blue lines on it, and between the blue lines, a scrawl. Tattered and yellowed, it was still legible after all these years. "Your mother wrote this to me. I didn't see it until after . . . until it was too late to save her. . . ."

Then he read it aloud.

"I have heard that everyone has one GREAT LOVE in their lives. ONE GREAT SECRET LOVE. I didn't know till I met you that I would have one. I thought I'd always feel alone and maybe get married and have kids someday but never really know REAL LOVE. I look at my mother and I think, THAT'S GOING TO BE ME IN TWENTY YEARS. Married with kids, cleaning, keeping my mouth shut, wishing something better for my kids. But when I saw you the first time, last spring, I knew just by looking in your eyes. I mean, I'd seen you before, you know that. But I had never really SEEN you. Did you know it too? It was like there was a chalk outline, or maybe a halo around you. When I looked in your eyes it was like looking into an ocean that was there just for the two of us. I knew that you were the one. I knew that there would be no others. You are my ONE GREAT SECRET LOVE. I don't know if we will always be like this, but I know that I will never ever forget you. NEVER. I want it always to be like it is between us right now. ALWAYS. No matter what happens. And things do happen. I know that. I know that sometimes love is not enough of a miracle to cure everything. I just wanted you to know. What we did together is what I wanted. It was PERFECT AND RIGHT."

When he finished, tears were in his eyes. The breeze picked up. The islands ahead were emerald and plum in the October dawn that edged the horizon.

Not so very far from humankind, he thought.

*Close, but not too close.*

*Far enough to learn together who we are. To set ourselves free and still control it.*

Then, behind them, the sound of the explosion.

His son shouted, "Fire! It blew up! Holy—"

Stony didn't look back. He didn't care if the Crown place was destroyed or burning.

Life could continue in an unimaginable way.

He closed his eyes and saw nothing but darkness. Then an aura emerged, a glow of light in his mind, the orange and yellow Moonfire—and she was there.

*She was there.*

A being within him now, a being of Moonfire and cool green shadow.

Lourdes Maria. Her hands open as if accepting what he would offer up, accepting the gift he was about to return to the cosmos. He saw her within himself, within his son. Her eyes no longer dark, full of pain, but golden and warm . . . her voice smooth, sure, but still she was there, as she had been at fifteen, eternally young, eternally faithful.

And the gift, the gift both of them offered to the universe, to the momentum of mankind and all that would be in the future, was there in their son. At war perhaps with his Other nature. The Outcast that was within the Storm King. The weakness that was within the power.

But beyond that, *she* was there as well.

*Your voice.*

*Your face.*

*Your spirit.*

*Your heart.*

*Your purity.*

The Isle of Avalon grew distinct through the dissipating

haze and light misty rain of morning as a fiery sun grew along its low hills.

*If I remember one thing*, Stony Crawford thought as he watched the sunlight break like glass against the slate sea, *it will be this. One thing from all that I was to all that I will be, this one thing burned into my memory, for Lourdes and me:*

In the boat, his son watching the morning as it came. His son, his and Lourdes's son, the light of creation within, but the human flesh and blood of his mother and father too. Perhaps that was the strongest prison for divine fire that had ever been created.

*Lourdes, see through my eyes. See him. See you within him.*

*Your purity.*

*Your heart.*

*Your soul.*

# BLACK RIVER FALLS
## ED GORMAN

"Gorman's writing is strong, fast and sleek as a bullet. He's one of the best."
—Dean Koontz

Who would want to kill a beautiful young woman like Alison...and why? But whatever happens, nineteen-year-old Ben Tyler swears that he will protect her. It hasn't been easy for Ben–the boy the other kids always picked on. But then Ben finds Alison and at last things are going his way...Until one day he learns a secret so ugly that his entire life is changed forever. A secret that threatens to destroy everyone he loves. A secret as dark and dangerous as the tumbling waters of Black River Falls.

"Gorman has a way of getting into his characters and they have a way of getting into you."
—Robert Block, author of *Psycho*

——4265-7                                    $4.99 US/$5.99 CAN

Dorchester Publishing Co., Inc.
P.O. Box 6640
Wayne, PA 19087-8640

Please add $1.75 for shipping and handling for the first book and $.50 for each book thereafter. NY, NYC, and PA residents, please add appropriate sales tax. No cash, stamps, or C.O.D.s. All orders shipped within 6 weeks via postal service book rate. Canadian orders require $2.00 extra postage and must be paid in U.S. dollars through a U.S. banking facility.

Name_____
Address_____
City_____ State_____ Zip_____
I have enclosed $_____ in payment for the checked book(s).
Payment <u>must</u> accompany all orders. ☐ Please send a free catalog.

# ROUGH BEAST
# GARY GOSHGARIAN

"[Treads] territory staked out by John Saul and Dean Koontz...a solid and suspenseful cautionary tale."

—*Publishers Weekly*

A genocidal experiment conducted by the government goes horribly wrong, with tragic and terrifying results for the Hazzards, a normal, unsuspecting family in a small Massachusetts town. Every day, their son gradually becomes more of a feral, uncontrollable, and very dangerous...thing. The government is determined to do whatever is necessary to eliminate the evidence of their dark secret and protect the town...but it is already too late. The beast is loose!

_4152-9                                    $4.99 US/$5.99 CAN

**Dorchester Publishing Co., Inc.**
**P.O. Box 6640**
**Wayne, PA 19087-8640**

Please add $1.75 for shipping and handling for the first book and $.50 for each book thereafter. NY, NYC, and PA residents, please add appropriate sales tax. No cash, stamps, or C.O.D.s. All orders shipped within 6 weeks via postal service book rate. Canadian orders require $2.00 extra postage and must be paid in U.S. dollars through a U.S. banking facility.

Name_____
Address_____
City_____State_____Zip_____
I have enclosed $_____ in payment for the checked book(s).
Payment <u>must</u> accompany all orders. ☐ Please send a free catalog.

# Elizabeth Massie

# Sineater

According to legend, the sineater is a dark and mysterious figure of the night, condemned to live alone in the woods, who devours food from the chests of the dead to absorb their sins into his own soul. To look upon the face of the sineater is to see the face of all the evil he has eaten. But in a small Virginia town, the order is broken. With the violated taboo comes a rash of horrifying events. But does the evil emanate from the sineater...or from an even darker force?

___4407-2                                    $5.99 US/$6.99 CAN

**Dorchester Publishing Co., Inc.**
**P.O. Box 6640**
**Wayne, PA 19087-8640**

Please add $1.75 for shipping and handling for the first book and $.50 for each book thereafter. NY, NYC, and PA residents, please add appropriate sales tax. No cash, stamps, or C.O.D.s. All orders shipped within 6 weeks via postal service book rate. Canadian orders require $2.00 extra postage and must be paid in U.S. dollars through a U.S. banking facility.

Name_____
Address_____
City_____ State_____ Zip_____
I have enclosed $_____ in payment for the checked book(s).
Payment <u>must</u> accompany all orders. ❑ Please send a free catalog.
    CHECK OUT OUR WEBSITE! www.dorchesterpub.com

# WHEN SHADOWS FALL

## BRIAN SCOTT SMITH

Martin doesn't believe his aunt's death is an accident, and he and a couple of buddies are determined to find the truth. But when he starts sneaking around the house of his aunt's new "friends," he never expects to witness a blood-drenched satanic ritual. But he does see it, and more important, the witches see him!

Suddenly Martin is in a horrifying race for his life. He has to stop the witches before they stop him for good. And he has to do it before Halloween night, the night of the final sacrifice, the night when the demons of hell will be unleashed on the Earth, the night when shadows fall.

___4313-0                                    $4.99 US/$5.99 CAN

**Dorchester Publishing Co., Inc.**
**P.O. Box 6640**
**Wayne, PA 19087-8640**

Please add $1.75 for shipping and handling for the first book and $.50 for each book thereafter. NY, NYC, and PA residents, please add appropriate sales tax. No cash, stamps, or C.O.D.s. All orders shipped within 6 weeks via postal service book rate. Canadian orders require $2.00 extra postage and must be paid in U.S. dollars through a U.S. banking facility.

Name_____
Address_____
City_____State_____Zip_____
I have enclosed $_____ in payment for the checked book(s).
Payment <u>must</u> accompany all orders. ❏ Please send a free catalog.

# DRAWN TO THE GRAVE — MARY ANN MITCHELL

**"A tight, taut dark fantasy with surprising plot twists and a lot of spooky atmosphere."**
**—Ed Gorman**

Beverly thinks that she has found something special with Carl, until she realizes that he has stolen from her. But he doesn't just steal her money and her property—he steals her very life. Suddenly she is helpless and alone, able only to watch in growing despair as her flesh begins to decay and each day transforms her more and more into a corpse—a corpse without the release of death.

But Beverly is not truly alone, for Carl is always nearby, watching her and waiting. He knows that soon he will need another unknowing victim, another beautiful woman he can seduce...and destroy. And when lovely young Megan walks into his web, he knows he has found his next lover. For what can possibly go wrong with his plan, a plan he has practiced to perfection so many times before?

___4290-8                                    $4.99 US/$5.99 CAN

**Dorchester Publishing Co., Inc.**
**P.O. Box 6640**
**Wayne, PA 19087-8640**

Please add $1.75 for shipping and handling for the first book and $.50 for each book thereafter. NY, NYC, and PA residents, please add appropriate sales tax. No cash, stamps, or C.O.D.s. All orders shipped within 6 weeks via postal service book rate. Canadian orders require $2.00 extra postage and must be paid in U.S. dollars through a U.S. banking facility.

Name_____
Address_____
City_____ State_____ Zip_____
I have enclosed $_____ in payment for the checked book(s).
Payment <u>must</u> accompany all orders. ❑ Please send a free catalog.

# HOWL-O-WEEN
# Gary L. Holleman

**Evil lurks on Halloween night....**

**H** ear the demons wail in the night,
**O** ut of terror and out of fright,
**W** erewolves, witch doctors, and zombies too
**L** urk in the dark and wait for you.
**O** ther scary creatures dwell
**W** here they can drag you off to hell.
**E** vil waits for black midnight
**E** nchanting with magic and dark voodoo,
**N** ow Halloween has cast its spell.

___4083-2                                    $4.99 US/$5.99 CAN

**Dorchester Publishing Co., Inc.**
**P.O. Box 6640**
**Wayne, PA 19087-8640**

Please add $1.75 for shipping and handling for the first book and $.50 for each book thereafter. NY, NYC, and PA residents, please add appropriate sales tax. No cash, stamps, or C.O.D.s. All orders shipped within 6 weeks via postal service book rate. Canadian orders require $2.00 extra postage and must be paid in U.S. dollars through a U.S. banking facility.

Name_____
Address_____
City_____ State_____ Zip_____
I have enclosed $_____ in payment for the checked book(s).
Payment <u>must</u> accompany all orders. ❑ Please send a free catalog.

# SHADOWS

## Kimberly Rangel

### WHERE TERROR RULES...

In the distant past, in a far-off land, the spell is cast, damning the family to an eternity of blood hunger. Over countless centuries, in the dark of night, they are doomed to assume the shape of savage beasts, deadly black panthers driven by a maddening fever to quench their unspeakable thirst. Then Selene DeMarco finds herself the last female of her line, and she has to mate with a descendent of the man who has plunged her family into the endless agony.

_4054-9                                        $4.99 US/$5.99 CAN

**Dorchester Publishing Co., Inc.**
**P.O. Box 6640**
**Wayne, PA 19087-8640**

Please add $1.75 for shipping and handling for the first book and $.50 for each book thereafter. NY, NYC, and PA residents, please add appropriate sales tax. No cash, stamps, or C.O.D.s. All orders shipped within 6 weeks via postal service book rate. Canadian orders require $2.00 extra postage and must be paid in U.S. dollars through a U.S. banking facility.

Name_____
Address_____
City_____ State_____ Zip_____
I have enclosed $_____ in payment for the checked book(s).
Payment <u>must</u> accompany all orders. ☐ Please send a free catalog.

# *ATTENTION HORROR CUSTOMERS!*

## SPECIAL
## TOLL-FREE NUMBER
## 1-800-481-9191

*Call Monday through Friday*
*10 a.m. to 9 p.m.*
**Eastern Time**
*Get a free catalogue,*
*join the Horror Book Club,*
*and order books using your*
*Visa, MasterCard,*
*or Discover*®

*Leisure*
*Books*

**GO ONLINE WITH US AT DORCHESTERPUB.COM**